# MEN ON WHITE HORSES

by the same author

TEA AT GUNTER'S
A KIND OF WAR
THE KISSING GATE
THE DIAMOND WATERFALL

# MEN ON WHITE HORSES

PAMELA HAINES



COLLINS
8 GRAFTON STREET, LONDON

For my godmother and aunt
MARJORIE ARMSTRONG

My very grateful thanks to Ron and Gwen Storm Gillings, Becky Storm Murrell and Captain Arthur and Mercy Gibson, all of Robin Hood's Bay, Yorkshire, who gave so generously of their time and their memories.

William Collins Sons & Co Ltd
London · Glasgow · Sydney · Auckland
Toronto · Johannesburg

First published 1978
This reprint 1984

ISBN 0 00 222392 9

Set in Linotype Baskerville
Made and printed in Great Britain by
William Collins Sons & Co Ltd Glasgow

# PART ONE

# 1907

Florence
Monday 28th September 1907.
St Cyprian!

Helen dearest,

So long since I wrote. Such a lazy brother (but what a charming one too!) Now I write to propose myself for a visit, at last. If I am welcome. I imagine however – and now be honest – that the Yorkshire breezes blow a little more gently when you know I'm coming, and that we shall have some time together.

And time together we must have. I have some very important news. I could almost say I'm crossing over to tell you since I don't think I could put it in a letter (are you not absolutely dying of curiosity?) It will amaze you, you will say 'never!' You will say 'but Frederick darling, you can't!'

Enough of not telling you. I want to see your face when – I want to see your face anyway. It's been nearly eighteen months and I did vow (you made me promise when you married into the frozen North) that I'd bring you the warm wine of the South every single year.

Shall we promise now this time, not to quarrel? Why do we, when we want so much to be with each other? And yet, every time. *Basta,* I think.

As to what you mentioned. Yes, money has been a worry. And no, you are not to slip me a little bag of sovereigns. Too often have I – Do you realize that it's fifteen years already since *you* were relieved of worry?

Autumn again soon. Wild boar with chocolate sauce and pine-nuts. Do you remember how you used to eat as a girl? And *now* – Whereas I who picked at my food then . . . Just lately I have been eating very well. A week in Rome, guests of the nobility – cousins of a friend of mine. The Antici-Montani. Quite remarkable what inbreeding can do. He (the Marchese) is just a poor thing. *She* is magnificent. The son and heir and his wife nonentities. The grandchildren, with one sad exception, very pleasant – but what happens next? Will they marry 'in' again? I may add *en passant* that they are Blacks of course. 'Dyed in the ink' – as they say here. The ultimate too, a Pope in the family; rather far back but undeniably *there*.

Sunset nearly and only ? more days until I see you. I shall let you know. Sunset, and before Matteo closes the shutters, the Apennines – indigo, and the city itself below, fading a pale rose colour. Why wonder that watercolours are such a snare, such a temptation?

How is Edwina, my *godchild* (I love that word)? And Philip, head-in-air Philip? And little Cora? And of course your Tom, your lord and master (surely you have found some method of getting your own way?)

Until when? Your brother (*tuo fratellino* who loves you),

Frederick.

---

The wind whipping the leaves, sending piles of them scurrying. Excited. That's the way everything is, she thought. It's not just me who's excited because he's coming. The sky is too. The weather.

Great gusts, bending branches of the rowan trees, leaves flurrying. She could see them from the window seat on the landing, looking out on to the garden and the park. Craning to the side a bit, she could just see the coach house and some of the stables. But she couldn't see the road *he* would come along.

The motor had gone to York to meet him, and Mother had gone with it because Uncle Frederick was her brother, her younger brother. He called her Helen. Mother and

Helen were two people really. One was gay and a bit like a child and liked having her own way. The other looked pinched and fretful, walking about with her shoulders rounded, talking a lot to Aunt Josephine. Aunt Josephine was Father's sister. She and Mother whispered together at the foot of the stairs. Once when Edwina had been in the drawing-room (and shouldn't have been), hiding behind the curtains because she'd been at the piano:

'I feel it here,' Helen said, her mother said. 'Just here. Under my heart really. I'm so afraid of – heart trouble.'

'Indigestion. It comes there, I know. But it's indigestion *only.*' Aunt Josephine coughed. 'How is the other trouble? It's not from that?'

Perhaps Helen-Mother shook her head because there'd been nothing more to hear. They'd gone off, and she hadn't been caught.

What hope had she now of not being discovered – curled up like this on a window-seat? She thought, I could steal out to the stables, then I've a better chance of seeing the motor arrive. I could go and see Arthur, I could say, 'I wanted to see my pony, I wanted to see Macouba.' She could tell him, 'Uncle Frederick's coming today . . .'

'Edwina, *Edwina*!'

She couldn't escape. Even if she pretended not to hear her name, others would. It was Tuesday, her afternoon for French with Miss Norris in the schoolroom. Nurse might be on the prowl, although Sarah the nursemaid was taking Cora for a walk and Aunt Josephine was resting. Father was away till the evening.

'Edwina!'

Caught. Now to sit with that terrible schoolroom clock. It went: not tick tock, but tick tick tick tick.

Miss Norris spoke French in a funny voice, quite different from the one she used for geography. She wasn't a person really, a human being. To begin with she was cold, so cold that she must surely be cold inside too. She had fat fingers, red with cracked chilblains. Her hands hadn't gone down even in the summer. The cracks had just healed but the fingers were still fat. The rest of her was spiky. Her hair was spiky too and mousey. When she bent over you could see her skin through it; corridors, little partings.

'*Je m'appelle Edwina* – please, Edwina. *J'ai huit ans. Répétez après moi –*'

It was her nose was the worst. It seemed to have been twisted into a hook with a twiddly bit at the top. It couldn't have been a very good nose because she got colds so often. But it was the drip at the end which was really the worst. It hung, unbelievably, then just when Edwina was sure it would fall . . . It was like watching icicles on the wall in winter.

'After me, please. *J'ai huit ans* –'

'You're more than that. You said once – you're thirty-eight.'

'Don't be impertinent. There is never any need to be personal, Edwina. Even the youngest child in France –' she sniffed loudly. The drop went upwards – 'half your age, can manage these phrases.'

I'm too little to learn French, she thought. I heard Aunt Josephine say that. Philip doesn't have to go through all this – it's different for boys. They've sent him away to school. I wish I had his pocket telescope. It cost a whole half-guinea. I could see three miles with it, I could see *him* coming.

'*Encore une fois. Je m'appelle –*'

Tick tick tick tick. So many yawns, so many years between each tick.

'How long till four o'clock?'

'Another half-hour.'

Another *half-hour*.

'Don't you think it would be rather nice if you could say a few little sentences to your uncle? *Bonjour, mon oncle. Je –*'

'He speaks Italian. He lives in Italy –'

'All educated Italians speak French perfectly. It's a well-known fact.' She rubbed at her swollen forefinger. 'Well-known.'

But what's that noise outside the window? It's the motor,

chuffing round to the front entrance. She shouldn't have let me sit where I can see out with only a little twisting. 'Miss Norris, he's here, he's here – Uncle Frederick is here!'

Nothing to stop her now, running, running down the narrow stairs from the schoolroom, along the twisty uneven corridors, across to the wide landing. There you can see down into the hall of the Hall. The bell's gone, there are servants there already. Aunt Josephine has opened her door, is coming slowly out. But I am flying, frock flying, pinny flying, hair flying, down, down the stairs.

'Edwina, Weenie, darling – ' I'm the first person he sees as the door is opened. He's wearing a cape coat and he smells wonderful, of different cigarette smoke, of some special scent. His face is all lovely shapes and shadows and lines and folds.

Mother is there. 'Be careful.' Sharply, 'She's heavy, Frederick.' Uncle Frederick, letting her go a little: 'You look wonderful, Weenie. So *big*!' Turning his head: 'Just those two suitcases. Not the gun.' Then still holding her, hand round her waist. 'Ah, Josephine. How good to see you, Josephine.'

'I have French, I had French today. Uncle Frederick, *je m'appelle Edwina. J'ai huit ans . . .*'

'We've had such a summer,' Aunt Josephine said, a sandwich in her hand. 'Rain, cold. Hardly more than half a dozen good days. If you'd seen the Bank Holiday outing for the villagers – '

'Frederick wouldn't know,' said Mother. 'The sun shines on him every day.'

Edwina tried to sit up straight but it was uncomfortable. She felt she could see him better if she poked her head a little. Just to be here in the drawing-room with him a full hour before she usually came down (and without Cora now), that was treat enough.

'Frederick has some news for us,' Mother said. 'But he won't tell.'

'Tomorrow, I promise.'

'No, I can't guess,' said Mother excitedly, as if she'd been asked to. 'Tell, do tell.' She made a little latticework of her fingers, peeping through them coyly. 'You've taken up singing professionally? No? You're going to be singing-master to some ancient Florentine family?' She clasped her hands together, put her head on one side.

He seemed to be enjoying the game. 'No, no.' His voice which often had an odd squeak to it, rose: 'But you're surprisingly – You're not hot but you're not cold.'

Aunt Josephine said suddenly: 'You're teasing Helen, Frederick.' She looked at him disapprovingly, a scone in her hand. 'It doesn't do to get her overexcited.'

Aunt Josephine ate a lot. She had moved on to plum cake now. Edwina for excitement could scarcely eat anything.

'The sea,' she burst out. 'The sea, tell me about the sea.'

Mother raised her eyebrows. Aunt Josephine saved her by saying: 'The crossing, Frederick. I've been appalled by the weather lately. The high winds.'

'The sea,' Edwina persisted, knowing she was doing wrong, willing his attention, 'what was it like? Was it angry?'

'Little Edwina,' he said, 'it was all tossedy about. If you can imagine. Great white horses. I only went up on deck so that I could tell you about it.'

His hair was a funny colour. The same really as Mother's. Not brown, not gold, white, grey, but an odd colour like polished pewter. Philip had it too. Nothing like her own thick black, with its fearsome straightness, its will of its own, springing back, full of tangles ('cotters' Sarah called them, tugging with the horn comb), not like Cora's tumbling light brown curls with their little bits of gold.

They had stopped talking about the sea. She was happy really just to watch. Mother had rung for more hot water. She let her gaze go round the room. The piano. It was something called a Bechstein. Mother's wedding present from Father. 'Do you play?' she'd heard someone ask once. 'Very little now,' Mother had said, twisting her rings, pushing the sparkling diamonds up and down. (Father had bought them for her. He was older than Mother so he had a lot more money. He had found her many years ago without enough to eat, in a foreign country, and he had put her on the back of his white horse and ridden with her back to England. These days he rode a horse called Kendal Brown.)

But now surely it was Edwina's piano? It was she who loved it. She'd found it, stroked the keys, struck them – what joy that first day when they'd sprung into life. Looking over now at the piano, silent, she could feel right down inside the terror of delight it had given her. It had come from her fingers, no, from inside her, no, from inside the machine, the wooden frame. It stood open, you could look in; when she struck a hammer went up and down, velvet, furry-covered. And yet, the sound came from her.

A lump of cake with a cherry in it fell on to the strap of her patent leather shoe. She wondered if she could rescue it without anyone noticing.

'. . . and in those circles you move in, this encyclical – you think that's the end of Modernism?'

'I heard only something about Tyrell. Excommunication.'

'That seems a bit excessive – '

'Oh, I have no patience with that kind of thing. Jesuits are always one extreme or the other. If you remember, in France – '

Aunt Josephine: 'I'm sure I don't know what it's about . . . I can't feel at home with Romanism – it's one subject Helen and I don't discuss.' She crumbled sandcake between her fingers. 'Why we can't all worship together . . .'

Tea was all cleared away. She had picked up the cherry without anyone noticing, but she had had to eat it. And just at that moment Cora and Nurse had arrived.

'Oh, but how she's grown – Helen, you should have told me. No longer a baby, a little girl! Come here, Cora – '

Nurse let go of Cora's hand and she ran forward, all simpering. Her ringlets bobbed as she moved. Edwina thought that just a little bit ago her mouth would have had treacle on it, running down the chin. They'd have given her treacle with nursery tea to make up for not coming down.

But horrors, Cora was going to sing. Rolling her eyes up:

'"When Nurse has tucked the bedclothes in And stumped across the floor, She says that not a single soul must come in through the door."' She held her hands in front of her, swayed on her toes: '"There's someone comes to see us then who Nursie says is dead, Dad used to call her "darlin' heart" but Muvver was her name . . ."' It went on and on, rather fast without much stopping for breath.

The agony was over. Uncle Frederick asked if Edwina couldn't do anything? 'Can't, *won't*,' said Aunt Josephine, but not unkindly, as if to show she knew Edwina had more sense than to make a fool of herself like that, with that song.

'Isn't she learning the piano?' he said to Mother.

Edwina was about to speak. 'There's hardly a hurry,' Mother said. She yawned prettily; she had small, very sharp white teeth. 'I mean to do something about it in the spring.'

'Helen has been far from well,' Aunt Josephine said.

'Ah that,' said Uncle Frederick, looking at something on his coat cuff.

'Ah yes,' Aunt Josephine said, pursing her lips, looking out across the darkening garden. Winter coming. Soon curtains would be drawn in the afternoons. 'Ah yes. It will come on to rain, don't you think?'

'I want a room of my own. I want to sleep by myself.' Sitting at the nursery table, in nightclothes now, eating bread and milk. Horrid, only just warm, with the milk tasting funny.

'What's that, what's that? What did Miss Edwina say?' Nurse asking Sarah. Sarah replacing the heavy iron fireguard, rearranging the towels, white, yellow marked, smelling scorched and a little soapy as they hung on the horse.

'Philip does, Philip has one – '

'That's different,' Nurse said briskly.

'Why is it different?'

'Time enough for that, time enough. You may not like sleeping alone. And what would little Cora do without you?'

Nurse had two small lines engraved on her forehead, just above her nose. They were something to do with her headaches. The lines looked like two little slits: the ache got in through them. Her name was Kettlewell, Ada Kettlewell – she'd seen it written in a little red book with an elastic band which Nurse left lying about. Sarah was much more fun. She came from a village called Beckhole in Goathland, which was a land of goblins and fairies and hobs. Horses in their stables would often be found in the mornings sweating and shaking as if they'd been on a long journey, which they had, because a witch had ridden them all night. (It was easy to prevent this, though. You had just to hang up a horseshoe, open side down, and all would be well.)

'She's to say her prayers, Sarah. See she doesn't get in without.'

'Mother's coming up to hear them.' Pause. 'Uncle Frederick's coming up –'

'Nonsense, certainly that's nonsense. If your uncle's here, she won't. Nor will he I dare say –'

'He said . . .'

'Come along then. Say what you have to say.'

Nurse didn't like it. Roman, she said, your prayers are Roman. Sarah told Edwina once, 'They're not right, she says. Looking up to, making a fuss over a woman. God's a man.'

In Mother's room there was a small praying place. A candle in a holder, a statue. Mother had let her light the candle once, when Edwina wanted a little sister. (Yes, she had really wanted a little sister. She had been that foolish.) Mother, with a face only half serious, had lit it, and then shown Edwina the beautiful lady. Beautiful with a delicate bloom on her cheeks, tendrils of dark hair, a dress with a pale blue girdle like the sky. 'Our Lady,' she was called. 'Not your lady,' she said to Nurse. 'Mine. Mine and Mother's.'

'And Cora's,' said Nurse sharply. 'And Cora's, miss.'

First the 'Our Father'. Nurse knew that. Then:

'Now go on and say it. Say the rest.'

'Hail Mary, full of grace, the Lord is with thee . . .'

On Sundays, Philip and Father and Aunt Josephine walked down the village to the Norman church up the steps. She and Mother went off in the dog cart – or in the motor in winter – to some friends' house three miles away where there was a small chapel. There, a priest in a lacy robe spoke in Latin. Mother drank coffee afterwards and Edwina, warm sweet tea with a sponge finger to dip in it. Once near Christmas she had been offered a chestnut, all sugared, in paper.

'And blessed is the fruit of thy womb, Jesus. Holy Mary, Mother of God . . .'

'Is that you, where are you, Little Bear? It's your uncle, Ricky the Great.'

He didn't come near enough. She wanted to put a hand out but she was suddenly too shy. 'Are you in a hurry, have you got time?'

He took her hand between his, laying them on the counterpane, caressing, rubbing it.

'Your news, what were you talking about downstairs?'

'*Tomorrow,* little curious one.' His voice had a laugh in it. He stroked her hand. 'You haven't told me *your* news – '

'There's nothing.'

'Nothing?' He was feeling the tips of her fingers.

'I – ' she began and swallowed. Then in a rush: 'When I go to the piano, when I sit down at it, I go mad, I go wild excited, I can't explain. My hands, they run away with me. I can feel all sorts of things – ' She rushed on: 'I don't sing properly, you see. It's a nosy sort of voice and then the tune isn't right, I can hear I'm not right. So she says I'm not musical . . .'

'That dance we did together last time – remember?' He spoke in a hushed voice as if it had been their secret. 'You can dance – '

'I'm not good. Cora's better already. And then I have to go to this dreadful dancing class – '

'Tell.' When she'd finished, pressing each of her nails as he spoke: 'What exactly happens at the piano?'

'It's as if it calls me or my fingers want – sometimes I go and make a noise on it.'

'Tomorrow,' he said then. 'You can show me.' He released her hand, laying it on the counterpane.

'Aren't you going to tell me more about the sea? About Italy?' (Stay with me, stay with me, don't say 'I'm going'.)

'I must go. Tomorrow – '

She lay back hopeless, the visit already over. It could not be that he would go out of the door. He leaned over and kissed her. She reached out to try and hug him but she wasn't quick enough.

'Escaped, I escaped,' he whispered. 'Kisses. Good night. Good night.'

Then she heard (but didn't see, couldn't bear to open her eyes) him tiptoe out.

She thought she must have been asleep for a while. There was a glow still from the fire. The flickering nightlight made funny shadows, almost frightening. From the nursery came the rattling of cups. A light shone under the door.

She propped herself up on one elbow. Cora, on her back, was making whimpering, snoring sounds.

'He'll make the mistress *more* difficult. After he's left, we'll be for it – '

Nurse's voice. Her sister must have come up to see her. She was housekeeper to two old ladies in the village. Edwina didn't like her. She was all the bad things about Nurse and none of the good. Worse altogether than Miss Norris who was – well, not *bad*, just ugly and that she couldn't help.

'Coming all the way from Italy – he's not Italian then? They've neither of them the *blood*, as you might say.'

'You might say indeed. He has very foreign ways. I thought he was going to kiss my hand.'

A chair was scraped back. 'Little Miss Hoity Toity – she'll be pleased?' Nurse's sister had a softer voice; you had to strain to hear it, but it hadn't any kindness in it. When people talked about the milk of human kindness, she imagined it running, sweet and strong, with honey perhaps. Nurse's sister didn't have it.

'Oh, there was no doing anything with *her* today. But the Master, he's not always so pleased. After all, it's the sister he married. I note he took good care to be away today – '

'Keep your voice down. Your own nursery, you should know when your voice carries. Miss Cora – you've got an easy one there . . .'

Talking about me like that, Edwina thought. Silly old cows. The voices went on. They were talking now about their brother who was a sailor. He was with his ship in the East. 'He said . . .' 'Never!' exclaimed Nurse. Their voices became hushed.

Edwina grew more restless. Suddenly she slipped her feet on to the thick wool rug, then creeping, holding her breath, she crossed the cold linoleum. Perhaps she was going to sneeze – then (thank you, God) she was past the door. Past the baize door too, down the staircase along the corridors, out on to the big landing. It was brightly lit, too brightly lit. She could hear the piano in the drawing-room. Her mother, stumbling over something with lots of soft notes.

There was a small velvet chair just under the main stairs. She'd be safe if no servants came by. Silence. Then she could hear murmuring voices. She wondered if her father was in there. She felt nervous, then cold, shivered, hugged her cotton nightie to her. The piano again. Little trills – and then, oh but then, Uncle Frederick singing. Not in French, but not Italian either; the sounds were wrong for that.

*'Dein,'* he sang, on a high note, the word again and again. *'Dein ist mein Herz!'* ('What time do we dine?' the grown-ups said.) The sounds rolled over her. It was the sea again. Sometimes the piano galloped: horses now, being ridden over the wild sea.

*'Den Morgenwinden möcht' ich's hauchen ein,*
*Ich mocht' es säuseln durch den regen Hain . . .'*

(I'm not interested in a calm sea. I'm not.)

*'Ihr Wogen, könnt ihr nichts als Räder treiben?*
*Dein ist mein. Herz und soll es ewig bleiben!'*

Uncle Frederick was riding. Nothing but nothing could be more beautiful, more exciting. She was unable to bear it. His voice was the wind whipping up the sea, then he was fighting it, was riding it again. All those white horses galloping . . .

The song was over. Another, give us another. More, Uncle Frederick, please, more –

*'Edwina!'*

Oh, who but Aunt Josephine, seeming to appear from nowhere but really coming out of the drawing-room, padding towards her, embroidery in hand.

'Whatever are you doing downstairs?'

But then Father was there too. He didn't seem too cross, just disapproving, the sort of voice, of face, that meant a little thunder now but all over soon. It could even be he was a little amused because he called out when he'd lifted her up, holding her carelessly, a bit as if she were one of his dogs: 'Helen – come and see what I've found. Look at this scallywag –' He hadn't been in the drawing-room; he'd come out of the library probably.

Aunt Josephine tut-tutted behind them. 'Nurse has her sister with her. It makes her careless.'

Mother said: 'Nurse can't be everywhere. It's very wilful of Edwina.' She looked far away, as if she'd been snatched from a dream. Then she seemed to gather herself and said in a little, cold voice, 'Children can be such a nuisance. Frederick, you have no idea.'

'And never shall have?' He didn't look at her, leaning back, an elbow on the piano.

She wriggled out of her father's arms. 'Slippery,' he said, 'slippery as a little fish.' He was very strong. Beside him everyone in the house, except perhaps Aunt Josephine, looked small. His red face and grizzled head with its tight curls. She saw him always as a great oak tree. However much Mother might order the servants about, it was always

Father who decided what might be and what might not: 'Father says no', and that would be that.

She met Uncle Frederick's eyes. He looked as if he'd been watching her a while. They had a hooded look. The room smelled warm, a smell of wine, some flowers from the hothouse.

'She must go back.' There was a silence. Suddenly the mantle of Cora descended on her. 'Nunky take Edwina up,' she said. 'Me tired. Weenie won't go up if Nunky don't take her.' She put a finger in her mouth, rolled her eyes round. 'Feel icky,' she said. 'Very icky.'

'She must go up immediately.' Father said it sternly this time. She thought he was coming to do it. 'Nunky take Edwina,' she said, beginning to cry, the tears coming easily, her finger back in her mouth.

Mother said, 'Frederick – your back,' as he gathered Edwina up in one, bending awkwardly to do so.

The light was still on in the nursery. If Nurse had gone to bed she'd have looked in, noticed her missing. When he'd laid her in the bed, tucked her up, he leaned over, his cheek against hers. She could smell drink again, sweet, winey, rich – she thought too she could smell the music; it was as if he were still singing.

'Good night, little silly . . .'

Afterwards she could hardly remember his going. Her head sinking down into the little pillow, the room whirling round, such tiredness, dizziness almost. 'I *do* feel sick,' she thought triumphantly; and a moment later was asleep.

It was Saturday and she didn't have any lessons. Out of the window she could just see the Spanish chestnut; everything beyond was covered in mist. Nurse said, 'The peacocks were up to their worst this morning. Given me a nasty head they have.' She was short-tempered with Cora, dressing her roughly, forcing her stiff little resisting arm into the holland overall. 'Your breakfast's up already. I don't know what we've all been doing . . . Miss Edwina – you think better than well of yourself, I dare say, but *I* know –'

Plainly Nurse didn't know – about last night. Waking early, she'd heard the songs still in her heart, knew suddenly, lying there, that *she* could have played the piano for him. And – then, excitement draining away, she remembered: those black squiggles, those curly tails. When she'd mentioned them to Nurse once, 'Difficult,' Nurse had said, 'they're very difficult. You have to have special lessons for that. It's not like reading a book, you know.'

'They're off shooting, I hear,' Nurse said now. 'I hope they can see something in this mist.'

'Bang, bang,' Cora said. She pranced across the room, pulling her ringlets in their curl papers away from Nurse. ' "There was a little man and he had a little gun and his bullets were made of lead lead lead he went to the brook and shot a little duck right through the middle of the *head head head*".'

'Stop it now,' Nurse snapped, 'stop it now.' She turned on Sarah: 'You've taken the button hook. Look for the button hook immediately.'

'Head head head,' chanted Cora.

'I'll give you head,' Nurse said shortly, banging the brush against Cora's head. Cora wailed. 'Ssh now. Nursey never meant it – Miss Edwina, stop *staring* – Nursey, come to Nursey. It's her poor old head. Those peacocks . . .'

Gathered together for the shoot, they managed to look like the big print hanging on the stairs. It was from many years ago. The park was the same but the trees in the garden looked younger, stiffer too, as if they'd been stuck into the ground just for the occasion. Figures stood around with guns slung. Peacocks walked with tails up. It was the same place. She often used to think that: it's the same place. And the people in the drawing, perhaps they were the family? Illingworth. Her name, until she married, then it'd be lost, nothing to do with her any more. All along the dining-room walls were pictures of people who looked, if you stared hard enough, in some way like the family now. There was even a child just like Cora. Strange to see Aunt Josephine's head,

Father's high cheekbones, his heavy shoulders. And all wearing such old clothes, like something out of a history book.

Of course Uncle Frederick was going shooting too. He looked beautiful but not quite right somehow. Fussed: he looked as Nurse sometimes did when she was fussed, but he wasn't impatient, irritable as she'd have been. He looked just a bit desperate; even – a little silly. He was in the wrong place. He should be over the sea in Italy where life was exciting, an adventure – even if the people were cruel to little songbirds. Only, sudden thought, what was the difference, big birds, little birds? They were all off now on to the moors to shoot birds that today were going about quite happily, that had got up in the morning to tread delicately about the heather or to swoop upwards on the wing, so beautiful, right across the skyline. The beaters had come – they'd be beating them out so that they had to fly up, had to be there for the guns.

She ran forward suddenly. 'Don't shoot anything.' She clung to him. 'Promise me you won't kill anything – ' Uncle Frederick looked embarrassed, she thought he was going to shake her off. His mouth had dropped a little.

Her father said stoutly: 'Get back, please. Go on – there's a good girl.'

'He usually misses,' said her mother, laughing. She didn't seem angry but looked gay and happy. 'Don't you, darling?'

'The truth,' Uncle Frederick said, 'she speaks the truth. There are things I do better.'

The motor had been brought round. They were all getting in, arranging themselves. She wanted them suddenly to be all gone. The mist had cleared, the sun was coming up, it was going to be a beautiful, beautiful day.

'My uncle's here,' she told Arthur. 'He's staying.' She pulled at the end of her riding crop. 'Well, aren't you interested?'

'Aye,' he said, 'aye.' But she knew that he wasn't. He went on saddling Macouba, adjusting the girth with care. She'd come out early, before he was ready, so eager was she to be off.

'Which way shall we go? I choose where we go today . . .'

As they set out, 'I saw they was off shooting,' he said. 'Pass a few years and you'll be along.' He reined in Otterburn, who was always mettlesome in the mornings.

'Yes, yes.' She loved Arthur, liked just to watch him. He didn't have a beard like most of the gardeners, didn't even have a moustache. It was a long sharp face and the skin always looked dark, shadowy; his hair very black and usually greasy. Whatever mood you had, he'd always treat you the same – slow and rather fond. She knew he was fond of her so she wanted him to like Uncle Frederick, and also to care about music, about sounds. And he did. He'd stop suddenly when they were going, say, through the woods. 'Hear that? That's a yellow'ammer.' Or: 'Reckon you could hear beck already – if you're quiet like.'

'Arthur, would you like not to work?' They were halfway down the village, turning by the little bridge. A cart laden with bracken blocked their path. She wondered what it was like to drive a cart, to work all the time. She would never have to work. Mother had said so.

'You mean – be badly?'

'No, I mean – to do what you want, all day.'

'Aye, well, I don't know.' He leaned forward: 'That stirrup of yours. I'll just – ' He smiled slowly. 'Folk that works are folk that works.'

They rode into the woods. 'I'd like to work,' she announced.

'Happen you will then,' he said, going a little ahead of her, to pull back some branches, so low-hanging that they might have trapped her. The story of William Rufus, in the big book in the library: the drawing which had haunted her for nights – She rode on to safety.

'How's your littlest girl? Emily, how's Emily?'

Emily had been born the day before Cora. Edwina had disgraced herself when they'd brought her the great news ('the stork has brought you a very own dear little sister'), saying coldly: 'Arthur has one in his house too. *She* arrived first, *and* they've got six others . . .'

'Up now with Macouba's head,' Arthur said, coming

alongside. 'She's right badly is Emily.' His mouth closed in a funny way.

'Does she have a cold, I've just had a cold. Lots of yellow stuff came out – I had to have a clean handkerchief five times.'

'It's t'kink cough. She were at it all last night, sick and all. They sick up with it.'

Otterburn, chafing, reared a little then broke into a slow canter. Arthur was taking him out for Mother. All her horses, Father's too, were named after snuffs.

'When Cora gets Macouba, can I ride Dry Toast?' she called, trotting hard after him.

It was a long afternoon waiting for them to come back. She did some colouring for a little, then grew restless. There were some copies of the *Catholic Fireside* Mother had bought her. She flipped through the pages. The children's section always annoyed her. A Mother Salome from St Mary's Convent in Cambridge wrote it and the words were all hyphenated, often in the most surprising places. She stared a long time at 'dis-tress-ed'.

Through the bars of the nursery window she could see one of the trees bending in the breeze; green-brown leaves grew thickly still at top and bottom, but the centre was bare. A leaf would swirl upwards, hang in the air, fly, then sink slowly to the ground. She imagined them all lying deep, stacked.

'I want to go out with my hoop.'

'But it will soon be tea, it's tea soon.'

'I want – '

'All right,' Nurse said grudgingly.

She wanted really to take her hoop out into the village, running where the carts and carriages, the odd motor came along, where the stream babbled the length of the main street. The village children played by it, even *in* it: *she* was only allowed to look at it formally, walking at Their pace.

Out in the garden she bowled along for a while, flexing her gloved fingers, then she pulled off her tam-o'-shanter, hanging it on the branch of a tree, and began to run. She could feel the darkening sharp afternoon cold on her cheek-bones. She shook her hair, tossed her head. It made her feel better. I'm me, she thought. Whatever happens, I'm *me*. Her hoop bowled over the damp crushed leaves. Looking up she could see the tracery of the elms, dotted with rooks' nests. She changed direction, hitting the hoop harder and harder, making time go faster till Uncle Frederick came back. Then oh joy, she was just near when she saw, heard, them coming. Flushed, happy, running to meet them – and *they* looked pleased too: except Mother, being helped out, she didn't look so pleased. Her father, red-faced, contented, walking in that way she knew meant the day had gone well – lots of fresh air, a good luncheon, a good bag, and now a good appetite again.

Mother said at once, 'Where's your hat, naughty girl?'

Uncle Frederick said, 'Nice thick hair, keeps out the cold.' He reached out and touched it. She threw herself into his arms, burying her head in the tweedy coat which smelled like and yet unlike him.

'Steady,' said her mother sharply as she nestled, burrowed. She added with a little sniff: 'You won't be able to do that soon. You haven't heard the news – '

'Why won't I?' she asked, coming out, reaching down for her hoop, searching for the stick. 'Why not? I shall if I want – so there.' She said it defiantly, thinking she was being criticized, expecting to be scolded.

Her mother said, more sharply this time, with a little toss of her head, 'Frederick – your uncle – is going to be married.'

'Oh,' said Edwina, in a little voice. She wanted suddenly to run indoors. But she stood instead squarely, feet planted outwards in the way Mother didn't like and had asked the dancing mistress to do something about. 'Who to, if I may ask?' (She had heard grown-ups say that: *'if I may ask?'*) 'A lady?'

Her father gave a snort, turned his head away, then blew his nose loudly. Uncle Frederick said easily, 'Yes, Edwina, a lady. Except that actually she's a baronessa. She has a title, you see, and is Italian.'

'What more natural,' said her mother acidly, 'when you live in Italy. Although there *are* English people in Florence – '

'Really?' Uncle Frederick said. 'I was scarcely aware. An English colony. I'm only part of it, after all – '

'It's only too obvious you're part of it,' she said shortly, walking in ahead of him, ignoring Edwina.

'What's her name?' Edwina asked. 'This Italian lady's *name*?'

'Adelina,' he said, turning to go in. He said it as if it were music. 'Adelina.'

She was about to lose him. She knew right down inside, in the part which would turn to water, sending her running fast to the lavatory, thinking all of me's coming out. Indeed she had already lost him because he must even now be thinking more of this Italian lady than of her. When they married she would belong to him. My wife, he would say. When he travelled or got his luggage together or made a list of what he had, he could put: a wife.

No one mentioned it. It was as if the topic were either not very important or perhaps so important that you didn't talk about it at all. She sat next to Aunt Josephine, who'd been out visiting sick people all afternoon.

'I saw Arthur's little girl.' She handed Edwina a skein of embroidery cotton: 'You do this for me, child.' Then: 'She seemed very unwell. She has whooping-cough. The older ones are recovering but hers is distressing to see – racking her whole frame.'

The room seemed lonely, although they were all there in it. The piano beckoned. She thought: if they went to sleep like in the story of Sleeping Beauty, all sitting about just as they are, I'd go over and sit down and music would flow out of me. I would bang and thump and then stroke the notes, then dance on them. Then just touch like feathers, ripple like water does, then bump bump, little knocks. Then my hands spread wide, as wide as they'd go, great thick sounds, telling myself what I was feeling, that I was happy yet unhappy, that I was *me*. I would wake the dead, I have such strength in my fingers. She felt thumb and forefinger pressing the skein of cotton, as if she would rub it away.

'Careful,' Aunt Josephine said. 'You're not untangling that at all. You're not helping.'

Uncle Frederick must have felt bad, though. He must have felt the need to say something, because he came up before dinner, sat on the end of her bed.

She was tired, so tired. 'Can I tell you something?'

'Yes.' He leaned forward.

She hissed into his ear, angry, suddenly so angry she could have killed him: 'I thought you were going to marry me.' She had only just thought of it, what was wrong. She wailed her whisper: 'I thought you were going to marry *me* . . .'

Uncle Frederick was to go to church with them. He was carrying a leather-bound book. Mother carried always a book called *The Garden of the Soul*.

Edwina imagined it to be full of plants, imagined a soul, something like a heart, but sprouting from it a profusion of lovely flowers – pansies, lilies, carnations.

They went in the motor, Uncle Frederick sitting opposite Mother, and Edwina beside her. Mother looked pretty today but fractious, tired. She was wearing a new hat with a purple satin lining, the brim turned up at one side, with a lot of ostrich plumes. Her coat was furry inside and with a big fur collar. Uncle Frederick had fur on his collar too.

'Can I see your book?' She took her hands out of her muff.

'Careful, little one. It's very old. A Missal.'

'Frederick, show me,' Mother said prettily, reaching out for it first.

'Adelina's engagement present. I mean to be very much holier. It's a family heirloom. They have so many, though, that it's not as *épatant* as you might think – '

Mother had taken it and was examining it carefully. The pages were thin and looked uncomfortable to read. There were two languages in two columns – she couldn't make out either. Their markers weren't the usual simple silk but dyed an elaborate pattern and plaited thickly.

'Quite a family,' Mother said. 'Quite a family.' She turned some pages. 'I don't think Father had hoped as much as that for us.'

'But you've done well enough – ' He fiddled with his gloves. 'After all, what are we, were we, but adventurers?'

'We still are,' she said definitely, a little flatly. 'You, certainly.' She was still holding the Missal, turning the pages idly, almost a little roughly. 'Why?' she asked. 'What I want to know is *why*?'

'I've just told you – '

'That's not all about you. Adventurer. Yes. But the other – now you won't be able to . . .'

He looked suddenly white and angry. Edwina asked to see the Missal, but she didn't want to look at it when she got it. Except that it smelled old and unusual, it was boring. 'How do you use it?' she asked.

'I was a great success in Rome. I am approved of. One of the oldest families – '

'Perhaps you should have aimed for Gladys Vanderbilt? Two *million* there. American Sphinx, indeed. And what's he? Hungarian? A Count?'

He said sharply: 'I shall have to be content with what I *have* got, won't I? Not exactly two million, but – ' He shrugged his shoulders, stared straight ahead of him. They seemed to be speaking as if they were alone, as if Edwina, all ears, had suddenly become invisible. 'It's not necessarily going to affect my private life. I can still – I've always been discreet.'

'Really?'

'Would I have been accepted if otherwise?'

'*I* don't know how the minds of old Florentine families work.' She leaned forward: 'Perhaps with this fresh blood and after all this inter-marrying they'll expect a beautiful child or two?'

'Perhaps.' His lips were pressed close together. '*Ora, basta.* No?'

They were silent for a moment. Then Mother burst out: 'Going back twenty years – perhaps you should have completed that which you began?'

'*That which you began!*' he repeated mockingly. 'You can say that here?' He shifted awkwardly in his seat.

'You think I've forgotten, don't you? Don't you?'

'*Bada, bada. La petite.*'

'As if any girl could forget –'

'Cruelty and bad taste,' he said in a thick voice. 'You're capable of both.'

'Edwina,' Mother said sharply, 'you've had that Missal long enough.'

They were nearly at the house where they went for Mass. It had a long winding drive, unlike the Hall which gave almost straight on to the village. As they were getting out of the motor Uncle Frederick mislaid a glove. He began to fuss: it was the same agitation she remembered before going shooting, so that he looked suddenly more like someone's mother, or aunt.

'But where is it?' he cried agitatedly. 'I *had* it –'

'Oh, come in without,' Mother said easily. But he was still put out. Edwina felt it as they wound through the corridors to the chapel. Two small boys were preparing the altar, lighting candles. She angled to kneel between Uncle and Mother, but felt that she would rather have been beside just him. She grew restless and looked about her. Mother tapped her on the hand.

Mass was mysterious. (Nurse said: Mumbo jumbo.) But she liked the sound. It was foreign and exciting. But it was safe too and familiar, because as Mother had explained once it had gone on for nearly two thousand years. Father and Philip, Aunt Josephine, the people who went up to the Norman church in the village, their ancestors had changed religion because it was too difficult to be good; and they'd stolen the churches while they were about it. The people who owned this chapel, their great-great-great – even farther back – some of them had actually been killed for going on praying this way. The red light, with its warm glow, showed that Jesus, the real Jesus, was there: safe in the little house, the tabernacle.

A glow like the light wrapped her round now. The warmth of the room, people breathing (the oxen's breath warming the baby Jesus). She felt safe – not the terror with music, with her fingers, with her feelings for Uncle Frederick. This was the safe world. You had only to love Jesus, which was easy, and all would go well. For ever and ever, until you died. And then – heaven.

So much on the table, so much shining silver, starched linen, green branches, hothouse plants. A special smell, of Sunday. Coming down to luncheon. Then upstairs to rest: until Grandma Illingworth's visit at three-thirty.

She came every Sunday. Straightaway after luncheon the whole house would seem to tauten. The nursery bell rang just before she was expected so that Edwina and Cora, tidied up again after their rests, could be downstairs in the drawing-room, waiting, tensed up like everyone else. The clock in the hall would strike the half-hour; the church clock, the little French clocks in the drawing-room, the clock on the stairs and – almost exactly after – the bell outside.

And in she came. She was a ship, a galleon, in full sail. Her skirts always inches wider round than anyone else's. Her hair always at the same height and always – brown-grey, not white at all – tightly knotted as if she were angry with it. Then that funny face, almost in a way like Punch (you could see in Father, in Aunt Josephine, how the mould had been used again, but softened). And oddest of all: when she smiled, when she spoke, the most wonderful, awful thing would happen to the bottom half of her face. She seemed to chomp. It would widen – Edwina would watch, always marvelling that it could go on widening so far and not split.

Sailing on, into the drawing-room, to *her* chair. Hers when she'd lived at the Hall, it had arms and a high back and was faded purple satin. As always she was followed by Miss Kinross, her companion, on tiptoe, apologetic almost for being there (although she'd have needed to apologize even more if for any reason she'd dared not to be). She carried Grandma's cushion, Grandma's crochet, and her smelling salts, and also one or two mysterious bottles in a large bag. A red liquid and a pink liquid.

Grandma sat down. And this was the funniest thing – it was as if, like in the fairy tales, everyone was altered just by her coming in. By her waving her magic wand. She, Edwina, so often pushed about, told where to go and what not to do, would feel suddenly important, all right. Father, Aunt Josephine, Mother, became, as she looked at them, half their real size.

Last of all, Harry the footman brought in Bath Bun. He was an aged pug dog and was placed on Grandma's lap, on a special crochet mat. His head slightly up, he looked round him, watching. Edwina thought he often gave looks of scorn to save Grandma's energy.

'Frederick,' she announced. 'I see we have Frederick amongst us.'

'Present,' Uncle Frederick said merrily. He wasn't, never seemed afraid of her.

'And what have you got to tell me, Frederick? News from the Court, news from sunny climes?' She chomped while she waited for his reply. Then: 'Quite a snap,' she commented, passing on, leaving Adelina behind.

They all had to speak up for themselves: that was the routine. Cora was, if not exempt, not taken very seriously. Soon she would be. Philip when he was there would go white with worry and forced attention. Giving an account of yourself, it was called.

Father was spoken to sometimes as if he were a little boy. 'Tom,' she said today, 'I've spoken to Holmes, I'll thank you not to suggest that he holds back on the east copse – I was very displeased when I heard. That's not the way to make the most of the estate.'

'Yes, of course. I'll see to that, Mama.'

'*Edwina* will tell me the capital of France – '

It came out quick, cheeky. She felt pleased. The sun shone.

'The capital of Italy.' Easy.

'The capital of Spain – ' Oh dear, not easy at all. She'd heard of it, but . . . She opened and shut her mouth like a fish. Uncle Frederick, sitting next to her, leaned over as if to tie his shoe lace, banged against her, breathing 'Madrid', turning it into a cough.

'Come on,' said Grandma, twisting Bath Bun's ear, so badly that he began to shake it.

'Madrid,' shouted Edwina, 'Madrid, Madrid.'

'Child, I'm not deaf. Done well though. Please to be a little quicker next time. Helen, how is her French? I would like to hear that some German was being thought of, I have a great respect for the Germans – their ambitions, their capacity for hard work. I should like Philip to visit there. A spell at Heidelberg perhaps, Tom?'

'We could see,' Father said a little uneasily, crossing and uncrossing his legs. 'He's after all only thirteen.'

'A tour of the whole Continent,' Uncle Frederick said. 'The Grand Tour is probably still the best. So much culture – even if it isn't taken in, isn't followed through, some always remains. Even for women,' he added, glancing over at Mother, who wasn't looking at him.

'Bother culture,' said Grandma, prodding Bath Bun absent-mindedly. 'Surely it is nearly tea-time?'

Tea was more relaxed. The worst was over. And she wouldn't stay very long afterwards, just enough perhaps to play a game of cards with Edwina and Aunt Josephine. A more complicated version of 'Snap': 'Snip, Snap, Snorum', which she'd played as a girl.

How she ate! At one time Edwina had thought, until Philip laughed her out of it, that all grandmothers ate like that. Up and down went the large jaws, on maids of honour, curd tarts, seed cakes, Battenberg. The chomping really came into its own, with of course lots of licking of her lips before and after. Often too she licked her fingers, afterwards wiping them on her big embroidered napkin.

She pronounced on Votes for Women. Her remarks were addressed rather challengingly to Mother, although it was she who'd brought up the subject. It seemed to be something she didn't approve of.

Mother didn't respond. Politics left her cold, she said. Perhaps Frederick had something to say, about the women of Italy? 'You have a special knowledge after all.'

Father said: 'I heard this rather pleasant story about Asquith, opening some university buildings in Wales, I think. The students asked him: "Are you in favour of Suffrage?" His reply was: "That's a subject I prefer to discuss when ladies are not present . . ." '

Bath Bun yapped. He sat on a small chair beside Grandma, a plain napkin fastened around his neck with a gold pin. Miss Kinross had to tie it on. She became very nervous while doing it, the more so because Grandma snapped and chomped at her: 'Be careful of him. You'll throttle him one of these days. He's only restless because he's hungry. Poor little currant bun . . .' He drooled. He drooled a lot in fact – hence the napkin.

' "He is foolish who supposes
Dogs are ill that have hot noses," ' said Uncle Frederick.

'What profundity,' said Mother.

'Landor's, not mine – I was about to remark that Landor had a Pomeranian, a little yellow pom, who commented on everything. Who was *asked* to comment on everything. A wag of the tail though, not a yap. *He* inspired that rhyme. I couldn't aspire of course to such profundity. I had the memory from a very dear old lady whose mind is quite crystal clear about Florence in the 'forties – though not, alas, about Florence in the twentieth century . . .'

Bath Bun yapped again. *His* opinion. Usually he had a saucer of tea about halfway through the meal, or when he began to look restless for it. Edwina thought he was rather horrible. She felt he was sneaky – that if he'd been in the room alone with her he'd take note of what she was doing and then tell the grown-ups. She thought suddenly of music. Of the piano. If that pug found me playing, she thought, then he would hurry off, his legs going like a rocking horse, off to tell them all: 'Come on. Edwina's making a funny noise on that thing in the billiard-room. Come on. She'll break it, for certain . . .'

That was what she was frightened of later that evening, when it wasn't quite time to go to bed, and Grandma had gone and the grown-ups were out of the way resting. She wanted, she told Nurse, to go and see Macouba. He hadn't seemed quite right yesterday. 'Just for a moment.'

The billiard-room was cold. No fire had been lit. She thought that her fingers would be stiff. But when she'd turned the top back and *dared* to sit down on the little embroidered stool and spread her hands out, they started almost at once to burn.

She came down on the notes – six, seven sounds all singing together, and always the next sounds there in her head – only just in front of her hands so that she plunged and swam and made a torrent, a tempest. Her hands fed her head, then her head seemed to feed her hands and although it was there in the rest of her body – the tingle the glow the wild happy unhappy excitement – really it was coming all of it from the tips of her fingers. And so when the first rush had died down she let them stroke the keys, just the tips, her hands as wide as they would go. They would never open wide enough to receive all that excitement, growing and growing till she burst again and it was through, the sound flooded.

She never heard the door open. She screamed with terror as two hands came round her eyes. She should have recognized them though – she recognized afterwards, thinking about it, their smell: some kind of scent, something soapy, ferny, and soft.

'Is that what you do in here?' he asked. 'Is that what you meant?'

'You gave me a horrid fright,' she said sulkily. 'I'm not supposed to be here – '

He put his arm round her. 'That's not really playing of course, not what *they* call playing. But immensely exciting. You'll have to have lessons, Little Bear. If you want to do anything about all this, you'll have to have lessons. Shall I perhaps arrange what I can before I go? Then by the time I come again . . .'

'When's that, when's that?' She felt the cold suddenly, thinking: he's going. And remembering too: when he comes again he'll have her with him.

'The spring. We are to be married at Easter. We shall probably come over as part of the honeymoon.' He tightened his arm round her: 'I'm hoping, Edwina, it won't be too cold. Adelina isn't strong. That has been one of the worries – if she should be where it's very damp and chill.'

'What might happen to her?'

'If she gets really unwell then – she might be taken from us.'

'Taken where? Who by?'

'She might die.' He pursed his lips, kissed her forehead. He smelt so beautiful. 'She might go to Heaven, Edwina.'

'Was he riding one of *her* horses?' The teacups rattled. Nurse's sister was there yet again.

'Very smart he looked, I'm sure, *she* was astride of course. The Master – if looks could kill. She's very defiant about it. *His* influence, I should think.'

'They'll ride like that in foreign parts . . .'

'. . . Something to do with her life before she married. She must have learnt odd ways.'

'Very odd, I should say. But then, she and Mr Illingworth – there's an unlikely pair to be pulling a carriage. You must wonder. I should. Indeed I should.'

'Not at all. I always make it my business to find out – things. For that marriage, you can blame the old one. The old Mrs I. Always bothered about abroad she was. Sending her son off every few years. That's what *I* heard. But not

Miss Josephine – oh no. She's only a girl of course.'

'Yes. *And?*'

'One of those trips it was. Germany, I think, or was it Switzerland – one of those *continental* places. He's at this hotel, you see, and who's there but *her* and that brother. And *not able to pay their bill* – '

'Your voice, Ada. You'd best mind – '

'Of course the Master's there and sees it all. The next thing is – he pays up. And Bob's your uncle. No one as soft as men. In no time at all it's wedding bells . . . I don't doubt she was very charming – she's all charm when she wants, you know. And pretty too, I'll give you that. There'd be no resisting her, I'm sure. And him, that brother, it'll be the same. Make friends as easy as – Not with *me* he wouldn't though. "Oh Nurse, is it all right if I come up and visit little Weenie?" That foreign charm. Let him try, I say – '

Rattle, rattle went the teacups.

'He'll not bother you, Ada. I shouldn't fear – '

'Indeed. They say he's met up with a *titled* lady. Cook said . . . You'd be surprised what I overhear.'

'Still, it's a funny sight, Ada, a woman riding like that! Didn't she write to the *newspaper* about it?'

'She did. About how natural it is. Natural indeed. If God had meant ladies to open their legs like that . . .'

There were six of them at the dancing class, not counting Madame Lambert who taught them and Miss Bowser who played the piano. The girls were: Clare, Muriel, Violet and Edwina, and the boys: Ned and Laurence. Violet was dark like Edwina but very beautiful with it. Her smooth hair, her motionless face reminded Edwina of nothing so much as wax fruit – Muriel was her younger sister. Clare, the daughter of the family where Edwina went for Mass, was dark also, but sallow too and a little sullen. Her lip curled back when she talked or smiled. Ned she loved to watch. He was quicksilver. Pointed too: head, nose, hands and above all feet. His dancing shoes even, seemed more pointed than anyone else's. His eyes darted. His hands flew about.

But Laurence was serious, solemn almost. His dark hair lay flat and polished, his face too was polished like wood. He always did exactly what Madame Lambert said – yet it came out wrong.

Madame Lambert had been a dancer herself once, a ballet dancer. But that had been nearly forty years ago in eighteen-seventy something. The dancing they learned was a mixture. There were steps which really were ballet, there were floating sorts of dances, there were attempts to be fairies. Finally, there were the 'real' dances: the waltzes, the polkas, the mazurkas. Then they took partners, but because they were uneven, two girls always had to dance together.

'One two three, one two three,' went Madame. The sleeves of her mauve dress were very loose and the arms which peeped from them were all crepey, somehow matching the material. She seemed to have difficulty rising on her toes. It was hard to imagine her as the light-footed ballerina, drawings and photographs of whom were all round the walls (Examining these was always encouraged: 'If you want an example of pas de deux, see then how I am poised in this picture . . .').

Ned was her favourite. He could move so quickly and easily. But he laughed at her. They all knew that. He would pull faces, shake his head, flap his ears while her back was turned. Laurence was her unfavourite. He didn't seem to mind being shouted at. He took everything absolutely calmly. When corrected, told to place his foot to the left ('Your *left*, Laurence,') he did so with goodwill. His face wore an expression of perfect peace. It was all beyond him. It made no matter what he did.

Sometimes he would talk to Edwina, in the odd moments. 'My father is a composer,' he said today. 'He writes music. He sits in a room all alone. Sometimes he goes to concerts where they're playing what he's written.'

She listened in wonder. That anyone should do that all day, every day of their life.

'Sometimes he says, "I'm very fatigued. I worked on the Fantasia until three in the morning." '

She marvelled.

She determined that today she would have him as a partner. As Madame began pairing them off, she said: 'I dance with Laurence this time. You said so last week – '

Madame had said nothing of the kind, but obviously she didn't like it suggested she'd forgotten, so: 'Yes, yes of course. Edwina then with Laurence.' The music started up. Edwina envied Miss Bowser, hunched, one shoulder higher than the other, dark hair screwed in an unsuccessful knot, banging out the notes . . .

'Oh see me dance the polka!' Laurence was very bad. 'Oh see me having such fun!' He was red with effort, but still unmoved. When it was over, he said: 'My mamma doesn't wear corsets.'

'How do you know?' Edwina asked, shocked.

'You can tell of course. Her frocks are called Liberty Gowns, because they give you liberty. My sisters are at art school, one is in Paris. I am going to be a diplomat. I shall arrange history.'

'Tra, *la*la, lala*la*la . . .' 'In the Shadows' by Herman Finck, thumped by Miss Bowser.

'Laurence Wethered. You are *not* attending . . .'

'How long's he staying?'

'Only three more days. Then it's back to the land of hokey-pokey. Little Miss-you-know-who will be *quite* impossible.'

Click of knitting needles. 'Have you tried the fizzy tablets? It says they melt down the walls of all the little fat cells, gets rid of the oil in them . . .'

'Remarkable . . . I hear that little one of Arthur Pickersgill's gone home. They've too many.'

'Too many. Have you got the Ally Sloper? We might win, I dare say. Read it out – I don't have my spectacles – '

'"A maid from the Emerald Isle
Met a Yankee who'd gathered his pile
Determined to wed him
She carefully led him . . ."

'You can choose from "aisle, beguile, crocodile, fertile, Gentile . . ." '

'What about "up the aisle"; that fits, doesn't it?'

She hated the monkey-puzzle tree. Dark and spiky, its shape was evil. Today in the afternoon breeze its ugly branches waved slightly. She thought it was something to do with death, and moved on. Her feet dragged through a pile of fallen leaves. 'Can I go out? I want to go out – ' But now she was here she didn't know what to do with herself.

It was cold and crisp, the sun suddenly glowing through the bare branches in the park. The coloured songbirds, the ones Uncle Frederick had given them, darted gaudily from branch to branch in their house near the peacocks. She walked on, farther than she was meant to go: past even the cottage where the head gardener Mr Ramsden lived with his brown bowler and his chestnut beard and his fierce temper. Through a broken gateway to the old overgrown garden no one ever visited. Elderberries, a thistle tree, thick nettles. Neglected, dank.

Death, dying, going home. The leaves beneath her feet, some crinkly red, some sodden, were dead. She had had a sister who'd died, born before her. The grave was visited. What would I feel like if Cora died, what would I *feel* like?

Suddenly, from the long damp undergrowth, bounding out, came the small tight body of Spot, Arthur's dog. She recognized him from the time Arthur had brought him to the stables. Rolling about in the hay, lying quiet when told. Now he rushed up to her, squirming. He seemed to be three small rolls, his head foxy and pointed. Emily loved him, used to dress him in an old sunbonnet, Arthur said.

Emily was dead. She played with Spot a little, throwing him a stick, pretending a tug of war. Then he wanted her arms. He nestled, one paw hanging over. Floppy, unbelievably heavy. I'll never manage, she thought, determining there and then to take him home. She was afraid for him: the carts going by, a small dog caught under the wheels – finished.

No one was about when she went through the Hall gates. The main street was quiet, almost deserted. Arthur lived in a small lane, the end cottage, in the shadow of the Norman church with its steps up to the railed pavement.

One of the children opened the door to her. A dark boy in dirty jersey and torn woollen knickerbockers. He looked surprised.

'Aye,' he said, screwing up his eyes, 'that Spot?' He called inside: 'It's Miss Edwina, Mam, brought back Spot –' Massed behind him in the small room was child upon child, pairs and pairs of eyes behind great manes of hair, watching her. She could smell cooking, something with oatmeal.

As she stepped inside the boy clouted Spot suddenly across the ears: 'That's for running off.' Just then Mrs Arthur came in. Edwina had seen her before: Christmas, the annual cricket match, a party once in the grounds of the Hall. Now, thumping down the tiny stairs, red in the face, wisps of hair stuck to her anxious face, she looked quite different. 'Sit you down, miss.' She shook a dirty flat cushion off a chair. A small boy with no shoes on hit out suddenly at his sister who began to yell. The big boy cuffed them both. Edwina had never seen anything so quick, so efficient. Two strokes to one, two to the other. 'Give over,' he said.

'*You* give over,' Mrs Arthur said, in a flat voice. 'Cock of t'midden – He plays father,' she said to Edwina. 'Always playing Dad. What will ye take, summat to drink?'

Edwina said primly, sitting upright on the uncomfortable chair, one of its legs shorter than the others so that it fell forward continually: 'I've hardly come any way, thank you. I don't need anything.' The younger children were all staring at her, looking wonderingly at her fitted coat, tammy, bright red scarf, shiny black buttoned boots. One little girl had on broken-down boots too big for her, and laces in only one.

Mrs Arthur asked cautiously: 'Should you be out – baht your nurse?'

Edwina said, 'I'm allowed to go where I please this afternoon. Miss Norris is taken ill.'

A stack of oatcakes stood drying on a stool in front of the range. Others were piled in a scuttle. It was these she had smelled. She felt cold and empty and awkward.

'I'm sorry about – Emily.'

'Aye,' Mrs Arthur said. She wiped her hands on her apron. One of the children said, in a squeaky voice: 'She wanted a orange. Afore she went she asked for a orange.'

'When had she seen one?' Edwina asked, then answered herself: 'They were given out over Christmas. I remember. We gave them to everyone, to families –' Her voice sounded wrong, it came out tight and loud.

'D'ye want to see her?' Mrs Arthur asked dully, and when Edwina nodded: 'I'll take ye then.'

None of the children followed them up. Emily didn't look as Edwina had imagined. All that coughing. She'd pictured a red face puckered up, damp hair. Here was a little wax doll. Tiny. Lovely. She looked at her for a long time. Mrs Arthur had her hands clasped together. Her eyelids were pink and puffy and the skin all round her nose dry and sore. Edwina turned. It was then that the idea came to her.

Mrs Arthur said: 'She looks bonny, eh?'

Edwina nodded. Then she said, as if plunging into cold water: 'Would you like Cora?'

Mrs Arthur frowned.

Edwina said, 'I mean – you've lost Emily. Would you like to have Cora?'

'I don't – I mun go down.' She looked confused, puzzled.

But it was so clear to Edwina. 'We could give you Cora. She's the same age. I'm sure if I asked Mother. She's too small to bother where she lives . . .' Her voice trailed away. Something was muddled and wrong, wicked wrong.

Mrs Arthur's face crumpled, frighteningly – almost as if it were paper that Edwina had screwed up in her fist.

'Who on them sent you?'

'No one,' Edwina said. 'No one. I just thought . . .' the words faded in her dry mouth.

'Can't folk be left then? Can't they be left in their grief, but ye've to come saying things like that?' She had laid her head down on to her arm.

'I'm going,' Edwina said, 'I'll go. I'm sorry – ' She crashed down the stairs. The children were sitting in a small circle. 'What's up?' called the boy, coming towards her. But she'd already got her hand on the latch.

She ran all the way. She was lucky and didn't see anyone. She'd timed it well too: all was quiet in the nursery. Nurse was mixing paste for Cora's scraps. German scraps: Hansel and Gretel and the house in the forest; the sugar house. Edwina couldn't look at them.

'Lost your tongue?' Nurse said after a while. 'Left it with the peacocks again?'

Uncle Frederick's last day. It was to have been wonderful – sad and happy at once, because although there was the sorrow of his going there was also to be an outing. Just her, and Mother and Uncle Frederick. They were to go into York, and have luncheon there. Uncle Frederick was to buy her a present . . .

But she woke with a feeling of doom and dread, the taste of yesterday afternoon still in her mouth. She looked at her best clothes laid out. The little red cloak, her muff, the cream cashmere dress with the wool lace neck and cuffs.

Katy, one of the housemaids, came up after breakfast just when she was about to be sent to the lavatory. 'Miss Edwina – she's to go downstairs *immediately*.'

Nurse said: 'She's to open her bowels first.' Edwina paid no attention. She knew anyway that if she sat there half an hour nothing would happen. Inside she had turned to stone.

Everyone was in the drawing-room. Standing. Her father glanced at his watch just as she came in. He looked grave and sad.

'Ah, Edwina!' he said, almost as if surprised to see her, as if he'd just recognized her. 'Ah, Edwina!' Uncle Frederick, darling Uncle, didn't even look at her. Aunt Josephine stood grim, silent, her mouth pulled together.

Father said: 'You know why we've sent for you?' She shook her head.

'Come along, Edwina,' Mother said sharply.

'No,' she said stoutly. 'No, I don't.' Her voice wavered.

Father said: 'Did you go to Arthur Pickersgill's cottage yesterday?'

'Yes,' Edwina admitted.

'What possessed you, what came over you? I cannot believe that a child such as you – It's *preposterous* –'

'We are *all* ashamed,' Mother said. 'Frederick was quite horrified.' Aunt Josephine could be seen nodding. Uncle Frederick's face was still turned away. 'Your own sister. And you distressed Mrs Pickersgill terribly. Arthur told Cook. She saw fit to tell us. I could not believe my ears.' Aunt Josephine nodded again in grim agreement. Edwina thought that perhaps Uncle Frederick looked far away because he was trying hard not to come in and take her side. Certainly *he* would understand that she meant it for the best. But he was thinking perhaps already of the sun in Italy, of the palaces and the white marble, of his voyage across the sea?

'. . . to say *nothing* of the risks of contracting whooping-cough. Naturally there will be no treat today. Your mother and uncle have decided not to go out either – You have spoilt the day for them as well as for yourself. You will stay in the nursery all day, without talking. Bread and milk only to eat. That may perhaps calm you down and get rid of some of the ideas you seem to have been possessed by . . .'

She said, 'I meant it nicely. I meant –' But it sounded hopeless. The words faded away. She had indeed been possessed. Otherwise how could she, how *could* she have offered them anything so purely awful as Cora?

A day so terrible, that could have been so happy. A wind started up, damp blowy rain against the high nursery windows. She didn't want the bread and milk. Couldn't have eaten anything. She sat with her hands on her lap, just staring in front of her. Nurse, who knew it all, treated her like a leper. She said: 'Go and sit on your throne again.

The poisons will go back up if you're costive.' With her next breath she muttered, 'Your own sister – ' She rushed over to hug Cora. 'Nurse's little darling, you'll never leave us, will you? *Will you?*'

The weather had grown really cold. It would soon be Christmas. She was making Uncle Frederick the most beautiful Christmas card that had ever been seen – drawing and painting, cutting out and sticking, pasting down fluffy wool. It was a snow scene but she drew the sea on as well.

Mother had again that pinched, slightly yellow look. Aunt Josephine was very solicitous, fussing about her sitting down. 'It's never been so bad,' Edwina heard Mother say: 'Beef tea only this time. And peaches, I crave peaches.' She complained of the smell of the camellias, the tuberoses. 'So sickly,' she said fretfully. The hunting season was six weeks old now. She said wistfully: 'If I were only on French Carotte now, setting out – how well I should feel. I know it would do me good . . .'

Philip came home. He and Edwina had little to say to each other. There was a diabolo craze at his school. He practised throw and catch all day, frequently and angrily disentangling the cord from the spool. Miss Norris complained because he came into the schoolroom to show off. A champion, Edwina learnt, could manage eighty-five catches a minute.

The undergardeners brought in great piles of evergreens, holly, ilex, yew. The Christmas tree was arranged downstairs. The whole look of the house changed. Sarah told her that if she went out to the hives at midnight, just before it became Christmas, she would hear all the bees humming.

Christmas was wonderful. And she was invited to a party two days after.

'Whoever is Laurence Wethered?' her mother asked, turning the large floppy invitation over. It was very beautiful, and had a picture of fairies dressed in gossamer garments just entering a wood, watched by elves and gnomes, all drawn in pale browns and greens, rather spiky. A witch lurked amongst the trees.

Laurence's house was very untidy. Lying about the hall were tennis racquets, croquet mallets and other summery objects. Mrs Laurence herself – Edwina thought of her as Mrs Laurence – was huge. And made to look more so by her great peacock-blue flowing gown with bits of gold on its wide loose sleeves – how different from Aunt Josephine who was all boned in, right up to the chin. Perhaps Mrs Laurence had no bones at all, so loose and plump and soft did she look: crowned by curly greasy yellow hair and a face of shiny red and gold.

She beamed on Edwina. 'You little darling.' Violet appeared from nowhere. '*All* you lovely little things!' She put an arm round Edwina. She smelt exciting, strong, heady. Laurence stood there suddenly. He looked tidier, more solemn than ever. 'My little wooden soldier,' said his mother, patting but not looking at him. Then she said:

'Laurence's Daddy is not even attempting to compose this afternoon. He will come in and play the piano for you all later. Now he is in his study with the 'cello . . .' And sure enough, a little way away, the 'cello could be heard. Oh, oh, thought Edwina, what a wonderful world, what a wonderful life. May this afternoon never end.

And for a time it seemed as if it wouldn't. It spun on and on delightfully. In the corner of the room was an enormous bran pie – just to look at it was good, to imagine plunging one's hand into the warm soft dark: to choose, to reject, to choose again . . .

All the dancing class was there. Mrs Laurence was overwhelmed by Violet's beauty. Lifting her chin, examining her face: 'You lovely little thing! I could *paint* you I could – '

They played Musical Chairs in the great dark-walled room with its exciting eastern drapes and its weird smell as of some exotic fruit. Ned said (she was surprised that, quicksilver, he wasn't still in): 'The girls *pushed* of course.' Edwina had not dared to push. Mrs Laurence didn't seem to notice things like that so that there was a lot of cheating. Then one of the older daughters came down to help – fair and large like her mother, but newer and not so shiny. 'We can't have this,' she said, going over to one small boy who, pushed by Muriel, had burst into tears. Laurence was still in. There were three chairs left now. Ned said: 'I say, don't you think it'll be rather bad form if Laurence wins?' His eyes darting about, he told her what he'd got for Christmas. His great-uncle, who was a major-general, had come and played – or rather fought with him, massed his lead troops for battle, showed him all about strategy. 'Strategy,' Ned said, 'is how you work out beforehand what the other chaps are going to do, then you do it first –'

They were surprised by the end of the game. Laurence had won. 'But that wasn't right,' the daughter said.

His mother said: 'Let the little man win, Ginny.'

'Nonsense,' said Ginny, in a loud stage whisper, 'Mummy, he *can't*, he mayn't.' She announced: 'We're going to do that last bit again.'

'No, really,' said the boy who'd lost. Laurence made no effort this time, strolling only. The other boy, who was called Hal, sat down easily and was declared the winner.

There were three more games before tea. She was so happy she couldn't believe it.

Tea was a splendid affair. She couldn't take her eyes off the walls. They were decorated with panels which looked very much like the invitation, except that instead of fairies there were young men and swooning women. They all had very long bodies and looked as if they might snap in two if a storm got up.

Oh, it was lovely to be greedy. She put the almond paste from her cake on the side of her plate to enjoy at the last. Then she turned away for a moment, looked back – and it had disappeared. It was after that things began to go wrong. She knew who'd taken it – the fat boy on her left, who said he lived in York. 'My father's a doctor,' he'd said proudly. Now he was half smiling, smirking triumph at her. She didn't want anything else to eat. A minute later she felt a sudden urgent need to go to the lavatory. She had to climb down, with everybody looking, and go over and ask Ginny, who took her down a corridor to a door with a curtain over it. When Edwina went through this and tried the inner door, it was locked. She rattled it.

'That will do,' said a deep voice.

She ran off and hid in the hall behind a coat stand, squeezing her legs together. And trying not to think of the cracker cake she would be missing. There was the sound of flushing, a tap running, and then out came a very large Norfolk-jacketed man with a drooping reddish moustache and red face. He walked away with his head bent forward in the direction of the back of the house.

She ran in – but already it was too late. She'd forgotten the silk party knickers with their button fastenings on either side. She got one lot undone and then – out it came. A sudden warm torrent. There was no stopping it; she watched horrified, unable even to raise herself on to the big wooden throne, a great pool round her.

What shall I do? Her feet were all right, just a little damp on her socks, but *that* part, the part Nurse always spoke ill of, was very wet: between her legs, misery. And the floor! There was a little towel hanging on a hook nearby. Bending down, she rubbed very hard to mop it all up. Then she stuffed the wet and smelly warm towel behind the pipes. She washed her hands thoroughly, like she'd been told to, and went out.

But it was all spoilt. When, not too long after, the famous Marius Wethered, Laurence's wonderful father, came in – and yes, he was seen to be the same man who'd kept her waiting – she could enjoy none of it.

He looked stern, a little mournful, walking as she'd seen him walk away from the lavatory. Mrs Laurence said: 'All these little people, Marius, have been asking for you to play.' She whispered something to him. He smiled, a visible effort, and then as if one smile bred another – just like Nurse said – he gave them all a talk, smiling away.

'Primrose, my wife, has been telling you I write music. Well – I don't.' Pause. 'Some wonderful little beings – I call them Mannikins – do it for me. They come to me and they say, "Here, listen to this!" Then they play it in my ears, sometimes on my hands, and I go to the piano and hey presto, there it is! Sometimes they're happy tunes, sometimes sad. Often they're music to go with the lovely drawings that Primrose, Mrs Wethered does . . . Let me play you a little . . . Here's a dance that the lovely ladies of the Court do, while they're waiting for the knights to assemble for the jousting . . .'

It went on a long time. She wanted to think it wonderful but somehow it wasn't, although parts of it were sweetly pretty. She could have danced to it if she hadn't a wet bottom. The children all sat round politely, full of food and drink.

'Do any of you little ones want to play the piano for Daddy? Then you can say you've played before a great composer – '

Clare walked up. Edwina was full of anger and shame. When she heard Clare tinkle, she thought, if that's all you have to do . . .

She had looked forward so to the bran pie, but that too was spoilt. When it came to her turn she could think only of wet: it was as if she could see a creeping dark patch coming off her hands. The fat boy waited behind her. After a while – perhaps he felt guilty because he'd stolen her icing: 'You smell,' he said, in a loud whisper, coming up close and hissing in her ear. 'You *smell* . . .'

Mother's riding clothes came all the way from London. Today she was in dark green, her breeches covered almost by her safety skirt and the long coat over it all. Her face was very set, her head a little on one side. Aunt Josephine, worried-looking, stood beside her, as if to protect her. 'This icy weather, Helen . . .'

Father said angrily: 'The going may be rough. What *is* this nonsense?'

'Nonsense to you all. I'm going on French Carotte, quite the gentlest – I wish I had as soft a mouth.' She glimpsed Edwina on the stairs. 'What are *you* doing here?'

It was a beautiful day. Only a little mist, a winter sun across the hoar-rimmed ploughed fields. She watched them go off to the meet. Father was on Brown Rappee; Philip, very smart and superior, riding Comore. Soon she would go herself. 'Out of my way, *ma'am*,' he'd said, passing her on the stairs. He had little time for her these days.

She kept thinking all day about something happening to her father. She thought of him usually as so definite, always there. An oak tree. The worry stayed with her. She couldn't say anything to Arthur when he took her out in the afternoon – Cora in the basket saddle – because she was shy with him still. Offering them Cora. It would come over her suddenly, a blush inside, a blush outside. He'd never mentioned it. He'd been if anything nicer to her than ever.

But everyone came back safely. It had been a good day. Father, his back to the fire, gave an account to Aunt Josephine. '. . . wind in the west, good for scent . . . We found in Wilson Wood. A big dog fox . . . headed him back up Bowdin Gill . . . crossed the full length of Rilsdale West Moor. Over an hour's run – hounds killed him at the low end of Lumb Moor . . .'

Mother looked tired but happy. Her skin glowed. 'I was right to go,' she said. 'I feel wonderful, wonderfully fit.' When Cora was reciting she was very animated and clapped longer than usual. Philip looking this way and that, fidgeted. '*Don't*,' Aunt Josephine said irritably.

A good happy healthy winter's day, in the New Year of 1908.

She heard a bell ringing in the middle of the night. Then doors banging in the distance; other doors outside. She was wide awake now. She wanted to creep out and discover what was happening, but something made her afraid and instead she lay absolutely still, tense, her fingers like claws.

'Tell me,' she said to Sarah first thing in the morning, 'tell me what's happened?'

'She's just a bit poorly –'

It was Mother she should have worried about. Mother might die, and never know that Edwina loved her.

Two days later: her first piano lesson. She was to go to a Miss Batterhurst, who'd been recommended by Lady Warren whose daughters had learned from her twelve or thirteen years ago. Mother had said: 'She was quite good in her day or so I'm told. She studied for a time in Germany – ' Now she lived with her sister, a three-mile drive away. Edwina disliked her at first sight. Her house smelled of mothballs.

'I am rather tired today,' Miss Batterhurst said, getting slowly out of her chair. She had a very white face, the blood had all run away from it and gone to her hands instead, which were very red. She was hunched when she sat down and even more when she stood up. 'You cannot imagine how fatiguing – ' she gave a small, half-finished yawn, red hand held to mouth, then raising her voice a little, called imperiously: 'Millicent!'

'My sister,' she explained. 'She doesn't have enough to do.' There was a rustling from behind the brown heavy curtains at the far end of the room – Edwina had thought they were another set of windows. A small frail woman shuffled out. She wore a widow's cap on her scanty white hair and black rosettes on her slippers.

Sitting down in a comfortable chair alongside the piano, Miss Batterhurst said: 'Ring for a drink, if you please.'

Her sister pulled the bell rope. 'What sort?' she asked in a quavery voice.

'I haven't introduced you,' Miss Batterhurst said, more as a statement than an apology. Then: 'She will have some cocoa. For me, the usual.'

The cocoa was very gritty, skin formed rapidly while she was trying to drink it and she could feel a moustache on her upper lip. 'The usual' turned out to be a yellow milky drink in a thick glass. 'Your nog,' Millicent said, taking it from the maid and bringing it over.

'Now we can begin,' Miss Batterhurst said.

Edwina had thought she would be allowed just to sit

down and make that wonderful wonderful noise, and that then she would be shown at once – but at once – how to read what was written on the music sheet, there up on the stand. But it was not so. Miss Batterhurst, yawning still (she seemed to have caught it from herself, so that each yawn led to yet another) held a little ivory stick rather languidly above Edwina's fingers. She showed her that she must use all five fingers: *'thus'* – forwards and back, up and down, up and down, hand held just right. It was easy, and quite without point. But it was as if Miss Batterhurst's fingers itched to use the little stick. At the end of the lesson suddenly, she leaned over and rapped her.

'I hear you're meant to be quite talented. We all have to begin the same,' she said wearily. 'And we all end the same, I sometimes think.'

Edwina wanted to cry with the disappointment. She rubbed her knuckles angrily, but Miss Batterhurst didn't notice.

'Millicent!' she called. 'Ring for her to be shown out – if you please.'

'She's lost it, of course.'

'No question. The Master – if looks could . . . He was quite sharpish with me even, he should have stopped her, no doubt of it.'

'She's very wilful – '

'*Very*. And there's one who's inherited it . . .'

'. . . She's only to give him another boy and she's done. It's not much to ask.'

'It's not. Old Mrs Illingworth, she's made it quite clear – one boy isn't enough. Master Philip, a cricket ball could hit him tomorrow – And the sickness about! Two days and he could be dead. Bowel inflammation – there's a possibility . . .'

'Indeed – '

'If she'd just pull herself together . . . Of course there've been other misses – without benefit of hunting.'

'Still, hunting – it's *asking*, isn't it?'

She drove everyone wild. She knew it and could do nothing about it. It was as if she was compelled to ask again and again: 'But what's she look like? What's her *wedding* dress like? What'll she wear on her feet?'

No one could tell her anything. Then at the end of February there was a photograph, sent to Mother. Tinted most delicately, it showed someone of such fragility, such a pale, fair person – that Edwina was more puzzled than ever. On that last visit she had heard Mother say to Uncle Frederick: 'She's Black, I suppose?' And he'd answered, 'Yes, a little. But not of course like her Roman cousins . . .'

And now this picture. She took her puzzle to Aunt Josephine. Aunt Josephine didn't laugh, but she smiled at Edwina. Blacks, and Whites, she told her, were just *names* – like Roundheads and Cavaliers. 'And you've learned about those from Miss Norris. But, as to quite what these Blacks *are* – well, your uncle explained to me once but . . .'

She seemed quite stuck – to get no further, but Mother coming in, overhearing, said: 'Oh *Blacks*. It comes from when they made Rome capital of the new Italy – what, forty years ago, and the Pope who'd ruled Rome always was ousted and a king took over. Some of the old families sided with the Pope and some with the new King – they're the Whites of course. Feelings run high. It splits Roman society right down the middle. I hope I have it right? Trust Frederick to get himself involved with some such nonsense.' Then she lost interest. She said to Aunt Josephine, 'She has some lovely clothes. Frederick has chosen many of them, I believe.'

Perhaps Aunt Adelina was like a doll for Uncle Frederick, something for him to play with, cosset, dress up – as she dressed up her doll, Victoria? And like perhaps, that lovely cut-out paper doll she had seen once and coveted: that stood up in camisole and drawers, ready for you to press on to it any one of a dozen outfits . . .

They were to arrive in the afternoon, for tea. They had been a few days in Paris, said Aunt Josephine, and would be very fatigued. She read out of the *Morning Post* that there had been heavy torrents, even snow.

But today was bright, spring-like, April: racing clouds in a blue sky, light wind through the trees. She could see the arrival from the window, but not clearly. Excitement, emotion misted her sight. Uncle Frederick's back was turned: he was helping *her* out of the motor. And yes, she was just like a doll, because small – smaller even than Edwina had imagined.

'Come back, Miss Edwina!'

As she flew down she knew she would fly as always into his arms. But then, there at the bottom of the stairs, amidst all the bustle – the new aunt, the little dark woman who must be her maid – she couldn't do it, was able to do nothing but skulk, in that same place where she so often hid eavesdropping.

He called her out. 'Weenie. Little Bear . . .'

She couldn't answer, was suddenly too muddled for anything. Her thumb went to her mouth. Stuck there. She heard him say: 'We'll leave it now,' and then a voice like a bell, talking to Aunt Josephine. Aunt Josephine explained: 'Helen is resting.'

Uncle said: 'Adelina will have to lie down. She is really done up – the journey.'

There was nothing for it but to come out and present herself. The doll had been dressed in a long fur coat, even more silky and beautiful than Mother's, and a high-crowned deep red hat. 'Ah, Frederick – *carina,*' she said of Edwina. Edwina leaned forward, and it was then that she noticed a smell, a scent about the doll. She thought, I would remember that smell anywhere. She disliked it at once.

The luggage was coming in: trunks, suitcases, boxes, hampers. Edwina had never seen so much. The maid was directing in sharp excitable English. A maroon-coloured hat-box covered with labels and drawings caught Edwina's eye. The picture of a lake and the words 'Grand Hotel, Brissago' – she could read no more.

Tea. That was an ordeal. Aunt Adelina's English was good really, but she didn't speak much, although she was very animated when she did so.

Often, very often she stole a look, a stare almost at Edwina. Uncle Frederick said: 'Still no Helen. Perhaps – after the meal – we should go up?'

Aunt Josephine said, 'I wouldn't think that at all advisable – '

'Her health is not good?' Aunt Adelina said. 'Is still not good?' She glanced over at Uncle Frederick. Edwina thought: It's something about her eyes. But then just when she'd pinned it on the eyes, she realized it was the nose, the just-so arrogance of it. Then, no – it was the mouth.

She *couldn't* like her. She knew for absolutely certain that she didn't, never could, never would. There was about her that something – quite different from Miss Batterhurst or Miss Norris or Madame Lambert, people she felt 'humpy' about. This was *real* dislike. 'I dislike her,' she said to herself.

And still Mother didn't appear. Although Cora had been brought down now, all simpers and ringlets.

'I should like to see this fine Philip,' Aunt Adelina said. 'I should like to see this fine young man.' But he was away with a schoolfriend, and his birthday present, a gleaming new Rudge-Whitworth bicycle.

'How was the sea?' Edwina asked. 'Uncle Frederick, how was the sea?'

'*Manners*, Edwina!' said Aunt Josephine.

'The sea, my little one. The sea.' She thought he was with her, that he understood, but he added only, playfully: 'What of the sea? What about it?'

There was a pause. Then: 'Oh, that sea!' Aunt Adelina exclaimed. 'I can't support it. The rocking – '

'But it was like a mill pond,' Uncle Frederick said. 'I imagine she's thinking of the hotel, Josephine. That felt, in those gales, *that* felt as if it were rocking – '

'Weather really is the most unreliable thing,' said Aunt Josephine. 'It can't be trusted in the northern hemisphere.'

'Absurd,' Aunt Adelina said, but she pronounced it without the 'b', '*assurd*, Frederick. That boat never remained still . . .' She had Cora on her knee and didn't seem to mind when she stroked and pulled at the silk net panels of her tea-gown. 'But see how *pretty* she is, Frederick!' Now she said suddenly: 'We shall have the presents, I think? We can't wait more, Frederick, for your lovely sister.'

And what presents . . . The best were the Easter eggs. Cora had a huge sailor one which stood up and inside had six floating toys for her bath. Philip's, they said, was a soldier egg with a regiment and cannon inside. (Too babyish, Edwina thought.) She had a doll inside hers: the most lovely doll, completely dressed down to the last detail – primrose yellow, silk, lace, appliqué, underskirts almost as beautiful as the frock. Even a tiny parasol. She wanted at once to love it. (But who was it from? Which of them had given it her?)

The drawing-room door opened suddenly as if angrily pushed. Mother stood in the doorway. Swayed in the doorway, it seemed.

'My sister!' she exclaimed loudly. '*How* delightful . . .' Aunt Josephine had already got up stiffly, but quickly. 'Helen, you've woken too suddenly.' She put her hand on her arm.

Mother shook her off. 'Allow me.' Her voice didn't sound right. It was louder, much louder than usual but not so clear. She stood still for another swaying few seconds then came over to Aunt Adelina. 'My dear. *Welcome*.' She held her tight – too tight, because Aunt Adelina shook her head, tried to move back.

Uncle Frederick said: 'Don't I get noticed? Your own brother?' He said it uneasily, with a little laugh almost.

She stared hard at him for a moment, then: 'But of course, darling,' putting her hands on his shoulders, turning a cheek to be kissed. 'And now can I see all the lovely presents? Lovely presents – '

She enthused over them all. How she enthused! They were each – and most especially hers, *too* charming, too sweet, too *deliciously* pretty . . . Only Adelina could have chosen them. 'Frederick hasn't the taste. He never had. And of course, I may add, he isn't accustomed to spending money . . .'

Aunt Adelina looked surprised. She had an expression almost of pain. She put her hand to her throat, then she opened and closed her eyes several times. Mother was making a fuss now of Cora. Aunt Adelina, with a visible effort, remarked: 'I have been saying – how pretty, how sweet . . .'

'Isn't she? Can we hope, you and Frederick – perhaps those curls – they're our family by the way, our mother – perhaps we shall see them again? Shall we, do you think, Frederick?'

Aunt Josephine said: 'I think you should sit down, Helen dear. Helen hasn't been well. It's the wind – the *east* wind, I mean. She has trouble sleeping – '

'Nonsense,' said Mother. 'I sleep. *How* I sleep.'

'*Beata te*,' said Aunt Adelina, in a quiet voice.

'You poor thing,' Mother said. 'How I pity people who can't sleep.' She raised her voice.

But Aunt Adelina was getting up. Uncle Frederick at once leaped to her side – a little too late perhaps. 'All right – all right?'

'I think,' she began, touching his arm. She looked across at Edwina, but their eyes didn't meet. Then leaning back she fainted dead away.

It was to be two weeks, the visit. She'd thought, oh what heaven, two whole weeks of him – but somehow it didn't work like that. Firstly she had her lessons to do, just the same. Perhaps he could have sat with her, Miss Norris wouldn't have minded. Sat there and read a book. Anything, just so that he was there. She ached for him. It was worse, because he was there somewhere, but not with her.

He wasn't with her because he was in the library with Aunt Adelina who lay on a sofa and ate little delicacies and sipped toast water and lemonade at all hours of the day. When it was fine enough she sat in the revolving wicker arbour outside. Mother, who would have sat in it perhaps, had taken almost completely to her bed. She got up once, to go with Uncle Frederick to York. Edwina saw them leaving. She was fussing over his appearance, standing back and looking at him, head on one side. Then: 'What beautiful boots,' she exclaimed suddenly. 'Oh my dear, aren't they beautiful?' It seemed to Edwina almost as if she were saying: 'Aren't you beautiful?'

She came back laden with parcels – little presents for her and Cora, even something for Adelina. 'Poor Adelina,' she said in her 'false' voice. 'She is seeing absolutely *nothing* of Yorkshire.'

Aunt Josephine kept suggesting that Mother had overdone it. And probably she had, since, although in an odd pushy mood, she kept saying that really it had been rather a tedious day. They had had tea at Terry's. She thought that she shouldn't have drunk chocolate. 'I'm always foolish in that respect. Frederick knows that . . .' And it had been cold, in spite of the sun. She had counted on its being warm.

Next day she was back in bed.

'I don't like my aunt,' she told Arthur, urging Macouba on as they went up the winding road to the woods.

'Nay, what's that? She's a *good* woman.'

'No, my new aunt. The Italian one – '

'Aye, well. It's not all folks likes what's new. You'll take to her, soon enow.'

'I don't like her,' she said obstinately. 'She smells,' she added, greatly daring.

But he didn't hear. Like the day she'd said: 'How do you know, Arthur, that Macouba's a *boy* pony?' She'd had to ask five or six times, saying: 'I *did* say, Arthur,' before he answered. 'Manes. Take a look at manes. Short is boy and long is girl.'

'What about their tails though?'

'That's different. Folks cut them. But manes – if it's a boy, it won't grow long.' Then he added: 'Best not to talk of it.'

Today she just let him not hear.

'. . . I thought I didn't much care for *him*, but I've even less time for her.'

'Titled though, isn't she, and all?'

'A title indeed, you needn't give much for their titles, they're not worth the breath they're spoken with. And the *fuss* she makes. Has everyone running. You should hear what they say downstairs. I hear it's "I can't drink this and I can't drink that, and I always have milk boiled." When you think of the fine milk we have here. Then the hothouse grapes weren't sweet enough. Cook said she thought she was wanting invalid food, but the jellies – none of that. Lemon, always squeezed lemon, most unsuitable, I should say, and none to be had in the village.'

'Do you think?'

'Not at all. Not at all. I feel certain about that. Not that *I* can judge but Cook says, not a question of it. Anaemic, she thinks. Old-fashioned green sickness . . .'

'And *her* – how is she?'

'Oh, *her*. I could say something about that. There's been a little, you know – the day he arrived. It's not often but it's happened before – It's not very nice and then she's upset inside after.'

'If I were the Master I'd hide the tantalus key – '

'Total abstention, I've said before. It's the only way. Thank God we were reared teetotal.'

'Another child – that's what's needed, Ada. Give her something to think about . . .'

She thought, I won't say anything about the piano until he does. But he said nothing at all for nearly the whole of the first week. Then: 'I nearly forgot – Helen tells me you *are* learning. Are we going to hear something?' He seemed all interested, eager.

For a moment she thought of spilling it all out: 'Oh, but it's *hateful*. Three months – whenever I want to play, she raps my knuckles. Perhaps playing's wrong – because it isn't work . . . My fingers and thumbs feel as if they'd been put into those prison things, the ones in *Every Little Girl's History* . . .'

Instead she said, 'All right, thank you.' And when he asked what she was doing, she said, 'Two exercises by Czerny.' She was proud that she could pronounce it. Churney.

He didn't ask her to play.

In the garden, pushing Victoria in her pram, she had to be careful to keep away from the wicker arbour – turned round always to face any sun there might be – because Aunt Adelina would perhaps be lying there, doing her embroidery. It was very beautiful, Edwina had to admit that. The little round wooden frame, the linen held taut, the beautiful stitches : she loved best the one called spider.

But one day, like in the fairy tales, she went too near the spider's web.

'Edwina!' It was a gentle call, so she pretended not to hear. But then it came again, and silly her, she went nearer.

'Come in a little moment, Edwina.'

She left her doll outside. 'I must put the hood up,' she said slowly. 'In case it rains – '

'Come and sit beside me,' Aunt Adelina said, patting a wicker chair. She was lying on the chaise-longue, her embroidery beside her. 'You would like some lemonade? It's so rinfreshing. Please, take yourself a glass.'

Edwina drank. It smelled in the arbour. Now when Mother used it again it would have this smell. Old fruit, something in church, and then something sweet and wrong, bad.

'I have been wanting a chat. I like that word. I have been wanting a *chat*, Edwina. You are my niece now and we have met each other hardly.' Edwina hung her head. 'We are both a little bored, no?' When Edwina didn't answer she went on : 'It is boring, perhaps? *Annoioso* we say. It is like to "annoyed", the sound, yes? *I* am annoyed. Frederick is out, they go to see friends. Friends of her. I am not strong enough. Josephine, your Aunt Josephine, she is out also.'

Edwina, ill at ease, rubbed the toes of her boots together.

Aunt Adelina said suddenly, crisply: 'When you go in – so soon as you are in, will you tell them they are not bringing my tea outside?' She leaned forward, touched Edwina's hand. 'Will you come and see me?'

Edwina thought she meant at home, in Florence, in Italy, over the sea. 'Yes,' she said. 'Yes, please.'

'Then ask your nurse,' Aunt Adelina said. 'And please to come about five o'clock. Before I rest. It is just to knock at the door.'

'Aunt Adelina told me to – '

'I never,' Nurse said. 'That *is* likely.'

But she gave in. Edwina wished she had not. Aunt Adelina was lying on a velvet sofa, cushions all round her. She was dressed in white, with a lot of heavy lace round the high neck. The sleeves had lots of little tucks. She was eating a sugary sweet from a beautiful box, all mauve quilted with paper lace. She clapped her hands like a child. 'So you've come! Sit down – ' she patted a small chair near the sofa. 'Please, eat one! You are allowed?'

She wasn't allowed. It was that perhaps Nurse had meant. But it was like somehow one of the fairy stories. The witch – was it Hansel and Gretel? – coming out of the little sweetmeat house. Tempting them. Now she had eaten, she would have to talk.

'So,' Aunt Adelina said, 'they are not back yet. I am very *lonely*. Imagine, at home I have been used to four brothers, two sisters – I am the baby. Already my first brother has five little ones . . .'

She talked on. Once she offered Edwina another sweet, then took one herself – they were a sort of jelly with nuts inside – wiping her fingers on a small handkerchief. Edwina licked hers. She realized she didn't have to talk after all: only to listen. And then suddenly: 'Do you like your mother, Edwina? She of course does not like *me*. Not at all. I do not, either, like her.'

There seemed no answer to that. For a while there was an

awkward silence – but then as if she had never said it, getting up from the sofa, Aunt Adelina said: 'You like clothes, no? I show you *many*.'

Hanging in the immense wardrobe, lying along the shelves, in the drawers underneath – dresses sparkling with gold and silver, furs, enormous hats with lace, with roses, feathers, ribbons, satin embroidered with pearls, frothy blouses, coats and boleros. Black, gold, cherry, turquoise, dove grey. Pleated silk skirts, dustcoats, a coarse fur jacket, a gauzy wool motoring scarf . . .

'This – you like this? And this?' As she lifted each garment she would fling it on the sofa, across a chair. 'This coat is sable. These last days they have been hunting too many in Russia – the dogs make them climb into the trees and then the men, they have them down with big sticks . . . This blouse, the lace is called *point Flandre*, and this, *point d'Angleterre*. This is from Ireland . . . And this coat, guipure lace. You see my skirt is shorter than your mother's – more the fashion . . . This to wear underneath, you call it cami-skirt . . .'

It was too much. They lay scattered, abandoned, in great heaps. Edwina asked, should she put them back? But no, Aunt Adelina said. No, her maid would do it.

The game was over. But just when Edwina thought she could go, Aunt Adelina, lacing her fingers together, asked: 'Do you sing, or recite perhaps? Say something for me.' She paused. 'No, you are right not to. I shall rather see you do something with your body. You go to dancing class, no?'

'Yes,' Edwina said, thinking of Laurence, who had not asked her to his house again (and how could *she* ask him?)

'Show me, please.'

Edwina went through a few steps, in her stockinged feet. Slowly, clumsily. She lost her balance and had to clutch at the mantel. Then she stumbled, and a moment later fell.

Aunt Adelina was laughing. 'Can you sing? Perhaps at singing you are better?'

Edwina hated her then, knew that she hated her. She thought of her playing the piano for Uncle Frederick (she hadn't heard him sing this time, hadn't hidden in the hall).

She imagined her settling down on the stool – which wasn't arranged for her but for Mother – taking off her rings, so large, violent-coloured, the colour of blood and dark green forests . . .

'Look, we have nearly the same name. Edwina, Adelina. So pretty.' She took hold of Edwina's hand. It lay limply in her palm. 'I like us – you and me – to be friends. I am used to nieces. I have many, already nine.'

'Yes,' said Edwina, then impulsively, 'I'd like to see them.' Wanting suddenly to meet an Italian child, imagining it quite other.

'Then you shall visit us.'

'When?'

'Oh – when?' She let go of Edwina's hand. She looked suddenly bored. A yawn began but she stifled it. 'When you are older.' She looked around her. 'When you are *fourteen. L'età di Giulietta,* no?'

Later she said to Uncle Frederick: 'She will visit us. It is arranged. When she is fourteen . . .'

Such an itching of her hands. At first she felt it inside; an ache so that if she could only sit down at the piano, could only *use* them. These days it was as if Miss Batterhurst had tied them up, put them into splints as for thumb-sucking, finger-biting. One two three, up and down with the scales. She never bothered to practise. It was all so easy. When indeed she did go to the piano now she would just sit and stare – hearing all those beautiful sounds in her head, but afraid that if she tried nothing would happen. And yet one day quite suddenly Miss Batterhurst had said, 'Really, Millicent, the child is quite remarkable.' To Edwina: 'If I weren't so tired – I would speak, I think, to your mother – '

Then the shutters had come down again.

The ache in her hands passed off. Now it was only an itch. Not a pleasant tickling but an itch, hot, scratchy. She began to tear at each hand, right, left, right, up and down the palms. In the dark, half awake, she thought that they must be bleeding, so savagely had she scratched. When she fell asleep she must have still been tearing – growing frantic, thinking: Uncle Frederick goes tomorrow. Thinking: one last scratch, this will do it, *this* will stop it . . .

'She has eczema,' Nurse said. 'What a horrid sight.'

They put strong-smelling creosote on her hands. She had to take nux vomica and at night, quinine. Socks were put over her hands, tied at the wrists. In desperation she rubbed them together and ointment seeped through.

She couldn't go to piano lessons. When later in the summer she was well enough to return, she refused. Mother said: 'I knew it was only a fancy. All that trouble.'

Mother was in bed a great deal that autumn, and over Christmas. It was to do with a baby, Sarah said.

'Where do they come *from*?'

'From God, of course,' said Nurse, 'although it may be different in *your* religion. God gives it to the stork and he brings it.'

'Why can't a peacock do it?' Why not?

Sarah explained: 'They can't fly high enough. Can't get to Heaven first. Asides, they're not gentle like storks.' There was a picture of a stork, his precious bundle in his beak.

But when he brought the baby he had not been quite gentle enough. It was dead. Mother was very ill: she asked for Uncle Frederick. Edwina cried in the night for the little brother who was not.

# PART TWO

# 1911

Grandma Illingworth was carried in, supported under the arms, wrapped round in rugs. Her arrival was much the same ceremony as when she came to tea. It was just that she had come to die.

'I am dying, Edwina,' she said, when Edwina was taken up to see her. She was in the big room in the west wing. Bath Bun was with her and barked protectively when Edwina came in.

'Sit down, child.'

Aunt Josephine nodded to Edwina to obey. She was sitting in there already with her knitting. A dark blue leather-bound book lay on the table at the end of the large bed. Edwina read out the title.

Grandma corrected her. '*Woothering Heights*. By your age,' she said, 'I had stolen a copy from my father's library. And read it – '

Aunt Josephine said: 'Not really suitable – '

'What do you know about it, Josephine?' She tossed her head about in the bed. Her skin was browner, muddier and her lips looked sore and dried. There were medicine bottles and cups and spoons on the table beside her. One of the maids brought up a tray. 'I can't eat,' she said angrily. As she lay there in the long silence, the chomping began. A memory, was it, of eating?

Aunt Josephine looked over at Edwina, a little lift of her head, of her eyebrows. 'That's enough. You should go now.'

But Edwina didn't want to. Grandma said suddenly, 'Bring your chair nearer,' her voice sounding higher than usual, a little cross even but commanding still. Edwina lifted her chair. 'Don't scrape its legs like that. *Don't*, child!' But when Edwina sat down near her, waiting expectantly, she turned her head away, closed her eyes. 'Josephine, read again, please.'

' "Heathcliff was hard to discover at first. If he were careless and uncared for before Catherine's absence, he had been ten times more so since . . ." '

Edwina folded her hands on her lap. The palms, cracked, had begun to itch. Between her fingers the skin was weeping. (Why did they use this word 'weeping'? Because that was exactly what it was. Her hands wept for the piano, to make music.)

' ". . . Therefore, not to mention his clothes, which had seen three months' service in mire and dust, and his thick uncombed hair, the surface of his face and hands was dismally beclouded . . ." '

'Is Edwina still there?' Grandma didn't open her eyes.

' "He might well skulk behind the settle, on beholding such a bright, graceful damsel enter the house, instead of a rough-headed counterpart of himself, as he expected. 'Is Heathcliff not here?' she demanded, pulling off her gloves, and displaying fingers wonderfully whitened with doing nothing and staying indoors . . ." '

Edwina got up to go. Grandma took no notice. She only said fretfully: 'That bit again, Josephine, that bit again. And my food – I'll eat my food.'

It was so hot. All that summer it had been hot. The hottest summer she'd ever known – and the saddest. She woke every morning sad, only she didn't know why. It wasn't to do with the baby's death – that was long ago now, more than three years.

It was long ago too since Arthur's Emily. The eldest boy was very big now, looked almost grown up. He worked in the vicarage garden. In her mind both deaths had got a little mixed up. She felt, just sad, as if something was lost.

And of course, her piano, her music was in a way lost. Since she'd said that day, 'I don't want to go, I won't go,' nothing more had happened. Whatever good things Miss Batterhurst had had to say, she'd no doubt been too tired that day to say them to Mother.

Mother. With her, she couldn't do right. It was as if she'd set out along the wrong path, and Mother said only, that's wrong, that's wrong – but couldn't or wouldn't set her back on the right one.

'Look at me when you speak to me.'

'I was, it was just – '

'Take that saucy expression, that impudent look off your face . . . What's this I hear? Miss Norris says that in French – '

'I want to learn Italian.'

'It's not for you to decide . . . Edwina, your life is mapped out for you. You don't realize, I think, the benefits of security. To know exactly what is going to happen . . .'

All right. She, Edwina, in only five or six years' time was going to be brought out into the world and looked over. 'When she comes out,' they said, puzzling her. Then the next step on from that: a lot of dancing and dressing up, and waiting. You waited, she thought, and then suitably, someone said, I want to marry you. Then she would go to live in a house just like this, only *she* would tell Nurse what to do and Miss Norris and everybody. The Philips and the Coras and the Edwinas would appear. They would be very perfect and beautiful – she would never be nasty to them as Mother was to her. But what will I *do* all day? she thought suddenly.

The feeling in the house changed, as if they'd settled down to a long siege. She heard them say: 'She may last for weeks.' The doctor came every day.

While they were out riding, Arthur said: 'You should of seen her, t'old mistress, hunting. Hedge-hopping she was, while she broke a hip. Never got over that. Seventy she'll've been.' He frowned. 'And never good-looking. She were never a good-looking woman. Your father he takes after t'old master. Miss Josephine, too. She does an' all.' He smiled. 'I reckon for a woman that's not maybe best . . .'

Arthur talked to her a lot, much more easily now. It was almost back to the old days, how it had been in the beginning. (Only: she would blush, hot colour flooding everywhere, when she remembered her visit to their house; what she had said.)

But death wasn't all that far away and came quite suddenly in the night.

Edwina, that afternoon (when in the July heat she should have been learning French verbs out in the garden house) had been sitting at the bedside again. The tray today had on it a jug of lemonade, and some curd tarts, very freshly baked, sprinkled with spice. She'd wanted, nervously hungry, to ask for one.

Aunt Josephine talked about the weather. She found it trying. 'It's difficult for our invalid,' she told the vicar.

She was still reading to Grandma from the blue leather copy of *Wuthering Heights*. It made Edwina think, she didn't know why, of Uncle Frederick (two whole years now since she'd seen him). Knowing the book so well, Grandma asked only for bits of it. 'I'll have the part when . . .' And Aunt Josephine would strive valiantly to find it. Edwina could make nothing of the story on this account.

There was a character called Joseph. ' "I'd rayther, by th' haulf, hev 'em swearing i' my lugs froh morn to neeght," ' read out Aunt Josephine, ' "nor hearken ye hahsiver – " '

'That won't do,' Grandma said, suddenly coming to life. 'You're prissy with the accent, Josephine. Your namesake too. You never were a bonny reader.' She wanted the account of Heathcliff's death. He had 'a queer end', one of the characters said. Edwina listened fascinated.

Aunt Josephine stopped reading. Half asleep, Grandma chomped. The room smelt now. It frightened Edwina. Bath Bun, on a cushion, growled menacingly when she came near. He ate three of the curd tarts in quick succession, then he had a saucer of tea with some of the honey from the garden. Grandma, waking up, said petulantly, 'We supported *six* hives, in my time.'

In the middle of the night the bells rang. Edwina came out of her room. Nurse tried to stop her.

Grandma was dead, they said in the morning. Edwina went in to see her. It wasn't like Emily. Nothing about it was like Emily. There was a great rightness about it all – and no beauty at all.

The day after the funeral – as if one life ending meant another beginning – they told her about school.

'You know that Clare goes to a convent? She's very happy there. We thought . . .'

It would be a strange world. It would be like a foreign country. 'Where is it? When would I go?' Question upon question. She irritated them. She said, inspired suddenly, 'Can I learn the piano there?'

'If you want,' Mother said, without interest. She added: 'It's by the sea, by the way.'

By the way. A school, a convent school. *By the sea.*

She went with Mother into York, to buy uniform. She needed a blue serge skirt and black woollen stockings. Blue bloomers. White Peter Pan collars. Brown leather hockey boots. On and on and on. She found it impossible to imagine the life at all. She would go in September and not come home again until Christmas. Mother had been in convents in Belgium and France and gone home (often a hotel) only once a year.

She wrote to Uncle Frederick. 'I'm to go to school by the sea, and sleep in a dormitery. I shall be in between Whitby and Scarborough on a peak sticking out. The Romans built one of their forts there and the Danes came and put a standerd up with a black raven. Now it's a convent with nuns and you can see the sea I think from the dormitery. I know there will be wild days and great white horses, and then I will think of you,' she added lamely.

She didn't like the letter and thought of destroying it, but Mother had already sent up for it. So she folded it over and over again, smaller and smaller. She put a heart on the outside. 'From Edwina!'

She was taken in the motor. Mother came too. All the way there she hardly spoke to Edwina. She seemed to have her mind elsewhere. Her gloved hands lay on her lap. Her nose twitched a little. She was wearing a hat shaped like a cavalier's with yellow silk satin round the brim; it matched her amber necklace. She looked very beautiful.

They had sudden glimpses of the sea, then it would disappear again, tantalizingly, so that they were into the valleys. Farm after farm was laid out on the hillside like a giant map. Bracken-gathering had begun; they passed a big party, the cart going up. There was a mellow warm haze over everything. A sleepy content. She was part of it, and not part of it. She was leaving all this and yet not leaving. She wasn't going very far from home. It would still be Yorkshire. She hadn't even changed Ridings. Why isn't there a South Riding? she asked insistently. Nurse had no idea, so was angry to be asked (like the day she'd asked about 'peacock'. How to spell it. Was it anything to do with pee? Nurse had gone a fiery red). But it turned out that Riding meant a third, in the old days. Who'd decided then which three it was to be? 'Winds,' Aunt Josephine said. The North wind blew, the West, the East, but on no part of Yorkshire did the South wind blow. She had really concerned herself, she said, with the weather . . .

But already, suddenly, we are nearly there. There's the Home Farm, and nearby, the house where parents who came from a long way stopped: because there were girls from Ireland and South America, India even. She was glad that Mother, that no one, would have to come and see her like that.

There were square stone gateposts but no gate. The drive was straight and not very long; elm trees stood on either side. The convent itself, dark red, enormous, spread out across the top of the cliff in the afternoon sun, while behind it, so very beautifully, so endlessly, effortlessly, the sea stretched away so still she couldn't tell, in the heat haze, where it ended and the sky began.

'Isn't it lovely,' she cried out. 'Oh, but that's lovely.'

'It's a tolerable building, I suppose,' Mother said. She adjusted her hat. 'I hope they give us some refreshment, some tea. In this heat.'

The tall thin woman with the pince-nez and the small mouth was Reverend Mother. They had tea in the convent parlour. Edwina knew that Clare had an aunt who was a nun here. Sitting there, on the stiff embroidered cushion, she wondered: Does Clare call her 'Aunt' or 'Mother'?

She was offered a drink – milk in a little cup instead of tea. And some small sugar cakes. Reverend Mother didn't eat but sat, her hands folded on her lap. She and Mother paid scant attention to Edwina. The talk was of Clare, and Clare's home; of other pupils; of people and families they both knew. Then of Mother's schooldays.

Her gaze wandered round the parlour. Over the fireplace was a statue of the infant Jesus in robe and crown. Ornate drawn-thread work, like Aunt Adelina did, covered the backs of the chairs. There was a piano, shut, over by the window.

Suddenly Reverend Mother turned towards her. Her hands moved to one side of her lap. 'Well, Edwina. Do you think you are going to be happy with us?'

She had not thought about being happy. Happiness was, after all, what happened when you died. Here, now, it meant only something frightening perhaps which happened at the piano. She started, jumped a little as if caught in some guilty act. Reverend Mother was looking at her, head bent forward slightly, a quiet smile beginning on her lips. She had to answer, very soon. 'I shall like it very much,' she said sturdily. 'And I'm going to work very hard. I'm going to study a great deal.'

Reverend Mother seemed a little taken aback. Looking more towards Mother, she said: 'Indeed. Of course. Study *is* important.' Then to Edwina: 'But other things are important too. As I'm sure your mother will agree. Accomplishments – so that you can fill your role socially, your place in society. *God's* place for you. Accomplishments are important, because they are necessary. Study, academic study is perhaps more of a luxury. I may add that no one before, ever, has actually declared their intention of studying. Usually,' she smiled wanly, 'we have to persuade.' She turned once again to Mother. 'Girls – naturally and rightly – have other interests.'

If she craned her head she could perhaps see out of the window, round the corner, to the gardens and cliff, the sea.

'Edwina.' Mother spoke sharply. She wore her small frown which was really a scolding.

Edwina paid attention again. But Mother was going. Gathering up her gloves, uncrossing her ankles, patting the amber-ribboned hat. She looked suddenly young, very young. It was as if Edwina could see underneath to the girl. Mother had been to school, to strict Belgian nuns, French nuns. It was Uncle Frederick who had stayed at home, who had had tutors. She wanted to say: Mother, don't go. In a sudden confusion of tiredness (she'd hardly slept last night) she thought for a moment that it was Mother who was to be left: to the mercies of this gentle nun with the pince-nez and the thin lips.

'We shall take good care of Edwina . . .'

Mother's dry kiss at the parlour door. The warm late afternoon. The small bustling nun who appeared it seemed from nowhere and gripped her by the wrist. 'I've come to take you to the girls.'

But first she was shown up to the dormitory. Later the maids would unpack her luggage for her.

Her bed, white curtains round it, was at the end of the long room as far away as possible from the window, and the sea. The nun, who was called Mother Cuthbert, pointed to the next-door cubicle. 'Frances won't be back till Wednesday, Clare of course is ill, otherwise the dormitory is full.'

As they walked towards the door, 'The sea,' Edwina said, 'can I go and look at it?'

'What's that? You call us "Mother", please.'

'The sea. Can I go down to see it, *Mother*.'

'But not at all, we don't go to see the sea. The girls sometimes go for a walk on the sands. With one of the younger nuns, of course, or Mademoiselle or Fräulein. It's a steep climb down . . .'

She was in the lions' den. Brought into a room where

girls, girls, girls were massed together, huddled, chattering. Mother Cuthbert said: 'Where's Meresia? Someone look for *Meresia*, please.' The chattering stopped and then began again. Edwina was alone, even though they seemed to crowd round her. Girls of her age, girls of all ages, girls with bosoms which could be seen pushing out of their dresses, girls with grown-up expressions and voices. A babble.

'No time before supper, dears . . . Guess what I've been told – I can learn Latin . . . "Amo, amas, I love a lass" . . . You'll never guess who's teaching Geography . . . Did you know Hermione's brother climbed the *Matterhorn* . . .'

A girl with a lot of teeth came forward: 'Are you new? I'm Babs,' she said. 'You're lucky sleeping next to Fanny. You'll always be in trouble, in a row. She's fearfully naughty. Term doesn't begin until Fanny comes.' She introduced two other girls: 'This is Vita and this is Madge.'

Edwina explained about Clare: 'I went to dancing class with her. She's not well. She's in Switzerland till the end of the month.' They hadn't known that. 'She often looks pasty,' Vita said.

It was just then a big girl came in, asking: 'Where's Edwina?'

'I'm Meresia,' she said a moment later, smiling at Edwina. 'I'm your guardian angel.'

She was so beautiful, this girl who'd been asked – and seemed pleased to be asked – to watch over her. Babs explained: 'A new little one always has a big girl to take care of her. Meresia will see to you, and show you everything.'

She wasn't like anyone Edwina knew; more like she imagined an angel. The navy skirt and blouse which looked so ordinary, so Aunt Josephine somehow, on the other girls, looked on her as if specially made and chosen. Her voice was a little breathless, her mouth full of something rich and warm. Fair hair in tendrils over her forehead was tied with a bow behind but clouding out. She had very long, very slim feet. She put an arm round Edwina's shoulders. 'I'll show you over.' As they went along the wide shiny corridors, their voices echoing, statues surprising her at every turn:

'The classrooms – they're just along there . . . this is where your veil is, you'll need it for chapel, after supper . . . the dining-room, through there . . .' She turned. 'If you have any problems, or anything worries you – you'll come to me, won't you? Won't you?'

At supper she sat next to Madge who was small and plump with furry cheeks, apple red. They had mince on toast. Madge told everyone the meat was poor quality: 'My father deals in meat,' she told Edwina. 'He doesn't handle it of course but he *knows* about it.' She said it a little defiantly. 'What does your father do?'

'Nothing,' said Edwina. She felt ashamed. Then she thought of some things he did do, but it was too late. Babs was already talking: 'Meresia's mother is a famous actress, did you realize? Lydia Merriwether. Only that's not her real name. She came to the school once.'

'What about her father?'

'He plays the piano or something. You'll like Meresia. She looked after me when I first came. I was only nine.'

Edwina asked: 'Which is Clare's aunt?'

'Mother Scholastica. She sleeps in one of the dormitories. Otherwise you don't see her too much with the girls. Sometimes she reads to us.'

There was a space at the table where Fanny should have been. They kept talking about her. People said, 'When Fanny comes – ' A court without a queen. 'I wonder what Fanny's doing? Fanny wouldn't eat this. Fanny has all sorts of special things, because – ' But no one, suddenly, could remember why.

A nun passed the table. She was very pointed. Everything about her, features, habit, shoes, hands, was pointed. But not like Ned; she wasn't like him. She seemed to float from table to table. As she came back, she paused a moment at theirs.

'Mother Anselm,' explained Madge, wrinkling her upper lip. 'She's looking for Fanny. She's got her nails into her.'

For chapel she had to wear a black veil. They sang: 'O purest of creatures, sweet Mother sweet Maid.' By the end of the first verse she knew the tune.

In the dormitory behind the white curtains she arranged her pictures on the bedside-table. A photograph of the Hall in a leather frame (a farewell present from Father). A miniature of Aunt Josephine painted from a photograph. Mother in a riding habit, posed in a studio. They took up nearly all the table. (But why nothing of Uncle Frederick? Why had she not asked him?)

After they had prayed and Mother Cuthbert had settled them, she lay very still, hoping to hear the sea. But she couldn't even imagine it. All she heard was a cough, or some heavy breathing, girls turning over in bed, rude noises – she thought they must be already asleep if they made those.

It was strange, and it wasn't home, but it would be all right. She said twice the name Meresia. It sounded lovely: like a flower, like a summer breeze, like the sea perhaps.

Everything was new, that was what tired her. A face coming round the curtains: '*Vigilate et adorate . . .*'

'You're meant to answer "*Deo gratias*".'

'*Deo gratias.*' Next, fastening the black lisle stockings on to the liberty bodice, brushing hard on the hair which always stuck out. Mass. Breakfast. Lessons.

Lessons. Arithmetic, History, Geography, French – it was all different. In history they were doing the Stuarts. She knew nothing about them. There was a picture in their books: 'When did you last see your father?' For most of the lesson she stared at it. The desks were strange with sharp corners, the exercise books in their brown paper covers rustled and creased; the classrooms, closed for the holiday, smelled inky and dusty.

Then during French the windows were thrown open in the September afternoon heat, and she smelled the sea.

'Are you sure you're all right?' Meresia asked at tea-time.

'No questions, darling? Nothing worrying you?'

Edwina said, 'Is it true your father plays the piano? For a living? All the time?'

Meresia laughed. 'Well, no. It's the 'cello actually.' Then she said affectionately, in a pleased voice, 'People usually want to know about Mummy. It gets a little tedious. Because it's only her work, after all. She's just always done it. She's so beautiful.'

'Is she as beautiful as you?'

'Oh no,' said Meresia, 'I'm not beautiful.'

But just then Babs, who'd been staring out of the window, came back to the table.

'You ought to be sitting down,' Meresia said.

'I saw the motor,' Babs said. 'Fanny's here.'

After tea and an hour's reading, they had Benediction because it was Thursday. Edwina had never been before. It felt warm and loving. Madge next to her was singing loudly – she prodded Edwina and showed her the right page. But some of it was in Latin. *O salutaris Hostia* they sang as the host came in all flashing gold, winking metallically from its many spikes. At the back of the chapel were the nuns, hidden by a screen.

Then this girl came in late. Into the row just in front where there was a gap. She had the reddest hair Edwina had ever seen. It looked almost angry because it was so thick, so determined. She had never seen so much hair on someone of her own age.

*Tantum ergo* . . . they sang. Fanny – for it must be – had a piercing soprano. The girls on either side, Vita and Marion, kept glancing at her. Every now and then she tossed her head as if her hair, although of course neatly tied behind, was in her way.

The monstrance had flashed. The priest was reciting the Divine Praises: Blessed be Jesus, the Virgin Mary, St Joseph her most chaste spouse (who had chased him? Herod's soldiers?). Many of them made no sense to her. She stared at the back of Fanny's head and began to feel sleepy.

Fanny was there at supper, a little further down the table. They were having onion soup, rings floating on the top. The bread, which was home-made and crusty, was cut already in squares. Everyone was reaching, some quite rudely. 'Pass the bread, *please*.' Edwina didn't want to scramble, seem hungry, because Meresia, sitting at the head of the table, supervising, might see her and think ill of her. Mother Anselm was walking about again. Once she paused quite a long time at their table. Edwina thought they had done something wrong.

'Is that Frances back with us?'

Fanny only smiled. It was Madge who said, 'Yes, Mother.'

'Then kindly don't let your excitement interfere with those who have already settled in, please, Frances.'

She moved on. The chorus began: 'Where were you in the summer, Fanny? What did you do? Where did you go?' No one seemed to mind that she'd nothing exciting to tell. She said: 'I got a gramophone, my dears. For my birthday. And ten records to go with it. I played it every day.'

She didn't seem to have noticed Edwina except to glance at her as they sat down. Madge said now: 'This is a new girl, Edwina.'

'Why have you come here?' Fanny asked directly. 'Oh, her,' she said about Clare. '*I* came because my governess died. They decided not to get another. I live in Whitby by the way, do you know Whitby? Well, I'm in St Hilda's Terrace, a tall house with a lot of steps and a bit hidden from the road.'

Her face: she wasn't pretty at all when you really looked at her. Her eyes were too small and she was too pale, her features almost puckered. Somehow, Edwina thought, I'd expected her to be beautiful.

They had cocoa to drink. It came round in a large jug. 'There's bits of skin in mine, ugh,' said Fanny. 'Did you ever see anything so disgusting? I prefer chocolate. All frothed up with cream, like I had when they took me to Austria.' There was stewed apple in a big earthenware dish. Meresia served it out. When Edwina tasted it, it tasted suddenly of home; as if the soft yellowy green, the mush and the running juice encapsulated the smell and sound and feel of home. Nursery dinner on autumn days – warm enough still to bowl her hoop in the garden, to watch the peacocks, stand and stare at Uncle Frederick's singing birds. It all came over her in a great wave so that she thought she would drown in it, be washed away by it. And there was the whole evening to live through, and worse still the night. And then tomorrow and tomorrow and the next day and the day after that. She could never bear it. A lump rose in her throat, closing off speech, tears tickling the backs of her eyes. She put her spoon down.

But no one had noticed. Fanny was still holding court. '. . . and then I absolutely refused to wear all those garments, I mean, the hottest summer ever, I just flung . . .' Mother Anselm, passing the table, looked at her. And passed on.

At the beginning of the French and German classes they always prayed. *'Je vous salue Marie pleine de grâce, Heilige Maria . . .'* Fräulein taught them German and Mademoiselle, French. At mealtimes, both could be seen, spotty and unhappy, sitting at a special corner table with the mistresses. Both had pale faces and greasy hair – and of course, spots. But Fräulein looked somehow as if she could manage, while Mademoiselle had a little frown all the time, as if she would like to cry out but had forgotten how.

The afternoon of that first Saturday they all went for a walk on the sands. They had to wear gloves. (Mother Anselm promised a blackberrying expedition next week, *perhaps.* Fräulein would take some of them, and no, of course, Frances, berries would *not* be picked in gloves.) They were to set out from the lawn and the formal gardens behind the main building, then along a winding sandy path leading towards the steps down from the cliff. It would be quite a long walk.

The girls were all going up to each other and asking, 'Can I walk with you?' Edwina counted up and saw that, oh horror, they were an uneven number. Someone then would have to walk with Fräulein; she feared it would be her.

She stood there uncertainly, she wasn't used to being uncertain. Her gloves felt clammy, the skin on her hands sore. She never thought about the piano now – Mother hadn't done anything about it. Her hands felt swollen and useless, might as well cover them up. Fanny was standing near the stone statue of the Sacred Heart, pulling on her tammy. She'd come out a little late. Madge said, 'Can I walk with you, Fanny?'

'Sorry, no. I'm walking with Marion today.' Madge looked around her for a while, then she turned to Edwina, 'Would you like to walk with me?'

What made Fanny so popular? She couldn't think what it was. It made her angry almost. She would like to be like that. It was something to do with, probably, the way Fanny was almost always in just a little bit of trouble, but not too much, not enough to bring down trouble on all of them. She'd never had a friend and thought that she'd like Fanny for one. And yet – she wouldn't. She thought, you can have both feelings at the same time. So she thought, I'll wait for her to choose me.

The tide was right out. It had a strange beauty, the sea so far away, like a memory. She wanted just to walk along the shore, looking at it, not talking. Chatter, chatter went the girls, still a crocodile. She tried to ease herself a little away but was called back. The sound of the gulls screaming overhead filled her with sadness so that the tears sprang up again. She thought irrelevantly, suddenly, music is the most wonderful sound there is.

'I'm homesick,' she said to Madge, because that covered up her not talking. She knew it to be true. But Madge merely said: 'One girl was so bad once they had to come and fetch her because she wouldn't *eat* – ' She stopped abruptly. Fräulein was calling for attention.

*Achtung!* They might, if they were very careful not to slip, play tig among the boulders. 'Frances asks special.'

There was no talking in bed at nights. She would have liked to talk to Fanny. Fanny somehow held the secret of how to cope, how to manage in this place which was almost all right. The novelty, the newness of everything pressed down on her so that she had always to be thinking, what do I do next, where should I be now?

Sunday was letter-writing day. She had already heard from Aunt Josephine, telling her what the weather had been like with them and that Mother had been out cubbing on French Carotte. She'd imagined she wouldn't hear anything till she'd written to them, and reading the large clear writing on the thick deckle-edged paper she felt a rush of affection for Aunt Josephine, that only she had thought that Edwina would want, immediately, a LETTER.

'Fancy hearing so soon,' Madge said, adding proudly, 'My father writes every Sunday and they get mine on Monday, so we always cross each other's news. It's rather silly, isn't it?'

Meresia, stopping her in the cloisters leading to the classrooms, said: 'I don't want to be in the way but if there's anything – ?' Edwina thought of telling her, of saying, I want want want to be at home. She imagined then that Meresia would hold out her arms and, small plump ugly hard, she would sink into the sweet-smelling cloud that was Meresia's hair. When it gets too bad, she thought, that's what I can do. I can always do that if it gets *too* bad.

She had never thought she would be so homesick. In the mornings, all fingers, she struggled with the buttons, the suspenders on her liberty bodice. She was reminded of the shame of Laurence's party. It was terrible that she should miss even Nurse. (But not Cora. She thought, I haven't come to that. Then she would be overcome, thinking of Cora reigning supreme, lifted above Father's head, carried on his shoulders, her corkscrew curls tossing.)

Outside the dormitory was a bag with her name. On Monday she would have to put in it bodice, knicker linings – two pairs – the knickers themselves, vest, stockings; their name tapes all sewn on by Sarah. Every last link with home. When they came back to her they would have been washed by foreigners, by strangers.

To pass the time along, to cope, she prayed. At unlikely

moments: in the lavatory, changing her shoes in the gym, gazing across the gardens at the sea (so often hidden from view, so little a presence. In her fantasies it had beaten against the very walls of the classroom). The prayer was simple and sometimes had words and sometimes not.

In the chapel in the evenings they sang to Mary Queen of Heaven, Star of the Sea, Stella Maris. Maris, Marisa, Meresia. In the statue in the chapel she was palely beautiful, with hands outspread. Another larger statue stood in the grounds in a small grotto, roses growing all about. She was Bernadette of Lourdes' Virgin – the Immaculate Conception.

One week, two weeks. Soon she would have been here *three* weeks. It was the month of the Rosary now and every evening it would be the Joyful mysteries, or the Sorrowful or the Glorious. (Perhaps if she asked, hinted, Uncle Frederick would send her a mother-of-pearl rosary like Clare, newly back from Switzerland, had?)

She was beginning to sort out the girls – a little. Babs, Gabrielle, Madge, Vita, Marion, Clare, Fanny. Fanny she had scarcely spoken to except to say 'excuse me' as they bumped coming out of their cubicles. Madge was the most – chummy. That was the word for it. Indeed too much so, because when she leaned near Edwina to make a remark, she smelled. Not like Aunt Adelina; this smell was like carrots in a stew, sweet and woody and faintly unpleasant. But better than Babs's breath (she tried to say that fast as a tongue-twister) when rushing by, she'd asked Edwina some question, blowing over her the fishy smell of her malt and halibut liver oil, eaten with a spoon after breakfast every morning.

The nuns were not so numerous really. She kept out of the way of most. She felt that like Nurse and Mother they would find her always a bit wrong. Some of them had nicknames: Aelred the Unready, Bede the Rosary, Edward the Confessor, Scholastica the Rubber Band (Clare didn't like that, she heard), Anselm the Angry.

There were other nuns, dressed differently, who were called Sister not Mother. They were there, Edwina was told, to do some of the same work as the maids. It was just as holy to be Sister, it depended only which God had called you to be. 'A Sister would be *most* unhappy as a Mother,' Clare explained scornfully.

Clare's aunt read to them the third Saturday, while they embroidered. She had a high voice and a small hooked nose. Although she was pale she wasn't sallow like Clare; and she was light and thin. You could tell just by looking at her habit, which seemed too heavy for her. Indeed Edwina had noticed already the heavier the habit, the thinner the nun underneath. Mother Scholastica had darting eyes; she would look up frequently from the book, survey them all sewing, then dart back.

Edwina had barely begun to learn embroidery. She was doing chain stitch, horrible bright green stalks for daisies on some coarse brown cotton material. Her thimble wouldn't stay on and had been jammed with waxed paper from the embroidery thread packet. She took it off because it was uncomfortable and promptly jabbed her finger. The blood oozed out interestingly.

She was sat next to Babs. Mother Scholastica was reading a story about Angels, by Father Faber of the Oratory. Babs whispered that he was a friend of the family, 'We've a picture of him in the dining-room.' The story was called 'Philip, or the Pains of Children'. The heroine was called Edith. The similarity of the names embarrassed Edwina: she felt that everyone around knew she had a brother of that name. But this Philip: beautiful, dying in terrible pain, 'his face as white as the chalk bank when the sun is not on it', was much loved by Edith who 'Wore a frown upon her brow which never ought to be seen on a child's forehead'. But her guardian angel appeared to console her. He had a transparent body 'and in the midst of it where his heart should have been was a great bright sea with a harp rising up out of the waters – ' (Mother Scholastica held up the coloured illustration) – 'and when he trembled it made a kind of hushed music like the sound she once heard in the piano when she ran against it in the dark.' The story had a very sad ending:

Philip lying dead on Mother's knee. But Edith saw too that Jesus was sending millions of angels with graces for souls in sorrow on earth. These graces came from Philip's pains.

'Well – I hope you enjoyed that,' said Mother Scholastica, closing the book and raising her eyebrows. In the still of the classroom, Edwina could hear the trembling of the angel, the harp upon the seas.

At meals Fanny was to be envied. It wasn't just the extras, the egg for breakfast every morning but also the vegetarian meals. Only the day before yesterday, when they had had mutton no longer hot, the grease beginning to set white, she had had an enormous mouth-watering cheese salad.

'What do you do on Christmas Day, Fanny?' Edwina had asked, speaking just as the thought came to her.

'Open Christmas presents, silly, the same as everyone else.' She looked surprised, a thin cress stem caught on her chin. 'Except that I probably get more of them than other people.' She looked round at her minions.

'I meant goose. Pheasant, turkey – you know.'

Fanny pursed her mouth up. Her eyes looked very small. 'I eat them of course. You're the goose.' The others all tittered.

It was like that a lot of the time. She didn't think Fanny or indeed any of them meant to be unkind. That was just how it was. She felt like a piece of the furniture.

Any time or place when Mother Anselm wasn't around, Fanny seemed to be in charge. In French classes she would amuse herself drawing little sketches on her *cahier*, leaning back and admiring them afterwards. She sat in the front row but one. Exasperated one afternoon, Mademoiselle, the tears hovering as usual, protested: *'Mais voyons, Françoise – c'est un peu fort.'*

'That word *"fort",'* Fanny said, putting down her pencil, 'it means "strong" usually, doesn't it? "Fort" too, like there was a Roman fort here once. And then there's *forte, piano-forte* in *Italian*, isn't there?' She smiled sweetly, a dimple showing.

Mademoiselle was placated. But when the class was over she asked Fanny to stay behind and clean the blackboard for her. Edwina hung around and then as Fanny came out to begin the walk along the cloisters, she ran after her. Alongside, she said casually but in quite a loud voice: 'I have an uncle who's married to an Italian lady. She has a title and they live in Florence, and she has relations who live in a big palace in Rome.'

Fanny turned round. 'Oh, but how ripping. Oh, but lucky you.' She tossed her head: 'Have you been there?'

'No. I shall though.'

Fanny said, 'I shall go everywhere.' She looked ahead of her. 'Anywhere I want. I shall do everything – ' She turned to Edwina: 'Sometimes – don't you feel, don't you want to get *out*?' She waved her arms, over in the direction of the grounds, the cliffs. 'I just want to get out. Over there – '

Over there was what Edwina longed for. 'The sea,' she began.

'Oh, the sea,' Fanny said scornfully. 'That's nothing. The sea, it's just *there*.' Then she said suddenly, companionably, putting an arm round Edwina, 'Is your aunt a princess? Tell me all about her . . .'

It was letter-writing day again. She sat at her desk in the main hall: Mother Cuthbert presiding, hawk-eyed with her funny beaky nose and darting eyes and, sometimes, kind smile.

Carefully she wrote, her new Waterman pen obstinately blobbing (her blotting-paper was speckled all over): 'Dear Uncle Frederick, I like it here . . . Mother has forgotten to arrange piano lessons but I play in my head a lot. You can hear the sea sometimes in the dormitery . . .' Then she added a postscript: 'Please send me a photograph of yourself.' She shook her pen. A great blot appeared like a tear.

'See you in Switzerland,' called Fanny in passing. It worried Edwina all morning. 'She must have meant during afternoon break,' Vita said, 'because she's got a special drawing lesson now.' But: 'Switzerland?'

It turned out to be only a circle of trees, grassy in the middle with rocky mounds all about, and further out in the grounds than you were meant to go during break. When she arrived there, panting, Fanny was already scrambling up and down the mounds. Luckily there was a screen of trees further back so that they couldn't really be seen from the building. 'I thought that was really interesting – about your aunt. Your uncle too. Let's talk about what we'd do if we had *all* the money, all the time, all the – everything. Let's talk about it. What would you do?'

Edwina caught the mood. She ran up a hillock, scuffing her shoe on a rock. She was on the tallest of the mounds: hand on forehead forming a peak, she gazed out to sea.

'I'd buy a grand piano. The largest in the world – the grandest in the world. And a great marble hall to play it in. And then I'd play it all day. Every day, all day – '

'You are assy. No, but really you are. I've noticed you – it's all going on in your head, isn't it?' She didn't wait for an answer. 'I'd *hate* to learn the piano. I told them I wouldn't. They mostly do what I say, like being a vegetarian – I just decided when we had tubes in the meat. They said "of course" and wrote to Reverend Mother. I shall stop when I'm tired of it.' She came down and stood in the circle. 'By the way,' she went on, hands thrust in pockets, 'I'm adopted. That's very private of course. You mustn't tell a soul.'

Edwina shook her head. 'How *terrible*. Have you known a long time?' She tried to imagine finding out suddenly that Mother wasn't Mother.

'Always actually. Lots of people know about it.' She pointed northwards: from where they stood you could see little of the curving coastline, misty already in the afternoon light. 'Bay. Robin Hood's Bay. I've an aunt there I go and see. She's my mother's sister and she's married to a fisherman. You aren't really meant to know that. My mother came from Whitby. She died having me.'

'What about your father?' Edwina was open-eyed.

'He came from Whitby too. He was lost at sea. Before I was born.'

It had been mild when they first came out but now a wind was getting up from off the sea. Edwina shivered, hunched her shoulders. 'Let's go back,' she said. She could not bear to think about 'lost at sea'. How could Fanny just stand there, idly kicking at a loose stone? 'It's cold. And they might find us. Mother Anselm might find us.'

'Oh, her,' Fanny said. She made a funny sign, hands lined up, thumb to nose, little finger to thumb. 'So,' she said.

'What's *that* mean?' Edwina asked.

'It means what it means.' She made a series of rabbit hops. 'Anyway, we hadn't finished saying what we'd do. You did all the talking. I think – I want – I think if I could choose I'd marry a very very rich man, with a title. I *shall* marry a rich man – probably a foreigner, and then live in some simply splendid way.' In the distance they could just hear the bell for afternoon classes.

'Hurry,' Edwina said.

'I shall have my boiled egg every morning in a gold egg-cup on a little gold dish with a gold egg-spoon. Queen Victoria did that. Did you know?'

She had settled into a routine now. That was the way you coped with life. She had always been at the convent: home was another world. Already it was the sixth week and it was Meresia's turn now to wake them all in the morning, to go through the dormitories parting the white curtains of the cubicles, saying '*Vigilate et adorate.*' The sound growing less as she passed down, then loud again: '*Vigilate et adorate.*'

'What's it mean?' Edwina asked Babs.

'I don't think it means anything,' Babs said, giggling. 'It's just Latin.' So Edwina asked Meresia when next she saw her. It was a chance to talk to her because she never had anything to say when Meresia asked her, as she did now, 'Are you all right, is everything all right?'

'It comes out of the psalms, darling,' Meresia said. 'It

says "take care, watch out. And adore", pray, you know. It's rather lovely, isn't it?'

The days were long though, very long. But dark and short too at the same time. It was November. The month you prayed a lot for the souls in Purgatory that they might get to Heaven quicker. Every time she said, 'Jesus Mary Joseph!' or 'Most Sacred Heart of Jesus I love you' or 'May Jesus Christ be praised!' she could gain an Indulgence and make their wait a little shorter.

It rained and rained and a gale blew so that there was no question of a walk by the sea. The trees in the grounds swayed in the harsh wind, losing the last of their leaves, their branches bent to and fro, only the trunks staying firm. She thought of her father and longed for him. If she could lean against him and be comforted. What would he do if she were to run to him and ask? 'Father – Daddy (as some people said) can I lean against you?'

Once when they were outside for recreation she ran off and stood very still, her whole body pressed against the trunk of an alder tree. She didn't think she could be seen. She wanted to clasp it and after a while, taking off her gloves, she felt the rough bark on her fingertips. Perhaps she could feel it with her lips too.

Mother Scholastica found her. 'What*ever*, my dear?' And as Edwina stood away red in the face, fumbling for her gloves: 'Some girl must prefer pagan gods?' Her eyebrows were raised and she wore the expression, somewhere between laughter and surprise, which could be seen when she read to them on Saturday mornings. But she didn't say anything more and just walked on. Edwina felt quite sick, certain that she would tell Clare (or would she?) and imagining that the superior Clare would mock her in front of Fanny.

Nothing came of it though. The days just went on, and on. The next week when the gales had risen so that the sea and the wind could be heard all night she lay in bed and turned the sound into music. In her mind it thickened and grew all interwoven. There was a tune and yet not a tune. Beautiful patterns of sound: her fingers itched for them.

Mother had arranged for her to go to the dancing classes. She wrote to Edwina about it. Madge asked: 'Who's your letter from? Father didn't write this week – Of course he has a lot of business letters to write always. Has your father?'

'He has no business,' Edwina said. It sounded odd (mind your own business, people said).

'I shall leave the white of my egg,' Fanny announced. 'Any takers? *Quis*?'

'*Ego*,' said Marion.

'You are a hoot,' said Babs. 'Really.'

Meresia had a letter. Edwina saw her reading it, intent, little finger at corner of mouth, hair catching the light.

She finished her letter from Mother. She was to go to the dancing classes, starting immediately. Mother had forgotten to deal with it before. 'Dancing is important. As is deportment. You will need both, Edwina.' She had written to Reverend Mother, she said.

Nobody enjoyed the classes and she soon understood why. They were given by one of the Maycock twins: bachelors who lived in a big house about five miles away and came over once a week. Osbert and Cecil. Osbert taught the piano.

Cecil was short and a little stout with crinkly hair which bushed out and protruding slightly pointed ears. His manner was rather prim. Vita said they sometimes called him 'Miss Maycock'. Edwina wanted to laugh when he stood with his back view to them as he pirouetted – oh lovely word – showing them how it was done. The funny stiff way he moved, elbows crooked, dancing with an imaginary partner. He seemed reluctant to touch the girls. That first class: 'Next time,' he said, 'we could do something a little more daring, I think? Perhaps,' he suggested, 'if we are all very very good then I shall show how the *tango* is done.'

'As if we didn't know,' Marion said afterwards. 'And anyway – it's a sin.'

Madge said to Edwina as they were coming out of embroidery, 'Of course the one that teaches dancing's all right. It's the other one – '

'How? What do you mean?'

'Oh, I couldn't say. It's just something I heard. It's not something you exactly say.' Fanny was just behind and she asked: 'What's that?'

'Oh,' she said, when she'd heard what Edwina had asked. 'Oh, *that*. Personally I never allow it.' She walked on past them.

Madge went very red. 'That girl. She thinks she owns Whitby . . .'

But when Edwina asked Fanny later what it was all about she said, 'My dear, I've no idea. I just made it up. To spite her. She's so assy.'

Two days later she said to Edwina: 'Will you be my friend?'

'I might,' Edwina said. 'If you're nice to me. And pay attention to me at mealtimes.'

Excitement, anticipation. Babs said: 'Have you heard? Her mother's coming to see her – Meresia's mother. She's in something in York, and she's motoring over for the afternoon.'

Edwina knew what she looked like because of the photograph. It hung incongruously in the hall amidst St Joseph, Our Lady of Perpetual Succour and the Adoration of the Magi. She'd spotted it the first week. 'Love and best wishes' scrawled at the bottom in thick black ink, 'Lydia Merriwether'. Jewelled and befeathered: ostrich feathers, she was nearly buried in them. Meresia's eyes gazed out, but they didn't smile and the mouth was smaller, the fair hair tighter curled. She looked a little proud, Edwina thought. A little teasing too.

She was to come on a Sunday and in the afternoon they were sent for a walk on the sands. They were all of them afraid they would miss her. Fanny in the infirmary with a sore throat, had to.

Madge was Edwina's partner for the walk. She talked all the time, full of grumbles. Edwina let it flow over her, like the sea rippled over the little hillocks near the water's edge.

'. . . and then Father says, or well it's Mother who says, you can't expect servants to care, can you, they're only servants – '

The motor, it must be the motor, was just drawing up to the front door as they came in crocodile with Mademoiselle, up through the grounds to the Girls' entrance. But it was possible by needing to go to the dormitory to be just on the balcony corner above the hall. Madge and Edwina, Vita, Babs.

She was all furs today. But white, like the ostrich feathers. Her face could scarcely be seen. And she was tiny: in the photograph she had seemed not only plump but large, a blown-up Meresia. Behind her hovered an even smaller, ball-like man with a face like a monkey. He was rubbing his gloved hands. Two nuns were there and the bell had already rung for Reverend Mother. Meresia, in her Child of Mary ribbon, came hurrying over the slippery parquet floor. Edwina thought that she looked anxious.

Babs whispered, 'That little man, that's her *agent* – '

'What agent?' hissed Edwina, who had feared that it was Meresia's father. Reverend Mother was to be seen approaching from the right. The girls put their heads out once more and then fled. 'Agent!' How exciting that sounded – in her mind it was associated with foreign adventures, the sort they read in the library on Sunday afternoons. And it was to see them in the library (or just to see the library?) that Lydia Merriwether came on her conducted tour.

It was hard to see who had intended to come through the door first but in fact it was Lydia Merriwether who burst in, burst through, a nun almost flattened at either side. She was followed by Reverend Mother and then, closely, by the small dark man, bowing and smiling, rubbing his hands, looking round at all the girls. They sat neatly, library books open on their knees.

And then suddenly her voice, loud, clear, thrilling: 'Reverend Mother *dear* – could they have tomorrow as a holiday? I should so like to give them that.' The sun of her smile shone on them all. Meresia, hovering, smirked.

'Of course,' Reverend Mother replied, a little drily. How could she say otherwise? Mother Aelred told them that they must all say thank you.

Like royalty Lydia Merriwether moved amongst them. A smile here, a word there. The little monkey man smiled at each one of them but didn't speak. Edwina smiled back.

As Lydia Merriwether came by, her scent which had seemed to fill the room made Edwina gasp. As it wafted by on her furs, now thrown back on to her shoulders, she seemed to eclipse Meresia as some tropical plant would push from view an English hedgerose. She will not do, Edwina thought, picking up words she had heard her mother use. She really will not do.

It came very suddenly, the feeling of Christmas. It was for her a feeling of happiness because when it came, then soon, only three weeks now, she would be home. She could feed Macouba with sugar lumps, ask him if he had missed her, bury her face in his neck, hope that she hadn't grown too big for him.

It was Advent and she must make sacrifices. She could not make too many. Thus she could help the sailors at sea, the fishermen, the pagans in Africa, people in mortal sin that they might come back to God.

A jar of wheat stood on a tray outside the classroom. Another empty jar beside it. If she made a sacrifice (and it could be something very small, like eating up semolina without saying ugh – and without telling anyone you hadn't) then you might move a grain from one jar to the other. You could do it too by saying those same indulgenced prayers: 'My Jesus, mercy! Mary, help!' (100 days each time) or 'Jesus, meek and humble of heart, make my heart like to thy Heart' (300 days once a day).

Fanny moved grains by the handful. Yawning in the dormitory at night. 'My dears, I'm just *worn out* with ejaculating . . .'

They had finished praying for the souls in Purgatory. Edwina had not had to pray for Grandma Illingworth because, as it was explained, it didn't apply to her. She had been a Protestant. But if Edwina wished, she might pray for her; there was no harm in trying. It was a confused idea. Wanting exact answers she floundered in a sea of misunderstandings. What of the small brother who had died, unbaptized? He could not be of the Kingdom of Heaven. She asked Clare who would be sure to know since her aunt was a nun.

'He's in Limbo, you goose. How could he go to Heaven if he wasn't baptized?' Perhaps, Edwina thought, they had done it secretly, hurriedly; perhaps when he'd been born he hadn't been *quite* dead? But she could never ask her mother. 'It's really no good you praying about it,' Clare had said. 'Anyway, Limbo's quite nice – it's just that it isn't Heaven. I mean, they're all naturally happy there.'

'What do you mean?'

'Not *super*naturally, of course. Goose,' she added.

Because she seemed to know so much, Edwina mentioned Grandma Illingworth and Clare said: 'Oh, Protestants. They *can* go to Heaven. But only of course if they really thought being a Protestant was right. They have to be invincibly ignorant.' Those didn't sound the words to describe Grandma Illingworth. Clare had looked fierce suddenly: 'Are you *sure* she never thought perhaps Catholics are right?'

Edwina relaxed. It could never have been. Never could she imagine those champing jaws going up and down, up and down on the Catholic faith.

Meresia asked: 'Are you looking forward to going home, darling?' Edwina said yes, and asked, was she?

Meresia smiled, 'Oh yes. Daddy will be home except for Christmas Eve.' And when Edwina asked her where she lived: 'In Warwickshire. We're not far, you know, from Stratford – where Shakespeare came from.' She pushed back a stray curl.

On the last evening there were carols, and a Christmas play. They were promised roast chestnuts after. The big girls acted while the younger ones watched. Our Lady was played by an Irish girl, whose blue-black hair stuck untamed from out of her short white headdress. Meresia was the Angel Gabriel. Even the shapeless white garment (a priest's surplice?) couldn't spoil her beauty. The stage lights shone on her hair and the false gold band. One wing – she must have knocked it making her entrance – was slightly askew. A loud stage whisper suggested that it should be straightened. The corners of Our Lady's mouth twitched; Meresia hunched her shoulders to hide the giggles. Behind Edwina a nun tut-tutted.

The backcloth for the Visitation scene had been freshly painted by Meresia and another girl. It was the most beautiful scenery Edwina had ever seen. Purples, browns, soft green, and a haze going out over the hills that Mary had crossed to bring the joyful news to her cousin. And further away still – the sea. Real to her although she couldn't smell it: just as she knew it wasn't so far from the walls of where they sat.

They sang 'The First Nowell' and 'Angels from the Realms of Glory'. The chestnuts tasted of her happiness, her sudden longing to be home.

The best time was before Christmas. After was horrid. A lot of her presents had been useful and none of them what she'd asked for. Philip had been given a penknife with all the kings and queens of England on it. He wasn't very pleased with it. She coveted it but would never have asked him for it.

He'd grown very tall, would be like Father perhaps, but he had a very small, very round head and an expression which was discontented and a little fretful at the same time.

She didn't like him really. Coming back when *she'd* been away, she saw him as a separate person, not just family. They were no longer all 'family'. Once you'd been away, really away, it was never the same again.

Indeed no one wanted really to hear about the convent. Except Nurse. Nurse surprised her not only by being very friendly but also by her insatiable curiosity about it all. 'What do the nuns wear at night-time, in bed? Do you know, do you see?' Edwina imagined her relating it all with relish to her sister. Superior knowledge. 'And shifts. Do you have to wear one for the bath?' No, Edwina explained. But Mother had had to of course, in her convents in Belgium and France.

Mother. It wasn't any better really. It was as if they were each in different rooms speaking to different people.

'The convent. Is it any good? Do you enjoy it?'

She hadn't realized she was meant to *enjoy* it. 'All right. It's not too bad . . .'

'And the girls? You've made some friends?' Under her breath: 'For God's sake say you've made some friends – '

'There's Fanny.' She said rashly, 'I like Fanny the best. She's the most interesting – '

'Ah, but does she like you the best?' Her mother shrugged her shoulders.

Edwina flushed. She thought, I'll refuse to answer that one. Let her think what she likes.

New Year's Day, 1912 now, was fine and bright and mild like an April day. Mother went out hunting; Cora went too and was blooded. Edwina would have gone except that she had a bad cold. But it meant that in the evening Mother was in a good mood and when she was called in to see her she decided to ask straight out for what she wanted.

Mother was lying back in a loose grey robe with big pink roses on it, sipping lemon tea and smoking, flat strong-smelling cigarettes.

'Can I have piano lessons?'

'What, here, now, in the holidays?' She arched her eyebrows.

'No, I mean at the convent. Like I have dancing lessons.'

'But Edwina – you were so trying when you had them before.'

'She wasn't any good – '

'*You* weren't any good. Those terrible noises you make which Frederick, dear Frederick, says are so *special* – they won't do. One has to practise scales, arpeggios – '

'But I do. I would.'

Her mother had lost interest. 'I don't see why not. If you

want.' She shrugged her shoulders again: 'After all it is an accomplishment. Just, please, don't bang – '

'Then I'll just do tinkly tunes when I think you're listening.'

'Edwina!'

'I'm sorry.'

'I should hope you are. When I've just said yes there's surely no need for sarcasm.' She paused. 'Your trouble is that you take everything *au sérieux*. Perhaps I can put it another way? If you could just remember – for heaven's sake – that music isn't *serious*.'

So she could learn. Oh thank God, thank Uncle Frederick, thank Our Lady who surely now would be in the practice cubicle with her. Thank them all. Thank you.

'Edwina, come back, please. I can't bear the way you stand. It's so – squat. That's the only word for it. You don't have to stand square all the time as if you were about to fight someone. And your hands. They're all thrusting, as if, as if – Anyway, I must say they look quite unsuitable for playing the piano. They're working hands.' She said it with surprise and discovery almost: 'They're working hands. No, keep away from me with that cold. Look at Frederick's hands. Frederick's. They're so long. And so thin, the fingers so thin . . .'

Her cold was nearly better but she had a head, a nose so cotton-wool-filled that she could hardly breathe or think. She went out into the garden. It was mild still. The birds were deceived and thought it was spring. As she stood in sight of Mr Ramsden's cottage, looking through to the broken gateway, she could hear them singing. Hedge-sparrows, a robin, hopping, rustling. There was a fine tracery of bare branches, the sun behind them. Her thick muffler hid her mouth so that she could breathe only with difficulty.

A sudden shaft of sunlight illumined the gateway, the trees beyond. Meresia stood there smiling – and was gone.

She was sure that she'd seen her, the light haloed about her hair, a golden aureole. 'Come back,' she said out loud.

And then felt stupid and silly. 'Come back,' she said again. But not unhappily. Meresia of course hadn't been there. A trick of light. Something in her mind. But oh, she was happy. So happy, because in seeing her that moment, she knew that she loved her.

Come back. Oh Meresia, come back. I love you.

Everyone seemed nicer in a way that second term. Madge appeared almost glad to see her. Fanny actually was. And even Clare gave her some sort of welcome. Perhaps it was that they were all fellow sufferers?

There was a new girl in their class: Annette, tall with freckles and lank hair. She'd just come from India where her father was in the Army and she was rather shy and homesick. She was in trouble almost immediately. She had brought with her several books; one of them was Oscar Wilde's *The Happy Prince*. Mother Bede, who was in charge of the library, said: 'I shall have to confiscate this. I think perhaps your parents – ?'

'But they're only fairy stories,' said Annette, her lower lip trembling.

'I want nothing by that man in this convent.'

Mother Anselm, who was standing by, chipped in to say that Annette mustn't argue. Nor should she interrupt. The book was removed.

'What about Oscar Wilde?' Madge asked. 'I've never heard of him.'

Nor had Edwina. 'He wrote witty plays, I think,' said Clare.

'But what was wrong? Didn't he believe in God or something?'

'Of course he did, he was Irish,' said Clare.

'Actually, I know all about it,' Fanny said quietly. 'He dressed up as a woman. You're not allowed to, by the law. Unless it's a play or a fancy dress or something. They sent him to prison. That's why they won't let us have the book, because he went to prison.'

'How awful,' Vita said. 'To go to *prison*.'

Fanny seemed different this term. Edwina didn't know why except that she looked older and at the same time more accessible. Like the sister she would have liked?

The weather was cold again. Her fingers in the frosty January air tingled with the excitement of playing the piano again. Tingled with the salt in the air, from the sea – the first thing she'd looked for when she got back. Lying in her cubicle the first night, thinking of it just outside the windows, the tide up, rushing against the cliff. Her soul could escape whenever she wanted.

It was a new year. Anything could happen, everything would happen, if only because she loved Meresia – and was to learn the piano again.

She had become afraid to speak to Meresia, yet it didn't matter. There was always time. It was enough to look at her, to watch her. I could be her guardian angel, she thought, if only I were asked, if only I were older. O my love my dove my beautiful one. When she heard that, when they were reading from the scriptures, she thought of Meresia's bosom, that it was soft like a dove's. It could be seen rising and falling beneath the school blouse, a downy softness. Breasts. They were called breasts. She had never seen any, imagining them growing like angel's wings on to the small nodules, the pimples which she could feel beneath her nightdress, saw when she lay in the bath. Nothing would come of them. Nothing could.

Madge was jealous that Fanny and Edwina were friends. She said to Edwina, 'Fanny only makes a fuss of people for a while. She won't want to know you next term.' She sneezed several times in succession.

There was some sort of fever running through the school. Annette was the first to go to the Infirmary, then Madge. It appeared that Mr Maycock (Osbert) had it too, so that her first piano lesson was postponed. Her hands flared up and she had to go to Mother Infirmarian where she was given some sticky ointment and an acid drop.

Perhaps she had had to wait too long for the lesson, perhaps it was just that she was sickening for 'flu herself, but when the longed-for day came – it was all wrong.

I do not like thee, Doctor Fell. It upset her from the start that he should look so like Cecil and yet not be him. The only difference was that Osbert wore a little goatee beard. The resemblance gave her a shock even though it was expected. She was a little frightened of him too, because Fanny had said the day before: 'It's very odd they don't have a "dragon" here. Other schools do. My cousin does. There ought to be Mother Somebody or other, sitting there. It's in case he leaps on you . . .'

He looked her up and down. 'And well – how are we? I *do* hope we're going to like each other.'

'It makes me feel very funny,' she said boldly, 'you looking so like – '

'How odd if we didn't.' His voice was a lot deeper. That made her feel funny too.

'Don't stare so,' he said after a moment, irritably almost. Then smiling – he seemed able to turn his smiles on and off very easily: 'I think perhaps, although you are quite the young lady, we could dispense with *Miss* Illingworth and call you by the name your parents chose so specially for you. And what was that?'

'Edwina.'

'Edwina. How beautiful. I compose sometimes,' he said. 'Nothing ambitious of course, nothing for the halls of fame. But I can think already of a little piece entitled "Edwina". It might go a little like this – ' He played a few tentative notes then, as if rubbing them out, began again, then stopped abruptly.

'Some have been published, as a matter of fact. Privately, naturally. But with a dedication to all you lovely little girls. He smiled again, only not with his eyes. 'But *revenons à nos moutons*, as the French say. Play for me, Edwina.'

He nodded approvingly, his lips pursed together. 'We have had lessons before, I understand?' When she had finished, 'Quite strong little hands,' he said, lifting the one nearest to him, then dropping it quickly. 'What have we here?

Is it catching?'

'It's eczema,' she said angrily, staring at his crinkly hair. 'I just get it. Sometimes I wear bandages and a lot of cream. But not when I'm playing – '

'How disfiguring,' he said. He looked away. Then he turned and pinched her cheek, playfully almost. 'No trouble though with your maidenly soft cheek and brow? Except that little frown. I don't like that little frown.'

'It's when I'm concentrating.'

'Shall we – a little *détente* perhaps? We put too much into our playing. That Scarlatti was only a little show-me piece for your teacher, and he can see that you're going to be very good – don't spoil it all by being earnest.'

It was Mother all over again. She was so angry that when he said, 'Let me hear some Scales. Do you know – B minor?' she attacked it with a sort of furious gusto and played two others he hadn't asked for.

'Oh, you dear little Roman Catholic girls,' he said. 'Really. You are all very dear.'

The minutes were running away. She felt that she hadn't started. He asked her to sight-read. It was a piece in six-eight time, the composer not marked. She surprised herself at how easily her eyes raced ahead of her fingers. She felt far away, flying, forgot she was with him. 'Turn the page,' she said in a commanding little voice, suddenly catching sight of him sitting there.

'We have heard enough, I think.' She felt like screaming. It was the most terrible feeling to be stopped like that, at that moment. Her stomach knotted.

'Nice supple little fingers, ah yes, nice tone.' He reached for a pile of music on top of the piano. 'We shall have to stop soon.' Figures passed the frosted glass of the door. It must be change-of-class time already. 'I have to be careful not to tire myself,' he said. 'It has been quite a debilitating illness.'

He set her a lot of work. She could feel his eyes on her and didn't like them.

'Perhaps you're the sort of young lady who likes to choose

for herself what she'll play, what she'll practise, eh?

'No answer. That means of course that you are. We shall have to see about that – shan't we, Edwina?'

Fanny, Fanny, Fanny. She was Fanny's friend. Fanny's equal. Although she wasn't always absolutely sure that she liked her, looking sometimes at that small cat-like face, the way her mouth curled, the pale skin and the brilliant slash of auburn which was her hair.

It was Fanny who said, one of those understaffed evenings (several of the nuns and big girls were ill too): 'Who'll dare me to run absolutely STARK NAKED from one end of the dorm to the other?'

'I dare you, Frances Perrott . . .' Edwina came out of her cubicle and said, what about her?

'I dare you, Edwina Illingworth . . .' She did it too, only she kept her navy blue knickers on so that she only got half the bet. She thought she would die of terror. Certainly she could be expelled, might be expelled. They all peeped out and watched Fanny: once round and back. She looked strange, something from the woods, her hair flying, her bottom very pink.

Because they couldn't be supervised as much as usual, they told stories after lights out.

Fanny was first. Hers was smugglers, in Robin Hood's Bay. 'One wet and windy night . . . these smugglers were escaping the Excisemen and this house had tunnels underground, you could pass the casks of rum and things along through to other houses . . .' The story was very long, with appropriate noises. Outside the dormitory a real salt wind lashed the windows. '. . . but then the two smugglers got into a fight and the big black-haired one killed the other down there underneath my grandfather's house . . . and now, every 17th March, if you're sitting there at half past eleven at night you can hear it happen, all over again . . .'

How spooky, and only a few miles from where they lay. They shivered with enjoyment. 'I made it up,' Fanny told

Edwina later. 'From some things I read.'

But for Edwina it was Clare's story which was the frightening one. Because it was true. Clare's brother at Ampleforth had told it to her. It had actually happened to a boy there.

'His name was Michael and he'd committed this Mortal Sin. He'd had plenty of chance to go to Confession because they had it every week but he was frightened to, although of course he should have realized it was God he'd be telling it to and not the priest in the Box. Anyway, in the middle of the night one of the other boys woke up and he saw Something Black sitting at the end of Michael's bed.' She paused. 'He could even hear it breathing – ' She warmed to her story. 'Next week's Confessions, and Michael still didn't go. That night, the Black Thing was halfway up the bed . . .'

Edwina pulled the bedclothes over her head, then remembered that it was her turn to keep 'cave'. In the evenings the nuns usually wore soft slippers.

'. . . and the *next* week the same – so the boy decided to tell Michael about the Black Thing. But Michael just said, 'You must have imagined it' and went very red in the face. The Black Thing came *again*, only this time his friend saw it move – nearer and nearer and nearer and nearer till it was right OVER Michael! His friend screamed and screamed. Lots of monks came running in. But Michael was dead – and the Black Thing gone . . .'

'Oh Clare,' Babs said, 'honestly.' Annette, her first night back in the dormitory, had begun to cry quietly. Fanny asked in her clear cold little voice, 'What was the sin that he committed?'

'*I* don't know,' Clare said indignantly. She added righteously: 'What's it matter *what* it was, if it's a Mortal Sin?'

The Devil was real. 'The little devil', people said when someone was a little naughty, but really it was serious. Evil, devil, evil, was all about us – the Devil was scheming, doing his utmost to get everyone. Struggling for every soul. He had so much power, so much, that lying in wait he might yet make a nonsense of everything, of all the beauty, of all the possibles, of all she felt pulsing inside – her certainty that she would win. I will and I will and I will, she would say over and over to herself, not even certain what she meant. Life, death, tripping you up over something so small. Mortal sins, fish eaten deliberately on a Friday, Mass missed on Sunday . . .

But you could turn to Our Lady. Pray to her that she might save you. *Salve Regina*, Star of the Sea, *Respice Stellam.* But even as she rested in this she heard the voice of Mother Anselm yesterday, stopping Fanny who had been telling them about the boys at Whitby on the harbour wall: 'This is how they walk, this is how they whistle – '

'Frances, please! Kindly remember, when a young girl whistles, Our Lady turns her back.'

She had thought being in the Infirmary would be fun: it had looked attractive and cosy one time she had peeped in. But she hadn't reckoned with feeling ill. She ached so in every bone and was so dry and thirsty and slightly sick all the time. There was a Scotch girl, Jean, in there with her – one of the big girls. She called Edwina 'pet' and lent her two books and an illustrated magazine. Her eyes ached too much to read at first but when she felt a little better she looked at the magazine and read all about the *Titanic* which was so big that it could carry as many people as lived in a small town. There were photographs, drawings, descriptions. She was transported.

But in the evenings her temperature would go up. The fourth night she dreamed that she and Meresia were the only survivors of a shipwreck. It was the ship she'd read about but it had on it only everybody from the convent. All, all were lost and although it happened in the Bay they were washed up on some desert island. It was hot, so hot. They had a little fresh water. She was gasping for it but there was only enough for one. 'You have it, Meresia. It doesn't matter if I die. I can always go to Heaven. Meresia, drink it, please drink it.' Meresia, weak and only half alive, drank it and she rewarded Edwina with the most wonderful smile. When she spoke though she had Jean's voice. 'Thank you, pet. Come nearer, pet, so that I can kiss you.'

'Have you heard of the Curse?' Fanny asked, climbing up one of the hillocks. They had escaped to Switzerland. 'Periods. About your thirteenth birthday they put some towels under the mattress. Gabrielle got the giggles when she found hers.'

Edwina thought she would put off bothering about what it was until the summer. 'Just ask me if you don't know anything,' Fanny said. She pulled Edwina's tammy back off her forehead. Edwina pulled it down again and snatched Fanny's right off. 'If you're clever,' Fanny said, 'you can feel not very well and get breakfast in bed. You just have to say to Mother Infirmarian, "I've got my bad time." '

She seemed obsessed with the idea. Over the next week or two she kept pointing to various big girls then saying behind her hand to Edwina: 'She's awfully pale. Perhaps she's got her Period.' One day she showed Edwina the chute where the used towels went. There was no one in the cloakroom at the time. 'That's where you put them to be washed. Ugh.'

'What about the nuns?' Edwina asked, thinking out loud.

'They don't have Periods,' Fanny said. 'You are ignorant. Periods are to do with having babies. If you don't have a baby when it's time to they just stop. It's a very big subject.' She bit her thumbnail. 'Can you come and stay with me at Easter? Write on Sunday and ask them – '

The meal gong went. Edwina made a rush for the door. 'Bags I a seat near the pipes . . .'

They went into Retreat just before the end of term. It was only for a few days but it meant no piano lesson. Although she still didn't like Mr Maycock she was so quietly, so deeply happy to be playing once more. Scarcely a twinge of homesickness all the term. Fanny couldn't understand why she watched the clock, anxiously waiting for practice time to arrive. Ten minutes with the set work, then twenty blissful, terribly short ones with any Mozart sonata from the pale-blue bound volumes she'd found tucked away in the library (bequeathed perhaps by some nun on entering?).

A Retreat. She was frightened that perhaps, some time in the silence, in the sermons, she might receive a Vocation. For it didn't matter whether you wanted one or not. Mother Edward had confided to them that she had received hers like that. It was the perfect setting for God to speak.

But if He were to speak then He would have to raise His voice above Fanny's. She spoke everywhere. In every nook and cranny, whenever there was a chance to whisper anything. Mostly they talked in the lavatories, standing on the seat, leaning over the partitions, keeping cave for big girls who might report them. That Retreat they needed – however many times was it? – to be excused.

They were meant to read a lot of the time. Fanny had a book about Catherine Labouré and the Miraculous Medal and Edwina was reading Thérèse of the Infant Jesus's *Story of a Soul*. The second day an unexpected spell of fine weather began and they were able to walk about the grounds with their books. There was one place a little nearer than Switzerland called Montmartre. It was a short avenue of trees and they walked up and down this, clutching their volumes, heads bent, hoping they looked like nuns reading their breviaries.

In fact Fanny had a new obsession. They both had. Edwina had given her the magazine with the *Titanic* in it and she had read it enthralled. It was the stuff of great imaginings.

They played a game, walking up and down Montmartre: 'By the way,' Fanny said, 'I have a thousand pounds to spare. I think I'll probably reserve my own suite and private promenade deck.'

'I'm 883 feet long,' Edwina said, '92.5 feet wide and I can do 22.5 knots. I'm bigger than the *Kaiser Wilhelm* –'

Fanny said: 'I shall take one of the private decks with Elizabethan half-timbered walls.'

Edwina: 'Five hundred and fifty people can dine in my first-class saloon and I have climbing plants on the verandah of my mahogany-panelled smoke-room.'

Fanny: 'I think I'll have my luncheon in the Café Parisien – no, on second thoughts I feel like a Turkish bath. Or shall I go in the gym, or play racquets, or shall I take a swim?'

Edwina: 'My reading- and writing-room has a great bow window. You can see the sea and the sky – '

'It says here in this advertisement,' Fanny said, 'that all the first-class passengers have Vinolia Otto soap. What do you think the others have?'

'Watch out,' Edwina said, 'Mother Anselm. Coming in to starboard.'

She fell in love with Whitby, and Fanny's house. But first of all with Whitby. Ever since she'd had permission to go, she could think only: I shall be able to have as much sea as I want. However much she loved, and had loved from the first day, the view from the convent gardens, the great wide sweep of the bay, the changing sky, the gulls wheeling by as she walked through the cloisters from the classrooms catching her breath in the sudden salt breeze – the sea had never been near enough.

Now she would be able to walk on the sands without her gloves, perhaps with her shoes off even? Stay till the last minutes for the tide, walk far far out when it had nearly disappeared.

Whitby. Skinner Street, Church Street, Sandgate, Grape Lane, Boulby Bank, Spital Bridge, Baxtergate, Flowergate – All that first afternoon she made Fanny walk about everywhere, homing back always to the harbours, to the sea. Fanny only wanted to go to the Westcliff Café for an ice. She grumbled: 'I think you're quite assy. I wish I hadn't invited you.'

And then Fanny's house. It seemed, after the Hall, so welcoming and small, standing half hidden by foliage, there in the terrace. Blossom was out on the trees, the front garden frothy with it, green leaves everywhere, and sunshine all that first day. So many steps to the tall house: Fanny skipped up them. 'Home, home,' she said. 'My home.' Proprietary.

Marmee ('It's after *Little Women*,' Fanny had explained) was greyer than she'd expected. Greyer even than Aunt Josephine. And silent too, although she was very welcoming. At tea, once or twice when she'd made a remark, she'd hold her head, run her hand over her forehead, push back a wisp of hair and ask: 'What did I say?' She seemed to go to some place not inside herself but far far away. Only it couldn't have been a fruitful journey because she came back none the better, but rather as if she'd lost something. Often she watched Fanny anxiously, protectively almost. She wore glasses, and taking them off to clean them she said to Edwina: 'If you are really interested in Whitby, our son has a fine set of prints in his room.'

'Oh, those,' Fanny said, wanting Edwina to hurry and come upstairs with her. She wanted to show her everything with possessive pride. Edwina had a room of her own: she had thought she would have to share with Fanny but their rooms adjoined – hers had been a night nursery once. To reach it you went down some steps. There was also a bathroom all to themselves with a big geyser. 'Don't you know how to work them?' Fanny asked.

They sat curled up together on the bed and talked and played Fanny's gramophone. Mostly the same record, 'Lily of Laguna', because she'd only just got it, but also there were two Irish songs, one jolly and one sad, sung by John McCormack.

Mr Perrott was even older than his wife but very jolly with it and not grey at all. Some people never did grey, Fanny told her. With him it was a family thing and since he hadn't by sixty he never would; although that wouldn't help her, she said, being adopted.

'He may tease you,' she'd warned. 'It just depends.'

Edwina wondered what it depended on. But he said to her only, looking at her closely after shaking hands: 'I'd expected a large girl. Fanny wrote us and the way she described you – we'd expected a large girl.' He lifted his eyebrows in query.

What was she expected to answer to that? She said defensively: 'I was bigger when I was eight, than my sister who's eight is now – '

'Best goods come in little parcels,' he said, patting her head.

They were both allowed downstairs for the evening meal. Fanny had a green velvet band round her hair. Herbert, her brother, wore glasses like his mother and had some of her manner, together with a slight stammer and a snub nose. His brown hair had an auburn tinge.

Treacle, brown gold, shone on the pudding. There were raisins inside. It seemed to Edwina the most perfect meal. The most perfect evening. She knew she would be happy, that she could let herself be happy, for a whole week. She and Fanny drank some of the wine, watered down. Mr Perrott said, 'This is a kind of celebration. We love to entertain Fanny's friends.' Herbert and Marmee echoed that. The taste of the wine reminded Edwina of something. The ghost perhaps of Uncle Frederick? The smell of his breath as he carried her late upstairs. She longed suddenly for Meresia's presence. It needed only Meresia sitting across the table to make everything perfect.

'Fanny,' Herbert had asked, 'are you going over to Bay?'

'Of course. And Edwina.' She turned to her father: 'Edwina can come, can't she?'

'But yes.' He had put on little steel-rimmed glasses to pick the bones from his fish. 'But yes.' He looked over his glasses at Edwina. 'You've never been to Robin Hood's Bay? You know you could almost cast a stone there from the convent windows. Have you tried? It looks its best in the spring – I think. Fan, you ought to take some colours along.' He said to Edwina: 'She really has quite a knack with a pencil and brush. What are your talents?'

'I think,' Edwina said, because it sounded better than 'I know', 'I think I'm very good at the piano.'

'She can play for us after the meal,' Marmee said.

Herbert said, 'We can have a musical hour.' It turned out that he sang very well. Marmee accompanied him in 'Pale Hands I Loved', which Edwina found very sad but which made Fanny restless and giggly. Then he and his father sang a duet from Gilbert and Sullivan, 'A Policeman's Lot is Not an 'Appy One'. Edwina joined in the chorus. She hoped they were not going to forget to ask her to play.

'And now, Edwina,' Herbert said, escorting Marmee away from the piano. She got up at once and crossing over to the stool, turned and gave a little bow. 'Sonata in C, K.330 by Wolfgang Amadeus Mozart.' Fanny tittered. But far away; another time, another place.

She played. Her fingers remembered with ease. They forgot only that there was an audience. At first she played simply, sitting very upright on the stool: a small gift to them for her happy evening, holding everything back a little so that it was precise and grateful. Tilt of the wrists, arch of the fingers, the happy hours with the blue album. And then the hunger began. Her hands first, her arms, her shoulders, then rising, growing from her chest to her heart. She had become all music. She need never stop, must never stop. Purely happy, why do I ever do anything else? she thought.

A pause. The first movement over, triumphantly. The second movement – but they had all begun to clap, Fanny the loudest. Her father had come over to congratulate Edwina, hand on shoulder, a pat on the head. 'There's a good little girl.' From behind, Herbert said, clapping again, 'You played really *well.*'

'But there's more, lots more – '

She was not meant to continue. It was like cold water, the realization. They had thought that was her 'piece'. The feeling was terrible, terrible.

'We shall certainly hear it then. You must certainly play again.' Another pat on the head. Final. But the hunger was still there, gnawing.

' "Caedmon's cross but that's no reason why *you* should be," ' Fanny said, standing in the doorway of Edwina's room.

' "Smoke Telfer's PickTwist and you'll be all right",' Edwina said tiredly, finishing off the advertisement. Fanny picked up a magazine from the table. 'Do you like everybody?' she asked.

'Very much.'

'It's funny, when you think they're not my real parents – '

'I think you look a bit like Herbert, actually,' Edwina said. The thought had struck her while he was singing.

'Oh, perhaps,' Fanny said. 'They say that's the funny thing about being adopted. It even happens with animals. You know, people and their dogs – '

'It happened with Bath Bun,' Edwina began.

'I say,' Fanny read out: 'This woman – she's an American millionaire's wife – she says she spends *eight* thousand a year on clothes. My dear, can you imagine? I'll bet she looks like a war horse.'

'We ought to go to bed,' Edwina said, yawning. 'Race you to get undressed – '

'After my Turkish bath,' Fanny said, stretching and yawning too, 'I shall go into the cooling room – Wait a minute till I remember it right – yes, Bronze Arab lamps hang from the ceiling, the stanchions are carved with intricate Moorish patterns. Wait a bit – '

Taking her up, Edwina said: 'Five hundred and fifty guests can dine in my first-class dining-saloon. The menu – '

Fanny said, interrupting too: 'It doesn't mention the other classes. Do you think they get any dinner?'

Such happy days. She bored Fanny with her love of the town, her love of the harbours. One morning she got up at five and crept out, unbolting the door like a thief, breath held. For a couple of hours she walked about, content to do just that. Climbing the hundred-and-ninety-nine steps to the Norman Church – square, grey, hazy in the pale early light – going slowly, savouring the sight of the roofless Abbey, its sandstone arches appearing out of the mist. Up and up till as the haze cleared she could turn and see below the red-roofed town. In the churchyard she looked at Caedmon's Cross, wandered round idly reading the tombstones. Then the Abbey again, and out, out over the steel grey water. 'Lost at sea'. She thought of Fanny's father. Walking down the steps again, she thought too of Fanny's mother. What was it like, not to have your baby die, but to die yourself?

She was back in by seven and only met one of the maids. Fanny was half awake, rubbing her eyes. 'Oh, go back to Brazil where the nuts come from,' she said.

'Can I see your prints?' she asked Herbert, wishing someone so pleasant was her brother instead of Philip. He was delighted to show her. There were twelve of them, all round the room. Fanny stood behind Edwina and yawned. 'If you don't want to see them again, get away.' He was friendly but firm.

Walking round, he pointed them all out. There was Whitby Theatre on fire nearly a hundred years ago. The old drawbridge over the Esk – ships used to be tied to its timbers, he said. Then the swivel bridge which came after, packed with carts and carriages. The Abbey, looking quite different, complete with a big central Tower and its great West window. The salvage of a coal boat: she liked that one the best of all. The painter had signed his name on the stern of the wrecked boat.

Herbert gave her a pile of writing paper, headed with yet more views. She thought at once that she would write to Uncle Frederick on it, imagining him already reading the long letter, thinking of her, forgetting Aunt Adelina.

Fanny yawned again. 'I can draw better than that. I can draw just as well as I want. So.'

They were to go by train. Cook, Mrs Ibbotson, would take them as she had a friend in Bay. The excitement: Edwina had never been on a train before.

Although it wasn't a very hot afternoon, Cook panted and puffed climbing up into the carriage, mopping her brow as soon as they'd sat down: 'I hope you girls aren't going to talk and jump about all the way.'

'She's not really Mrs,' Fanny had explained earlier. 'They're just called that out of politeness. No one would really marry anybody so fat and ugly.' She was in a showing-off mood and talked most of the time just to irritate Cook; putting her head out of the carriage window when she'd been told not to. 'This time ten days where shall we be? Back in that horrid nunnery. Lots of spiders in my bath trying hard to make me laugh ...'

Then suddenly it was written: Robin Hood's Bay. And Fanny, jumping out first, said: 'It's miles to the village.'

Cook said: 'I'm surprised, I'm sure, your auntie doesn't send the cart up to meet us.' She was puffed already before setting out on the long walk down the hill. The sun had come out now and she screwed her eyes up against it. They came past the Victoria Hotel and soon after there was a stretch of open land on the cliff top. The convent stood out, clear in the afternoon light, across the wide sweep of the bay. Edwina wanted to stand there for a few moments but Fanny had already run on ahead. She was left with Cook – who grumbled. It was something about a tradesman. The pork wasn't what it should have been. 'I know it's no concern of yours,' she told Edwina, 'but folk have to tell someone.'

A horse and cart passed them in the street, the horse pushing his head up against the sun. They'd passed the house of Cook's friend now, but she would come back. Fanny wanted to go right on down to the sweet shop, near the water. That exasperated Cook more: 'You can't arrive at your auntie's all sticky-mouthed.' Edwina too was getting angry with her.

Then they turned up a little lane off the main street and Fanny, ahead once more, knocked at the second house. A small dark boy answered, wearing braces over his shirt, his trousers a little too big; long black stockings, wrinkled. 'Mam – it's them!'

A voice came from the back. 'She's in wash kitchen,' the little boy said. He stood, half smiling, half scowling, looking down at the polished step. 'Well, let us in,' Cook said crossly.

'Jack, didn't you fetch them in?' Fanny's aunt, opening the door wider, standing there smiling, pulling at her black apron: 'Come on, then. Mrs Ibbotson. Fanny.' Fanny darted forward and kissed her. She coloured. Like Jack she was dark: he had her big eyes, pale skin drawn tight over the cheekbones.

Fanny said: 'This is my friend from school – Edwina Illingworth.' Inside there was a fire and two or three chairs drawn up to it. Auntie, who was called Mrs Mitcham, said to Cook, 'A cup of tea, Mrs Ibbotson?' But Cook shook her head. 'I'll be away up to Jane's.'

'Ben'll come for you then, when it's time for the girls.' She sat down heavily, tiredly. 'Now, Fanny?' She laid her thin hands in her lap. 'Now then?'

Fanny began to prattle. There was no other word for it. A lot of it was swanking. She talked about school mostly: a paper chase, the latest dares, her drawing lessons. She included Edwina in her account. But it was all exaggerated, more than life-size. She seemed perfectly at home though. It was Edwina who felt stiff. She stared hard at the kettle, gleaming black on the hob, coming up now to the boil. Jack was standing behind his mother. His eyes darted from Fanny to Edwina. She smiled at him, but he didn't smile back.

Auntie made the tea. Half amused at Fanny's tales, half mocking, it seemed. Fanny talked on, her legs pushed out straight towards the fire. Her aunt watched her face closely all the time.

They ate some little cakes with blobs of jam on the top. Jack kept darting from behind Edwina's chair to snatch another. 'They're a treat for him,' Auntie said. She asked Edwina about herself. Fanny seemed to remember then to ask after the rest of her family. There was an Uncle James, she'd told Edwina, who was married to Auntie and didn't talk much, and a cousin Ben who lived a little way on down, another cousin Robert who always came along to see her. And Grandad.

Auntie said now: 'You never asked after Mercy.' Fanny said hurriedly, 'Well?' and Auntie said, 'I'll fetch her down.' Edwina asked Jack then if he liked having a little sister, but he just scowled. Fanny said, 'Of course he does. Everyone wants a sister.'

Mercy had damp curly dark hair and red sleep-flushed

cheeks. Fanny played with her for a while, pulling at her fingers, then tiring suddenly, passed her to Edwina. Edwina was surprised at how warm she was: so Emily must have been.

Fanny asked: 'Can we go out in the village?' Jack said then, 'Can I come too, Mam?' Once out, he skipped ahead of them, running back every few yards. Edwina felt they were an odd trio. In some ways it was like a procession: Fanny kept looking around her as if she were someone of importance. She said to Edwina, 'When people see me, I expect they say things like – "Oh, there's Annie Mitcham's little niece going by –" '

They were nearing the sweet shop. Jack skipped backwards: 'Fanny, you got summat for me?' He put out his hand. Fanny took a penny from her drawstring purse.

Edwina stood still, down in the Dock, looking all around her: up back at King Street which she hadn't visited yet, imagining delightedly all the little lanes, passages, which must lead off it – many of them maybe with their own surprise view of the sea. Then she turned, and stared out over the water. The sight of the convent gave her a shock. She couldn't believe: it looked so near.

'You can walk it easily,' Fanny said, 'when the tide's down. Or along the cliffs, if you're careful – '

Inside the sweet shop the woman serving seemed to know Fanny. Two small children came through from the back and crept behind her skirts. 'It's Fanny,' she told them and then: 'What time are you away? Will you see the boats?' She gave Jack his penny-luck bag. She told Fanny: 'Ben goes out with the men now. Sin' New Year he's been.'

Fanny said to Edwina: 'Don't get too near.' They were standing at the Wayfoot, the narrow slipway leading to where the fishing cobles were launched. The tide was coming up and every now and then a wave rose higher than the rest, surprising them. Edwina just stood there and got her boots wet. 'What a mess you look,' Fanny told her. 'I doubt you'll get them dry before the catch comes in.' She began walking up again. 'You've never seen it rough,' she said. 'You'd be frightened.' 'Speak for yourself,' Edwina said, but Fanny affected not to hear and just walked on. As they passed the fish shop on their left, she said, 'Last summer when I was here early in the day they let me do skeining. So there.'

'So there, what?' Edwina had had enough. But Fanny turned on her her full scorn. 'Skeining mussels, of course. Bait, for bait, ignoramus.'

'You sound like Philip,' Edwina said angrily. 'You sound like my brother, like boys do – ' She followed her sulkily up the steep road.

Auntie put her boots to dry, and lent her stockings and some waders which were much too big. Dressed like that she watched the catch, although she'd missed the first sight of the cobles, brown-sailed, coming into view.

Fish, there seemed to be fish everywhere. It was more exciting than when she'd watched on the quay at Whitby. Here she was part of it, even if that meant listening to Fanny's superior explanations. ('Threepence a pound for that, I should think . . .') The men she couldn't sort one from the other: what wasn't covered by sou'westers, or beards, was all voluminous oilskins, and legs lost in great leather thigh boots. But later, when they were all back at Auntie's, it was suddenly all very simple. The room full of them, changed and washed and come to see Fanny: individuals.

Grandad came in with Uncle James. He was very big and you could see too that he was Auntie's father by the way his eyes were set. The nose was more beaked though, and he had this lovely beard, so thick, so luxuriant: the best she'd ever seen.

Uncle James, who was just as quiet as Fanny had said, sat without saying anything very much at all, just tickling Jack and making him excited so that Auntie in the end spoke sharply. Grandad said to let him be. He had his hands to the fire and Edwina looked at them fascinated: the hair grew as thick there too as she'd ever seen. Hands, she thought, I shall always be looking at hands. Hands make music.

But now they were greeting Robert. Fanny jumped up to

rush and hug him, pulling on his neck. He was as fair as all the others seemed dark. And tall, big. When he'd sat down on the cushioned squab under the window and Fanny had come and sat beside him, Jack, restless, came over and tugged at him.

It was then that Ben came in. ('He's my cousin too,' Fanny had said, 'but another family. I have a *lot* of relations, you see. Almost everybody here, almost everybody in Bay is related to me.') For a moment he stood in the doorway, frowning a little. His brows met nearly in the middle. He wasn't very old, only perhaps a couple of years on from her – not like Robert who looked about twenty – and not very tall: taller than her, just. But it was when he came right into the room, crossing over towards the fireplace, to where Grandad sat on one side – it was then she noticed. Oh, she thought, oh, but he walks just like me.

She recognized it at once. It was a way of moving so that she knew exactly how he felt: it feels, she thought, as if *I* were walking. A great sudden wave of kinship so strong that when he was shown her, when Fanny repeated, 'That's my cousin,' she said almost, very very nearly came out with: 'and mine too.'

Fanny had sat herself on Grandad's knee now. Ben sat, legs a little apart, Mercy in his arms, up and down, bobbing, plunging: 'This is the way the gentlemen ride, eh?'

There was some question of when they ought to go. 'You'll take a bite?' Someone would have to go up and tell Cook. Fanny said, 'She likes to stay on talking to Jane. No one'll worry if we're with Cook.'

'Too heavy, lass,' Grandad told Fanny, but he didn't move her off. They sat around companionably. Fanny wasn't talking so much now. They ate fish and chips sitting round the table with its shiny oilcloth. The paraffin lamps had been lit, they made odd shadows across the faces so that staring (for weren't they all strangers until today at least?), she saw Ben watching her. He grinned. Sitting opposite: grinning, then saying: 'Eat chips first. They're cold quicker.'

'Daft,' Auntie said. She looked tired now. A bit cross too.

Grandad had said, half jokingly, about the tea: 'What's this then?' holding up the mug. 'Been washing again?'

Uncle James said, placatory, 'It's weak enow, but – ' She flared up: 'It said on packet – it did now – as good in second water – '

Edwina said, 'I like it like this. I don't like it strong.' They all looked terribly surprised that she'd spoken. Grandad looked at her suddenly, approving, making a clucking noise with his tongue.

It was time to go. Ben would walk them up to Jane's.

Then after they'd collected Cook, he said he'd come up to see the train off. He loved trains. Fanny had been buttonholed by Cook, and Edwina found she could walk a little behind with him. They stopped then on the cliff top. There was a steamer caught in the evening sun. Ben said: 'She's for Sunderland. My uncle, he's her captain.'

'Have you ever been right out to sea?' Edwina asked.

He imitated: ' "Right out to sea." What's that?' He was laughing. Then he said something she couldn't catch. 'Where'd we go today then?' he asked laughing, grinning.

'*Real* sea,' she persisted. Fanny appeared: sent back to fetch them. 'Like that steamer. Like the *Titanic*. Had you heard of that?'

'Aye. I heard on it.' He was still laughing at her.

Fanny said, 'I might go on it, the *Titanic*. To Rhodesia. To see my Uncle Clive.' It was the first Edwina had heard of it.

Ben didn't seem all that impressed. Cook could be seen making angry signals. They walked on, more hurried now. From an alley nearby a dog ran out, spotted black and white, feathery tail. Ben made as if to chase it, and as he moved, it might have been her. ['I hate the way you walk,' Mother said.]

On impulse she called, 'Ben,' and then as he turned, opening her purse, she took out a silver threepence. 'Give that to Jack for goodies. He wanted – '

'It'll go on lasting stripes.' He put his hand out. 'Right then – You can trust me.' He took it from her: the skin on his hands was worn, parts calloused. He smiled again: what she'd thought earlier was a frown was just his brows going together.

'I'll trust you,' she said.

One of the maids, crouching down, making up her bedroom fire for her: 'Cook heard of it,' she said, 'there's been a big boat gone down.'

'Is the lifeboat out?' Edwina asked, thinking already that she would have to go and look. But just then Fanny was in the room, panting, eyes excited: 'My dear, have you *heard*? The *Titanic* –'

She couldn't sleep that night, couldn't rid herself of the image of Uncle Frederick. He rose above the waves, fighting, riding the great white horses. She thought, he is going under. In the bed she turned and tossed. These icy waters.

It was her last day there. The atmosphere was funereal. They sat with Cook in the kitchen for a while. Fanny read out of the *Daily Mail*: She could not have enough of it. Edwina didn't want to read about it at all. Cook told them that one of the workers, the builders, in Belfast it was, had scrawled on the side of the ship, 'Invincible to God and Man.' 'What can you expect?' she said.

Fanny said, 'Just listen to this – "Why," cried one lady, weeping because her father was aboard, "the captain can press a button and save everybody . . ." '

Cook stirred sugar into her tea. 'The waste. It cost near on a million, they say –'

The first day of term Meresia wasn't in uniform but came along the shining corridors in a white ninon dress strewn with flower motifs, with a big sash and a picture hat. 'Have you *seen* her?' breathed Annette. Glimpsed and then lost again she was seen to be, as Edwina had always known she was, much much more beautiful than her mother. The most beautiful person in the world.

Several of them were to make their First Communion at Corpus Christi. Edwina didn't wonder what Christ would taste like: although it wouldn't be ordinary bread, she knew it well from Altar Pudding, Clare's favourite. Hateful remnants of unwanted Communion hosts, trimmings, stirred up with gooseberry jam. Ugh. (Jesus, Mary and Joseph assist me in my last agony, 100 days.)

Mother Bede was in charge of the dormitory this term. Usually they only saw her in the library at weekends, when they chose their Baroness Orczy or their Rider Haggard. She interfered more than Mother Cuthbert. When she came round at night she really looked at everything. Even their knickers. White knicker linings must be turned inside out each night for an airing. 'Otherwise they get so stuffy.'

Meresia had a letter one morning at breakfast and could be seen to be fighting back tears. It was the second week of term. Marion, who had a pash for Jean, did some spying. She told them: 'Jean said, "Meresia's parents are going to be separated."' Annette said she didn't realize Catholics were allowed to, but Clare explained that it was all right so long as they didn't marry anyone else.

Edwina lay in bed imagining Lydia Merriwether saying, 'I want to be separate, I don't want you,' to Meresia's father. She thought she would probably declaim it like an actress. The worry for Meresia kept her awake. When she did fall asleep she dreamed she was riding a donkey, the saddle loaded with baggage. She knew she should hit it to make it go, but even though she had a big stick, she couldn't. There were some steps in the distance leading up to a high building. Standing on them was a small woman, very hideous, dressed like a nun, but in brown not black. Her face was brown too and wizened. Edwina was afraid of her at once, but she knew that she must be brave so she dismounted and walked up to her. She held out her hand; 'I'm Edwina,' she said. 'And why would I speak with you,' the old woman said, 'when I'm a person who's shaken hands with Queen Victoria?' She stretched her arm then and touched Edwina's hands. It was so painful, prickly, burning. 'You're a witch,' Edwina said. Then she woke up. She was already scratching at her hands; looking at the dreaded eczema.

She had her first piano lesson the next day. He looked as hateful as ever. He was wearing a brown velvet jacket with a red rose in his buttonhole. She stood awkwardly, head right up, hands turned out behind her back.

'Ill met by moonlight, proud Edwina.' She looked away. 'Don't tell me you lovely little girls don't know your Shakespeare.' He patted the piano stool: 'Sit down, please.' She sat on her hands, knowing it was a silly thing to do. He pulled at her arm. She struggled. 'Titania!'

'My name's Edwina.' She laid her hands resignedly on the edge of the piano. He picked one up, looked at it then dropped it carelessly. 'I thought so.' Then suddenly changing his manner; 'Well, *Edwina*. I've written a piece for you as promised. *La voilà*. "Edwina".'

It was horrible, she thought. It reminded her of 'In the Shadows' and 'Narcissus' at Madame Lambert's dancing class.

'Well, *qu'en penses-tu*? Do you like it?'

'Yes.' She remembered her manners. 'You're very kind.' Then she added: 'It doesn't sound like me really. Not like I am.'

'What are you like?'

Her answer was to get out her music, set it up and begin to play. Sitting with him she felt that she played mechanically, like a doll. He scarcely listened to her. He was adjusting the angle of the rose.

'I'm glad you like it. I shall put it in an album.'

The next week, he played it for her as she came into the room. 'Quite my favourite piece for the moment,' he declared. 'Composition. I know my good fortune in having the gift. A good fairy at my christening perhaps?'

He picked up her hand. 'A little better. What have we been doing? Zambuk, Cuticura – sticky ointments?' She shook her head. 'Anyway,' he said, '*Revenons à nos moutons*. I think some Chopin. For the end-of-term piece. What do you say to that? All fire and passion.' He touched her hair: 'So thick. When you play it sets up an electric charge perhaps? Couldn't you be a little calmer? Yes, we'll allow you the Chopin, I think.' For sight-reading he produced something very hard: it was as if watching her walk with ease he was willing her to stumble. It was difficult but she could – just. Seeing always a little ahead, her body played it.

That was why she minded so much when, pulling his chair round and back a little, he laid his hands on her shoulders, lightly. He'd done that before. It was an insect tickling, buzzing. But today he moved his hands down further, touching the stuff of her blouse. She went on playing. He had found where her breasts were beginning to grow, the little bit at the end, the nipple. He pressed it. 'We ought really to do some theory,' he said. 'Minor thirds. Give me an example of a minor third – ' All the while he went on massaging, working at her. She wondered if perhaps she should say something. She supposed she would have to suffer. Certainly, she couldn't tell anybody.

It was May now. There was meant to be a procession to Our Lady, through the gardens, through Switzerland and Montmartre and back to the grotto where Our Lady of Lourdes stood. 'O Mary we crown you with blossoms today, Queen of the Angels and Queen of the May . . .' But there was a sea fret and by afternoon a wind blowing off the sea; fat drops of icy rain, mist again by tea-time. Summer had not come after all. Instead they stayed in the chapel and sang the Lourdes *'Ave Maria'*, with its rising rising *'Ave's'* – so high that lots of the older girls couldn't reach them. Mother Cuthbert had a musical-box statue of the Lourdes Virgin which played this. She brought it into religious instruction class.

Uncle Frederick wrote: '. . . We shall probably come in August. How you will have changed! Are you still sometimes a Little Bear? I hope so. We have been nearly all last month with the Antici-Montani, staying in their lovely palace. Rome is so beautiful in the spring. The children in the family are all much older than you. Stefano is already 25. There's also Eugenio, Ersilia and Maddalena. Taddeo at 17 is the nearest in age. They are all great fun except sadly Eugenio who is not quite right. He hasn't really grown up, you see. How glad your parents must be that they have three such fit and lovely children. I was really glad too to hear that you have made such a good friend at the convent . . .'

'Slimy tripe, ugh,' Fanny said, pushing her helping down behind the hot pipes (cold now, in summer). Mother Anselm was safely at the far end of the refectory. Edwina said, 'You're lucky Meresia didn't see, thanking the chance which allowed her to say the beloved's name.

Meresia at the head of the table seemed in a dream, fork halfway to her mouth, stationary. Edwina wondered what she would say if she told her about the music lessons and Mr Maycock. Not that she ever ever could, ever would. It was still going on, only these last two weeks it had been worse. Yesterday for instance her nipples had felt raw and sore. Lying in her cubicle that night, tender where the vest fabric had rubbed them afterwards, she'd thought that she didn't want them touched again, ever. Her hands felt sore too and hot. She laid one of them between her thighs. It was warm there but at the same time cool and refreshing. It comforted her. Then she remembered that she ought to have her folded hands on her chest. It had been Mother Cuthbert who had shown her, her third evening. 'On your back, my dear, with your hands like this. Then if you should die in the night . . .'

Clare had said that *she* always lay like that: otherwise she didn't sleep. When Edwina did so it made her feel always very peaceful – and in the winter very very cold. The cold of death perhaps? But now, her hand between her legs, she felt only this curious comfort as if someone, who wasn't Edwina, was bringing peace to her. It was too as if something or somebody stirred and fluttered, a bird in her entrails, moving and growing between her legs. Then, cool peace, so that she drifted into sleep – and what would it matter if she *died* like that? There was music too. Where did the sea begin and the music end in this cool comfort of her hand which played, without moving, as she lay so still?

'In order to receive the Blessed Sacrament worthily what

is required? In order to receive the Blessed Sacrament worthily it is required that we be in a state of grace and keep the prescribed fast. What is it to be in a state of grace? To be in a state of grace is to be free from mortal sin and pleasing to God . . .'

'Even if you eat something without meaning to after midnight, that does it,' Babs said. Vita had read about a girl who absentmindedly ate a chocolate she found lying about the very morning of her First Communion. 'It was terrible – she couldn't disappoint all the people who'd come and spoil the whole day. So she committed a mortal sin.'

What with worrying about accidentally eating, and looking anxiously to see that Meresia was in the chapel, and not getting the giggles, Edwina forgot to pray or to *feel* anything at all. Suddenly, it was all over. Communion breakfast, presents: Fanny said she'd spoken to the priest and it was all right if you'd eaten candle grease or bits off your nails, because they weren't food.

The sun shone for the procession in the afternoon. Edwina's flowered wreath gripped too tight and set her head throbbing. 'How can you grumble when you think of Our Lord and the Crown of Thorns?' Clare told her. 'Yes,' Edwina said indignantly, 'but He was famous for it.' She and Fanny were at the head of the procession. They had to scatter rose petals, kissing them as they did so. Whenever they'd practised, Fanny had got out of rhythm, irritating Mother Scholastica, who was in charge, beyond endurance. 'Frances, you are doing it expressly.' Now, on the afternoon, Fanny had begun a violent attack of hay fever. Pink-eyed, runny-nosed, the basket of petals shaking with every sneeze. 'Jesus my Lord my God my All,' they sang, following the Blessed Sacrament between the elm trees.

It filled her with shame and fear, the idea of telling Meresia. And yet she felt such a relief, such a quiet joy when she'd made the decision. For how long now she'd wanted, desperately needed, something to say to Meresia that would hold her for more than a few seconds. And (why had she never thought of it before) Meresia would surely solve it all?

The day before the next piano lesson she looked for her, finding her after tea walking along near the Lourdes grotto, on her way to tennis. She and Hermione, racquets under their arms. She said, heart thumping: 'Meresia, can I talk to you?' Hermione went on ahead. 'Meresia,' she began, and then dried up completely.

'Yes, what is it?' Meresia said patiently, then, 'What's the matter, darling?' as Edwina began or thought she was beginning to cry.

'Come along and sit down,' Meresia said, taking her arm, leading her over to a bench near the grotto where Our Lady looked down on them, arms outspread.

'It's my music lesson – '

'Yes?' Meresia frowned, looked doubtful. 'I suppose?' she began, then: 'No, tell me – '

When Edwina had finished, 'Oh darling,' she said, 'how awful for you.' (She had believed her, completely, without question. Not as Mother, who would surely have said: 'But is it *true*, Edwina?')

'How truly awful for you,' she said again. And then, oh joy of joys, putting her arm round her, holding her close, she said very gently: 'The best thing of all would be if you could try not to worry any more – *forget* about it. Just – ' she paused – 'just if it comes into your mind and you're still upset – then you could pray for him. To Our Lady. Because he must need our prayers or he wouldn't do anything so – ' she hesitated, searched for the word – 'impure. So awfully immodest.'

And then releasing Edwina, sitting up again, no longer the Child of Mary speaking but the child perhaps of Lydia Merriwether: 'Oh gosh,' she said, 'what an awful mess. I mean – had you told anybody else?' Edwina shook her head. Meresia bounced a tennis ball up and down, holding the racquet with easy grace: 'It's just – that it makes sense of something someone said, oh ages ago, and two girls, I know, have given up piano. Just saying they weren't interested any more.'

'I couldn't say that. Ever.'

Meresia turned. 'You're – rather good, aren't you, darling? Jean heard you practising once.' She stooped and picked up the ball. 'Anyway, leave everything to me, won't you?' She put her arm round Edwina again.

They walked back to the building together. She felt a sort of excited peace, so that she didn't ask for anything else. It was how she would have liked to feel with Uncle Frederick.

HELP POLICE. HORRIBLE THEFT. The beautiful bejewelled crozier, clasped in the wooden hand of St Hilda, the statue near the Lady Chapel, was found without its jewels – those gleaming rubies, emeralds, winking diamonds, palely glowing amethysts. The pride and joy of the convent. News of the theft went the rounds, was chewed over at mealtimes. The jewels were from Mother Scholastica's dowry, Edwina learnt: part of the enormous whispered sum she'd brought in with her. Clare, white-faced, was the shocked centre of the drama. Mother Scholastica was seen to look no different.

The police came. Not the helmeted perspiring figures of the picture books, but important ones, in dark suits with Gladstone bags and confident expressions, and large walrus moustaches. Mother Aelred asked for hands up of those who had visited the chapel after evening prayers. The police would like a word with them. It may have been that something was noticed. No stone must be left unturned, she explained, leaving in the air an image of the grounds being searched on hands and knees. And indeed the two important police could be seen, bending, looking at footmarks, examining window panes.

Fanny was interviewed. They were really nice to her, she told everyone. One of them patted her on the head and said he had a daughter her age at home and he only hoped that *she* would have been as helpful.

She had been back to chapel, she'd told them, to say some special prayers for a Novena to be finished by the Feast of the Precious Blood. The detectives had been most awfully impressed and asked her all about the Precious Blood and how did you do a Novena? She'd told them too about the Nine First Fridays and what the Sacred Heart had promised Margaret Mary Alacoque. 'It's wonderfully easy to get to Heaven if you know the way,' the other man had remarked. Marion said: 'I'll bet you were glad you went in to pray. Jolly things like that never happen to me.'

'Don't be assy,' Fanny said, '*of course* I wasn't there – '

They were good detectives though and found their man: the ne'er-do-well husband of the woman who did the rough at the farm guest-house. He had hidden all night in the organ loft, waiting his chance. He was traced as far north as Newcastle, but the jewels were gone. False ones gleamed now in the crozier.

'All those who have music lessons with Mr Maycock,' Mother Aelred announced, 'please come to me for extra work. It is not certain,' she added, 'that he will be able to come back this term at all. Arrangements will be made . . .'

Arrangements were not made. There were only three weeks of term left. She practised as hard, harder, than ever. One hot afternoon in early June, she was called to the parlour. Meresia said, 'Daddy, this is Edwina.'

He was only a little taller than Meresia, with grey receding hair; he put on a pair of glasses immediately after shaking hands, as if to look at her more closely.

'You're going to play for me later?' The surprise was still total. A message during break while she and Fanny were wolfing down cold toast left over from the mistresses' breakfast.

He'd come in his own motor, with a chauffeur. They were to go on a picnic, to Goathland. The chauffeur was rather young and wore a very long coat and had spots on the back of his neck: from where Edwina sat she found that she was looking at them for a lot of the time as they drove inland, towards Wheeldale Moor, the red brick of the convent on its rocky promontory fading, growing smaller; soon the sea would be left behind.

'How did you order, arrange, such weather, my darling?' But Meresia just smiled at her father and said it had been lovely all the week. Today she wasn't wearing her Child of Mary ribbon, but had mufti on: a cream-coloured skirt and a blouse with a lot of hand crochet round the neck and wrists. On her it looked more beautiful than anything of Aunt Adelina's, ever. 'Are you happy?' she asked Edwina. She sat holding hands with her father.

Of course she was happy. And even more so when they'd settled down near the heather, not far from the Roman road, the slightest of afternoon breezes stirring the bracken. Seeing the signpost marked 'Beckhole' she had told them about Sarah. It was so easy because everything she said was right. She couldn't believe in her happiness.

Meresia's father was very gentle and easy with Meresia. She couldn't imagine being friends with her father. The way Meresia said, 'Daddy, do you remember that time – you know, that concert, that man we met . . .' Turning to Edwina perhaps: 'If you could have *seen* him. We were in Paris because – no, but it's too much – ' laughing, overcome by the memory and the happiness of the memory.

The chauffeur sat a little way away after he'd brought the hamper over. He was reading a pink newspaper which he held down in the breeze. He had food beside him which he didn't seem very interested in. Edwina wondered what it was like to eat apart like that. It was the same as the nuns, and yet not. More like Arthur perhaps?

After tea, she took her shoes off, wiggled her toes in their black lisle stockings.

Meresia's father said, 'Take the stockings off too. I would.' Edwina giggled, and Meresia said, 'He's like that. A tease.' But he seemed to her really a serious person; his face so firm and quiet, the jawline like Meresia's.

'We should drive down to Beckhole then, for Edwina.'

She told them: 'There was a Dragon. It ate lots of beautiful maidens (Sarah's face by the fireside, hoping Nurse wouldn't come in), and of course he breathed *fire*. But then he got slain by a very brave man called Roland Burden who fought him for half of a whole day . . .' She thought as she spoke of Meresia being carried away by the monster to his lair up in the hills. She saw the limp powerless body, that curious softness of Meresia, so that everywhere you placed your hand you would meet only yielding flower-scented gentleness. A rose without thorns.

The idyll was almost over. They were back at the convent, and 'Which piano would be best, I wonder?' Meresia said. The parlour one wasn't too good, but it was the most convenient so she played to him on that one, feeling the damp resistance, the sweetish raisiny smell coming up from the keys.

When she'd asked what she should play, he'd said: 'Something you have by heart. Two pieces perhaps, one for execution, one for touch and feeling.' She gave him some Mozart and then a Chopin waltz she had been trying on her own. She wanted tremble, glitter when she was playing the Chopin but when she tried half-damping the pedal, it stuck – she hadn't wanted to risk the smudgy sound of it full down.

'That was sort of drier than I meant, in that last but one section – because of the pedal.' She found herself talking easily.

He nodded. They spoke a while then he said: 'I think you sing in your mind, sing while you play. That's so, isn't it?'

'Yes.' But she had never thought of it before. He talked to her then, Meresia looking on approvingly, eagerly almost. One had, he told her, to be enormously careful. 'I've seen so many spoilt – and especially with the piano. Not all can be Mozarts after all and triumph over the whole problem. Little Master Solomon who played before the Queen earlier this year, they say he won't do anything like that again until his studies are finished. Admirable – if it comes to pass.' He smiled, then turned to Meresia: 'I don't want to predict anything. One can't anyway; but I think quite seriously that there is something very definite here. *Quite* a gift . . .'

When Reverend Mother came in a little later he spoke to her with great authority. It seemed to Edwina that in a few golden minutes everything was arranged. Her parents would be written to. He knew of someone excellent in Scarborough but who would be abroad this summer. It would be best to practise gently until the autumn. He said: 'If I can help again?' and then as they shook hands finally: 'I think your future could be very interesting, don't you?'

The first disappointment was that Uncle Frederick didn't come. Not his fault, but Aunt Adelina's. In late May she had been quite seriously ill and now the specialist said there was no question of travel. She would convalesce in a spa. Next year, he wrote, they would try to do better.

Macouba was Cora's pony now. Edwina said that she didn't want another, that she wasn't interested any more in riding, and especially hunting. She watched Mother's scorn and yes, anger, when she said this. Father told her that she must please herself. His mind was already ten days ahead, to when the grouse shooting would start. Also, he was very taken up with a breeding experiment: crossing a foxhound with a bloodhound. The fruits of his efforts were to be seen romping and rolling in the sun in a wire pen near the stables.

She saw them often, because after the first week of the holidays she was down every day with Macouba. He had strangles, and it was Edwina, not Cora, who cared. Throwing rugs over his shivering frame, coaxing him with hot bran mashes, helping Arthur poultice his glands. She was there when the vet came to lance the swellings. She and Arthur talked. It was like the old days. His eldest boy worked in their garden now: Mr Ramsden shouted at him.

Meresia wrote to Mother about the new piano lessons. Edwina was shown the letter. Mother and Father said how kind it was of Meresia's father. Edwina told them that he and Lydia Merriwether were to separate – she felt important knowing about it, yet sad at the same time.

'Mother Bede explained. It's because of their work. They can't be in the same place at the same time. Sometimes God wills it that way, she told us . . .'

'You could spare me your convent phrases, Edwina,' Mother said, with a dry little smile. Edwina was eating kedgeree, pushing it about with a fork. 'Your manners,' Mother said sharply. She rose from the table, taking Meresia's letter. The envelope remained on the table.

That evening, in her room, a chair against the door, Edwina practised over and over and over again that beautiful, beautiful handwriting. 'Mrs Thomas Illingworth' – each individual letter – rows and rows of Meresia's 'a's', 't's'. This is what my handwriting will be like, she thought. I will take Meresia into myself, become part of her.

Fanny was to stay at the end of August. Afterwards Edwina would go back with her to Whitby. Now, it was just to wait for her coming. Through a succession of rainy days she played the piano in the library, infuriating Philip. He told her: 'You'll go mouldy like cheese if you sit indoors all the time. You heard the Pater say – you ought to play with Cora . . .'

'*You* play with Cora,' she said savagely.

'And I ought to tell you this, you're awfully rude to the Mater. I thought you were the one being brought up a Catholic. I thought you were meant to be holy . . .'

'Saint Philip,' she said angrily, letting fall a cascade of notes. And then, triumphant discords – I hate you, Philip Illingworth, you're hateful . . .

Fanny's visit was a great success. Mother thought her beautifully-mannered. During her stay they were allowed down to dinner wearing their best white dresses. They drank a glass each of half wine, half water. A lot of the time Fanny spent seated in the park, drawing with great care and verisimilitude a picture of the Hall (complete with peacocks) which she coloured in and gave to Mother as a present.

On the fifth day of Edwina's visit to Whitby, she and Fanny went over to Bay. It was to be an all-day excursion and they were to take with them sandshoes and enough food and drink for a picnic on the beach or up on the cliffs. Marmee said: 'I trust you girls to do whatever Cook says.'

Cook was as trying as last time. Worse really. She hinted at reasons why she didn't feel her best. 'You girls will know soon enough,' she said, 'and I'll thank you in the meantime to show a little more thoughtfulness . . .' Later she said,

'Nature doesn't bother if it's a lady or a cook when it's a certain day of the month . . .' She was going to make a nice cup of tea in the train, she said, and proceeded to set up the spirit lamp and all the paraphernalia. Edwina was very alarmed and thought that the carriage, which she imagined to be all of wood, might burst into flames. For most of the journey she read anxiously the fire precautions and instructions set between the framed sepia views of Whitby and Sandsend and Scarborough.

But then they were rid of Cook and might go down on the beach. Oh, but it was lovely to be back. It was almost as if she, and not Fanny, belonged here. She was a Foreigner, she knew that (Fanny had explained to her, furiously turning the gramophone handle for 'Everybody's Doing It', 'You're a Foreigner, Edwina, I belong . . .').

Fanny's aunt told them, 'Ben's off sick.' A fish-hook had caught in his eye, and though it wasn't damaged for ever it hadn't healed yet. He wouldn't be going out with the boats for another two or three days.

The tide was more than halfway down. They sat on a rock not far from where King's Beck ran into the sea, and had their picnic early because the air made them hungry. Further out among the rock pools there were the summer visitors. The little girls had tucked their dresses in their knickers – such an expanse of prints and hollands and dimity. Some of the boys were very foolishly dressed, Fanny said. She and Edwina were still hungry and when Matussi's ice-cream cart came down they both bought strawberry ices.

Edwina was trying to get her tongue down to the bottom of the cone, when Ben appeared. His eye looked bad, the bandaging important and serious. It had brown marks on it. Edwina asked him if it hurt.

'Did it – ' he grinned. She asked, when did it happen? Fanny was taking off her shoes and stockings and looked uninterested.

'Monday was a week. I was up at Dr Wilson's Tuesday, when he's over from Whitby. He saw to it.'

He sat beside them on the rock. 'Since you've stockings

off I'll show you summat in pools.' When he took them out over the scaurs he had them on his left so that he could see with his good eye. He showed them brittle stars, crouching down by the pool. Edwina bent close to him. She watched his hands – they were shaped like hers, but worn clear, polished almost so that they reminded her of pebbles just washed by the tide. Her own had dry scaly patches – a bout of eczema just ended.

They walked up back a roundabout way because Edwina wanted to explore. Fanny, who'd hurt her little toe on a stone, took the direct path. Alone with Ben, Edwina talked. Between being shown this house and that, she told him about the piano. They'd just had a Visitors' Concert, he said – she should have come and played then . . .

Later, for tea, they were very crowded. There weren't really enough chairs. Instead of going to borrow more, Robert said: 'Edwina can sit on Ben's knee then. I'll take Fanny – '

'No, thank you,' Fanny said, pushing her fingers through his hair. 'They smell fishy,' she said, sniffing them. He gave her a playful smack. '*Cousin.*'

But Ben sat down and quite simply put Edwina on his knee. 'Pass us our tea then,' he said.

His knees felt firm and hard, when he shifted a little the bony part went into her. She rocked a little and unbalanced. But even when it was uncomfortable, she felt happy – where she should be, strange but familiar. She had that feeling she had sometimes when she was very tired, light-headed, I have been here before. She thought she would like to stay for ever.

That night, she wrote to Uncle Frederick:

'I've been twice now to the most beautiful marvellous place, it's called Robin Hood's Bay because they think Robin Hood hid here one time when the sheriffs were after him. Not so long ago there were smugglers and Fanny's cousin Ben showed me a place called the Bolts, where they got away. I am sending you four pictures of Robin Hood's Bay . . .'

She asked Marmee for a stamp and posted it at once. Fanny looked at the name and address. 'I must write to my Uncle,' she said. 'Uncle Clive. Any day now he may invite me to go out to Rhodesia. He's probably struck gold, which will be very convenient for me . . .'

Mother Scholastica read to them while they embroidered: *Three Daughters of the United Kingdom.* It was about three girls at a convent and she read it in a light uninterested voice. Edwina guessed that the holy girl who was certain she had a vocation would never become a nun. It would be the most unlikely one, which was Beatrice de Woodville, noble scion. 'I bet you a bob,' Fanny said.

Edwina had graduated to drawn-thread work. She thought the most lovely moment was when, triumphantly, all the threads cut, she was able to pull – one lovely long stream. She saw herself already, a whole tablecloth made: point de Venise, araignée: then those intricate bobbles which hung from the antimacassar in the convent parlour. What Aunt Adelina did with such skill she too would be able to do. She would make it for Uncle Frederick, tossing it at him carelessly, in front of that smelly cow. 'By the way, *I* made this . . .'

'Uncle Clive sent me a photograph,' Fanny said at the beginning of term. 'I asked for one because I'm sick of seeing your funny floppy-faced Frederick in your cubicle.'

'*He's* floppy-faced too,' Edwina said when she saw him. It was a snapshot only and he had screwed his eyes up against the sun. 'It's fearfully hot out there,' Fanny said, 'it's Africa, you see. I wish photographs could be in colour then I could see what sort of eyes and hair he's got.' She read from the letter: 'I am the one in the middle – pig in the middle. The other two sport rather splendid moustaches, as you see, but I have never favoured one. What about *your* sending me a new picture, and one too perhaps of your friends?'

Both pictures were taken in the garden in the early autumn sun with Fanny's new Kodak. They sat grinning in their school-dresses. When a few weeks later the pictures were developed, Edwina looked at them unbelievingly. She thought that she would never forget that afternoon, that it was preserved for ever on the sepia paper: she and Fanny with their arms about each other. Because it was the very next day that they had the Fight.

White Peter Pan collars – worn with their school dresses. Often they washed them at night, drying them on the hot pipes. Edwina washed hers, she remembered doing so, but then in the morning, Fanny's was missing. 'That's mine,' she announced, coming into Edwina's cubicle. 'It's *not,*' Edwina said.

Is, isn't. Is, isn't. 'Give it to me!' Fanny cried, for all the world as if it were something of importance. As suddenly it did become. For she snatched it from Edwina. 'You shan't have it!' Edwina ran after her out into the aisle of the dormitory.

'I always get what I want,' Fanny jeered. 'Always. I would die if I didn't.' Holding on to the collar she leaned forward and tugged at Edwina's hair. Edwina pulled hers back and at once, as soon as it was in her grasp, she wanted never to let go. That great handful of red hair, horrible, how could she ever have thought it beautiful? I hate her, she thought.

They'd begun to kick and struggle. Other girls had come out of their cubicles. Someone tried to separate them: 'For heaven's sake. There's a nun coming.' Fanny's forehead, white and stretched, the hair pulled back, eyes popping. A vicious kick from her. Then like cold water, Mother Anselm's voice.

'Frances, Edwina! In Mother Bede's dormitory too – like little animals. Into your cubicles, please.' She clapped her hands. But almost at once she called Fanny and Edwina out again. 'Apologize to each other, please. A shocking exhibition. You should be ashamed. Girls who made their First Communion.' Edwina knew suddenly that if they'd been able to go on, if she'd been left to it with her fists, she'd have won. I am a witch, she thought. My pricking thumbs, the power in my hands. I can always win.

'*Ashamed,*' Mother Anselm repeated, turning to go.

All through the first classes, Edwina felt sick, shaky. Then at break, as if nothing had happened, Fanny pulled her aside: 'We're not supposed to know, have you *heard*? Meresia's parents are getting a divorce – It's all round the big girls.'

'I thought they were Catholics,' Vita said. Clare added: 'It's not allowed ever – Whom God hath joined let no man put asunder – Even if he's drunk or beats you or things like that – '

'You can tell it's wrong anyway,' Babs said, 'because when you've done it even the King and Queen who are Protestants don't allow you to walk anywhere near to them at Ascot.'

'That just shows,' Marion said. 'I bet Meresia's ashamed ...'

And indeed Meresia did look ashamed, or upset, or both. Edwina forgot all about the morning's fight: thinking of, sorrowing for Meresia, remembering the picnic.

He jumped up and down on the little piano stool beside her, his short legs swaying to and fro; every now and then giggling happily, throwing forth some excited comment, some new idea.

'We shall have the most wonderful times together. I see that already. Let us try . . . Ah now – listening finger always, *thinking* wrist – Remember that . . . Now an exercise. We come down on the keys, like this – but from different heights – *so* . . .'

His name was Franz Hengelmüller. His sister and Meresia's father had studied the 'cello together. Although he had an Austrian father and many cousins over there, he himself had been born and bred in Yorkshire. 'I die here, of course. But first I live . . .'

She was to come every Wednesday from three to four, travelling on the train from Ravenscar with the visiting art teacher, then coming back alone. One of the lay sisters met the train.

Third teacher lucky. 'Lovely, wonderful,' he cried at once, the very moment her first piece finished. He took her seriously too. 'We are going to work very hard – together.' All that excitement and enthusiasm she had: well, he had even more. Talking, urging, whirling round on the stool: 'Think, please – now we stop to think. The great teacher, Leschetizky, he said always – "Think ten times, play once . . ." '

She was to stay to tea every week. Cristina, his sister, was small too. Together they made Edwina feel a giant. The bread was cut very thin – or perhaps it only seemed so after school – the butter very lavish. Cristina wanted Edwina to take some cakes back with her.

Franz said: 'You don't have sufficient. I know. No school feeds enough.' He himself barely stopped to eat. He couldn't keep off the subject of music, letting his tea grow cold: 'But Chopin – he wasn't really at home on the piano – not the way Beethoven was. You know, in a large place, in a hall he could scarcely be heard? No, that is true – It was the approach for clavichord. The way you *think* Chopin played,' (but she had not thought at all), 'that was Liszt, perhaps Kalkbrenner. How they played him. You see, you need to remember this . . .'

Both grew excited when she said she didn't know Scarborough well. 'Oh, but you must, you must.'

'The sea,' he said. 'I am always happy by the sea. We are back from the Alps and it is the *sea* again. I like to listen. It is my music.'

'I love it too,' Edwina said.

'How are the lessons?' Meresia asked. Her eyes were no longer pink-rimmed. During the first half of term they had looked always as if she cried a lot and they never had a chance to heal.

'They're capital,' Edwina said, using without thinking and she didn't know why, a Philip sort of word.

'I'm glad they're capital,' Meresia said, smiling. And it was then she added, so casually, almost as if it were a nothing – standing there on the parquet floor of the hall, just in front of the big Sacred Heart statue: 'Daddy and I were wondering, would you like to come and spend a few days at Christmas? You could play, and perhaps meet some people and Daddy could give some more advice. Mrs Aveling, she's a singer –' she hesitated – 'she's coming to stay too. There could be some lovely music. Anyway,' she said, turning to go on, 'do think about it.'

Think about it. How could she think about anything else? All through lunch – the hard-boiled eggs in batter unable to nauseate her, watery cabbage not needing to be offered up – she made plans.

She was floating, dreaming still when later that afternoon she went off to practise. Today there were no rooms free. She would have, she supposed, to go in one of the dormitories. No fun that, because you could never be certain a nun wasn't behind the curtain saying her Office. But luckily this afternoon she'd seen someone she was sure was Mother Scholastica going along the cloister to Chapel. Her dormitory, St Lucy's, was one of the three with pianos.

There was a horrible painting of St Lucy up above the piano. Her eyes, like two peeled grapes, were on a plate which she was holding. But the painter had been cowardly because instead of dark empty sockets he'd given her a new pair of eyes, gazing heavenward. Today though the picture didn't worry her as she sat, eyes closed, dreaming again. Her hands were too icy to play so she warmed them a few moments on the hot pipes, singing to herself a tune that she made up as she went along. Then to the piano: scales, arpeggios, up and down, faster and faster. She took out her music, propped it up but it was no good. She was too excited.

She danced the length of the dormitory. O my love my dove my beautiful one. The shadow of Meresia's departure this term was lifted. She pulled the ribbon from her hair and shook her head, then with hair all about her face went over to the window. It was difficult to open and there was a wide sill, but it was unbarred. Resting on her stomach she leaned out, breathed in sea air.

A discreet cough behind her. She jumped down and saw, coming out of her cubicle, Mother Scholastica.

'Piano practising, Edwina?'

'Yes,' Edwina said defiantly.

'It looks like it. Very like it. Fasten your hair, please.' Then as Edwina fumbled, bending down and looking for the ribbon: 'Should you like Mother Anselm to know of this?'

'No, Mother.' The answer came out more cheekily than she

intended. She held her breath a little anxiously but Mother Scholastica said only, 'You are a very *odd* child.' Then suddenly, in an exasperated tone, 'You're good at the piano, aren't you? Something quite special? Why then why, when your life is mapped out for you so plainly, can't you appreciate it?'

Edwina, puzzled, stared at her. What did it feel like to be Mother Scholastica?

'You have been thoroughly irresponsible, is that not the case, Edwina?' She turned her head away, sighed heavily: 'Oh, I don't know. Really I don't – '

Edwina said, suddenly bold: 'Do you like being able to tell us off?'

'*What* did you say? You do realize how impertinent, how rude a remark like that is? Does your mother allow you to speak in that manner? Oh, I don't know,' Mother Scholastica said again. 'I'm wasting my time. Why am I here at all?' She shook her finger at Edwina: 'You have special lessons, set yourself up, you are not to be trusted.' She was very flushed. 'Little fool,' she said as she went towards the door.

Horrible, yes, to be reported. In fact she never heard anything more about it. Afterwards she realized that she had not expected to: in some odd way she felt almost that it was she who had caught Mother Scholastica out.

It was too good to be true and perhaps because of that, hugging it to herself, she didn't write home about it until nearly the last week of term. Meresia's father would of course have written. That first homecoming meal she could hardly wait to mention it. Philip wasn't back yet. Aunt Josephine was upstairs with a feverish cold and Cora was ill too, with a septic throat.

They didn't answer at first.

'Didn't you get it – my letter?'

Mother said crisply: 'We can talk about it after, Edwina.' Then in a bright voice: 'You are invited, you know, to a party at Clare's. Has she mentioned it?'

Edwina shook her head, splashing some soup as she did so.

Her father, looking up, said: 'Behave yourself. Those manners may do at the convent. They will not do here.'

Her soup plate was cleared away. When she tried to speak, Mother raised her hand, a signal that she was to say nothing while there were servants there.

It could only mean something awful, that they should keep her waiting like that. But then immediately after, Father said: 'Come along, Edwina,' and led her into the library. Mother was there too. She was sitting very upright, her hands folded in uncharacteristic manner: Edwina imagined suddenly that perhaps she wanted to smoke.

'About this visit,' he began, and then cleared his throat. He'd remained standing, not in the relaxed way he stood before the fire recounting his exploits on the hunting field but in a rather solemn, important way, which filled her with dread. Stern God the Father.

'I am afraid there is no question of your staying with this friend. Her father . . . we were of course very grateful that music lessons . . . But we had not at that time any idea . . . there has been unpleasant exposure in the newspapers. Unsavoury is the word, I think . . .'

'Tom,' Mother interrupted sharply, 'Edwina is not a child.' She turned to her and said in a very firm voice: 'Meresia's father is living at the moment with a person who is not his wife. Do you understand? They are not married, Edwina, so it is quite incorrect – *wrong,* rather, I should say. *Cela ne se fait pas.* You understand? Even when a divorce does take place, it would hardly be the *ménage* . . .'

She was not to go. What price Christmas then? What point the holidays? She cried all afternoon, a useless, exhausting tantrum, beating with her fists on the bedcover: when someone came, calling out that she was reading, resting, tired after the journey from school. Again and again it flooded over her that Meresia had left, that she would never see her again. At tea-time, white-faced and angry, she said: 'I should like Fanny to stay.' Of course, they said, mildly enough, of course. It could be arranged.

'It is perfectly sickening,' she wrote to Fanny, taking care to go out and post the letter herself. 'See if you can get hold of a newspaper.' She wanted too to write to Meresia, but when she tried she wasn't able at all. Supposing too, Meresia recognized the pale imitation of her own handwriting? Back went her face into the pillow.

The Party. She had to face the party. And Clare of course. It appeared that Cora was asked too.

Aunt Josephine. Her ally, or so she felt. But she'd been in bed for all the week before Christmas. Edwina had been loath anyway to involve her in the Meresia affair. What could she have done to help? In spite of her friendship with Mother, in spite of her looking so solid, her words didn't carry much weight.

A card came from Meresia. A little note inside: 'We were so sorry you couldn't come. Another time perhaps?' Fanny wrote too. She couldn't come, she had too much on. 'P.S. I found something in a newspaper.'

On Christmas Eve she became ill. From Cora whom she hadn't wanted to see, she'd acquired a throat, wretchedly thick and coated, so that it hurt whether she swallowed or not. Nurse was surprisingly kind to her. Sarah had left now to get married. Nurse was barely needed, although Cora would not be coming to the convent. There was no point in her leaving home, Mother said, since she was perfectly happy, and so good, and so *easy*.

But the party was inescapable. She was better, no doubt of it. Not feeling good, but not bad enough to stay behind. There was talk of cod liver oil and iron. She was growing. Mother looked with distaste on Edwina's growing.

Her hair wouldn't behave. Not just cotters now, but a horrible habit of not lying any definite way. It seemed to grow independently of her. 'I hate it,' she said, on the evening of the party: tugging at it herself, only to see it stick out, slightly greasy, at an angle. She would have liked to have had it washed for the party but it appeared that although she was not ill enough to stay at home she was not well enough for that.

Cora had new shoes and between looking at them in their drawstring bag for half of the journey, and patting her ringlets and tossing her head for the rest, she was an annoying companion. Edwina hoped to lose her early on at the party.

A great log fire burned in the hall and it was warm there but not upstairs where they put their coats. She felt hungry suddenly, the first time since she'd been ill, the first time really since she'd come home. She thought of pastry, mince pies, jellies, savouries, and wanted that part of the party to come quickly.

Clare in a new dress. Lemon georgette so that she looked sallower than ever and not very well. But who was this? She couldn't believe it. The party only half an hour old and there, standing in the doorway of the library, talking to two other boys and looking restless – as ever – shaking his head, turning it, moving from one foot to the other: Ned.

They were being marshalled together for some Highland reels to 'warm everyone up'. She pushed aside some people to get to him before he should move, imagining he might disappear. Quicksilver.

'Hello,' she said. 'It's Edwina Illingworth, from Madame Lambert's.'

He was pleased, was seen to be the kind of person who didn't mind at all being interrupted. He even introduced the other two boys to her. One of them called her 'Miss Illingworth'; the other, a dark thick-set boy, looked very much less pleased. 'As I was saying . . .' he remarked pointedly.

'Oh, but those classes,' Ned said. He turned to the others. 'Edwina and I, we went to these perfectly dreadful dancing classes – ' Then back to her: 'I say, do you go to school?'

'With Clare.'

'Oh,' he said, 'with Clare.' His eyes darted about.

*'As I was saying,'* the dark boy began, 'there's this first-rate notion of having cricket in railway carriages, like on board ship – but you have a pitch in every corridor and passengers can only come out of the compartment when an over's called . . .'

It was no good to feel snubbed. And Ned did say 'See you later,' as she walked away.

So much food. She ate prodigiously as if from some deep hunger. Three helpings of trifle . . .

'Are you all right, my dears? Are you all happy?' Clare's father, tall, thin, distinguished, a fragile figure looking as though he'd snap if bent at the waist. He wandered about as though sent on an errand which he'd long ago forgotten. His wife would murmur something and then his face would light up with recognition and for a few moments he'd move purposefully. Then: forgotten again.

For the first game after supper they were told very clearly where they might and might not hide. Edwina scarcely knew her way about and, looking for somewhere, was haunted by the story of the Mistletoe Bough, imagining she saw the skeleton dressed in its faded bridal clothes . . . She thought: I'll hide somewhere silly, so obvious that I'll be found at once.

At first it wasn't easy. Then suddenly, she came upon somewhere really likely: a sort of linen room, with tables stacked with towels and big baskets full of washing. The cupboards along the length of the wall were too narrow and too hot except for one at the end with two very deep shelves quite empty. The room had undrawn curtains and when she got into the cupboard moonlight filtered weakly through the panels and edges of the door. To make herself comfortable she had to sit with her knees drawn up. She felt warm and quite lively. Her head filled up with some sprightly Mozart, the rhythms insistent, so that her fingers itched. It flashed through her mind as she played: this is what it is to be happy, shut in a semi-dark cupboard, playing Mozart on my knees.

Voices. The light switched on – 'Try those cupboards.' A girl: 'No, they're just narrow linen places.' A boy: 'Try them all.' Sounds. 'One two three – no, they're all the same.'

'Ali Baba, in that basket, do you think?' They laughed and went off. The light still on.

Enough was enough. She had been successful. She turned the doorhandle. Nothing happened. She tried again. It seemed loose – suppose it came away in her hand? She pushed then instead. But nothing yielded.

I want to get out, she thought. I want to be downstairs, back at the party. She called out, 'I'm in here. Come and find me.' She banged on the door with her fists – but her hands, her knuckles, were too precious. She kicked instead.

She began to panic. The trifle rose acidly. She bit on a handkerchief to stop screaming. It was just then that the doorhandle turned. She gave a little high-pitched noise.

'Hello.' The door opening. 'It's *Edwina*, isn't it? I say, you have hidden well. Can I come in, there's chaps following – ' She moved over a little and Ned climbed in. 'This is awfully jolly. I couldn't – '

She interrupted, her voice a little tearful: 'You shouldn't have pulled the door to. Now it won't open.'

'No more it won't. Never mind. We'll soon be discovered.'

He was sitting as she was, knees drawn up. 'I can't see you properly,' she said.

'Feel me.' She reached out. His hair was very silky. She nearly put her fingers in his eyes. '*Hey* – Hey, that hurt. How old are you?'

'Thirteen.'

'Oh crikey, those dancing classes. I'm fifteen now – Those days one just did as one was told. Now I do what I want.'

'Can you?'

'There are ways and means.' He had his same urgent manner of talking as if in a hurry to get the next thought out. 'Not at school of course. But at home – Mother's always rather busy with being beautiful. It takes a lot of time, I can assure you. Father doesn't admire her enough. He's all tied up with money. The Baltic Exchange. Your mother's not like that?'

What was Mother like? 'No, not really – '

'You're not as fat as I remember. What sort of things do *you* like doing?'

'I play the piano very well.'

'Good for you, so do I, I play by ear a lot. Pick things up. I used to rather like operetta.' He whistled: 'That's the Waltz from *Countess Maritza* – '

'When do you go back to school?'

'Next week. End of.'

'Come and see us,' she said.

'Yes, yes I might. Thanks awfully.' He was restless again. 'This really is rather fun. I wonder if they'll find us soon? Actually I think I did give a hint to Woodward where I might be trying – '

'What sort of flower is that? It smells nice.'

'I'll give it you.' He pulled at his lapel. 'Let's put it in your hairband, here. All right? Hunky dory?' He eased his legs. 'I say, remember Laurence?'

'They went away just after you did. He's going to be a diplomat.'

'Is he *really*? What I'd – '

Voices. Noise. Banging at the cupboards. 'Come on out! The game's over. Is that Edwina Illingworth? They're looking for you. Your little sister is crying . . .'

A snivelling Cora, her bag clasped to her tummy, swinging her legs.

'You didn't need to *cry*,' Edwina said. 'They were coming for us in a bit. You're just too young to be asked.'

'Sucks. I didn't cry to go. I was crying *because* of going. So. Anyway I know something you don't – '

'Well?' She hated her own curiosity. 'Well?'

'The peacocks might have to go. Nurse said. No one loves them and they make too much noise. If they do someone is going to do a painting or take a photograph of them walking about – like those ones on the stairs.'

'Really – '

She remembered, felt in her hair. The flower had gone.

A new term. A new year. 'Keep some toast over from elevenses,' Fanny said. 'In this paper bag. I want to eat it with toothpaste. Annette says it's ripping.' They spiralled on pink Euthymol, making a fat pattern. Fanny was nearly sick. Edwina was.

'It might be better with biscuits,' Fanny said. 'We'll try

again.' Edwina said, as casually as she could: 'You didn't say what you'd found. In a newspaper – about Meresia.'

'That? Old hat now. It was all about some actor Lydia M. wanted to marry and the father wouldn't give her a divorce, but now she was getting one herself because of a Mrs something who's a singer. It was full of words like adultery and petition and cohabitation – I found it in Whitby Library actually – '

'You might have copied it out for me,' Edwina said.

'It wasn't *that* interesting,' said Fanny, shrugging her shoulders and walking off. As likely as not she would be in an odd mood for the rest of that day. She was full that term of odd moods, saying suddenly to Edwina for no reason: 'You're only sucking up to me because I've got tuck,' or 'Look at your phiz, who'd ever want a phiz like that?'

'Do you want to be my friend?' Edwina asked.

'What if I do: what if I don't? You can pair with anyone you please. I shan't invite you home though – ' They were standing outside when she said that, in the garden just where the formal part was about to finish and sandy grass took over, before the path led down the cliff. It was a day of sudden winter sunshine: Robin Hood's Bay, red pantiles huddled, was clearly visible. I must be able to go home with her. It was as if standing there she could fly suddenly over the sands to the small house in Bay and cups of tea and hot cakes and sitting on Ben's knee. She had belonged. She did belong – for no reason she could see. And Fanny was the key which opened the door.

*Three Daughters of the United Kingdom* dragged on. So did her embroidery. A spider with two legs longer than the others: all to be done again. And who cared whether Beatrice de Woodville became a nun or not?

Then those meals: Communion pudding again today. The gooseberry jam seemed to have fermented. Ugh. And yet when you thought about it, it was a step away only from the Body of Our Lord. 'Do you suppose,' she pushed the remains round on her plate, 'does anyone think that Jesus really sat with his apostles and they all ate this squidgy tasteless stuff. I mean, great grown men. Fishermen.' She thought of Ben and the others. 'Having *that* for their supper . . .'

'I heard,' Clare told them all, 'about a nun or it might have been a monk – at any rate they *live* on just that. So holy that the Body of Christ is food enough.'

Fanny, who hadn't touched hers, said, 'So what?' and tipped her plateful behind the hot pipes. From force of habit Edwina glanced towards the head of the long table. Hermione sat there now.

No Meresia. A dull ache, every night and often in the day, although sometimes it surprised her that it wasn't more. She had thought it would be unbearable.

Music, oasis in the desert of the week, that was what saved her. Those wonderful lessons. Whereas before she could do no right, now she could do no wrong. Mistakes, whether from carelessness or ignorance or over-enthusiasm, were something you learned from immediately. He too: 'I learn always from who I teach. Every day something. And my teacher said, when *I* was the pupil – '

She loved Cristina, because for Cristina too she could do no wrong. She had only to sit there and eat, and she was right. They loved her for being Edwina.

She was lent scores to take home. She read them at night with a torch under the bedclothes. 'You're mad,' Fanny told her. 'You're getting much too serious about it.'

She explained. She was going to play in public. It would be what she'd do with her life. As she said it, she knew that she had always meant to. And Uncle Frederick had meant her to. She would straddle the world.

'You are assy,' was all Fanny said.

Clare, who had coughed all the first month of term, went home for a week. She came back with a gramophone which they were allowed to play in the library. The records were mostly of a tenor called Gervase Elwes. Clare said he had been to stay often. 'Of course if you've never actually *heard* him sing *Gerontius* . . .'

These were Shakespeare songs. Mother Anselm approved. 'Blow blow thou winter wind . . .' The sound, faint but pleasing, was part of the white landscape, the February frost, the rime-covered garden, the grey sea.

Not Fanny's taste though. John McCormack, that was real singing, she said in the angry voice she used so often now. Madge said, smirking, 'You've got a pash for him.'

'Yes,' said Fanny hotly, 'I have, as a matter of fact.' She'd managed to get hold of a photograph of him and had it by her bed, next to the one of Uncle Clive. Mother Anselm, seeing it, asked: 'And who may *that* be, Frances?' Fanny said, 'That may be my uncle, Mother.' She smiled so as to make a dimple. 'After all,' she said to Edwina later, 'it isn't as if Uncle Clive is real either.'

Two days later Edwina, her partner on a dreary afternoon walk, saw her burst suddenly into angry tears.

'I want a father.'

'But you've got one.' Edwina said it without thinking.

'A *real* father.' Tears of rage, it seemed, welled up. 'I want to know all about my real father. I don't even have a photograph. And they – ' she flung her arm over in the direction of Bay – 'they close up. Like those mussels they're always skeining. Auntie just says, "He was a fine man." They even muddle me and tell me things like, "He lived in that house for a bit" then next time it's a different one. He came from away, they say. Then, he and my mother lived in a house built on to Grandad's because of him being at sea. That's *another* story – '

'But your family in Whitby,' Edwina said, 'you even look like them. That's really belonging.' Fanny just shook her head.

Later that day though, as if nothing had happened, the old Fanny: 'My dear, have you *heard*?' Leaning over the lavatory partition, 'An absolute deathly secret and you're not to tell a soul – Clare wasn't meant to but she wanted some of my plum cake – It's about her aunt. She's going. *Out*, assy. Into the world. She's lost her vocation. She's taking her money with her too. They're frightfully upset. We won't get butter on our bread any more . . .'

There was a letter-card from Meresia, views of Nice folded up concertina-like. The handwriting gave her an odd feeling. She must have tried, and succeeded, more than she thought. Meresia told her about the divorce. Now she was out here for the winter. 'I feel I've lived this sort of life for ages, and yet it's only eight weeks!' Then: 'Your music. I so believe in you. And so does Daddy. *You can do great things.* And remember the parable of the talents . . .'

All that morning she floated, along the corridors, through the classrooms. She would become the greatest pianist the world had ever known. To please Meresia.

She looked at Mother Scholastica with new eyes now. And Mother Scholastica too seemed to have different eyes. Alternately defiant or slightly tearful. Perhaps leaving wasn't so easy?

Then suddenly, she wasn't there any more. No explanation was given. One of the older nuns said: 'She's gone away.'

'Where?' Edwina asked boldly.

'She's gone for a rest. If you girls cared at all you would have noticed she has been in ill health for some time.'

'Without that money they'll be in ill health,' Fanny said.

They had finished the reading of *Three Daughters.* Marie, who'd wanted to be a nun, had married Beatrice's brother Reginald, Earl de Woodville. And Madge had married Marie's jolly curly-haired brother. And of course, of course, Beatrice had become a nun. Although she hadn't wanted it, all that time God had wanted her.

Edwina was filled with dread.

Home for Easter, she was disappointed not to see Mother Scholastica at Clare's for Mass. Evidently she had been there only a fortnight and then had gone abroad. Mother said she had looked pale and tired, with lank grey hair. To Father she said: 'You told me always what a spirited girl she'd been – she doesn't look as if she could say boo to a goose.'

'She was sharp as a nun,' put in Edwina.

'Well, she's not a nun now,' Mother said, almost with satisfaction. 'She'll find the way is not strewn with primroses.'

' "Say *au revoir* and not goodbye," ' sang John McCormack. Fanny stuffed a flannel petticoat into the papier-mâché horn of the gramophone. 'Isn't it lovely now, couldn't you just dance to it?' she said of 'In the Garden where the Praties grow'. She affected an Irish accent that she'd got off one of the older girls.

'Aren't we going over to Bay?' Edwina asked, for the second time. Fanny said, 'Oh, I can't be bothered.' She bought a new John McCormack, playing it immediately she brought it home.

'O list to the strains of a poor Irish harper . . .'

'The darling man,' she said. It was a day of warm spring sunshine, an April foretaste of summer. The windows were thrown open in her room.

'Remember his fingers could once move more sharper<br>To raise up the mem'ry of his dear native land . . .'

'I think you *ought* to go to Bay,' Edwina said.

Fanny said: 'Whose relations are they, for heaven's sake?'

But Edwina had stopped breathing. Spoken to, but not by Fanny:

'And when Sergeant Death in his cold arms shall<br>embrace me . . .<br>And lull me to sleep . . .'

She was all at once long and thin, no longer short and a little plump but very very tall. And frozen.

'Nice, isn't it, that one?' said Fanny, winding up the gramophone.

That summer of 1913 she went to stay in the Lake District. They had taken a house for the month of August. The time dragged. Sunshine or rain, the days and nights were too long. Then back home and most of September still to go before it would be school again.

Fanny saved her. Most of last term although they were still friends they'd been on the verge of a quarrel at least once a week. Now she found Fanny had taken for granted her coming to Whitby. And as usual she felt that Mother couldn't wait for the day she departed.

Two things happened on that visit. The first was that she began her periods which was embarrassing because she had to tell Marmee. Also she couldn't hide it from Fanny who was immediately jealous. In fact she was moody for nearly all the time although she lent Edwina her Kodak. Edwina planned to make an album of Whitby photographs all taken by herself. Herbert suggested the best subjects. The other happening was that this time they did visit Bay: in brilliant sunshine, which she'd come to think of as Bay weather, even though for so many days of the year the same wind and the same rain lashed both the convent and the village.

When they arrived they found that it was Ben's birthday and they were invited to tea at his house. They went there almost straightaway, taking Jack with them. The cake was just coming out of the oven. It had to be split open while it was still hot and then money put in. Edwina and Fanny wrapped the coins. Jack said: 'Reckon I'll get one. What I'll buy wi't. I'll get –'

'Counting chickens that's called,' said Ben's mother, shutting the oven door. She was called Damaris and she was as fair and creckled as Ben was dark and stocky, with a plump face that looked as if it could be jolly but had decided not. Jack was still hovering. She gave him a friendly cuff. 'Get away.' Robert had appeared and Ben's two sisters were giggling in a corner. The youngest, Becky, who was dark like Ben, giggled through missing front teeth, pointing at Fanny. Sal, who was about twelve and very fat, fair too, whispered something. Fanny tossed her head angrily.

The cake smelled delicious. All the coins were in now. Jack began again: 'I'll get – '

'What's he on about?' Robert said, pulling his ears. 'Fanny, hear what he had, Friday a week?' Sal called out: 'Lads get the luck – ' she nudged Becky and they both giggled. Fanny said in a superior voice, 'I don't know what you're talking about – '

Robert told the story, hands in his pockets, one leg up on a chair. A young man and his girl it'd been, in a motor. The usual: a fine drive down the village then the engine not wanting to start, to go up that hill. There'd been lots come out to help, all of ten, and Jack not the least. Pushing away. Very smart the motor was, a two-seater, and both of them really dressed up. Everyone pushing, nearly all little lads; the blacksmith he'd come and he'd given the biggest shove. Then the young man (he'd been wearing a scarf this long – Jack showed them, winding it round and round his neck – and on a hot day too) he put his hand in his pocket and brought out gold – a whole sovereign. Divided it up they had. *Two bob* Jack had brought home . . .

Ben's mother had appeared again and just at that moment Ben himself came in, rubbing his eyes, shaking his head. 'Birthday lad,' his mother said, setting some currant pastry on the table. 'You're not to eat nowt,' she said.

'I weren't – ' he began and then grinned. She said, 'He's been asleep. They were out early.' Robert yawned, and said Ben had done right. Fanny sat all the while with a little lift to her upper lip as if the room smelled. She ignored Edwina. Ben's mother told him to take a jug for beer up to the Mariner's. 'Keep him safe from the sly cake – '

'I'll go too,' Edwina said, jumping up, not waiting to see if she'd be stopped. In the street she asked: 'Is it true you sleep outside?'

'Well, in a manner – ' He showed her where some wooden

steps led up to a door on the first floor. 'That's it. In there.' He pointed up. She thought only how she would love that, to go up to bed each night from outside. 'Will you show it me?'

'Some time, aye.'

'No, now.' She pulled a face but he'd already walked on ahead. They climbed the hill together.

'Still at that school, are you?' She nodded. 'I often look that way like, when we're out.'

She said: 'I see the boats sometimes, if we're out in the garden or for a walk. Brown sails – '

He asked her about the piano and her music. She talked the rest of the way and then most of the way back. She stopped only when they met anyone and he got wished a happy birthday. They turned off left to go to the house. 'Can I take your photograph?' she said. 'Later. I've got a camera.'

'Get away, you don't want my picture.' He looked at her sideways. She persisted: 'But I *do*.' He laughed, shaking his head so that she thought he'd spill the jug.

She said, 'Will you be my friend?'

He smiled. Amused it seemed, but not surprised. 'Aye. If you like. I could be.' He had his hand on the door, just going in.

'Next time I come,' she said, 'we'll talk a lot.'

'What was all that then, going up Bank?' But before she could answer back, he was inside. Lots more people now. A confusion of aunts and grandparents, uncles, cousins, all come to see him this day. And no, they wouldn't have any of the cake, it was for youngsters. Chairs had been brought in. Enough. She wouldn't be sitting on anyone's knee.

And now the excitement of the presents. The best was a watch. It was lovely and very heavy. Someone asked, 'Will it spoil in sea-water?' And someone else said, 'Mebbe now, lad'll be on time . . .' Ben was very indignant. He said: 'Did I ever miss then?' and immediately everyone vouched for him, that he was a great timekeeper. He sat, the birthday king, surrounded by gifts, by goodwill. If she'd only known, been able to bring something . . .

But she was so happy. Only Fanny spoilt it, sitting staring in front of her, not talking. Ben's mother shrugged her shoulders once and winked at one of the grandparents but otherwise no one bothered. Even cutting the cake didn't cheer her, even getting one of the coins. It was Becky got the most. Jack none.

Edwina had hop bitters to drink but Fanny wouldn't touch them. Ben put on a funny paper hat that Sal had made him and everyone laughed and clapped. Then the grown-ups turned the younger ones out for a while. 'There's no way to breathe in here.'

They strolled down towards the Dock. Becky and Sal were still giggling. Fanny said as they reached the bottom of the hill: 'I suppose you're going to the sweetie shop to spend what you won – *I'm* going back.' Ben shrugged his shoulders, raised his eyebrows at Edwina, questioningly. She shook her head. The girls went into the shop. Ben and Edwina turned up Albion Street. 'Now then,' Ben said, 'you wanted to talk – '

'I've nothing to say.' Her mind was quite empty. Ben said easily, 'It's like that right enough. I'd to stand up in school once and say summat. Bye, I had it ready too. But there I were, dry . . .'

Blackberries, half red and half green. Ben picked out one, black, juicy, and handed it her. 'Next week, one after – we could have maybe gone brambling.'

'Next year,' she said, biting into it, 'next year then.' She hiccuped loudly. Then a moment later, again. They walked on a bit but she couldn't stop. Hiccup, hiccup.

'It's not funny. It hurts – '

'Fetch a long breath,' he suggested. 'Slow like – no, not that way – ' She tried again. He put his hand on her shoulder, patted her sharply on the back. 'Babies,' she said, 'little babies get that done to them.'

'You ate too much,' he said.

'*You* did – '

He turned and began to run off. 'Hey – this'll rid you of 'em.' He ran faster. They were higher up now. They hadn't taken the cliff path but were in what seemed to her like a small wood. She ran after him. He ran faster still. The ground had knotted roots, leaves brushed her face. Round and round, in and out, she was panting, her hair tangled. Then she surprised him, coming out the other side of a bush, pushing him down on the ground, tickling him. 'Hey, give over. Give over, I'll get 'em, I'll be hiccuping.'

'Does it make you dindle?' she said. 'That's what Sarah used to call it when we went all tingly. Sarah was our nurse-maid – ' The hiccups had stopped. She thought she must have frightened them away. She ran off then and he chased her. Then it was her caught, her being tickled. 'Go on,' she said. 'Do it again.'

'What?'

'That. Now it's me dindling all over. I like it when you touch me.' She wanted to say, 'I liked it when I sat on your knee,' but instead she said without thinking, 'I hated it though when Mr Maycock squeezed me, you know, up here.' She pointed. 'It was before I had any shape – ' He turned his head away. He had coloured, dusky, angry perhaps. 'What is it?' she said hurriedly. 'What did I do wrong?'

'Nowt.' Still not looking at her he began brushing grass, twigs from his shirt, his trousers.

'But I did.'

Head bent, he said, 'It were when you said – When you pointed.' He said angrily: 'I don't – I were just – it was play, playing catch. I meant nowt – '

'I never said you did.'

'Well then – ' But they were at cross purposes. He should have understood. She should have explained better. Suddenly she was angry, as furious with him as if he'd been her. Angry with him because he wasn't her.

'We'd best go back. Time – '

'You ought to know the time. With your lovely new watch.' She said it rudely.

He was a little ahead of her. 'I've spoilt your birthday,' she called, repenting suddenly, hurrying to catch him up. He said nothing to that. Perhaps he hadn't heard. She grew angry again.

'How old are you?' he asked. They were just going past the Congregational Hall.

'Fourteen,' she said angrily. 'I've been fourteen nearly a month.' He just said, 'Well, that's grand, isn't it,' kicking at a stray stone with his boot. They turned left, up past the fish shop. Two boys coming out greeted him. She thought, we will never be friends, not now.

She had planned to take the photograph of him down at the Dock with the Bay Hotel in the background. Now she didn't think she could.

Almost time to go. They were standing outside the house. She had the camera. 'Is that yours?' Jack asked. Wanting Ben to hear she said loudly, 'I shall have one of my own for Christmas. I've only to ask my father – he has rather a lot of money, you see.' Tears pricked. 'He is really rich I suppose you could say.' When Ben was obviously listening, she went on: 'We have twenty bedrooms in our house, *main* bedrooms. And acres and acres of land – ' Fanny kicked her.

On the journey back she said to Edwina, 'That was horrible, I hated the whole outing, the whole day. And you were the horridest thing of all. I shall never bring you again. Showing off like that – in front of my family . . .'

Fast octaves, as many as possible. ' "Shaking them out of my sleeves" as dear Liszt said. Now Edwina, *we* do it . . .' Oh, the joys of being back. Franz again and as much music as she could fit into her days. (Try, when looking out of the convent windows, when walking in the grounds, not to look north. Not to look towards Bay.)

An October afternoon. Cascades of notes, a difficult passage, repeat it, not yet right, take it more slowly – and then suddenly Vita's head round the practice-room door:

'You'll never guess who's here – '

Meresia. Perhaps it was Meresia. She remembered guiltily that she hadn't thought about Meresia for days, for weeks. And she had thought that she would love her for ever.

'It's Mother Scholastica, only it isn't – She's *Cynthia* now . . .'

Edwina and some of the others hung about watching for the visitor to appear. They were rewarded later that afternoon in the library. Lifting her head from Baroness Orczy, Edwina could hardly believe what she saw. It wasn't just the skirt, so hobbled, so fashionable that she had difficulty walking towards them – it was everything. The hair crimped into a mass of curls, peeping out from the angled straw hat, the fragility of the long umbrella. Greeting them all too, as if nothing had happened, sitting down with difficulty in one of the low chairs, talking to everyone, taking out a cigarette case and then a long holder and lighting up: 'Do any of you smoke?'

Fanny said boldly, 'I do as a matter of fact.'

Cynthia (how could one think of her as that?) said, 'Oh, I meant amongst the *older* girls,' turning away carelessly. She talked on. She thought she would probably spend Christmas in Austria. If they could only have seen this, that, the other. Everything was *too* this, too that. Life is very exciting, she told them. 'I have to make up for lost time.'

Fanny sat there looking sulky, angry, disturbed. Edwina felt that the world had rocked a little. God's in His Heaven, but – the proper order of things. It couldn't be right surely to have become so different? Oh God, she prayed, don't give me a vocation. It would interfere so terribly. She flexed her hands, the fingers restless.

The smell of Egyptian cigarettes lingered in the library all afternoon. Mother Bede, coming in, pushed up the sash windows, a look of disgust on her face.

A letter came from Uncle Frederick. 'November, and St Martin's summer here – I wonder how it is with you? I imagine gales and storms at sea and the winds howling round your cliff-top building! Nevertheless and notwithstanding (and this is my news), Adelina is absolutely determined that we shall pay a visit to this Robin Hood's Bay you speak of so often. She is *very* keen to sketch and to paint there and nothing less than a lengthy stay will do. Is that not delightful? Naturally you will be expected to join us for at least some of the time . . .'

'I don't know where I'll be in the summer,' Fanny said, putting the letter down. 'I may go to Covent Garden, you know, to hear John McCormack. I don't know – I might just go to Rhodesia. To see *my* uncle.'

Ned was the New Year surprise. He came to call just like she'd told him to, a year ago now, when it had been 1913. Philip was skiing in Switzerland with a friend from Oxford, Denis Kinross. Edwina was glad he wasn't there to spoil things. But Cora was. She tossed her ringlets and sucked up to him. 'I like you,' she said, her head on one side, ''cos you have laughing eyes.'

'You look nice,' he told Edwina. 'Not so fat. Remember the cupboard? I shall leave school in a year or so, by the way, I'd like really to go round the world – ' He played the piano in the drawing-room while they were waiting for Mother to come down. 'This is all the rage,' he said, singing something called 'Hitchy Koo', in a light tenor voice, standing up to play. It seemed he could never sit still. Then he sang 'Waiting for the Robert E. Lee'. 'The show's called *Hullo Ragtime* and it really is absolutely topping. If you're ever in London – ' Missed notes, relentless irresistible rhythms. 'My little lovin' Sugar Babe'. 'I think I've rather forgotten the words . . .'

Mother came in. She said, 'No, don't stop.' Ned had coloured. She postured, annoying Edwina. Her skirt, although nothing like Cynthia-Scholastica's, was too tight. She said, 'Really we must get the sheet music.' Then later: 'The Americans, they have such vitality, don't you think?' Her behaviour quite spoilt his visit. It annoyed Edwina even more that Ned didn't seem to mind. He had really, it appeared, come to see them all.

'He *specially* sang that one for me, you know,' Cora said proudly, behind Edwina on the stairs. 'Little lovin' Sugar Babe . . .'

'If you can tell someone is singing the music in his mind –

then that is good.' Franz jumps down from the stool. It is time for tea. 'I wonder always – Rubenstein's face. The expression, *very* intense. Cristina, what do you think, did you not think that always?' He claps his little hands. 'Good, Edwina. So good.' Then after tea: 'We take it very calmly, I think. When you are seventeen, eighteen – a year abroad. Salzburg, Vienna – I arrange something.'

And Uncle Frederick, he would be there behind her. He would support her. She dreaded often the thought of telling Father and Mother, that after school she just might not after all do the Usual. (And that other sickening fear that she might be Called – just as boys were called to be Fishers of Men. Only that thought reminded her of Ben. Guiltily, remorsefully, angrily, she remembered that she didn't want to think of him again, ever.)

Already it was June. About the coming summer holiday in Bay she felt a great tiredness. The tiredness turned into a case of mumps: Fanny and Edwina, victims within a few days of each other, lay in bed side by side in the Infirmary. There was toast to eat, but it hurt too much when she tried to chew. She found herself crying.

'Trust Mother Infirmarian,' said Fanny. 'It'll be ship's biscuits for supper. You wait.' Outside the sun shone but they could only think of their swollen pain. One good thing though – Fanny seemed to want to be friends again. Just recently her moodiness had given way to a combination of the old teasing Fanny and a new calm, sometimes silent one given to occasional secret beatific smiles.

'You look absolutely assy,' she told Edwina as they sat up in bed drinking soup. 'So fat in the face. Would you like to know something, by the way? I think I ought to tell you. I'm probably going to be a nun. It came to me, it was after Communion one day, that I have a vocation.'

'There's no hurry,' Edwina said with joy in her heart. That they should both be chosen was unbelievable, impossible.

'I think I'll make rather a nice nun,' Fanny said. 'I shan't enter here of course. But it'll sort out all that messy business about my parents, and not knowing them at all. And not belonging . . .'

Mother had arranged it all. She had been in touch with Marmee and taken her advice: Uncle Frederick and Aunt Adelina would be ten days at the Hall; then rooms with service had been booked in Bay, with a week first at the Victoria Hotel. They would be there all July and most of August.

Aunt Josephine wrote that Aunt Adelina had brought: 'A lot of hat-boxes, and a new maid who is Scotch, I believe.' Edwina pined in the Infirmary. In the afternoons she and Fanny were allowed to walk up and down Montmartre in the June sunshine. It was a wonderful summer. Out in the bay the sun, shot silver, danced on the waves.

Then, surprise: she had been meant to go home now – as was Fanny – but instead she was to go over to Bay immediately, to stay there the whole of Uncle Frederick's holiday. Fanny was invited to come over whenever she liked.

Forget about Ben and be happy. The day before she left she saw the cobles out at sea. I was silly, she thought. Babyish too, asking to be friends like that. Perhaps she could avoid him, perhaps Fanny would not be there too much. I shall be very dignified, she thought, and behave like a lady. I shall be a summer visitor.

The rooms they had taken had a piano. It would be all happiness and beauty. Fanny said excitedly that she would sketch, do watercolours. She and Aunt Adelina would set up their easels amongst the scaurs at low tide, or up on the cliff. It was to be hoped that Aunt Adelina would not sing in the evenings, squawking horribly so that people passing their rooms might hear and laugh.

But that first evening, eating together in the dining-room of the Victoria, even Aunt Adelina's presence, too elaborately dressed, too heavily scented, couldn't spoil the joy of reunion with Uncle Frederick. Just to look at him and to think that they would be together for weeks and weeks. She would play the piano for him as soon as they moved into the rooms.

They would go over to Scarborough, just the two of them, to visit Franz.

Aunt Adelina drank her soup delicately, putting the spoon down frequently and pausing. She was thinner this year and paler too but with the same hectic red spots high on her cheeks. She gazed round the dining-room, not paying much attention to Uncle Frederick or Edwina. Edwina was wearing her best dress, of white broderie anglaise, with a blue sash. She had wanted to wear one of the two frocks Aunt Adelina had brought as a present but she had been told, a trifle sharply, that they were for daytime. 'They are nothing.' (Delicate, fine, lace and embroidered insertions, a Claudine collar, care and expense written all over them, they were – nothing.) 'You shall wear them every day.'

She shan't spoil my happiness, Edwina thought. She smiled at Uncle Frederick. He smiled back. He was looking idly too round the dining-room : 'Quite a mixed bag, if I may use a shooting term.' Aunt Adelina smiled at him almost as if he were a child, approvingly.

'German there, I think,' he said, raising an eyebrow, then saying something quickly in Italian. Edwina realized he meant the group at the next table but one : a very small, very fat man with a wife who was bigger but just as fat, two blonde children who appeared to be twins and a young girl, their nurse. The man's voice carried : He was complaining. 'In my country,' Edwina heard him say to the waitress. 'In my country . . .' His soup was left untouched. Now he was protesting about the meat : he made signs to show he could not cut the beef. Edwina, sore still about the jaws, could manage hers, chewing it easily.

Aunt Adelina tapped her hand. She was not to stare. But she herself continued to look surreptitiously. So did the two middle-aged ladies at the next table. One of them whispered to the other at each new piece of bad manners. Uncle Frederick said : 'I think really this should be ignored. Edwina – when are we to meet Fanny?' Edwina, eating strawberries and cream now (even the German family had not spurned these), talked happily.

Her room, which looked out to sea, was large and comfortable. Before she settled she opened the curtains and then the window just a little. All these years of sleeping near the sea and yet so far from it: here she felt it was in the very room. When she woke in the middle of the night, moonlight was streaming across her face. She leaned out. The moon, a great orb, seemed to rest on the dark sea. Everywhere still. She thought, down in the village Ben is asleep. For a few seconds she fancied that she could hear him breathing, breathed with him. And then she remembered.

That first morning was for exploring. She and Uncle Frederick were the first in the dining-room. Afterwards they went for a walk – Aunt Adelina would not be up till eleven. As they came down New Street, appetizing smells wafted from the baker's on their left. Some children carrying buckets hurried past. It was then that she saw, coming in their direction, head bent in concentration, clutching a large tin: Jack. She called out to him.

'Where's Fanny then?' he said at once, looking straight at Edwina. He hadn't noticed Uncle Frederick or he was shy. But Uncle Frederick was looking at him: 'What's that you have there?' inclining his head, smiling interest. Jack took the cover off the tin. 'Our dinner,' he said proudly. Onion, carrot, stewing steak, liver, potatoes ranged round, and down one side a suet roll. 'I'm going up bakehouse wi' it.'

'And how much will that cost you?'

'A penny.' She was surprised how he'd grown this last year: just twelve and taller than her. You could see he was Fanny's cousin: although his eyes were larger and longer-lashed, they were set in the same way. He asked again, 'When's our Fanny coming?'

'We must let you go,' Uncle Frederick said. Then as Jack walked carefully off, 'He's very *beautiful.*' A funny word to use, Edwina thought. She put her arm through his: 'So much to show you, darling Uncle Frederick.' And as they reached the Dock: 'If you like drinking, do you know that from the Wayfoot you can see *five* pubs?' She added importantly: 'And there's some more you can't see – ' The tide was up. People stood around. She looked to see if anyone had noticed her Uncle Frederick – how beautiful *he* was.

The German family weren't in the dining-room at midday but the two elderly ladies were. One of them smiled and bowed. Then on their way out, they stopped by the table.

'Excuse me. Excuse me, but I couldn't help hearing you address each other in Italian. My sister and I – is the little girl Italian? We are *so* interested.'

'Interested,' said her sister in a loud, definite voice.

'I expect you have noticed, in fact I know you have – the quite appalling behaviour of a certain person. Our German cousins indeed.' She lowered her voice: 'We had wondered – a little word with the manager?'

Aunt Adelina made soothing noises. 'There is such a one in every hotel . . .'

'Our first visit here and he bids fair to spoil it utterly.' Edwina watched her, fascinated: she had a face like a tortoise, springing up from her neck as she spoke. Her sister was smaller and less wrinkled, more moist. Both had very tightly curled iron-grey hair which bobbed about as they talked. 'To get away, you see, has been such a triumph ("Triumph," echoed her sister). We are half Yorkshire, you see, on the *paternal* side, and were determined to visit the North. Mother is eighty-four and not at all accustomed to our going away. But we were adamant on this occasion. Off on our own, we said, to walk. We *love* walking ("Walking," came the echo). Our Father worked in the City and how he walked. Every day from Hornsey, wet or fine . . .'

Edwina's pudding was growing cold.

'. . . We have *quite* forgotten to introduce ourselves – The Misses Hodgson. Mabel and Victoria. Of course we had to stay here – the *name*. Such a coincidence.'

'I think,' Aunt Adelina said, 'there are many hotels named from your old queen.' Mabel nodded. Fortunately the conversation, if it could be called that, was running down. Later Aunt Adelina grumbled: 'We are not fortunate. These people shall attach themselves, Frederick. How to avoid?'

About three o'clock they walked out together, to go to the

beach. Aunt Adelina, carrying a frilly parasol and dressed in lilac with an underskirt which allowed only small steps, was looked at by everybody. Edwina thought, I don't mind. She isn't any real relation. But going slowly down the steps – what she hadn't expected: excitement, terror, delight – the thought that perhaps she might see Ben. Afraid that she might. Afraid that she mightn't.

Matussi's ice-cream cart was down on the beach. 'Hokey pokey – no?' Aunt Adelina said, pursing her lips. 'You know, Edwina, how they arrive at this? First it is *ecco un poco* when they try to sell. "Here is a little". Then it changes, because you English hear "hokey pokey".' She shook open her parasol. 'So pretty. Like hanky panky. You like hanky panky, Edwina?'

Fanny would come at the end of the week: 'I am saying the Little Office of the Immaculate Conception every day now, if we share a room in the new place we could say it together . . .'

Perhaps she was eager for Fanny to come. Perhaps she wasn't? On the Friday morning Aunt Adelina, who wanted some biscuits to keep in her bedroom, sent her out shopping. Crawford, the maid, had left the day before to stay with her family in Aberdeen. Edwina went into Storm's, the grocers. Several people were waiting. Being served was the German from the Victoria, Herr Brefeld. He was saying indignantly as she came in: 'But that you must have – you look for it.' He pushed his hands out in an impatient gesture. The boy behind the counter looked bewildered and flustered. 'We don't – what's it for then?'

Herr Brefeld made an exasperated clucking sound. 'To push, to push on the bread – *Verstehen*?' The boy had coloured and looked desperate. Herr Brefeld turned round as if to seek support. 'What do I do?' His gaze rested on Edwina, recognizing her. 'Well, eh?'

'I don't know.' She supposed what he wanted to be some sort of paste or spread. She said wildly: 'Perhaps the carter will get it for you, from Whitby – '

'Yes, yes,' he said self-importantly. 'Who is this Carter, Herr Carter?' He said to Edwina, 'Please to arrange and send to the hotel.' When she didn't answer at once, he repeated, 'Arrange, please!'

Edwina said, 'I'm sorry,' and then suddenly found herself crying. She felt, from behind, an arm go round her shoulders, clasping her roughly, letting her go again. She moved and recognized Ben's mother. 'Never mind. Don't you mind – '

There was a chorus of 'It's a shame – I never . . .' Mutterings. Herr Brefeld stalked out: 'Good day!' Edwina was served next. She asked for the biscuits in a shaky voice. She smiled at Ben's mother as she went out. She would have liked to say something.

In the afternoon Aunt Adelina sat on the cliff top, her easel set up, Uncle Frederick on a folding stool beside her. Edwina, restless, didn't want to stay with them. She walked slowly down the hill, looking at her feet most of the time. She was wearing one of the new dresses, at Aunt Adelina's insistence. Although it was cool and comfortable it made her self-conscious. No one else passing was so delicate and frilly.

Down in the Dock several fishermen were standing together, attending to lobster pots. One of them, bent over, in salt-stiffened cap, was Ben. At once she blushed: the colour creeping hotly from her belly to her face, to the roots of her hair. He hadn't seen her. To go, or to stay? Then he turned. He too coloured. She saw it flood his face. He didn't speak, just stood still.

'It's me,' she said, 'and don't say my face is fat. It's the mumps. Fanny and me, we both – I'm still swollen.'

'Aye,' he said awkwardly, 'well, it is.'

She rattled on nervously: 'Don't you like my dress? My aunt brought me two like this from Italy. I'm to be here probably nearly eight weeks.'

'That'll be grand then, won't it?'

A silence fell. She said suddenly: 'I'd better be getting back.' One of the men, older than her father and very grizzled, was looking at her curiously, as if about to laugh.

She blushed again. Now she was angry. 'I have to go.'

She ran off very quickly. She didn't look to see if he was looking. Her heart drummed. She felt sick. Oh Fanny, come and join us, soon.

When the gong went for a meal there was an immediate exodus from all the hotel rooms. Soon everyone could be seen assembled on the two balustrades, Herr Brefeld pushing to be first down. The staff had begun to try avoiding him: their waitress could be seen bracing herself before coming over. 'Prussian,' Uncle Frederick commented. 'Beating the French has done them no good.'

He and Aunt Adelina read the newspapers, their faces composed in a solemn expression they wore no other time. They remarked about the trouble in Ireland. Aunt Adelina asked what it was all about and Uncle Frederick, explaining rather vaguely, said he hoped it wouldn't lead to civil war. Aunt Adelina shivered and agreed. 'All so unpleasing . . .'

Sooner or later, Edwina realized, she would have to be at least once alone with her. Their last day at the hotel: 'Come,' Aunt Adelina said in the afternoon, 'We go up. She comes and sees me, Frederick. It is too hot to be the artist today.' As they walked up together Edwina found it in her to admire the pale linen skirt with its row of buttons running diagonally across. She thought: after all she is kind to Uncle Frederick.

There were two wicker chairs, one with a footrest: Aunt Adelina took this. Edwina had not yet been in her room, one of the best in the hotel (she and Uncle Frederick slept separately. 'Your aunt is such a light sleeper, Edwina'), and she had a good look round now, eyeing with mild curiosity the row of medicine bottles.

'Sit down, Edwina. We talk. It is so long – you remember we speak together my first visit to England? We arranged then you shall visit Italy. We said fourteen years and now it is we who come here instead. But next year – if all is going well. There is trouble in Europe, yes, but it will go – You come then, next summer. No?'

'Yes.'

Aunt Adelina looked at her intently, head on one side. 'So big, and before you were a *little* girl. I don't think you grow tall but you are – *come direi?* – quite already the woman. You like to be a woman, Edwina?'

(Oh let me out of here. Let me open a window and make the sea blow away the scent, the *smell.*)

'I can't choose, can I? I mean, I *am* a girl.'

'I say "woman", Edwina. Your mother, sometimes I think she is not so pleased to be woman.' She shook her head impatiently: 'But that is not what I mean, I don't explain well. Edwina, you like to eat a fruit? Please – in that basket there. You are friends with your mother?'

'Sometimes.' (And if I am to take sides, then I'm on her side, when I am with you.)

'She is not happy, Edwina. She and Frederick – when they are children, so uncertain. I make good care of Frederick, he is happy now. There is no thing he want. I give it all. But your mother – ' She closed her eyes. 'She has now this problem, Edwina. You know what is this little trouble?'

Edwina, biting into a plum, felt the juice run cool down her chin. 'She isn't strong. Like you – '

'Yes, she is strong, Edwina. But she is eager to drink. Sometimes, very much – then it is bad because she say things. She does what she doesn't mean . . . I have told Frederick: "Speak of this to her. It is only kind – " But for that he is obstinate. I tell you this Edwina only that you know, that you may be a good daughter.'

Edwina didn't answer. She looked instead out of the window. On the horizon, the calm line of the sea, a ship was becoming lost to view. Outside in the corridor some children ran by. One shouted, 'I'll tell on you – '

'Where is their nurse?' Aunt Adelina said primly. She sat up very straight: 'But why do we talk of these sad affairs? These *bad* affairs. Instead I show you some beautiful shoes they make for me at home in Florence. My feet, you see, are difficult – so high.' She swung her leg down: 'Look away please, Edwina.' A few moments later a silk stocking and a garter were laid across the bed end and she held up a bare foot, small and white, for Edwina's inspection: arching it, making patterns with her toes, twisting and turning the fine-boned ankle. 'I am fortunate, don't you think? *Peccato* that he is always hidden. Yours – are they pretty, Edwina? You don't answer – You are not upset about your mother, yes?' She stretched her fingers out delicately. 'We look at some clothes together. Before Frederick knocks at the door. Yes?'

God's doing. An act of God. Late afternoon and walking up to Auntie's to make sure they knew Fanny came to-morrow. She went a long way round, twisting and turning through the alleys. As she came out near the house she saw some milk had been spilt. It ran blue-white. She stepped aside to avoid it, then looking up again saw the house door open. Ben came out. He was carrying a large jug. They stood awkwardly, looking at each other for a moment. 'Jack's off somewhere,' he said. 'I'm away to fill this for her – '

'Can I go with you?'

He'd begun walking already. 'I'll not stop you – ' They didn't speak all the way to the public tap. She watched his face all the time. Halfway back he said, 'It's not so fancy, what they've put you in today.'

'I don't have to wear my best frock every moment. And anyway I dress myself – '

'Do you then?' They were at the door already. It was like before, only water now, not ale. He held the jug carefully.

'Be my friend again,' she said, agitated, desperate. His face altered. He had put the jug down, was pushing the door in. He didn't look at her.

'I was never owt else,' he said.

'Of course Mother favours one butcher,' Mabel said, 'and we another. We have to hide from her that the mutton is bought from Mr Crossley or she would leave her food quite untouched ("untouched," said Victoria). And she *will* use the same plumber that Our Father always used, not realizing that it is his son who has the business now. And he is no good . . .'

'Whoever are they?' asked Fanny, walking away from them along the beach; Aunt Adelina at her easel continued to give them half her attention. 'I'm not spending my holiday listening to their troubles – '

It was the old Fanny. Edwina had feared that piety might have taken over completely. She was to be there for only about ten days. They shared an attic bedroom, talking far into the night every night: Edwina in a small bed under the eaves.

'Your uncle,' Fanny said, picking her way carefully amongst the stones and the weed. 'He's – wonderful. When I first saw him there at the station. It's such a Christ-like face. I wonder, perhaps, if he's suffered terribly? He is – I'd never have guessed how he was from the photographs.'

'He's not at all like John McCormack,' Edwina said.

'Oh, *that* old potato. Your aunt though – I don't like her.'

'Nor do I,' said Edwina. The next ten minutes were spent most enjoyably, listing her horrid traits.

'Do you think they're happily married?'

'Oh, I think so,' Edwina said, surprised. 'I think so.' Fanny was pensive. Edwina said: 'Once when my mother was very angry about something she said to him, "*mariage blanc*, Frederick?" And he said, "What if it is – we are *happy*." '

'White marriage,' Fanny said. 'Everyone gets married in white – the woman, that is. I think that's a silly remark.'

A gull flew into the sun. Edwina said: 'Ben's promised to put us two in a boat, if you want. One day when he's free and the tide's up.' She paused. 'When he has his own boat he's going to name it after me.'

'My family,' Fanny said. 'Heavens, they are boring.'

In the evenings they made music. Uncle Frederick sang: Loewe, Schumann, Schubert. Aunt Adelina accompanied him always. From the horsehair sofa across the room Fanny, chin in hands, hung on his every syllable. Last of all Edwina played herself, often for an hour or more, while Fanny yawned on the sofa. Or so she told Edwina. 'I could have been upstairs praying. Your aunt at least has her embroidery.'

Aunt Adelina had her watercolours too, for the daytime. Her first finished paintings filled Edwina with horror. The convent and the Roman fort, although larger than life, were at least recognizable. But there on the sea was a galleon in full sail, while from the north peak rose turrets, battlements – a fairytale castle. When Edwina protested, she said in astonishment, 'But why, Edwina, it is the custom. Many artists make so. Now it is *more* pretty, *more* charming – no?'

No. Fanny, however, thought they weren't bad. 'At least they're interesting,' she said. But the donkey pulling Matussi's ice-cream cart had an opinion nearer to Edwina's – for as Aunt Adelina was stroking him that very afternoon, standing just a little too close, he kicked her.

The damage wasn't serious, mainly her ankle and her nervous system, but it was enough to make her an invalid for at least a week. Lying on the horsehair sofa, cushions under her leg, she talked to Edwina about Rome: '. . . You see my cousins certainly. But in *campagna* of course – when you are coming it is not season in Rome . . . Taddeo is the baby, you will find him very charming. And Ersilia, she is to be married this December. Maddelena, you don't see also, she is married woman in Siena. Stefano is oldest of all. One day he is Marchese. *Eugenio* we speak of with sadness. All is not well with him. He is child still, Edwina . . . Nine or ten in the mind, you understand?'

Each morning also Edwina read to her for half an hour. But most of the time Uncle Frederick sat with her. Fanny had gone back now. All three of them feared that Mabel and Victoria would hear the news and pay a call of condolence.

Long hot July days and Edwina was free. Freer than she had ever known. Fanny's aunt, black apron over red and blue striped skirt, sat on the house steps knitting in the sun. Edwina would sit beside her and talk. Some afternoons she took Mercy down on the beach. Often she was round at Ben's house. It was good, Uncle Frederick said, that she had these friends. He asked after the lovely little boy, Jack.

They were used to her in the village, she thought. Some days she looked across the bay at the convent, hardly able to believe in it, so different a world did it seem.

'I could walk it,' she told Ben. 'If I wanted.'

'It's nowt. When tide's down – '

She said: 'The farthest we ever got on a school walk was Mill Beck. And we had to wear our gloves of course.'

He looked at her wonderingly. She pulled a face and they both laughed. He'd finished for that day although it was only two or three: 'Seals were after salmon. We'd nowt.' She arranged then to come back with him for tea. 'That's what I told them, my aunt and uncle, I'd be doing anyway.'

'Bye! Cheeky. How d'ye know we'll have you?' She made as if to strike him but he dodged her.

They rested for a while on the cliff top, amongst the furze and the green bracken. She felt breathless, overheated. The sun had been high all day. White horses, their manes streaming, rode out over the blue-green sea. Nearer the shore they reared – frolicked.

'What's it like then, there? I can't rightly imagine – ' He grinned: 'Do they beat you?'

'It's just – We start off our day with a girl coming round the dorms and . . .' She heard her voice running on. Then as she finished her story: 'Of course a lot of what Fanny tells is make-believe. If you've been listening to *her* – ' She turned towards him: 'Of course I can't imagine being you, either. Do you like it?'

'I never thought on it – ' he was smiling. She persisted. 'Do you *like* your life though?'

'Well, I've – times I've thought – there's some in family go to sea and some fish.' His hands were drawn up round his knees. 'I might try for summat with Turnbull Scott. Furness Withy. Them.'

'But wouldn't you be away *ages* – '

'Could be nigh on four years. And everyone's hand rag

at the start. If we were away up foreign I'd not be allowed home. If I got my ticket though – '

'Ticket?'

'Captain's ticket. So you can sail a ship. There's nowt here in Bay, not really. It's a great fight. Wi' t' sea.'

'Wouldn't you be beastly seasick? I – '

'Seasickness, that's soon done with.' He screwed his eyes up in the sun. 'I can't recall like – I were on't soon as I could pull an oar.' He turned: 'What of you then?'

She told him all about the piano and how she was going to be famous. 'That'd be summat,' he said.

'Would you be proud?'

'Aye, I would.'

'If I couldn't play, I'd die.'

'Then you'll have to – '

'What, die?'

'Nay, daft. Play piano. I don't sing bad – And Robert – At Bay Fair, he won contest. They'd one out on quay.'

Silence fell. The sun beat down on her bare head, her hair ribbon hung limply in the heat. She supposed she should have worn her hat; Aunt Adelina would be appalled.

He said suddenly: 'I was thinking – '

'Yes?' she said.

'That time when you spoke of – when we fought like. I didn't do right.' He buried his head casually on his knees. 'That man – '

'It was the music teacher. This girl said to tell no one about it. I know he shouldn't have done what he did but I didn't know *why* he shouldn't.'

'It depends like who's doing it – I mean if you're wed or you're courting – it'd be a different – ' He paused. 'I'm sorry then. You know, for the way I were.'

Below them the tide was right down. She watched the sea, wondering what she should say, feeling suddenly very grown up. A slight breeze blew saltily the thin grass where they sat.

'You said just now – if you're married or you're courting – But what do people do then?'

'Find somewhere quiet, I shouldn't wonder.'

'I mean, what do they *do*?' It was Arthur all over again. She blurted out: 'I don't think I understand because Fanny or someone said about babies coming out when girls had periods but the man could stop them coming out – ' her voice tailed away. She felt the colour flooding her face.

'I don't know much about what happens – about what they get each month. But t'other – ' he looked down at his hands – 'did you want me to say? You're not – it's not a tease?'

'Yes, I do. I do terribly.'

He didn't speak for a few moments. 'That thing a boy's got, he puts it – there's a place for it she's got. He leaves summat and that makes a bairn grow. If he's not taken care – '

'Is that all you have to do to get a baby?'

'I reckon so.'

'Does it hurt?'

'Mebbe – if no one'd been that way before. I've not – ' He wasn't looking at her. He said, his voice a little husky, 'I've not been with a lass. I were a short while fancying – she's gone now. She lived up Bank. But it were nowt. A kiss and a cuddle.'

They were both silent. She looked down at her hands, free now of the dread eczema. His were clasped round his knees. He was gazing away right, to where the cliff path led through to Mill Beck. His hands were brown, short-fingered, square – just the thumbnails bitten, on the left hand a cut half healed. She was unable to take her eyes off them. The light breeze had gone again and the air was once more still, close so that an insect buzzing nearby seemed suspended in a cocoon of sound. She too felt suspended, timeless.

She put her hand out suddenly and felt for his. It was dry and very warm and fitted hers perfectly.

Locked together they sat without speaking, without looking at each other. Such long minutes. Afterwards she was to think they had been hours.

She went with Uncle Frederick to see Franz. She played first, and then sat with Cristina while he saw Franz alone.

Afterwards they all had tea together. Some of the talk was about the trouble in Europe – Franz said, 'I am such a person always to fear the worst – ' but most of the conversation was light-hearted. Afterwards Uncle Frederick told her that Franz had been full of ideas as to whom she should study under. A Martin Kaiser in Berlin had been mentioned.

The day after the Scarborough visit, a Sunday, Aunt Adelina was fit enough for her first walk out. They processed solemnly, Aunt Adelina grumbling about the state of the road. It was not permitted to make jokes about donkeys.

At the Dock, standing with a group of others, she saw Ben, Jack, Robert. Becky and Sal were there too. Ben was wearing a new navy-blue guernsey and looked hot. He saw her and grinned, even before she'd led Uncle Frederick and Aunt Adelina over.

'You are cousin to Frances? No?'

'Aye.' He'd coloured but he was smiling at Aunt Adelina. She was staring at his guernsey. Edwina had watched his mother complete the knitting only last week. It had been done on very fine needles, the pattern intricate; Edwina had marvelled.

'But Frederick – ' she turned – 'such a *design.*' She was staring at Ben's chest: 'They make me at home, in Florence. What do you call this?'

'A gansey,' Ben said. She repeated it after him. 'Pretty,' she said. 'They copy for me. Embroidery. I have then cushions so or to hang on the wall. But first I draw this. You will bring it to our rooms?'

Edwina was embarrassed, full of shame. She looked at Uncle Frederick to see how he was taking it. But his gaze was fixed on Jack who, lanky and self-conscious, was moving restlessly from one leg to the other, head on one side, awkwardly graceful.

'So, that is arranged?' Aunt Adelina said. Ben was to bring it up that evening. Edwina was determined she would ask him to stay and hear her play.

'A lovely boy,' Uncle Frederick said, walking slowly back up, Aunt Adelina a few steps behind them. 'Jack – is it?

Fanny's little cousin. I think I remarked the first day. The Italian boys – they're lovely, but of course very different. Smoother, more polished. This is like a colt, and furry, downy, like a peach.' He looked thoughtful. 'It's the northern air – '

She said, 'But what about Ben?'

'Ben?' He remembered: 'Oh, Ben. But he's a man,' he said, puzzled. She was puzzled too.

'Some are church,' Ben said, 'and some are chapel. That's all about it.'

It was the old confusion: the Norman church up the steps, Father and Philip and Aunt Josephine. The chapel in Clare's house. Only this was different: Chapel with a big C. All part of what the nuns called 'non-Catholic'. People minded one way and another. She'd asked Fanny once: 'Don't they mind in Bay that you're a Catholic?' and Fanny had said, 'I'm never there on a Sunday. And anyway if Marmee and everyone was kind enough to bring me up, then I've to live their way, haven't I?'

Edwina had walked up to the church once by herself (hoping to catch a glimpse of the vicar: 'He's a one,' Ben had said, 'all t'lasses, they've to curtsy for him . . .'). Opposite she saw the closed doors of the parish hall where she was to play in the Visitors' Concert next month. Where Ben would hear her.

She was cross with him. 'Why did you bring the guernsey *just* when we were sitting down to eat – so you didn't get asked in?'

But later when Aunt Adelina had copied the design Edwina had been the one to take it back to him. All the night before she had had it lying on her quilt. She'd put her hand inside it, where he had been, and kept it there until she slipped into sleep.

He took her up to the old church, up on the Whitby Road. A great many of his family were buried there. He showed her the graveyard almost as some proud possession. 'The daffodils in spring – champion. You ought – ' All around them gravestones, old and tilted, fallen, salt-etched and scoured, the writing darkened and scarcely to be deciphered: It must be wonderful, buried within sound of the sea.

'I'd like that – to be buried here. Would you?'

'It'd depend like – how it came about. If it's close in, if I'm washed ashore – '

'But you could die in bed – '

'Me? I'll not die that way.' Then he grinned. 'I'll show you me Auntie Ada. She was that keen was Auntie to lie here. One day at our house, she's on about daffies. "Eh, but they're lovely," she says, "I shan't mind going *there*." Then me dad tells her, "But there's no place, Ada – You'll have to get cremated and that's all about it." "Aye," she says, "aye, that's right," and me dad goes on, "But you've to go all of *fifty* miles for that, Ada." "Well," she says, "never mind then. It'll be a nice ride . . ." '

He pointed to a newish inscription: 'She had her way though . . .'

It was beautiful, all of it. And such peace. The hot sun beating down, but a gentle breeze off the sea ruffling the grass, the harebells fluttering. Years ago Aunt Josephine had read *Wuthering Heights* to Grandma Illingworth, dying in the big bed.

> 'And when Sergeant Death in his cold arms shall
> embrace me . . .'

Standing, blouse sleeves rolled up, collar turned back in the sunshine, she shivered.

'Quite a little oversight really,' said Mabel. 'We came because I think they have forgotten us. Although we volunteered our services ("Services," said Victoria). It is to be a *Visitors'* Concert after all . . .'

Uncle Frederick asked what exactly was their piece?

'The Nurse scene from *Romeo and Juliet*. By Shakespeare, you know. We have seriously thought of joining a local drama group in Hornsey – to raise the tone, you know – but while Mother takes so much of our time . . . I play Juliet and Victoria plays the Nurse ("Nurse"). It's a piece that Our

Father particularly enjoyed – we know it well and are completely word perfect.'

Uncle Frederick said that he would see what he could do.

The word 'War' – which like King's Beck had run through the village, now hidden, now visible – came out into the open. On the shore the tide beat against it, reinforcing it.

It's only a word, she said to herself. But suddenly there were Uncle Frederick and Aunt Adelina looking grave, speaking together over the newspapers, going down to the post office. A panic flurry seized her as she tried to sort out the moves and counter moves. Russia, Serbia, Austria, Hungary – why had she not listened?

Uncle Frederick, taking her aside, holding her hands, told her that he thought they should leave, should return to Italy as soon as possible. 'The news is not at all amusing. I think home is perhaps the best place.' Telegrams were dispatched. One was sent to Mother holidaying with Cora in Devon: it crossed with another calling Edwina home.

Only one morning left. 'Ben?' she asked in a panicky voice standing at the door of his house. 'That way,' said his mother, pointing through to the back. She was stooped over a large wash basket. Stretching up, she sighed heavily, pushing back the hair from her forehead. 'Eh, but I'm fair mafted.' Edwina too felt the close, stifling air, had felt it all the way hurrying to the house. 'Can I help? Go up to the drying-ground for you?' Ben's mother shook her head. 'Nay, that's for Becky. I'm late, and she's made off I don't know where.' She paused, then: 'Are you teasing him – our Ben?' She said it casually.

Edwina was taken by surprise. 'No,' she said simply.

'I'd thought mebbe. When I saw you first. But never judge a blade by t'heft they say. Fancy clothes or no – I'll trust you.' She stopped as if embarrassed. Then: 'They let you run free,' she said, 'I'll say that.'

'I'm going,' Edwina told Ben. 'This morning. Because of the War.'

'Aye.' He looked miserable. She was standing there awkwardly. He took one chair and she took another alongside, sitting at the table. On the oilcloth stood a mug of water, half full. She fixed her gaze on it.

They talked for a little while, in short half-finished sentences. She'd begin to tell him something but then thinking he wasn't interested, or that she was saying it badly, she'd break off. Then he'd do the same. Easiness had flown out the door.

'Where'll we walk?'

'I'm only meant to be getting some things at Storm's. I can't – ' She thought his eyes looked shadowed. She asked: 'Have you been out with the boats?'

'Aye. Three o'clock.' He smiled. 'And I'd three eggs to my second breakfast . . .'

'You're greedy.'

'I am.' He took her hand from her lap and clasped it in his. He said in a burst: 'I've felt – I don't rightly know. Since time on t'cliff – '

She held tight miserably to his hand. 'Can I sit on your knee?'

She pressed down hard, her head against his shoulder, face buried in his shirt. She smelled sweat and a tarry smell, something from the nets. If someone comes in, she thought. Cheek against his shirt, she felt for where his heart was. When she could feel it beating she wanted to cry.

'What's to be done?' he said roughly. His hand was gripped tight round her waist. She thought he was crying too, and when a moment later their faces touched, she knew that he was. Lips, dry and anxious on cheeks, on forehead, nose banging nose, then their mouths met and opened. He tasted of salt.

Our Lady Star of the Sea, may it never end. May I sit for ever on his knee . . .

Footsteps outside. Clatter. Voices. A guilty jumping apart.

They made their awkward farewells in public. 'You never heard me play,' she said unhappily.

'Nor I did. But you and Fanny – '

'Yes of course,' she said. 'When I stay with Fanny next. I'll be over. Of course I will.'

Of course I will of course I will of course I will, went the wheels of the train as it puffed out of the station, climbing up and away, through the tunnel. Of course I will of course I will . . .

Philip enlisted at once. Mother was preoccupied with this and also with Red Cross work, of which Aunt Josephine was the organizer. There was talk too of taking in Belgian refugees. Father had become very busy. The war might not, indeed probably would not last very long, but meanwhile there was a great deal to be done. No one had very much time for Edwina nor really any suggestions as to what she might usefully do. She began some knitting, because she was good at that.

Back at the convent she and Fanny and all their set had become big girls. They slept in a dormitory with wooden partitions instead of curtains. If you stood on the hot water pipes you could lean out of the windows and talk. You could see too, over to the gardens, and beyond to the sea. Those first golden September days she twice glimpsed the boats out. She needed only wings, and she would be there.

Then the weather changed, and she could see nothing for a sea fret. Other people grumbled of the cold, so she kept her window closed. War or no war, school life seemed much the same. Next year, she was told, she could be a prefect. On Sundays now she wore her Child of Mary ribbon, just as Meresia had done.

A group of Belgian nuns arrived. They wore enormous white head coifs so that their faces could hardly be seen, and walked around always several together. One of them taught dressmaking. She showed Edwina how to keep her sewing needle rustfree by rubbing it in her hair. To begin with everyone was sorry for them. This lasted about three weeks until one of them, a Soeur Clothilde, reported Babs to Mother Anselm because Babs had not moved out of her way as she passed. 'Your girls are *mal élevées, ma Mère . . .*' Everyone thought this was a terrible thing to do since Babs's brother was fighting in Flanders.

It was the day after this incident that they first heard the rumour about a big ship. All night there'd been a violent gale from the south-east. Vita, coming in late for breakfast, said: 'I think there's been a wreck – ' It was a Friday and the first class was RI. Reverend Mother interrupted a recitation of the Cardinal Virtues.

There was indeed a wreck. About a mile south of Whitby the *Rohilla*, a hospital ship, on her way to collect wounded from Dunkirk, had struck a mass of rocks near the treacherous Saltwick Nab. She was breaking up fast, her boats nearly all carried away by the rough seas: attempts to get a line across by rockets had failed. The Whitby lifeboat, which because of bad weather couldn't reach the wreck by sea, had been daringly and courageously brought on to the Scaur.

They prayed then, and again in chapel after eleven o'clock break. 'O Blessed Virgin Mary, never was it known that anyone who fled to thy protection implored thy help or sought thy intercession . . .' They heard that the lifeboat had rescued thirty-five before having to be abandoned. Fanny, going home for the weekend, was allowed to leave on an earlier train. Outside the classrooms the wind howled and moaned. The nuns had formed a rota of perpetual prayer. Many of the girls, Edwina amongst them, joined the vigil that night. 'Our Lady Star of the Sea, *Respice Stellam, Porta Naufragorum* . . .'

The next day the Scarborough lifeboat had no success. Nor did two others. Even in her dreams Edwina prayed. Then on the Sunday while they heard a special Mass for those already drowned, a nun came up to the priest during the sermon. It was all over. The Tynemouth motor-boat, after spreading oil on the troubled waters, had brought off the fifty survivors. Eighty-five had died (including the Catholic priest who'd been tending the one patient aboard).

Fanny was late back. She had stayed to help Marmee with two survivors they'd taken in. 'I went and stood on the cliffs on the Saturday morning. Herbert sent for me to come home but I wouldn't. It was terrible. You could see the people on the bridge – lots of them in pyjamas – but the worst was the ones all hanging on to the stern, there must have been about thirty, and oh God they just kept falling off. Then there came this absolutely giant enormous wave, it went right over them and – honestly I screamed, I couldn't help it – there was nothing there when it cleared. All gone. I just – you can't *any* of you imagine – all sitting in the library reading *The Scarlet Pimpernel* . . .' She was very white and shaken, and had to keep on telling the story over and over. Edwina thought perhaps it was because she had been thinking about her own father. 'Lost at sea.'

But gradually she became the old Fanny again. That November her indulgences gained for the souls in Purgatory impressed even Clare. But her moods see-sawed, taxing Edwina's friendship. She would keep asking her if she hadn't heard from Uncle Frederick? 'Perhaps his letters aren't getting through? If you only knew what I *felt* about him – '

At daily Mass it was the rule that if you were going to Communion you wore a white veil, so that the number of hosts needed could be calculated. Several days running, on the way to Mass, Fanny took a black veil. 'I dare Mother Anselm to remark about it,' she told Edwina. 'Anyway I'm going to ask for a special confession.' She said importantly: 'I think I have the screws . . .'

This dread disease, where the victim was no sooner out of the confessional than she needed to go back, had always been the prerogative of the big girls. Now they were old enough to have them too. Edwina was fearfully impressed.

'I definitely can't go to Communion and that's it,' Fanny said. 'I've had impure thoughts. Like it says in the Examination of Conscience. I've had them about *him* – your uncle. I just can't help myself. I love him so. Even if I wasn't going to be a nun it would be *wrong*.' Her eyes had narrowed to slits and her skin against the flaming hair looked whiter than ever.

Edwina said robustly, 'Well, if you can't help it, God can't blame you.'

'How do I know I'm *really* trying to resist every time? You just don't understand the screws – Or being in love either. I'm fed up with you. And Vita, and Babs, and Gabrielle – '

That Fanny should love Uncle Frederick seemed to Edwina natural enough. Had she not loved him herself since almost before she could remember? But that she, Edwina, on account of the love between her and Ben should take a black veil – she could make nothing of that. It seemed to her sometimes that she lived in two worlds: this convent perched six hundred feet up, and the village, which was Ben's home.

Towards the end of November Reverend Mother heard there was a possibility of raids on the East Coast and informed all the parents. Edwina feared that she might be sent for. Fanny and Madge, who would of course have been no safer back in Whitby, stayed on, but Vita and Gabrielle and some twenty others left, protesting.

Short cold dark days. Franz and music were her solace as ever. Going over to Scarborough and between times playing, playing, playing. Bach, Beethoven, Brahms: 'The three B's' as Franz called them: he told her of Brahms in the taverns, sitting the servant girls on his knee. 'I tell you this only that you see he is human. Then you don't play him so religiously. We must be serious only about the music, not with it.' The corners of his mouth turned up, his eyes were laughing.

He had relations in Austria (it had been only his parents who had settled in England) and she knew that he worried about them, that a political accident should have made them into the enemy. 'The name Hengelmüller – it isn't a *happy* one at the moment, you might say? But we don't change it, Cristina and I. Although we have *thought* about it . . .' He in his turn was worried for Edwina, that ideas for her studying abroad were for the moment ruled out. 'But I have other plans,' he said, looking secretive.

Advent, and the jars of grain once more: this year the sacrifices were for the boys in khaki, for the sailors too, in peril on the sea. Edwina had knitted already that term two body-belts, a balaclava and three pairs of mittens. 'You've just got quick hands,' Fanny said in a dismissive voice.

She was wearing a white veil as she knelt beside Edwina

at Mass the next morning. She had sorted out her scruples. Edwina turned the pages of her 'Welcome' prayer book. Which Welcome to give the newly-received Christ? She felt the stirrings of hunger. Because it was Wednesday it would be sardines for breakfast – she'd have preferred hot porridge. The chapel felt chill and outside the weather was grey, foggy. Only two more days now till breaking-up.

*'Ite missa est,'* said Father Walsh.

*'Deo gratias,'* they chanted.

She thought at first that the organ or the choir loft had fallen over, the crash was so loud. Fanny clutched at her. She put her own hand out, pulling at the bench. 'Oh God,' said Fanny and at that moment there was another crash. But louder. A pane of glass in the window beside them shattered. Fanny screamed.

Mother Anselm appeared in the aisle, hand held up to stop them rushing. There was another crash. 'In order, march out in *order*, please.' Her voice was drowned by another crash. As they grouped in the corridor outside the chapel, Madge started up an hysterical whinnying sound. 'Oh my God,' Fanny said again and again, clutching tight hold of Edwina. Another thunderous crash.

Mother Anselm was amongst them: angular, efficient. 'Everyone,' she began, '*everyone* – ' Madge's whinnying rose, high-pitched. Moving forward Mother Anselm slapped her briskly across the face, then as if nothing had happened: 'Outdoor clothes, please, girls. Gloves not to be forgotten – '

Fanny breathless, rushing into her cubicle and out again, pulling her tammy down. Her hair had fallen either side of her white face. 'The Germans have landed,' she said.

Edwina wasn't frightened. Just curious. It all seemed so unreal that when panic did come to her, five minutes later, halfway down the drive, she felt it as if it were someone else's.

'Move together in crocodile, please,' said Mother Anselm. 'Frances, you are out of line. When I say "scatter", scatter. When I say "run", run.' A second later 'Run!' she called, as the loudest sound of all came.

'If I live I promise to keep my vocation,' sobbed Fanny. She had on still her indoor shoes. The road outside the convent was muddy in the cold grey mist. In the distance to the left of them they could make out some black smoke. They had eased back to walking. Behind Edwina saw the whole community of nuns, the white coifs of the Belgians to the fore. Their own crocodile was accompanied now by Mothers Bede and Cuthbert and Edward. Mother Anselm in a fruity, vibrating voice began a hymn:

> 'Full in the panting heart of Rome,
> Beneath the Apostle's shining Dome . . .'

The nuns took it up and some of the girls. Louder and louder:

> 'God bless our Pope! God bless our Pope!'

An overloaded motor went by, then a chauffeur-driven one. It stopped near the head of the procession. Mother Anselm spoke to the passenger, a large grey-haired man. Three of the elderly nuns were given a lift. In the field alongside a bolting carthorse careered round, galloping in and out of sight through the mist. They were nearing the home farm now. A mother and two daughters came through the gateway as they passed: they had a pram and a small cart loaded with belongings. The mother had just a coat on over her nightgown. The eldest girl said to Fanny: 'Whitby's in flames.'

'Frances!' called Mother Anselm. 'Everyone keep moving, please. No conversations – '

Fanny said, in a sobbing voice, 'They've come. The Huns.'

They reached the main road. The mist was breaking now. Soldiers passed going towards Scarborough; army lorries, motor-cycles. Fanny wanted to run out and stop them. 'I'm going to ask.' When an officer got down from a lorry and came over to Mother Anselm, Edwina had to hold her back.

The farm girl was alongside again: 'They're here right enow. Down on t'beach. That's why there're all them troops . . .'

'Faith of our fathers, living still,' they sang,
'In spite of dungeon, fire and sword . . .'

Mother Anselm marched up and down, her arm with its flapping black sleeves waving an imaginary baton.

'Faith of our fathers, holy faith!
We will be true to thee till death . . .'

They were moving cross-country. The officer had suggested a farmer about a mile on who had a very big barn. While they waited there for the lay sisters to bring in the baskets of provisions, they sang the Lourdes *Ave Maria*. Fanny had calmed down completely. Edwina felt sick.

There were rations of Marie biscuits and a bar of Fry's chocolate each and an apple. The nuns had packed them some weeks before. Fanny said, 'I'm thirsty.' She ate Edwina's apple for her. They played Blind Man's Buff to keep warm and to pass the time. The nuns kept their gloved hands inside their sleeves, standing about.

Later when they came out to a wintry afternoon sun, she shivered; couldn't stop shivering. She wondered and worried if the boats had gone out. 'You might pull yourself together,' Fanny said. There was a curious flat feeling about the journey back. But it was over. And they were safe.

At home for Christmas, she read all about it in the newspaper. The German ships had come out of the Kiel canal in the night and after shelling Hartlepool, still under cover of the mist, they'd attacked Whitby and Scarborough. An angry sea caused the ships to roll and the shells to go wide.

Aunt Josephine was concerned for Edwina, watching her for signs of shock. Father, in his study, looked as if his mind were on other things: 'I shall expect to hear any plans for the future from Reverend Mother.' Mother was preoccupied: she hadn't heard from Philip, in France since October. Cora, jealous because she'd missed an adventure, affected not to be interested at all. Nurse demanded a detailed account.

The convent was not to be moved to the country, Reverend

Mother wrote. Although St Margaret's School at Scarboro' had left, and several others, she did not herself feel that such a raid would occur again. Decisions to return next term would have to be made by the individual families.

Edwina stamped her foot and protested that she must go. She was amazed at how violently she felt, how childishly she reacted. But her greatest surprise was the weary manner in which both her parents gave in. 'I don't see why not. If Reverend Mother is confident . . .'

In the New Year she went to stay with Fanny. A few days before she left, Philip's Oxford friend, Denis, came to spend his fortnight's leave with them. His parents were dead. He and Mother sat together and talked about Philip.

'Hark, hark, the dogs do bark!' was the name of a jigsaw puzzle Fanny had been given. It was a map of Europe, with dogs fighting all over it. They did it three times while listening to the gramophone. Fanny told Edwina that in the raid a pig had its back sliced off by a piece of shrapnel, and had to be destroyed. 'I wonder if they made it into German sausage?' One afternoon they went up to see the damage done to the western arch of the Abbey. Edwina said: 'Aren't you going to Bay this holidays?'

'But I've *been*.'

Why had she waited so long to ask? 'Did you see – any-body?'

'The same old faces. And the same old questions. "How are you going on at school?" I'd love to tell them: "I'm going to be a nun."' She thrust her hands in her pockets. 'The raid – they wanted to hear all about that. The boats were out at the time, you know. Only they were outside the ships – the ships had come so far in – and in the mist they just thought they were *ours*. Can you imagine? Ben was asking after you, by the way.'

'After me?' Her legs trembled.

'Yes, I think he has swoony feelings about you which could be jolly embarrassing. What a family I have . . .'

That night in bed she counted, laboriously, how many days since Ben had kissed her, since she had kissed Ben. The next day she went to Scarborough with Fanny and Herbert, to pay Franz and Cristina a surprise visit.

She could not believe it. On the upstairs windows of their house there were boards. Downstairs the outside shutters were closed. The small lawn in front was partly dug up: there were two big holes full of ice-filmed water. Red paint was daubed over the railings outside.

'All is past,' Franz said, 'we try to forget.' It had happened within a few days of the raid, but exactly who had stoned the house, defaced it, written slogans, wasn't certain. 'It was of course not our friends. We think it was from outside perhaps. Cristina has been very shocked.' He too looked shocked, as if more than the house had been attacked.

Edwina played some Mozart. 'You must sing for your supper, I think the saying is.' After tea they played a duet. Herbert asked for an encore: he seemed relaxed in the company. Yesterday he'd had a white feather given to him for the third time, even though his eyesight was such that he could not possibly have enlisted.

There was only a week left of holiday when she returned. Denis was still there but in bed with influenza. There had been a letter from Philip, behind the lines now in a rest camp.

She wanted to get back to school. The convent was more real; it was home. And it was near – as near as she could get – to Ben.

Reverend Mother may perhaps have regretted her decision, since only half of the pupils returned. But for the girls – except that there seemed too many nuns in charge – there was at first an atmosphere of daring and excitement.

Gradually though a routine became established and all was as before. A cold dark term with nothing to look forward to but Lent. Edwina heard from Meresia, who was engaged to be married. 'I'm nursing now. I came back in September and am at a big hospital in London. Devonshire House. What a long time ago that lovely picnic seems . . .' Clare, who spent nearly half of that term in the infirmary, told them that Cynthia-Scholastica was doing some sort of war work.

News dribbled in week by week. From Italy: Aunt Adelina was not well. The doctors took a serious view. Fanny heard from *her* uncle, Uncle Clive: 'I wish I were a bit younger, I'd come home immediately – How I would like to get into khaki. I think I could still teach the Hun a lesson . . .'

'How old is he?' Edwina asked.

'I never thought. He's younger than Marmee. About forty-something, I suppose.'

Easter 1915 Fanny came to stay with her, and was allowed to help Mother with some of the Red Cross work; Edwina went too. Fanny was on her best behaviour. Mother was particularly impressed.

Ned turned up to see them. It was a fine day and they all walked in the garden. He was in uniform: he had joined the artillery. 'I had to play around with my age a little, but when they found out they didn't do anything. I'm an awful genius at that sort of thing. I can't go out to France though, worse luck, till I'm nineteen.' Mother joined them for tea. She was very animated and talked a lot. Ned said: 'She's still very attractive. Why do you dislike her so?' They had gone out alone together to see the songbirds. 'I don't dislike her,' Edwina said.

'Remember in the cupboard?' he said, 'it was fun, wasn't it? Will you write to me? I'll write, from the camp. Or are you writing to a lot of chaps already?'

Before he left he played them ragtime again, at Mother's request. He sang too in a light voice. She felt a great rush of affection for him, and trust and fear. She wanted desperately to tell him: 'I love Ben and I don't know whatever to do about it.'

'Guess who's here?' Babs said.

If Cynthia had been a surprise eighteen months ago, now she was a shock. Smarter than ever, she was accompanied this time by an officer: a portly man with moustaches and a very red face. 'He's a colonel at least,' Vita said. 'He might even be a *brigadier*.'

It was the day before Corpus Christi. They were in the garden near the Lourdes grotto, picking blossoms to scatter during the procession. A June sun shone after three days of rain and chill. Cynthia had come out to look for Clare. Seeing her approaching, they tried to look as if they hadn't been looking. Clare was sitting on a bench resting.

The brigadier's name was Willie. It appeared that she drove him around. 'I used to *teach* these little ones,' she told him, waving her hand. Willie said with a laugh that they didn't seem to him so little. 'But that's how I see them!' she cried. Willie asked them what they were picking the flowers for and Fanny explained in her purest voice. Cynthia took out a cigarette with a nervous gesture, snapping open the case. 'Have you a light, Willie?'

'Of course, my dear.' There was enough summer breeze, the little breeze that always came off the sea. It would not light. His fingers cupped, tense with concentration, he bent over her.

'I'm going to show Willie round the school. Clare, come along with us, pet.' Clare rose listlessly from the bench. 'Very soon Willie and I are going to France. Frankly, I can't wait.' She looked around her, blowing a circle of smoke. She remarked casually to all of them, 'And what are *you* doing to help our boys?' They all looked blank. 'Well,' she said impatiently, 'aren't you knitting something? Weren't you taught to *knit*?'

Edwina was angry at being made a spectacle of like this. Her mouth was pressed hard, memories of herself caught in the dormitory not practising: 'I put my piano first,' she said priggishly.

'Oh that,' said Cynthia. Her eyes met Edwina's. Edwina stared at her and she looked away, blinking. All round her eyes were little fine lines: the eyes themselves, still for a moment, were anxious, almost, she would have said, frightened.

They went off in the direction of the house. Clare, the belt of her summer dress hanging too loosely, tagged behind them. Vita said: 'I can't think why she keeps coming back. The nuns can't like it, can they?' Marion said that she supposed it was to see Clare: 'But she could see her at home.' Fanny said, 'I think, my dears, that one should make *absolutely* sure of one's vocation . . .'

'. . . and after all our plans and hopes for your coming out to Italy,' Uncle Frederick wrote. 'Now it is not only you at war. Although here it has not been the same straightforward business. Three different factions with feelings running very high, even to fighting, so that it has been wise to keep indoors after sundown. Adelina has been very distressed by it all. She is no better, and has to spend two days a week in bed. We shall go to the mountains for the summer . . .'

No letter came from Ned. One morning after the post had been handed out she braved Mother Anselm.

'Letters were given out ten minutes ago, Edwina.'

'I was *expecting* one – '

'You know the rules. Parents, close relatives – a few family friends. In other cases, we make the decision.' She shook her sleeves. 'Does that answer your question?'

'No, Mother.' But Mother Anselm had already moved on, so that short of running after her, striking her, shaking her, there seemed nothing to be done. I'll never know if he's written or not, she thought.

Father was tired. He was an outdoor man. 'I'm not used to all this writing,' he said of the desk work that his contribution to the War Effort involved. The whole way of life had changed. Practising in the drawing-room, she could look out where once Prince, thick linen tied loosely over his hooves, had pulled the mower over the wide lawn. Now potatoes grew there. The younger gardeners had all gone. Arthur's eldest was out in France now.

She made bandages with Aunt Josephine, her mind far away: scheming, worrying how she could get to Bay. To tell Fanny would be simple – but unimaginable. Later in September she would be going over to Whitby but Fanny had announced already that she 'wasn't bothering' this holidays.

'Marmee says I must do what I want about it and not feel obliged.' She came to stay with Edwina at the end of August. Mother made a great fuss of her.

'Do you mind?' Fanny asked. 'She does seem to rather like me.' It didn't interfere with their relationship. They were now just two people who were often together, for the exchange of gossip, moods, worries, grumbles. How good to have someone to grumble with.

But oh, the moods of Fanny. She was just jealous perhaps of Edwina's playing. She affected to be bored by the whole subject. 'My watercolours are very important to me,' she said suddenly. 'My sketches.' It was the first Edwina had heard. Passionately: 'I just don't think you've any idea of what I'll be giving up when I enter. I mean, I might be asked to draw a holy card or an 'In Memoriam' – but I shan't be able to do real things. It will be a tremendous sacrifice. Could *you* give up the piano?'

Two weeks later when they were both in Whitby, Fanny's aunt sent a message. Could Fanny come over? There'd been bad news. She would like Fanny there. It wasn't a death.

Edwina went too. She didn't, thinking about it afterwards, feel quite sure how she'd managed to go along when she wasn't part of the family. She had just dressed and been ready when it was time to go. Herbert, not Cook, was to take them over.

'What can it be?' said Fanny in a rather bored voice, hiding nerves. Edwina, knowing that Ben wasn't dead, felt sure that it was a maiming. Inside the cottage, Fanny's aunt said to all of them – Herbert sympathetic, leaning shortsightedly forward: 'He went off Tuesday. Told us nowt. Right through to Scarboro' where they'd be sure not to know him. Not fourteen . . . We were teasing, others were teasing – his voice had cracked like. "You're a man," they said. Wicked words. He was wanting to go wi' t'men, full time. His dad had let him and all. Why's he want to make off then?'

But he had done it. Jack, the baby, run away to enlist – and accepted. However did he pass them? He must have given a false name, since at Whitby they knew nothing of him, nor at Scarborough. The truth had come out only when he'd gone missing and his friend, frightened and almost in tears, had told Jack's father.

'He can't go to France,' Herbert told them. 'He'll only have dared pass himself off as the minimum.' He felt certain, he said, that they'd be able to trace him. Everything possible would be done.

'This is a grand to-do,' said Fanny's grandfather, coming in out of the cold. It had rained with an unexpected chill wind all the afternoon; now it was growing dark unusually early. Indoors they had to light the oil lamp. Grandad told Fanny off for not coming over to see them. She dimpled. He said it was a shame she was too big to sit on his knee now. Then they all began talking again about the business of Jack. Edwina watched the door in a frenzy of worry and dread. Time, hurrying, hurrying.

Fanny's aunt said: 'You'll stay and take a bite? Ben's coming up, and mebbe the girls – '

He came, five minutes later. Careful with the door, they told him, so the oil lamp doesn't flare. Mercy, sitting on her grandfather's knee, wanted to go to him at once. 'They love him right enow, the lasses,' Grandad said, putting Mercy down. But she tired of Ben's knee and wanted to go back. How could she? Edwina thought, wishing only that she could so simply sit there. Throughout the meal Ben watched her – she didn't dare to look back. What if their eyes should really meet and betray them to everybody? She became tongue-tied, slopping her tea when she lifted it to her mouth, beginning sentences she couldn't finish. Fanny, sitting next to Auntie, had become suddenly very animated. She was showing off, telling them all she meant to do when she left the convent next summer. 'You see if I shan't become a clippie . . .' Herbert looked on indulgently. Ben, who seemed worried about Jack, asked him if he thought he'd be able to do anything. He asked the three of them: 'When have you to go?'

'Soon,' Herbert said, looking at his watch. Ben got up suddenly: 'Then I've summat to show Edwina. She'll mind on it, from t'summer.'

'Where is it?' asked Fanny's aunt.

'Up ours. We'll not be long.' It seemed to her impossible that everyone shouldn't notice something, but even Fanny didn't look interested. Outside it was chill and blustery, not like summer at all. He seemed happy not to talk but she needed to say something, anything. 'You never heard me play the piano,' she said.

'I never did. But I know how it is –'

'How?'

They were climbing the rickety stairs to his room. 'Like the sea,' he said. Inside the room they just stood there awkwardly. She looked around, wanting to memorize every detail.

'This is it, this is t'room,' he said. The bed had a blue patch cover, light and dark squares. She was sick with longing, with the need to touch him. She said almost sharply, 'What did you have for me?'

He had his hands in his pockets. 'Nowt,' he said, smiling.

He moved towards her. She moved. Once again they bumped, heads, noses. She had forgotten how he was, how he felt.

Their mouths were foreign countries, their tongues the travellers exploring them. She had not thought of doing it like that. Nor had he perhaps because when they stopped he said: 'That were a nice thing to do . . .' They were standing close together. She had her head on his shoulder. She felt very faint. He unbuttoned her coat and then parting it, put his hands over her breasts. 'Reckon I need bigger hands –'

She was dizzy with happiness. 'You'll go right in where my soul is if you press like that. Then it can fly out and join yours –'

'Have I got a soul then?' It was his teasing voice.

'Everybody has. "My soul is like to God because it is a spirit and is immortal, when I say that my soul is immortal I mean that my soul can never die –"'

'Daft.'

'But it's true,' she said.

'Of course it's true, it's just a daft way of talking.' There was a cleaned sea-urchin on the wash-stand. 'That's yours,' he said. 'I meant it for you.'

He had tight hold of her hands. He was frowning, brows nearly together.

'Oh, do we do right?' she said. 'I just think – '

Suddenly, angrily almost: 'You could've wrote,' he said.

'*You* could,' she said, stung.

'Where?' he asked simply. 'Where would I send it then?'

'I don't – ' she tried desperately to think. 'Home, but then – better not.'

'I love you,' he said.

'Yes, I know.' She couldn't say the words. Tears choked.

He said roughly: 'We'll have to be away. There's not a half-hour to the train.' He was looking at the birthday watch.

They didn't kiss again. She thought they dare not, for how could they ever stop? On the road going back, head bent against the wind, she heard a whistle go, very loud: pause and then start again.

'Telegram whistle,' Ben said. It was to summon the telegraph boy in the village. 'It'll be bad news – there's little else about.' He paused. 'I was thinking – I'd mebbe go in for a sailor.'

'When?'

He shrugged his shoulders. 'I'd only thought – ' She was grasping the sea-urchin so tight she feared it would splinter.

'He could've fetched that down hisself,' Fanny's aunt said when they saw it. 'Making her walk up – '

'He had some other things to show me,' Edwina said.

Three days after she'd gone back to school, Philip was killed, at the Battle of Loos. Reverend Mother sent for her to tell her: another girl had lost a brother also, and one of the younger ones a father. The nuns were very kind. Mother Bede, who thought Edwina looked shocked, insisted that she have breakfast in bed: a luxury, an occasional treat reserved for those who looked overtired, overwrought. Mother Infirmarian brought up toast and honey and told her that the souls of those killed on the battlefield flew straight to Heaven.

Washed clean, for them there was no purgatory.

She wrote to her parents, and worried for Mother. For herself she remembered only with shame that she hadn't really liked him. She felt a hollow sadness, a kind of sick regret – but on behalf of Philip, not herself, for what he would never now know.

Life went on the same. The best was Franz. Waiting always for it to be Wednesday and then when the lesson was over, counting the days again. They talked about her future. Franz said: 'I think you should apply to go to the Royal College of Music.' He would write to her parents. 'Leave it to me,' he said. 'I arrange everything. London, and where you live – *everything*.'

It was late November now. She wrote excitedly to her parents. They wrote back and didn't mention it. She thought perhaps that their letters had crossed, and didn't worry. She was busy practising for a school concert on the feast of St Nicholas: a special thought for the Belgian nuns.

She played Brahms, the Capriccio in B minor, and wished only that Ben were in the audience. She wore a white frock and a large blue bow tying back her hair. She was the age now that Meresia had been when she first knew her. Yet she didn't feel at all like Meresia, who had seemed so grown-up. She was not grown-up. Just restless.

When she'd finished she didn't wait for the clapping but went straight into the C sharp minor, in case they should stop her, because she had been put down for one piece only. But in fact she got an encore and could have played for much longer. One of the Belgian nuns took her aside and said that God had given her a great gift. Afterwards there were games, and a feast. It was only ten days away from the anniversary of the Bombardment. They said special prayers, their voices raised in thanksgiving that those who'd had the faith and courage to stay on, in that exposed place above the sea, were still safe. *Te Deum laudamus.*

The next morning a letter came from her father: 'There is no question at all of your going to the Royal College of Music – or any college, for that matter. We were a little surprised that you should have consulted with and made decisions with your teacher without first approaching us . . .'

In the music room, practising, she could do nothing systematic. Her hands roamed over the keys. Then suddenly with grim determination she began to work through the Brahms' Fantasias. But she could bring none of the joy of execution to them: could only thrust and press, heavy where she should be tender, aggressive where she should have been vibrant. Appalled at the sound she was making, ashamed, she sat there muttering, praying: 'Lord, I am not worthy that thou shouldst enter under my roof . . .'

Her father was angry before he spoke. She was angry too of course, but showed it by her cool greeting, her tart questions. 'No, I don't want any luncheon, thank you.' Coming down at six o'clock. 'Where is Father?' Saying aggressively, 'I want to see him.'

He was in the library, in front of him a mound of paper, envelopes of different sizes, forms in a toppling pile, a glass of brandy and a decanter at his elbow. Behind him on the wall, the War map, its little headed pins marking out the progress of the armies.

He didn't look up when she came in. 'Yes?' he said. 'Is it urgent? This report has to go up to York for the Wednesday Assizes.'

'Well,' she stared at him, so that he would *have* to look up. 'What am I going to do instead?' she asked angrily. She had been saying this to herself ever since. She'd wanted to write to Franz. She'd composed a letter several times over, but the bits of paper were still in her writing portfolio.

'I think you should sit down, Edwina.' She noticed that his face was very red, the blood rushing thicker as he spoke in his turn angrily: 'Perhaps you can explain your rudeness?' He had got up and was walking to and fro in an effort to keep calm.

She said obstinately: 'I want to go there –'

'I don't think, neither of us think from any indication you've given us, that you are old enough, leave alone responsible enough to live in London – '

'I wouldn't be living on my own – I just want the *chance* to learn. If I'm properly, fully trained, I can make a career of my playing. I can give concerts – ' She searched for further heights. 'I want – '

'We seem to be hearing a great deal of what you want. Why should you know what is best for you? How have you suddenly come by the experience and knowledge?' His forehead looked lumpy with veins. 'I had meant, wanted to speak to you calmly. But you have precipitated the whole discussion.'

She shouted at him, in a passion of terror that unless she fought for it, it would go beyond her reach utterly. 'If they say they'll have me, I've the right to go. I could get some money. I've the right – '

'Right! Women's Rights, I suppose. We are to hear of those now.' He was pacing up and down faster. 'Yes, you have rights. You have the right to be loyal and good. And to your mother and myself for a start. Your place is *here*, do you understand? Until you marry. I don't think you realize what your mother has been through – a son lost . . .'

'That's not fair, I only want to take my chances. I want, I want – '

'Lower your voice!' His hand was shaking. 'I think you had better go – '

She was shaking too. After a while, because she didn't know what to do with her rage, with her body, she went, like he had said.

New Year 1916. Philip's friend Denis came to stay. He was to go out to India at the end of the month, and talked about it at dinner in a quiet voice. He had blond hair in very tight curls and neat regular features and reminded Edwina of a more pleasant, more handsome Philip. He was polite to her in a cool way; once they had a short conversation together. He and Mother went for long walks when the weather allowed it and Mother wasn't working. Her behaviour was very emotional. She has lost her only son, Edwina told herself in excuse of her odd moods, her sudden lashing out at Aunt

Josephine, at Father, at Edwina.

She herself felt sullen and angry still, wanting only now to be back at school. Mother scarcely noticed. Father, busy, ignored her. It was Aunt Josephine who helped the most, sometimes just by giving her work to do and then praising it, sometimes by talking. Things always looked worse in the cold weather, she said. She knew about Edwina's disappointment. She said robustly: 'Everything passes. Even this dreadful War. And I might, it is just possible, be able to help you later. I have some means. Also, you will not be under age for ever you know.'

But she spoke of an unimaginable five years ahead. I have to get through 1916, Edwina thought. She wasn't sleeping well. Once she woke shaking, covered in sweat. She had been watching the sea through thick glass: grey-black water churning, white spray rising, thrown high in great spouts. Uncle Frederick, struggling, arms flailing, tried to lift himself up above the waves, the great white horses. He was calling her, but she could hear nothing. She drummed on the thick glass, panicky, shouting: 'I'm coming!' He rose and fell, struggling always. But even as she banged and shouted he rose again. She saw then that he was Ben. 'I'll save you,' she cried, hurling herself again and again at the glass, so violently, so despairingly, that she woke herself up.

'They got Jack back, you know,' Fanny said. 'Everything seems all right.' But she hadn't been over to Bay, nor could Edwina get her to talk about it very much. All those first weeks of term she was in a flat, frustrated kind of mood. She said to Edwina, 'The one clear *good* thing in my life is that I'm going to be a nun.'

Edwina said, 'You've never told anyone though – shan't you?' But Fanny just replied: 'Why upset them? It's going to be the most terrible shock to everyone. And Mother Anselm, people like that, I wouldn't give her the satisfaction. Just think how she'll feel when she hears . . .'

Franz showed Edwina a letter from Father. 'This I ought not to do, but you see it is not without hope.' Europe, which

Franz had evidently mentioned, was described by Father as 'a possibility we could certainly discuss in happier times'. Perhaps, Franz said, when she was eighteen they would allow her to nurse or even to join one of the services 'and then one day the War is over and life begins again'.

The spring weather was so beautiful that year that it felt almost as if perhaps life would begin again. Mother wrote to say that Ned was spending a fortnight's leave with them, at her invitation. 'He is stationed near, you know, but is about to move south. He seemed so reluctant to go home, and it is a tremendous help to have him here now that Denis has left.'

The temperature was nearly in the seventies when she went to stay with Fanny. She could never remember so warm an April, sitting out in the garden at the back, walking by the sea. It was then that she confided in Fanny.

'Why ever didn't you tell me you liked him? Just because I don't want to be spoony doesn't mean *you* can't.'

'It isn't that – ' She felt compelled to lie. 'I just like seeing him. I know he likes seeing me.'

'He's interested enough. I told you that. And he is my cousin so you might have asked my permission – '

Edwina was amazed. 'All right then. I'm asking.'

'Don't be so assy,' Fanny said. 'If you like though, we'll go over.'

It was almost like old times, travelling with Cook (who grumbled all the way that her friend was getting old and didn't listen properly). But first she'd written to Ben, just in case.

'If you wanted to write to each other,' Fanny said, 'he could write here, if it was holiday time. Marmee would never open anything. It would have to be addressed to me of course.'

They'd chosen a Sunday so that Ben would be free. Fanny was a great help, saying after they'd both walked up to Ben's and had a cup of tea: 'I'm going for a walk, everybody. Ben, you have to come too, but I don't want Becky or Sal . . .' Then on the path nearing the woods, she skipped off: 'I'm going to say my rosary quietly. You've got till half past.'

'What's up wi' her?' he asked. Edwina told him and he grinned: 'Well, she did us a good turn.' He'd taken hold of her hand, gripping it tight. She said: 'I thought I was only going to be able to sit and *look* at you.'

'I reckoned same – '

At first they only wanted to kiss. They found somewhere that seemed hidden. A wood pigeon could be heard just through the copse. The sea seemed very far away. He gave her his coat to sit on. Hands clasped tight, mouth to mouth – it was just as she'd remembered. No, better. Much much better.

'It's wrong,' she said, 'I think, what we're doing. From what they taught us, I mean – only, the language they use is a bit vague.' She said between kisses, 'I don't mind though, because it's you.' She could not relate it to anything. She had prayed and he had come to her.

'Have I to stop then?' He was laughing.

Apart, they talked, listening all the while for people nearby, for Fanny.

'What time's it got to?'

'You have the lovely watch,' she said.

He sat up straighter, pushing his feet out. She looked down at them and thought: why did I have to see Aunt Adelina's, when it's his I'd like to see bare? Why? She saw then that he was watching her. He said, his voice husky: 'I reckon it's worse – when you come.'

'What do you mean?'

'When we're out wi' boats, or summat needs doing, then I forget mebbe. But nights – '

She shivered suddenly. He said, not looking at her: 'There's not much for us – together.'

She sat choked, silent.

'There's not, is there?'

She wanted him to look at her. She said desperately: 'If you got your Captain's ticket like you said then I could sail with you, or I could play concerts while you were away and then we could be together whenever you came home.'

'And bairns?'

'Oh well,' she said, 'I'd be able, we'd be able to afford a nurse – ' It was so simple that she couldn't see why he too didn't see it.

He said angrily, looking at her now: 'That's daft. Well you know that – Like's best marrying like – There's more to it than love.'

'But you love me?'

'Aye, I love you.' She felt a great sadness. 'I love you right enow.' There were only minutes left. Another parting. She thought: I am him, he is me. It is only our thinking that's different. And how can that be important?

Behind them the wood pigeon cooed persistently. They got up to go. She dusted down his coat, and they went off to meet Fanny.

'Did you let him do anything?' Fanny asked. 'Touch you, I mean. Or kiss you?'

'No, of course not . . .'

There were ten days of holiday left when she got home. She played the piano when she wasn't helping Aunt Josephine. More Brahms: 'Variations on an Original Theme.' For no reason that she could think of it became associated with Ben, with her love for him.

Mother was edgy and difficult so that Edwina wondered about the 'trouble' Aunt Adelina had described. Aunt Josephine tut-tutted when she tried to mention it. The days dragged on. She was pining, love-sick. She could hardly speak for it.

Mother sent for her, one late afternoon. It was like being sent for at school, except then she was frightened only up in her head. Now she felt it in her belly as if she must defend herself, as if she had something to protect.

Mother was lying back on her sofa, smoking, a cornelian ashtray beside her.

'I want to talk to you about your sulks.'

'My sulks?'

'Yes, your *sulks.*' She drew lightly on her cigarette. 'Your utterly too childish sulks, I can't tell you how unpleasant I find them.' Then in an irritated manner: 'Sit down, can't you. It's the very way you *stand* – defiant, cocking a snook. It won't do.'

'What won't do? *I* don't care – '

'Don't be rude to me. You were rude and defiant when Tom spoke to you at Christmas. He made his reasons quite clear, it's not as if he merely forbade you – '

'It seemed like that, it sounded like that – '

'Don't interrupt me. You didn't wait for his reasons. You went off the deep end. If you'd stopped to listen, *if*, you would have heard that he had very good reasons. The very idea of a career in music. It makes one fear for your sanity.'

'Why? I'm good enough. Lots of people have said – '

'It's not proved, is it? Your duty is to stay at home for as long as you're wanted. Then to make a good marriage – if anyone will have you. No man will stand for arguing, sulks, forward behaviour – they don't like it. And they won't want to hear all you know and how gifted you are. This parable of the talents, that's not what it means. You could tinkle to give pleasure surely? If you weren't so selfish you could think of doing something for the War Effort with it.'

'What?'

She shrugged her shoulders. 'People like a nice tune. You play quite well after all.' She reached back to a small table behind her: 'My medicine – the doctors said – ' She sipped: 'Whether you marry or not you have absolutely no need to earn money. So why the career? If you *know*, had any idea what it's like to live, sometimes not even sure you can pay for the next meal, never being able to forget about money. *You* want for nothing.'

'But Uncle Frederick . . . He would want me to go.'

'Oh Frederick. He's had this bee in his bonnet always, always, about your playing. His judgement is nothing to go by – Look at the woman he married.'

'She's rich at least. You should be pleased.'

'Did I ask for your opinion?' Seeing her cigarette burnt out, she lit another. 'I sent for you, to tell you I won't stand for either your sulks or your defiance. I am a woman who has lost her *only* son, and I don't think that a mother who has made that sacrifice should be asked, expected to put up with conduct of this sort. In the face too of a perfectly reasonable edict. *You may not go, Edwina.* Do you understand?'

'No.' (Why was the whole matter being brought up again?)

Mother laid down her cigarette suddenly then, taking hold of Edwina, shaking her roughly, pushed her back against the chair. 'You shan't speak to me like that. Duty,' she said, 'don't the nuns ever speak to you of *duty*? Don't they teach you that obeying your parents is the same as obeying God?'

'Yes,' said Edwina sullenly.

'Why are you so *rude*? Fanny doesn't give her parents trouble, does she? Does she? Perhaps you could try to be more like her. That's what friendship is about surely? And take that miserable look off your face – what right have *you* to look miserable? What did Philip's death mean to you – you didn't give birth to him, did you? And that other baby, that son, I lost him.'

'I know. I know.'

'You couldn't possibly imagine what it could be like to carry for nine whole months, to go through hell. And now, I have nothing. Just you – and look what a bargain I have there.'

'Cora –'

'Yes, Cora. I rely on Cora. And Denis, when he was here. And Ned. Now Ned –'

'Ned's my friend.'

'What do you mean, *your* friend?'

'I got him first –'

She mimicked: '"I got him first!" You don't *get* people, Edwina. I think you've misunderstood something – as usual. Ned, quite simply, would rather be with me. Has he ever shown the slightest interest in being in your company?'

'Yes.'

'When? I should be very surprised if that's anything but

a fairy tale. Fanny now, he admired Fanny. I shouldn't mind if he were to take that further – '

'I should mind very much indeed.'

'How quite disgusting. You would, would you? Sour grapes. To fight with your best friend over a boy.' She drained her glass: 'But it would be for him to decide, wouldn't it? It's not really as if a girl, a woman has any choice in the matter.' She rearranged herself on the sofa, yawned.

I shall choose, Edwina thought. Nobody decides anything for me.

'Do go, can't you? I need to sleep before dinner . . .'

There was a letter from Uncle Frederick. Aunt Adelina had died ten days earlier. It had not been unexpected, he said: The outlook had been hopeless since the autumn. They had wintered in Rome with the Antici-Montani – they had had a suite in the palace and every care had been lavished on her. Because of the War there had been shortages, although their farms and estates had produced food otherwise unobtainable. She had not suffered too much: the end had been a gradual weakness. She had not been strong enough even to be carried to the Spanish Steps which she loved so much in spring – although they were a sorry sight these days: no flower-sellers, no artists' models, green-grey soldiers everywhere: 'The idea of a short war has gone . . . two of the sons are in the *granatieri*, the Grenadiers, against the old Marchesa's wishes. To be Black is still very important to her – that a Black should fight for the King! It is she, I will say, who has supported me throughout our whole ordeal. Without her . . . A debt I cannot hope to repay . . .'

Fanny said: 'I know I didn't like her, but I feel so much for *him*.' She said wistfully, 'I wish I could help. I wish sometimes I didn't have such a pash for him. It makes my life so difficult. Edwina, do you think I'll ever be a nun?'

'If you want to be – '

'Oh, I do. I do. Then I can love him purely. And I can

belong to a proper family and be all in one piece.'

That term, their last, they were prefects. It didn't alter their way of life very much. They still leaned out of their cubicle windows, talking long after lights out. No other friend but Fanny. She supposed that they were fond of each other: like sisters perhaps, how she imagined sisters should be, so that she didn't *think*, do I like her? But oh how she needed her, how they needed each other.

'You took Fanny,' Madge said one day, suddenly, bitterly, 'you had her *all to yourself*. After you and her became friends *none* of us had a look in – '

It had been partly true. She and Fanny had been different. Not for them the exchange of holy cards: dear fluffy ones inscribed 'To Vita in memory of . . .' 'Marion, remember *that* time in the dorm . . .' Even their conversation had been different. Once when Fanny had made some joke about how babies were made, Babs had said, jolly but firm: 'I don't like girls who talk about *that* sort of thing.'

It was an incident early on that term which made her realize her need to defend, to protect Fanny. It was the Belgian nuns again. They had not grown any more popular and now that food was short (dishes of lentils where once there had been meat) they were suspected – unjustly really, Edwina thought – of getting privileges. They ate separately from the other nuns, in a special annexe. Their food could be seen sometimes laid out ready as the girls passed to the dining-room. It did not look privileged.

The same Soeur Clothilde who had once upset Babs, accused Fanny now of bad manners, and bad blood. Fanny, in tears of rage, said: 'She told me I didn't know how to behave with ladies and that I came of a bad family, "The tree is rotten" she said . . .'

That evening at supper Edwina brought in a small paper bag and emptied into it the contents of two salt cellars. The next day, excusing herself out of the last morning class, she went to the annexe. No one was about. A small bowl of stewed fruit lay beside each nun's place. Carefully she scattered a teaspoon of salt on to each portion. Walking back to the classrooms, she felt much happier. And about ten years old.

'I think you ought to know. Ben's written to me. It's been opened of course but it's all right – '

'Can I *see* it?'

'Don't be so assy impatient! Here's the bit – he says he's going off, he's joining the Merchant Navy and he wants me (that's you) to write – '

She got the precious sheet of paper off Fanny, holding it with her fingers shaking. 'Your loving cousin,' she saw.

'. . . even though fishermen don't have to go, we're what they call reserved, I wanted to fight you see, there's four gone already and Sal's John last week . . . I knew you'd care to know and let others know . . .'

She said the next day, 'I'm going to try and see him.'

'You must be mad,' said Fanny. She thought she probably was, but in the event it was only to think and plan, and to watch the tides. And not to tell Fanny. She lay in bed those three nights, waiting, thinking. She did not dare to feel. In the daytime she was exaggeratedly good. Fanny, who was making an elaborate novena for the Feast of the Precious Blood, noticed only to remark, 'You're in a funny mood.'

A crescent moon, moon enough to see by. Dressing up warmly, a dark gaberdine skirt from her mufti, a shawl, her galoshes in a drawstring bag, she listened carefully: heavy regular breathing to one side of her, suffocated snores to the other. She tiptoed down the centre of the dormitory – if anyone heard the boards squeak they would think only that she was going out to the lavatory – opening the door slowly, gently. All those years of creeping down at home, concealed outside the drawing-room, listening, listening. But this evening, to get downstairs was only to begin the venture. They can only expel me, she thought.

The clock struck one. She thought as she moved along the corridors: If a nun sees me now, I'll say, 'I couldn't sleep, Mother, I thought a walk in the garden . . .' But nothing, nobody. Just silence, half light, the creaking of the door.

She would like best to be some giant sea-bird, landing then on the rocks outside Bay, or better still on the red pantiles of the village itself, the roof of his home. As she crept now over the dry sandy grass – the garden just left behind – she thought, suppose I am taken for a German spy? Suppose, suppose. She wanted to be quickly down but she wouldn't take a short cut. If she were to stumble, twist her ankle, if stones were to fall . . .

Then at last, down on the beach. When she stopped to rest for a moment, she felt her heart thudding. I am mad, I must be mad. Seaweed glistened in the moonlight, flat broad leaves, bubbles of bladderwrack. The sea itself, comfortably far out, rippled gently. There was little or no wind but the air was not close enough for thunder. She realized only then how much she had counted on the wind not freshening, on the weather holding. What would I have done if there'd been a blow?

The cliffs hung, threatening her. They had never done that before. Soft rock, that might fall. She had been creeping too close, it made her feel more invisible. She came out now a little. Wine Haven. Millers Nab. High Scar. Peter White Cliff. To remove the needle of fear, she named them, saying the words over and over again like a charm. Once, clambering over the wet shining slabs of stone, she stumbled and the salt water went up to her ankle, inside her galoshes, a damp stocking, a damp hem of skirt.

At Mill Beck she wondered if she should go inland and along the cliff top. But she kept to the shore, hating to stop even for a moment now because of the violent thudding of her heart. Perhaps she would die of fear.

The village lay hushed. Every pub shut, everyone abed for early rising. How still it was. And how great now the danger of discovery. Our Lady, Star of the Sea, who had guided her this far – Quietly, so quietly up the street. Don't breathe. And then carefully, up the wooden steps to his room. The steps creaked and she stood frozen, waiting. She had not thought: how to make him hear? Suppose, oh God, after all this he isn't there? Isn't alone. She tried the door, dared to try the door. It gave, opened slowly, silently. And yes, he was there.

She touched his shoulder. The slightest of whispers: 'Ben.' Then again, 'Ben.' He stirred. She moved the sheet back a little. Through the curtains chinks of moonlight showed her the quilt, its pale and dark squares. And suddenly his eyes open, wide. Jesus, St Joseph, Our Lady, not to let him cry out.

'Ah,' was all he said, 'Ah,' as if she'd touched him, as if she'd touched him *there*. She whispered, 'You're not dreaming.' She put out her hand. 'It's me, I came along the beach.'

He sat up. She saw he had his vest on. 'You never,' he said, shaking his head.

'I did.'

'You're daft – ' But his voice sounded pleased, proud almost. She was crouching by the bed. 'Shan't I get asked to sit?'

'Hush – keep your voice down.' Already they were touching. 'The walls they're thick, but it'll not hurt to take care.' He'd pulled back the bedclothes a little, climbed out. He sat on the edge of the bed. She was alongside. She said: 'I thought you'd wear a nightshirt – you've got your vest and pants on, you're funny.' He said, 'I've these on when we've to go out – to be ready quick like.' She asked anxiously then: 'Are the boats going out early?'

He had tight hold of her hand. 'Not till five or six, and I'll not be with them, I've things to do afore Friday. It's just – I were lazy.' Their heads were together, his breath, hot from sleep, on her cheek. 'You're that daft – to come here . . .'

'Do you mind?'

Their hands, joined together, lay on her knee. 'What d'ye think? That's daftest of all – '

She said, 'I'm going to take some of my clothes off.'

'There's place in bed.' His voice kept having a little choke in it. They were so awkward with each other. She thought, I should never have come, I don't know what to do now I'm here. If I hadn't, he could have gone quietly off and forgotten me. The very idea made her sick and trembling.

'Shall we lie together?'

'Aye.' Then as she climbed up he said desperately, 'If I've said nowt, it's not that – '

'I know,' she said. 'I love you.' At first they just lay and talked. She said all the things she'd wanted to say. It seemed easy in the half darkness. And for him perhaps it was the same. He told her about going away, about the Navy: how he knew it was right, that he'd had to do it. 'But when I come back, then – '

'When you come back.' His hands moved over her body as he spoke. She felt so warm, so secure. She had stopped too being afraid, stopped thinking of the danger. Why should she, how could she be discovered?

'Get in bed, there's place – you feel starved.' But she wasn't cold. And if she shivered it was with happiness, to be like this. 'I love you,' she said.

Where the curtain wasn't quite shut and the light came in, he pulled it tight. For a few moments they were silent. Their hands felt for each other. And then the fever began in the darkness. Mouth upon mouth just as she had remembered. Such clinging, and then the tongues that only a few seconds ago had been talking, lost, sucked up. Not explorers this time but desperate, those about to drown. Coming apart, only to join again, sinking, back down in the feathers of the bed. Then Ben above, over her so that she went down, down. If it was only this to drown . . . Softness and hardness, hardness and softness, everywhere the unexpected. Nothing as she had imagined. (What had she imagined?)

Wild drumming of her heart. Pounding in her head and the smell of danger. She was gripped so tight, his head buried in her shoulder, she could never have moved. It hurt at first, and she bit her lip because she couldn't cry out. She thought she might break inside, that something terrible was happening.

'I shouldn't then – '

She said, 'Oh but you must, you must,' terrified now that he might stop. She had not broken, she would not break. He lifted himself – her breasts hurt where they had been pressed. She noticed then how heavily he was breathing, a stranger almost, but his hands she recognized, the smell of them, pushing back her hair. 'I love you – I shouldn't then.' They were hands guiding a boat. And now too, it hardly hurt. And it mattered not at all anyway, the hurt didn't matter because although he was strange now, seemed a stranger, she had always known him. She *was* him.

Suddenly he lay beside her, panting into her hair. 'I minded,' he said; she thought he was crying, 'I had to be careful . . .' He began to cry in earnest, racked by great sobs. 'I shouldn't of – that's all about it, I shouldn't of.'

She whispered then, 'It's *you* they'll hear.' It was for her to stem his tears but she thought only that she would weep herself. She felt about for his fingers. Hands clasped again: so tight that she thought, how could they ever be prised apart?

'I did make it worse, coming here.'

'Never, you're never to say that – '

'Are you cross that I did?' When he didn't answer she said it again. He'd stopped sobbing. 'Don't ask daft questions.' He was indignant. 'Fondhead,' he said.

'*You're* the silly one.' They lay silent again. He seemed quite calm. Then: 'I'll have to look at time.'

'It's good there's a moon,' she said:

' "I see the moon, the moon sees me
God bless the sailors out on the sea . . ."

Sarah used to say that.'

'Sarah?'

'The nursemaid. I told you – '

Time wasn't real. It could not be heard ticking. Perhaps they would be able to lie here for ever, talking in low voices.

She said: 'Will you think of me, when you're out on the sea?'

'I'll never think of owt else. Get away – I'd sink the ship.'

'You're laughing at me – '

'Why not then?' He said despairingly: 'It's that – or blubbing like a lass – '

There had always been a time to go: the end built into the beginning.

'I ought to get ready.' Her clothes felt strange, uncomfortable. Clammy to the touch.

> "And when Sergeant Death in his cold arms shall
> embrace me . . ."

Fastening her blouse she shuddered: then trying to control herself, afraid he'd notice, she shuddered the more. So cold suddenly, so cold. An aching chill.

'You *are* starved. If I could fetch you back only . . . I love you,' he said. 'You'll mind always I love you?'

Charm against all the monsters that lurk in the deep. I love you, I love you. Our Lady, Star of the Sea – there was no time, no place you couldn't pray. Keep him in your care.

Mother Bede had her breviary open as she walked round by the box hedge, coming face to face with Edwina.

'What*ever*? Edwina – '

'I couldn't sleep, Mother. I got up early.'

'You've been beyond the garden. Look at your skirt. And your hands and arms. There's *sand* – '

'I'm sorry, Mother.'

Mother Bede looked at her closely. She didn't speak for a moment. Edwina felt suddenly, too suddenly to halt them, the prick of tears.

'You know that it's very wrong to go out of bounds. And for a *prefect* – '

'Yes, Mother.'

Mother Bede was gazing at her still. 'No girl should look so exhausted – Is it trouble of a spiritual nature?' She snapped shut her breviary: 'Go as quietly as possible back to the dormitory. I shall arrange with Mother Infirmarian for breakfast in bed.'

'Whatever have you done to deserve that?' Fanny said,

bursting into the cubicle. 'They've given you *honey* too . . .'

Now that she'd left school, Mother allowed her to go over to Franz once a month. There she could stay the night and in the morning have a second lesson. It made sense of that autumn of 1916. Ned had been in France since July. Mother scarcely discussed him, although occasionally a field postcard or an actual letter would arrive. This she would take up to her room. She wrote to him frequently though, saying always: 'I am about to seal the envelope, any message, Edwina?' Cora, nearly fourteen now, sharing a governess with a family of girls in the next village, although as objectionable as ever, was in this matter almost Edwina's ally. 'She's *hateful* about him. They were always going off together, laughing and talking. I had to *push* so as he'd notice me . . .'

The Brahms Variations: She had christened them now 'Ben's Air'. Calm, tender, changing to fierce, angular, ominous: storms at sea. For a little while lyrical, and then a burst of fragmented sounds. At the end, gentle, warm, relaxed. Peace, war and then peace again. That is how it will be, how it can be, she thought.

She had written to him but had heard only once, through Fanny. It was a letter Fanny could have (would have) read. Then things grew more difficult. Fanny became a land girl and was billeted in the Wolds. Her post lay about at home, collected when she turned up, usually unexpectedly. Difficult too, to keep in touch: at first Fanny wrote regularly but later, during 1917, gradually her letters ceased. ('This outdoor work, I'm one great yawn by evening . . . my hair isn't bobbed by the way – the only one of us – I want to be able to see it lying all about me when I'm shorn, when I take the veil after the war . . .')

Edwina's hair was not bobbed either. Except that it was worn up now, it was as heavy and difficult as ever. She too was doing some war work, Junior Treasurer of the Red Cross. She wore a smart uniform. Once a week officers from the nearby camp came over for coffee and there would be singing: she played the piano always. Cora, allowed to stay up, flirted and maintained that she was 'really almost fifteen'. Mother too was over-vivacious; the atmosphere was febrile. To sit quietly with one of the visitors, to look absorbed in conversation, was to bring her over: 'I hope you're not *boring* anyone, Edwina . . . really you should be passing the biscuits round.' Father was never there. Sometimes Mother spoke of her lovely hunters: 'They're all soldiers now. My beautiful French Carotte the second . . .'

That Christmas of 1916 Edwina spent a week in London with Aunt Josephine, staying with some cousins she barely knew. It was her first visit. Most of the time she spent with her aunt. They grew closer. Sensing the warmth of her affection (no one but Edwina to lavish it on, now Mother seemed to need her no longer) Edwina dreamed about confiding in her. Just sufficiently, so that letters – if there were any – could come to her safely. But how ever to broach such a subject, when even Mother's drinking could not be discussed frankly?

She went to Confession while she was in London. Mother had made no remark so far about her not going to Communion. Nor could she find in herself any sense at all of wrongdoing. But she felt somehow that she must regulate the situation. She couldn't face the chaplain at Clare's house, the possible questions, so she went now to Brompton Oratory. A weary-sounding priest, probably only too used to accounts of eve of embarkation passion, absolved her without comment.

Another wartime Christmas. In early February, one bitterly cold Sunday, the oak tree was felled. She came in from the village to find the house in commotion. Father lying in the hall, spread-eagled, breathing heavily – he looked to her massive as he lay there. Aunt Josephine explained that he was not to be moved. The doctor was on his way.

It was a severe stroke. He lived three days but without regaining consciousness. At the funeral in the Norman church up the hill, dry-eyed with shock, Edwina remembered how when she was small she had run between his legs, and been trapped there. She longed now for that pincer movement – gripped, held tight and safe. In bed that night she wept.

Mother was ill for two weeks after. Aunt Josephine said that it was partly the shock and partly 'her trouble'. 'She has been through a great deal, Edwina, and she is not well nourished. We are none of us really well fed . . .'

'I wish that I could see you,' Uncle Frederick wrote. 'It is very difficult here. That two of us should be widowed in a year. I am in Rome for the winter – the youngest Antici-Montani has been wounded in the head but it is not thought to be too grave . . .'

Cold winter, cold spring. Ned killed at Arras in April. Death was a familiar now. Mother, scarcely recovered, lapsed back again. It became obvious to all that she was drinking. Although not well enough to do any real work she would make sudden appearances, dressed, composed, apparently normal. This would last for several days, after which she would take to her room again. The officers still came weekly, their visits often coinciding neatly with one of her good days.

1917 turned into 1918. Spring, summer.

She had always known it, when the letter came from Fanny. The sun was shining on to the corner of the table where she read it. Outside it was hot, had been hot for nearly a week, but all that day she felt cold: a deep stone cold. Nothing could warm her.

She would have liked to go over to Bay. That she could comfort his mother she was certain. They would mourn as a community and she envied them that. Here she could say nothing, show nothing.

She could not play the Variations, 'Ben's Air'. Deathly cold, she could not play at all. And yet, as the days and then the weeks passed and it became autumn, what surprised her most was that she no longer believed in his death. He was, simply, not dead.

The action of a German submarine. 'All hands lost.' 'Lost at sea,' as Fanny had said so often, so proudly, of her father. But those last weeks of September she would stop suddenly, standing quite still wherever she was, as sure of his presence as if she could see him in the flesh. It was so precious to her, this sense, so against all reason, that she clung to it desperately as if she herself were drowning. It consoled her when Mother was difficult – and how much patience was needed there. It consoled her when she woke, at first to desolation, then (so sure did she feel that he was not truly dead) to a kind of peace.

'I can't remember why I sent for you – '

In the room the usual smell. A blend of her scent, Turkish cigarettes, and drink.

Edwina said: 'I'm only just back actually. It was very busy this afternoon.'

Mother was half sitting, half lying, in a wraparound *peignoir*, heavily embroidered. A glass in her hand, held carelessly: 'How boring you must find it all! Do you find it boring? I expect you wish you were doing some real War Work. Dressing up in a smock and breeches like – Fanny, is it? Or nursing – if you'd been older you could have nursed. You could still, of course. You could have gone to France. I'm not surprised Tom forbade any such goings-on – You're so headstrong, you're not safe. I know Frederick thinks he can control you, but even he . . .'

'Whenever has Uncle Frederick ever had anything to complain about?'

'Don't get so agitated. It's so unattractive. And *sit down.*' She reached for the box of cigarettes. 'That time at Robin Hood's Bay, I thought he said something. I don't recall. It could have been *Adelina* complained.'

Edwina said, stung, 'She's dead, so she can't defend me or deny it, can she?'

'Oh yes – she's dead. Like that marriage.' She lit a cigarette. 'That was dead.'

Silence. 'What do you mean?' Edwina asked, her voice wary.

'Mean by what? What did I say?' Sipping, and puffing, throwing back her head. 'How could any marriage with Frederick be anything?' she said.

Edwina said angrily: 'I think he's wonderful. He's – ' Her voice tailed away. She was near to tears already.

'Pass me the water, would you?' Mother was pouring from the decanter. 'No, leave it. Those hands – that dreadful eczema. And don't watch me like that. It is none of your business what I need – how much – '

'If you don't want me for anything, I think I'll go – '

'Don't be so priggish. Don't be so difficult. Surely, *surely* you can find a few moments to sit with a war widow – Yes, Tom lost his life as much through the war as if he had gone to France – ' She tossed her head. 'What exactly is it you have to do? If it's to play the piano . . . I've upset you about Frederick, haven't I? Edwina. Really. You *must* have realized that my Frederick, my lovely Frederick, was not quite like the others.'

A little cold nugget in her heart, in her stomach.

'No, I expect you wouldn't. These things are not much discussed at the convent. They weren't at mine.' She fixed her gaze on her feet, her embroidered slippers. 'You know that some men are more interested in – other men?'

'Yes.'

'Or in some cases, little boys. Little boys can be more to their taste – the little Italian ones, I believe, are very obliging. You understand my drift? Is your pure little mind opening like some seashell?' She put down her glass, lay back to finish her cigarette. 'It's not very important – He was always, is, very discreet. There's never been a hint – And money, you understand, he had to have money. She thought the world of him. And she didn't want – the other thing. I know that. The whole arrangement suited . . .' She swallowed hard then suddenly, her voice thick, as if blocked: 'What we had together, Adelina couldn't have known that. Couldn't. Just as a child like you can't. Can't know – can you? Can you?' She turned to face Edwina.

'I don't know what I can know. *Please* – ' The room had grown very warm. There was the smell of flowers, a hothouse scent.

'What we had together. Nothing before or since. If you've

been nearly to Paradise and then seen the gates shut – my God.' She poured another drink recklessly, slopping some round the glass. 'You see, I still call upon my God. Don't *stare* –' She took some of the drink hastily. 'The sort of childhood we had . . . what do you expect, never knowing one day to the next . . . always worrying about money. Dreading Father's face – there were a few years when I was at the convent, but then –' Her voice had a croak in it now. Edwina thought of taking the drink away from her, even made a move as if to do so, and then thought, what is the use?

'Together, you see, we were always together. After the convent. We were alone so much, needed each other so much. How can you *imagine*? Frederick and I, it was more than brother and sister. We knew about each other. Everything. What he felt I felt, what I felt . . . Those long tedious days in hotel suites all over Europe – Bruges, Montreux, Nice out of season, Köln. Was it any wonder?' She said bitterly, very, very angrily: 'You know what goes on between – you know what a man and woman do? Someone's told you?'

'Yes – of course.'

She lifted her glass. 'I didn't know. *We* didn't. Not then. We found out together. Or almost.' Edwina didn't recognize her voice. 'Unfinished, of course. Unfinished. Not *quite* – like everything Frederick does. A failure – no, a dilettante – even at that. So nearly, the act so nearly accomplished. And then we took fright. Nice people don't do that sort of thing, after all. Do you hear that, Edwina?' Edwina nodded dully. 'I might have had a child. Who knows? If he'd . . .' Her face had become very ugly, her mouth with its pretty teeth almost square: 'And then he dared to marry. Little boys I don't mind. But other women – When I first heard I was *so angry*. And I could hurt him, I was able to hurt him. "Perhaps you should finish that which you began?" I said to him. We were in the motor going to church. "Perhaps you should finish *that which you began?*" He didn't like that. He understood me –'

'I'm going to go,' Edwina said.

'Take that look off your face, you convent prude. One day maybe you'll suffer. Take that look off – '

Out of the depths have I cried unto thee, O Lord, Lord, hear my voice. Standing there, half in, half out of the room, rooted. Waves rose and crashed in her head. Great white horses rushed into the harbour, against the sea-wall. She knew for certain, finally, irrevocably, that Ben was dead.

# PART THREE

# 1920

'I can't believe it,' said Fanny, clutching the edge of the cupboard as the train swayed. She sat down on Edwina's bed. Behind the drawn blinds the French countryside passed them by. Edwina couldn't believe it either.

The furious excitement had begun that morning at Victoria. The first of April, at eleven o'clock. (Or had it really begun yesterday in York, the three of them boarding the London train, their tickets booked through to Venice?) An over-stimulated Fanny had spent most of the smooth Channel crossing being thoroughly sick. Sitting on deck wrapped up, she was brought champagne laced with cayenne – a remedy Uncle Frederick swore by. His father had given it him always, in the worst of gales: 'The better the champagne, the quicker the cure.' It made Fanny cough horribly.

But once on dry land she was herself again. Or what remained of the self Edwina had known. She was the same and yet not the same. That she had become beautiful, a beauty, was certain. Far from coarsening her, outdoor work had tempered her. Her eyes shone brilliantly against the unladylike tan of her skin. Where in the last year at the convent she'd been lanky, almost gawky, she was rounded, even graceful. But it was her hair that was still her greatest glory.

The first thing Edwina noticed about her when they met up again: that it hadn't been bobbed. 'I was the only one but I was absolutely determined. Sometimes though – at five in the morning with your fingers all iced up and the pins not wanting to go in . . .' She talked a lot about the farm work, the land. Nothing at all about being a nun.

They had got in touch again late in 1919, and met at Christmas, when Edwina had gone over to Whitby for a week. It was the first time she had left home for over a year; the first time she'd been away from the nightmare of Mother. Aunt Josephine, helping her, the two of them nurses, no longer called it Mother's 'trouble'. As firmly, desperately, they withheld from her what she now could not live without, Mother abused them, made mischief between them, cajoled them. And in the end was cured. Again and again Edwina thanked God that she had told her nothing. (If she had had that weapon. If she had had the name of Ben.)

For the moment anyway, free of the compulsion to drink, Mother had bought a new little bay. She was to hack it through the late summer, hunt it this winter. The season she would spend with Cora in London. She paid Edwina as little attention as possible.

Fanny burst with convent news: 'Cynthia-Scholastica actually got married, you know. I *think* to Willie. And you know about Clare becoming a nun? And then Meresia married the Hon. somebody – he survived the War, but he's only got one arm. Vita actually got out to France nursing. And Babs . . .' So it went on. It seemed to Edwina another world. '. . . and of course I wore my smock and breeches, to shock Mother Anselm . . .'

It had been Uncle Frederick's idea, the visit to Italy. He had written early in the New Year saying that it had been one of Adelina's last wishes that her promise to Edwina should be kept.

She had not wanted to go, because she had not wanted to go anywhere. But it had seemed churlish to refuse; and it meant escape from Mother. Then had come the proposal to take Fanny too. It had come in a roundabout way when Uncle Frederick was already over in England and the plans half made. But she had encouraged it, had thought: If I can't enjoy it, someone shall. And Fanny had not waited one minute to say yes.

They were to be away eight weeks. The first ten days were to be spent in Venice, then on to Florence to Uncle Frederick's home. The remaining weeks they would stay in Rome with the Antici-Montani.

'I can't believe it,' Fanny said again. 'When I get back home – it'll be so flat. You've got the autumn to look forward to, you assy thing – '

It was Aunt Josephine who had made *that* possible. Who

had suddenly offered the money, the support; had taken her side against Mother, had gone with her to see Franz. In the autumn, she would probably study in Paris. The piano. Something would really happen. She had to believe that by then she would come to life again. (Was not the sudden lift of the heart this morning – the castle and cliffs of Dover, the first scents, sights, sounds of France – was not that proof it was perhaps possible?)

'You can't *imagine* what a hard life . . . I only want to live an easy one now. My hands quite spoilt . . . There were good bits – like I liked haymaking. But all those petty rules – ' She pulled her kimono tight round her: 'Uncle Frederick looks as if he feels the cold. He looks chilled all through. Beaten down. I'm very sensitive to how he feels, even though I'm not in love with him any more – I think uncles are pointless. By the way,' she said, sticking her feet out in their fluffy mules, 'by the way, I'm not going to be a nun after all.'

Edwina lay back in bed. 'I didn't think – '

'I must have been mad. No, my dear, men are the thing. I think I shall probably marry someone rather rich. Remember how I used to say? Remember?'

She talked on. Outside in the darkness trees, fields, farmsteads flashed by. Edwina wanted suddenly to sleep. The day's tiredness accumulated as if she had been hit.

'Just look,' Fanny said, 'this dear little place to put a pocket watch. Don't you love it all? A bedroom on a train – '

Ben and his birthday watch ('Will it spoil in salt water?').

It was midnight almost. Fanny left. There was just the sound of pucketing wheels. Her bed seemed to rock. Out in the corridor a man was talking to the guard. Sleepier than she realized she half listened, '*. . . je pense que . . . non, monsieur . . . on approche Dijon . . .*' There was one more stop in the night. She half woke, then knew nothing at all till Fanny shook her. She had not expected to be so drugged.

'We're in Switzerland!' Lifting the blinds they watched together the morning sun sparkling on the blue lake: Vevey, Montreux. ('That's *Byron's* Chillon.') Just before Sierre, washed and dressed, they met Uncle Frederick for breakfast.

Fanny was full of excitement. The hot croissants, the chocolate, the black cherry jam. 'And butter,' she kept saying, 'all this *butter*.' A cup of chocolate held to her lips, 'What do you do all day now?' she asked Uncle Frederick. 'What do you do with your time?'

'Ah well,' he said. 'Good works. There's a lot needed. War wreaks havoc – children especially. I sing still – I read. I go out. People I knew before. My wife's friends – '

'And your wife's money,' Fanny said. Edwina blushed. She couldn't believe in Fanny's behaviour.

Uncle Frederick had coloured. 'And my wife's money,' he said. 'Have you tried rosehip jam – this jam?' he pushed the dish towards her.

'Thank you,' Fanny said. 'As a matter of fact I was only joking.' There was silence. Edwina looked out of the window, then glanced back at Uncle Frederick's face. It betrayed nothing. She thought, probably I have loved him all along.

The train drew into Brig. Domodossola, Pallanza-fondo Toce, Baveno, Stresa, Arona: Fanny read out all the names. At Milan she wound down the window and they both leaned out: a train full of soldiers waited on the opposite platform. A handcart with drinks came by and the soldiers hung out: *'Cabù!'* Two of them caught sight of the girls and called something, pointing. Fanny through cupped hands called back: 'We're nice girls, you understand, *nice* . . .' and laughed. Edwina said, 'You're behaving all the time as if you wanted to show Mother Anselm something.'

Fanny grew worse. During luncheon, she announced: 'I want a Fortuny dress, Uncle Frederick. While we're in Venice.'

'Oh yes – ' looking up from his salad – 'yes?'

'Will ten pounds be enough? I've been saving and saving.'

Uncle Frederick smiled. For some reason Edwina thought he was going to turn to her: 'And what is *your* heart's desire?' But he only said, to Fanny: 'I dare say we can arrange something.' It was like him to have heard of a dress designer, for one not to have to explain.

Venice. By the stone pier blue-bloused men worked boat-hooks. But a private gondola, black, smart, plush came to meet them. 'I do feel a *snob*,' Fanny said. 'Oh, isn't this the cat's whiskers – '

Such beauty. There had not been sunshine before Milan, but weather which anywhere else would have meant grey indifference, here made a misty watercolour. Coming out into the Grand Canal, she thought, it is like no other place. A barge passed by, a fluffy white dog in the prow, head held erect as if he were the figurehead.

The palace was by the water's edge. Aunt Adelina's friends, whose home it was, were away. Edwina's bedroom was large and chill and high-ceilinged, with three beds, all of them made up. She chose the largest. They were to rest till dinner-time. Fanny came in, to say that her room wasn't so big. 'It's very grand but not so grand as yours.' She tried the light, it was dimming already in the room. 'No, there's a message – the electricity isn't working. They haven't had it long. Candles are coming.' They came a few minutes later, an enormous candelabra, branching everywhere, then two more by the bed, one near the wash-basin, all greens and gold. Fanny left and she slept, as one drugged.

At dinner, she felt sick, a nagging pain round her temples. Uncle Frederick remarked that she was very silent. 'Indeed, you're a very quiet Edwina altogether, these days.'

'The War has tired me.'

'It has tired us all,' he said.

The headache was still there when she woke, only now it was worse. Her window gave out on to the water, a small bridge. Before she was properly roused she heard the faint splash of oars, footsteps ringing. Looking out, she saw rubbish floating by – torn paper, a bottle, cabbage stalks, some food she couldn't recognize. As she walked back across the chill floor, a mouse scurried past, disappearing near the faded wall hangings.

Yesterday was another world: today was sunshine, flamboyant jewel colours, sudden spring warmth. In St Mark's

Square, below the gold of the Lions, the burnished prancing Horses, grey pigeons clustered thickly. It was to be a day of sightseeing – not too serious, since they had a week. 'The air is champagne,' Fanny declared. She was more eager than ever today. 'Don't forget my Fortuny frock, Uncle Frederick.' He told her that she had made a tongue-twister. 'Fanny's Fortuny frock . . .'

They were to go up the reconstructed Bell Tower before midday. He said that before the old one crumbled, when it was thought to be really in danger, the bands had not been allowed to play, the midday cannon to fire.

Now they sat drinking coffee at Quadri's, to the strains of the 'Tritsch-Tratsch Polka'. The man playing the violin looked like Osbert Maycock. She saw it as some ill omen.

Her head had begun to throb continuously. Because of the wonderful weather they ate lunch on the water, a board spread across the gondola: Parma ham, veal, crusty bread, grapes, red wine. It was wrong not to be hungry, to have no appetite. In the late afternoon they looked at silver, lace, coloured glass in the Merceria. Light-headed, she found herself thinking – of a beautiful ruby-red goblet: I'll buy that for Ben. Then sick with her mistake she became aware more than ever of the throbbing, a giant heartbeat, shaking the whole of her.

At Florian's, the other side of the Square, Fanny drank chocolate and chatted to Uncle Frederick. He told them that Oscar Wilde had written *Salome* there. Fanny said to Edwina: 'I told you wrong about Oscar Wilde.' A quartet played the waltz from *Countess Maritza.* Edwina remembered Ned in the linen cupboard and thought that she could not bear the weight of loss and lack of hope. She said: 'I'm ill, I think.'

At once Uncle Frederick was all solicitude. He should have noticed. She had been too brave. She went straight to bed, shivering now. She thought of cholera, but the symptoms weren't right. 'I think you have to have diarrhœa,' Fanny said.

She drank mineral water until she felt that she would float and still her thirst was no less. The gondoliers' cries worked into her dreams, she didn't know if it was night or morning. A man in a frock-coat, white-moustached, came and took her pulse, examined her. Uncle Frederick came in after.

'*Malattia spagnuola*,' the doctor said, Spanish illness, had she met any? 'Spanish 'flu.' she said. 'Ah no.' He thought probably it wasn't that, that it wasn't serious at all.

Two days later Fanny had her Fortuny. An appointment was made at the Palazzo Orfei, and she came back triumphant. It had been a little more than the ten pounds but not much, and here it was: chestnut colour and very simple, all silk pleats. 'My hair was much admired, by the way.' She wore the frock that very evening, to show Edwina. 'I expect Uncle Frederick may buy you one when you're up and better . . .'

The days passed. Venice had become for her a place of foreboding, of violence done to the heart, to the body, animals beaten, booty secreted, murders in alleyways, bodies in the darkness of canals – places where the sun never came to disinfect, to cleanse. Venice was full of secrets.

Her illness had just to burn itself out. She was brought a clean nightgown four times a day. Growing stronger, she ate sitting at a marble table in the bedroom. A fire was lit for her, the weather cold and blowy again. Fanny came and sat with her. She had been out twice socially and had been much noticed. Yesterday it had been a prince: 'Can you *imagine* it?'

Florence, Firenze – When she was little she had thought they were two different places. But it had been always the magic city, the home of the beloved. Now, even though the journey had been a weakly dull affair, dozing head lolling in the train compartment, she had come to life suddenly in the carrozza, clip-clopping in the early evening sun. A wild excitement seized her so that when they passed near some stalls, the leather goods carelessly piled, all around her faces which seemed to her centuries old, she wanted to jump down and be jostled amongst them. She found herself asking question after question in a feverish rush. Fanny looked at her oddly. She had forgotten almost that Fanny was there, so far back in time had she gone.

Uncle Frederick's apartment was warm after the Venetian palace, by comparison almost cosy. But she'd been in it only a little while when she became aware of Aunt Adelina. Her ghost, here in this room among the yellowy-blue Lucca silk hangings, the heavy curtains with embroidered borders. She even fancied that there rose up from them Aunt Adelina's smell. Inescapable, since on one wall (and how poor beside the Mitti-Zanetti next to it) was one of her mockeries of Bay, with its strident blues and dull reds, its invading turret, spurious *tempietto*, pretty galleon.

She thought she would never have the smell out of her nostrils. It was then that she noticed for the first time the sofa cushions: their dense embroidered covers recognizable immediately. Ben's guernsey.

She picked one up, looking at it closely. If she screwed up her eyes she could make of it, dulling the colours, something like the original.

Another ghost. Oh welcome ghost – in spite of the pain, welcome.

She had not expected to wake up so refreshed. For a while she lay still, then she could bear it no longer. There was still cold water in the jug from last night – she splashed her face and then dressing quickly let herself out.

At first she just walked. She didn't know where she was but it didn't worry her. Shutters were being drawn back, blinds pulled up, trams half-empty still, passed her both ways. She thought, I'll aim for the Duomo. I will know it when I see it.

She came to it through the Via Pecori. Inside the cool dark

echoing interior, Masses were being said and for a few moments she joined in one. Then although she felt it wrong to do so she walked about. A bat flitted by her in the gloom. The thick pillars rose to the domed coloured sky like great tree trunks.

Outside, in a side street she stopped at what looked like a café: the proprietor was opening up, shaking a mat at the door. 'Café?' she asked, to be sure.

*'Caffé. Si, si, signorina. S'accomodi . . .'* Throwing a flimsy checked cloth over one of the tables, he pulled back a chair for her. She thought of asking for some lemonade but he had already disappeared, into the back.

When he came back he was carrying a saucepan in one hand and a cup in the other. A thick black brew was stirred and poured in, followed by several spoonsful of sugar. He stood over her smiling. She smiled back and after a moment a large woman, twice his size perhaps, came through the curtain followed by a small girl in a pinafore with hair drooping over one eye. They smiled too.

Then began a conversation of sorts. *'Sola?'* he queried. *'Seule, seule?'* and she nodded. They spoke of Firenze, that it was *bella*, that the Duomo nearby was *bello*. She too was *bella*. *'Tedesca?'* She looked puzzled. *'Inglese?'* She nodded. He said delightedly: *'Tedeschi, austriaci* – bad,' and shook his head. Then he said something quickly to his wife. She was back in a moment with a yellow sugary bun. Edwina wanted to refuse. *'Prego, prego,'* he insisted.

Some workmen came in and he excused himself. Still the wife stood there and smiled. *'Bella,'* said the little girl suddenly, reaching out and stroking the comb in Edwina's hair. Edwina got out her money. But first the woman and then the man refused, waving their hands, smiling. At the door she turned back and taking the comb from her hair placed it in the little girl's hand. As she went out she saw that she was already wearing it.

When she rang the bell, although it was a servant who answered, it was to reveal Uncle Frederick standing in the hall. He came up so close that she thought at first he was going to hit her. The servant had moved away. He said with a half-curling smile, 'How could you? Tell me how you *could* – '

'But I only – ' she flared up. 'Nothing could have happened to me. I was only walking, sightseeing.'

'Cheap behaviour. Sending me out of my mind. A *tease*?' He was almost crying. 'I'm in trust. What do you think I thought, imagined? I looked over the balcony, looked to see – you haven't been happy, you've been ill, disturbed about something. Your over-excitement yesterday. I thought of it all. *All.*' He went on, beginning to cry in earnest now, 'Helen trusts me with you. What could I say? What would I feel myself?' (A servant passed through the hall and she turned.) 'Don't bother, they don't understand, they don't know English.'

But oh my dear, she thought, they understand tears. She quivered with tiredness and upset. It welled up inside her that once she had loved him and that made her angrier than ever. He'd put his hand on her arm: 'What would I tell Helen if anything had happened. Answer me that!' His fruity voice had grown squeaky.

She couldn't help her anger then. 'I'll do *what* I please.' She pushed him off to run upstairs.

'Come back,' he called. 'Come back, Weenie – '

She slammed the bedroom door and sat still, trembling, stomach turning over. The weird sweet flavour of the yellow bun, rising in her gullet, filled her mouth.

It was a bad day. Uncle Frederick was cold and silent. She was too proud to address him directly. Fanny, who'd slept late and missed the upset, talked enough for both of them – exclaiming as the sights unfolded: 'Oh, Uncle Frederick, look at that gateway (arch, doorway, alley, roof, column) – I *must* come out and sketch . . .' She was cross with Edwina, hissing at her: 'What's the matter with you this morning?' She said accusingly, 'You've slept too much.' Uncle Frederick, overhearing, remarked suddenly, drily but lightly, 'We can't accuse her of *sleeping* – '

'Oh, I don't know what you are talking about,' Fanny said. 'Family. You can never understand what people mean when they talk family fashion.' She said the word 'family' angrily.

But in the evening it became all right. During the meal Uncle Frederick, more animated than Edwina had seen him for a long time, was both courteous and tender. Afterwards: 'Play for me,' he said, as if afraid she wouldn't. She did, because it was like saying 'I'm sorry' without the awkwardness, and because his asking had been 'I forgive you'.

She played a Haydn Sonata in F, drawing it out from memory, hearing it come back through the sounds, the feel of her fingers on the keys – My memory is in my fingers. (And so it would be, she thought, if I could touch Ben again.) She went through his sheet music with him, played some Chopin preludes, a little Liszt. Then, 'Sing for me,' she said, 'like you used to at home – Schubert, Loewe. You choose and I'll play.' 'The Shepherd on the Rock', 'The Youth and Death'. Then one of Loewe's that had frightened her in the far-off days in Bay: *'Der Schatzgräber'*. *'Meine Seele sollst du haben,'* he shouted it almost. 'My soul thou shalt have, I wrote down in my own blood . . .'

Fanny yawned ostentatiously. 'I'm tired,' she announced, making her excuses, not even kissing Uncle Frederick good night. He scarcely noticed her go.

'His "Erl King". Can we? I prefer it to Schubert's – '

'I remember,' said Edwina, 'I remember you did.' Because his voice was so beautiful they were together for a while and she thought suddenly – trying at once to forget and yet still remember all she knew – that perhaps Mother had felt like this sometimes: At one with him, so that it was all right after all.

A gipsy woman with a child in her arms tugged at Edwina's skirt. The child's face was covered in scabs. The woman muttered some word Edwina couldn't catch. Uncle Frederick pushed her away and she shouted at him.

'We're only at the station,' he said, 'and they begin – '

'She's cursing you,' Fanny said excitedly. 'Everything will go wrong from now on.' Edwina felt sorry for the woman and thought it would have been nothing to pass her a few coins. This was Rome after all. Rome was to be the best of all.

The last few evenings in Florence Fanny had talked incessantly of the Antici-Montani: 'Imagine, a Marquess – and to be actually *staying* there. I wonder what the son and heir is like? The loopy one, do you think he'll be frightening? And the one who was wounded – I think Taddeo's a lovely name, don't you?'

Edwina was curious too, but for her the Antici-Montani seemed always to have existed: they just were. All the same, images came to her that she couldn't rid herself of. For instance, that Taddeo would wear a bandage round his head. She saw him clearly, the white, bloodstained bandage above a weary suffering face.

Uncle Frederick seemed more than a little anxious that they should all get on together, that all should go well. To Edwina he said: 'It isn't just that I've told you all about them – I've also told them all about *you*. Naturally I'm eager that everybody shall like everybody – '

'Naturally,' said Fanny, looking sidelong under her lashes, a new mannerism she'd affected since arriving in Italy.

The palace came as a surprise, appearing suddenly in the street; she'd imagined something standing back, imposing. People made way as the motor turned through the open gates. She glimpsed a tree-lined courtyard, another motor, a carriage. The porter was tall and bearded and licked his lips almost continually as he spoke. Uncle Frederick spoke to him rapidly in Italian. Bells rang, echoing back across the courtyard, beyond into the distance, on and on.

A footman was escorting them along an endless open passage: marble columns, stone seats, busts on pedestals. It was dark and cool. A great lion with crossed paws looked at her. Then suddenly hurrying towards them, footsteps, and round the corner, a young man. He said at once: 'Uncle

Frederick!' Then to all of them, 'Here's – here is *Taddeo* –'

Oh, where was the bandaged head, the wan look? This person sparkled, shone, from gleaming boots to white teeth, to eyes blinking rapidly, excited: 'I come of course to take you up. I was quite unable to wait – I told them, bags I go down – did you have a rotten journey? Everyone is upstairs of course. It is good you are in time for luncheon. Stefano is not here yet, but the remainder of us –' In his over-excitement he seemed unable to stop. 'And this is Edwina – which is Edwina? And you are Edwina's friend *Frances*? No, don't introduce –'

They had come to the wide, worn marble steps of a staircase – he took them two at a time, rushing ahead, every now and then stopping to talk over his shoulder. 'I see you're already surprised – they are surprised, aren't they, Uncle Frederick, that my English is so perfectly good? We have of course had governesses, *English* governesses. By the way, I go to England myself in only two weeks, that is the sad thing I wanted to tell you at once. But before that –' He stopped, walking still ahead of them, hurrying down what appeared to Edwina a quite enormous corridor, doors on every side. They passed through two large empty drawing-rooms and at the third set of doors, stopped. Taddeo pushed ahead. 'Nonnina! They're *here*!'

So shining, so alive: he must have taken it all. At first sight she thought she'd never seen so lifeless a group. It was as if wax figures had been assembled to greet them. Five people: A small man with grey-white wispy moustache and receding hair, sitting beside a dark, sharp-featured woman. Another taller more severe-looking woman, grey hair scraped tightly back. Then, tiny legs swinging from a tall chair, the odd figure of a man with a little boy's face. He was staring, eyes slightly crossed, mouth hanging open. Last of all, and nearest to her, was a very very old woman, sitting sunk in on herself, a stick lying beside her chair.

Then suddenly, it was all different. The tableau dissolved. 'Frederick –' Slowly, painfully, one hand clutching the chair, the other her stick, the old woman stood up.

'No, no,' Uncle Frederick protested, 'please, not for us – '

'But *of course.*' Her voice was deep. 'Dear Frederick.' This was the alarming (and indeed she did seem so) Marchesa Vittoria. The dowager, Adelina's aunt. She held her stick as if it were a weapon, not a crutch. 'You are shown your rooms – of course our Taddeo could not wait. He is so *bon enfant,* but impatient . . .' She thrust the stick forward suddenly. 'Show me at once, which of these is *Edwina.*' Her voice boomed, a royal command.

Travelworn, tired, Edwina wanted only to shrink from notice. To escape this ogress. The few seconds she had been in the room felt like hours.

But even as she stepped forward, was introduced, greeted, patted even on the head, her fear left her in a rush. Was it something about the jaw, set of shoulders, line of nostril? The presence in the room?

I have nothing to fear, she thought. It is only Grandma Illingworth.

They were ten in the dining-room. Stefano had joined them now and Father Gomboli the chaplain. They sat at a large oval table. Heavy tapestries hung on the walls around. It was dark in the room and although not yet two o'clock an ornate chandelier had been lit. It was easy to be hungry – the smells were inviting – but difficult to eat. There was too much to look at. She could not take her eyes off Eugenio, the idiot son. When he had been introduced he had pulled a face, his upper lip wrinkled, his eyes rolling. Now, catching her looking, he stuck his tongue out quickly, then back to his soup. He ate noisily, his napkin tucked into his collar, yellow stains splashed on it already.

Stefano was seated next to her. She had been surprised when she saw him, because although she realized that she had in fact seen a photograph – from Adelina, she thought – it had been of a younger clean-shaven person. He said: 'My grandmother has told you already what a pleasure it is that you join us – ' His voice was very deep, not light like Taddeo's, but grave, authoritative. Where Taddeo had straight, almost sleek hair, his was thick, wavy above a luxuriant moustache. Dark, liquid eyes sloping downwards, giving him an almost arrogant expression: they could not, would not, she thought, ever sparkle. When he looked at her his attention was total. Possibly, probably, she thought, he is very good-looking.

What *he* thought of Fanny's looks was a lot less vague. Instantly on meeting her, his eyes had stayed on her just a little too long. Now Edwina saw him looking, looking, looking again. And Fanny had noticed. She was in any case very pleased with herself, over-vivacious, talking too loudly. It seemed to Edwina that the old Marchesa, sitting where she had a good view of both girls, did not approve. Taddeo, next to Fanny, continued to chat animatedly. The wispy-haired Marchese on her other side looked a cowed figure – when he did make a remark he had often to repeat it. No one had quite heard. His wife said: 'He asks if the Spanish fever is about in England, how you are with it?'

They spoke English, out of courtesy, Edwina assumed. Those who could not were silent. Taddeo had said, 'You don't know how we like to practise. All those spiffing ladies, their work to teach us must not be wasted.'

Stefano said to Edwina, 'He goes to England soon, you know.'

'I've told them. I go about my head.' He tapped it lightly. 'They are the most experienced of these wounds. Also, I've many friends and it is so convenient that our Roman season is ending as yours shall begin.' When Uncle Frederick told him that Cora was to be presented he exclaimed delightedly that he might then meet her. 'But surely I shall. And then I don't feel so bad that I go before in this way. I shall still be with the family. Perhaps later we *all* can meet?' He was carried away by ideas, plans. The old Marchesa looked on with an indulgent expression. His own parents seemed little interested. Fanny responding, countering, had a very high colour. She was waving her fork in a self-conscious manner, laughing loudly.

They were eating small savoury doughnuts, an anchovy

buried deep inside. Eugenio tipped his plate to make them run about. One fell on to the table, rolling towards his aunt's wineglass. The severe-looking Donna Laura, Marchesa Vittoria's unmarried daughter, had not spoken all through the meal. She looked now about to say something but instead pressed her lips together nervously. Norberto, the *maestro di casa*, passing the wine, scooped up the doughnut neatly.

Wine appeared in Edwina's glass. 'Our own,' Stefano told her, proudly she thought, 'everything, you know, is ours. And this excellent bread . . .' It was faintly yellow, very crusty. 'All is ours. We are so fortunate that we have fruit, grain, meat – '

Norberto was holding for her a large silver dish with what looked like slices of chicken. It was a Friday; from years of experience, even though abstinence had been lifted during the war years, she hesitated. Stefano said at once: 'It is not meat. Rather it is fish. *Tonno*. Tunny, yes?' She coloured and he said, 'I think perhaps you are rather holy?'

Fanny, wineglass in hand, said loudly, 'How assy – ' Eugenio, waiting to be served, banged a tattoo with his pudding spoon. 'I want,' he declared. His mother, sitting next to him, put a hand over his wrist. Taddeo said, 'But it's good to be holy! You know that we have a Pope in the family? And not one of the rotters at all – he's in the gallery of course. You shall see him.' Fanny asked his name. 'Paschal – three, four, I don't remember exactly – ' He waved his hand. She said coyly: 'Why not again then, why only *one* in the family?'

'Certainly it shall happen again. Perhaps the children of our children? But for now, Stefano and I, you see, we have other ideas. And Eugenio – ' he shrugged his shoulders, glanced over at his brother – 'well – he is hardly *papabile* . . .'

*'Taddeo!'* The old Marchesa drummed heavily three times with her forefinger on the table. No one spoke for a few moments. Eugenio, food on his plate again, was eating with gusto. 'I am a naughty boy,' said Taddeo. 'Nonnina, so *sorry*.'

Donna Laura, who had not spoken yet, coughed discreetly.

She said suddenly in a frightened voice: 'What shall your visitors see of Rome?'

Stefano, turning to Edwina, said quietly, 'We have many ideas – ' But Taddeo interrupting, announced: 'I am your *cicerone*. Stefano and I . . . you need no other. No, Uncle Frederick, it's not your work . . .' Edwina, feeling suddenly that she was being looked at, glanced over and saw that the old Marchesa was watching her carefully. Their eyes didn't meet. She coloured. Turning to Stefano to answer him, she saw that he too was staring, at Fanny.

Fanny clapped her hands. 'I want to see *everything*!' she cried. 'Please, when can we start?'

In the Borghese Gardens small children in white plush coats and white hats ran about. They looked hot. Their nurses, ribbons flowing, tried to keep them in order. The paths around the Piazza di Siena were shadowed by ilexes. Two girls came by walking very erect, an elderly woman watching their every step. Taddeo said:

'Oh, but that reminds me, that is how – Maddalena and I we have had just such a Miss.' He looked over at Stefano. 'Stefano has different memories. He is much older, you see.' Fanny asked, how old? Stefano said: 'Already thirty-two. Taddeo is the baby, he is only now twenty-three – '

'Tell us more,' Fanny said, 'about when you were young.' In the motor, driving through Rome, Stefano had said (in answer to Fanny's 'What's that, why's that?'): 'You must forgive, we are very ignorant. When we are children it was not the custom to explore. You understand me?' He said with feeling, 'Children – they were not the fashion. Those so boring afternoons. All the winter out with Miss in the landò – we ride to the Villa Borghese, Pamfili. And then when it is Sunday always the Pincio. And in the spring because we have no garden then to the garden of friends where we are running round the statues and are wet in the fountains. We learn *nothing* of Rome.'

But now, as they sat for a few moments out of the late afternoon sun, although she'd asked them to talk, Fanny was in fact doing it all herself. She prattled. She prattled as she had done on those visits to Bay, and perhaps because the four of them made a fine picture, people passing stopped to look. Taddeo said laughing: 'We are not accustomed to behave so, habitually we are awfully correct chaps.' Fanny told him that his slang was terrible, and that the sooner he got to England and changed it . . . He agreed humbly.

They walked through avenues of glossy magnolias. Further on the busts of noble Romans stood on marble plinths – many of them with broken noses. Napoleon was amongst them, odd man out: Uncle Frederick had told her earlier that he was there because Valadier, his architect, had re-designed the Piazza del Popolo, just below. On the gravelled terrace of the Pincio two small boys leaned over the balustrade for a spitting contest down into the square. A man nearby cuffed one of them and they made off. Edwina looked down: Below, motors coming through the Porta del Popolo circled the square. They appeared to her angular, anxious, without purpose. She looked beyond. The view coming into focus hit her.

Rome at her feet. Towers, churches, roofs, a misty bewilderment. The dome of St Peter's, Hadrian's Tomb – landmarks blurring then into the stretch of the Campagna. And beyond it all – the sea.

Stefano said, announced really: 'All visitors to Rome, it is here they must commence. The seven hills. But not exactly. I show you – '

Fanny, pulling her hat down, said: 'Taddeo, dear Taddeo, *tell* me, do you think I should get my hair bobbed?'

One of Aunt Adelina's watercolours hung in Edwina's room. She supposed it had been put there out of kindness. Fanny, pacing up and down ('I get so *restless*'), hadn't noticed it. 'Your ceiling's quite too perfect,' she said. 'Is that one of their villas painted on? I've just got cherubs and things – ' She sat down on Edwina's bed, 'Isn't Eugenio quite awful? And the marquess himself, he's pretty feeble. Of course your aunt came from that old dragon's side. Her niece. Isn't that right?

Only they're all obviously part of one great big overbred family. Your aunt married really fresh blood with Uncle *Frederick*. Then they didn't have children – '

'She was always ill,' Edwina said, recognizing and dreading the turn of conversation. Fanny said: 'I was thinking about that only the other day – if *nuit blanche* is a night without sleep then do you think *mariage blanc* – '

'I don't know.' Why did I bring her? she thought suddenly. I've had more than enough. Fanny peered at the watercolour. 'Is that meant to be *Bay*?'

Edwina said, 'Do you have to be so absolutely awful? I mean – like today. And then this evening at dinner – '

'What on earth? I never heard anything so assy. They *like* it.'

'And – how you were with Uncle Frederick.'

Fanny burst out angrily: 'You and Uncle Frederick! You take sides against me – I know.'

'Fanny, I never – we never.'

But Fanny wasn't listening. 'Turn that terrible painting the other way – I don't want anything to do with it. Bay – and uncles. They make me *sick*.' Her hair hung about her shoulders, vivid. Hissing at Edwina, she looked like some avenging witch: 'If I tell you something, will you promise to tell absolutely *nobody*?' She sat down again on the bed. She was half crying.

'I found out the most terrible – I went over to Bay because I'd finished on the land and I hadn't been, not really since Ben was lost. I went for the night, and while I was there, you know old Jane that Cook always used to go and see, they said she was ill and I was feeling all *gracious* in the morning so I decided to sit with her a bit. She was all alone and she grabbed my arm, looked in my face, "Who's that, who's that?" I said, "You know me – Annie Mitcham's niece – " but she kept on shaking her head, so I said in a saucy voice, "All right, who am I then?" and she said, "*Annie's*." I was pretty impatient by now, she was being so assy. "That's right," I said. She thought that was a great joke, chuckling away to herself.

' "Aye," she said, "you're Annie's right enow. Annie's *bairn* – Whitby, Annie was, but she'd kin here. It wasn't told, we none on us told . . ."

'I didn't know what to think. That was shock enough – Only there was worse to come. I was all agitated, I said, "But is Uncle James my father?" Only it didn't make sense, because then there'd have been no difficulty about keeping me. I was getting desperate – I thought someone might come in, and then I'd never know – people had been so close, they might just deny it all – '

She kicked off her slippers, drew her feet up on the bed. Edwina said, 'If I'd *known* – '

'She seemed to forget it was me there listening. "Fine goings-on," she said, "Annie falling like that – found herself a fine man she did, one with nowt to do but meet a bonny lass night times. And Annie's dad, he's away up to house, but the gentleman he's gone – been waiting, you see, to go off foreign. But his sister's there the while. His sister, they kept it, brought it up a lady, coming over here with all her airs each of her holidays – come to see her auntie. *Auntie* indeed. They give out the dad lost at sea . . ." '

'Oh my God,' said Edwina, 'Fanny, poor Fanny.'

'You couldn't stop her, she was telling me all – how her sister had seen them together in ways you couldn't doubt, and then Annie, who hadn't wanted to say who it was, she owned up, and my grandad – it seems he was a man everyone knew and respected so that when he came up to see Marmee his word was enough. And – Marmee said straightaway that they'd have me. Because Uncle Clive had been gone some months by then . . .'

She had her arms round her knees, hugging them. Her head bent. She was half sobbing all the time she spoke.

'I went back home and I tell you I didn't wait ten minutes to say something, I was so angry I thought I was going out of my mind, you can't imagine the feeling – choked right up to here. I could have killed, I could have murdered – and I shouted and shouted at them and then I started to cry. They were terribly shocked and frightened, I frightened them,

Marmee sent me upstairs to rest – and then I suppose they talked it over because she came in and I was a lot calmer and she said then that Uncle Clive had been living with them just before going to Rhodesia and how he'd never settled to do anything before and this career was to be the solution – she said I wasn't to think of him as anything but a wonderful person, he'd always been a perfect brother – it was just that he'd fallen in love where it wasn't suitable and I *must* understand the difficulties of it all, that there was nothing to be done that wouldn't have spoiled his chances of settling out there. And of course he felt *very* special about me and it was he who'd insisted I be allowed to keep in touch with my – with Auntie. *Everyone* had helped, she said, and one thing you could be certain was that no one in Whitby or Bay, no one would ever breathe a word – and then – just think Edwina – a silly ill old woman gives it all away . . .'

She straightened up, then she stared for a moment at Edwina. Her eyes were pink-rimmed, swollen. She said, more calmly: 'So that's how it is. Nobody is who I thought they were. I couldn't go back to Bay now. I feel so odd about – her. And Uncle Clive. That's the worst – I used to be so proud of him. Now I'm ashamed. Just thinking about – ugh . . . it made me sick – I didn't want to be a nun after that – '

'Poor Fanny,' Edwina said again, '*poor* Fanny.' She put her arms about her. Fanny, sighing heavily, groaning almost, pushed her face into Edwina's shoulder.

'I'm all of a muddle,' she said. 'Such a muddle. Tell me you are too – '

I am your *cicerone,* you need no other.

'. . . What do we show you today? It's not good to go *outside* everywhere when we haven't seen yet inside. So many rooms – You understand we don't live in it all and some are letted – on the ground floor for example. I'll show you everything. Stefano, he comes later . . .'

'. . . Here are the rooms where dear Adelina was, where she lived the last days – you see they are very beautiful . . . And here the rooms where Stefano will live. Stefano and his wife.'

It seemed to Edwina that the Palace had no end. And indeed, shaped like a figure of eight, it had none. Room leading into room into room: the eye could take in only so much. Images dissolved one into another. Ancient gold cornices perhaps, about damask-curtained windows, a mass of azaleas in oriental jars; paintings, tapestries, screens – and furniture. What must it have taken to furnish all this? Tall chairs, leather-armed, oak-backed, carved lionheads – all these fabrics and textures, gold, silk, satin, velvet. They were on the *piano nobile* where the present Marchese as head of the family lived. Coming along the corridor they met him now, wearing a mask. When he had passed Taddeo said, frowning a little: 'I must apologize, awfully sorry – he is afraid again of Spanish fever, someone must have told someone that they know one who has the symptoms and because of this . . . He will sit in the motor like that, perhaps go to the Club . . . It's – ' he made as if to empty his hands – 'he is not famous for courage.' Still talking all the time as he walked them along he said, 'He was, if you believe me, *very* good on the hunting field, that is where he has met Mamma.'

Fanny was very quiet. She had not spoken the whole of the tour. It had been Edwina who had made the appropriate comments, asked the right questions. She couldn't pretend she didn't prefer the subdued Fanny, at least here in Rome. But left over from the night before was a feeling of helpless sympathy: she herself could never have survived calmly such a discovery, such an upheaval. And underneath too, it was as if for half an hour she had been back to Bay. For had it not been Ben's kith and kin they'd been talking of?

'. . . Now you look at this tapestry. *Mille seicento*, I think, when it is commanded for a wedding . . .'

They stood at the head of a long corridor. Edwina said: 'You could play tig here. Or hide and seek – ' Fanny, coming to life suddenly, cried: 'Please let's!' She grew excited.

Taddeo, laughing, said, 'But it's not new idea. We've been many years – as children but also when we're much older. Myself and my friends most particularly . . .'

Stefano appeared beside them. 'I'm glad I find you.' Fanny had coloured: 'We're talking about playing catch, tig – '

*'Rollerskating,'* he said. 'That is the best. You see it is quite perfect here – Before the War at the home of friends and many other places there were parties. Adults, you understand. Every guest rollerskating – it was for a while very fashionable. I made so myself.'

Taddeo said, almost vying with him, Edwina thought, 'But the bicycles. The worst was the bicycles.'

'Bicycles?' said Fanny.

'But yes. Here, on the stairs. Myself and my cousins – Stefano then was too old, too serious – we ride down together *very* fast, three together perhaps. Really it is spiffing fun and just a little dangerous, which is naturally why we like it. Of course they tried to forbid but then we continue. And then one day it's not so good because we meet Norberto. He's carrying a tray, wine, glasses. Of course we had *warned* – "we're coming!" – but he doesn't hear. Imagine – the mess, the broken glass, the wine like blood everywhere. No one's hurt – except of course we don't do it any more.' He'd been waving his arms dramatically, miming with his body the bicycle descent. Fanny, listening intently, seemed to have come to life completely. Now he said: 'But we bore you with our memories . . .' She protested immediately.

'Now we go last of all to see Nonnina. She has her own front door of course. I *think* she expects us.'

Edwina felt her cheek self-consciously. She'd looked twice already in one of the enormous gilded mirrors to see if the marks had faded – for this morning after a night lying on the embroidered pillowslip, she'd seen clearly on her face the imprint of a bird's claw: creased lines, angrily coloured. It had crossed her mind that perhaps it might never fade.

'Here Nonnina has her Wednesdays, when she is At Home. My sister comes over often. You will meet her certainly . . .'

They passed through a large drawing-room – with a piano – through another room and another.

The old Marchesa sat alone. She was not doing anything – That surprised Edwina. Taddeo said: 'We have been showing – everything. Now we are all so tired.' He kissed his grandmother affectionately. 'We tell them the terrible story of the bicycles . . .' Chatter flowing, he sat beside her on the sofa. As ever he seemed unable to stop: she made no effort to restrain him, smiling occasionally, even laughing. Her hands were clasped tight over her stick. Edwina noticed them: gnarled, brown-spotted. Her dress was of dark silk jersey, lace at her wrists. She said nothing. But she watched Stefano watching Fanny. And she watched Edwina. Her gaze could be felt, didn't need to be seen.

*'Basta,'* she announced suddenly, *'basta,'* fingers opening and shutting on the cane, chewing the words. *'Basta.* You may go – today I am really a little *tired.*' Then just as they were about to leave, pushing her stick forward she said sharply: 'Edwina! I like you to stay.' She turned her head slowly: 'You will stay, please.'

'Now, at first, I wish to hear why you are so sad? You don't answer me? I hear something from Frederick – The War has not been good for you. Your brother – '

'Very early on.'

'And for that there is still – a hole?'

'No.' Edwina hesitated: 'I think I don't – ' Then she said firmly: 'I'd rather not talk about it. Any of it.'

This was acceptable. The old Marchesa didn't answer: merely nodded her head slowly to show assent. For a few moments there was silence. Then: 'If you wish to speak to me of this at some time, then I shall listen. You understand?'

'Thank you,' Edwina said. Silence again, which she didn't mind at all. She felt no need to speak, although she had a mild not unpleasant sense of fear. It was akin almost to excitement.

'I think perhaps you were not very fond of Adelina? I was

most fond. But blood is a strong affair, quite different from these bonds of marriage – I have however for Frederick great affection. That has come to me most naturally – Such a person needs a mother. And you also are quite devoted to him – ' It was a statement, not a question. She paused. 'Stefano, my Stefano. What do you think? You like him?'

'But of course.'

'There is no "*of course*" – He is very handsome, beautiful, no? And for the family very important. We must thank God that nothing has happened – this *stupidity* that they must fight. And Taddeo – ' she leant on her stick – 'fortunately he is *mutilato* only. But you will have seen that all is not well – there is too much fever, too much nervous life.'

And Eugenio? Edwina felt certain that he would be discussed next, but no. The old Marchesa, as if missing her cue, suggested instead that they should take a drink. Edwina was to pull the bell.

'This we have made many years,' she said, sipping and then putting down a glass of cinnamon-coloured liquid; she turned to Edwina: 'I understand that you are excellent with the piano?'

'I'm very serious. And yes – I'm good.' She mentioned Paris, and the old Marchesa asked sharply: 'You want to do, so?'

'Yes.' They finished their drinks in silence. Edwina thought perhaps she had done, said, something wrong. But the silence was not uncomfortable. Putting down her glass, the Marchesa exclaimed: *'Mah!'* Then was silent again.

'You may play for me,' she announced now. 'There is a chair before the piano – inside is music. Please choose.' She rose stiffly. Edwina took her arm. She didn't thank her but said merely: 'Some Weber, I think?'

The piano, when they reached it, was badly tuned. 'It is now some years since – ' But Edwina was happy to play. When the Marchesa had had enough, she raised her cane. Then as Edwina stood up: 'Quite an *exécutante*,' she said. She remained where she was, in a high-backed chair of blue velvet, while Edwina tidied and put away the music. *'Mah!'*

she exclaimed twice, clasping and unclasping her fingers over the stick. *'Mah!'*

In an upper courtyard Severina, a dark squat woman, sleeves rolled up, turned with happy abandon coffee beans in a roaster. Their smell filled the air.

'Whatever did she want you for?' Fanny asked. 'I don't think she likes me at all – and a great deal I care . . . Her reign is quite over, for goodness' sake. I'd be assy to mind.'

The smell of coffee beans faded away. They were completely indoors now: 'I never told you,' she said suddenly. 'That first afternoon, I'm sure I saw Annette's brother. There were some people painting near that kiosk where the band plays.'

'I don't know him,' Edwina said. 'I mean, I remember she had a brother – '

'I went to stay there once – they lived with this aunt – and I met him just for half a day. I'm sure it *was* him in the Borghese. But I thought how embarrassing if it wasn't and when we were with Stefano and everybody . . .' She broke off: 'This reception next week – it's a *princess*, surely, giving it? Can you imagine? I shall wear my Fortuny frock . . .' She stretched her arms above her head. 'I don't want my mood ever to change. I don't want to feel black and muddled ever again. If time could just stand still – '

But time going too fast was a good sign. It meant, Edwina thought, that you were alive. (In the grave, how it must drag.) And indeed it did seem to her that it was going if not fast, at least less slowly. There was so much to do – And because he had to go before they did, Taddeo seemed determined to make something memorable of their visit. She was grateful for this. Also, with him she felt quite at ease, however febrile his mood. With Stefano, less so. He treated her, it seemed, with a formal politeness, a kind but almost distant courtesy: it reminded her of childhood parties where one was told to be nice to so-and-so. Someone had said: 'Be nice to Edwina.'

Their days had taken on a pattern. At seven-thirty the hot

water came, at eight o'clock Severina brought breakfast: some cake-like bread in slices, occasionally rolls, some soft white cheese or honey, and strong but milky coffee. She and Fanny would take it together in Edwina's room.

In the morning someone would take them out. Occasionally it was the young Marchesa, but never her husband, and never Marchesa Vittoria. Most often it would be Taddeo with or without Uncle Frederick. Stefano might or might not. He had a great deal to do, it appeared, administering the estate, work that he took increasingly often off his father's feeble shoulders.

After luncheon (always a large meal although not so large as dinner) and a light siesta, there would be another outing. Once it was tea at the Excelsior, another time a visit to friends. Taddeo was always most assured, most confident of where, how, why. 'No, *not* this place – it has too much cake-walk about it . . . Piperno's – remind me, please, that we go there. The artichokes are very special, cooked in the Jewish manner . . .' Sometimes Stefano would disagree, and then Taddeo would appeal to Uncle Frederick: 'Dear Uncle Frederick, you are so experienced, you do agree?'

It would have been impossible to be bored. Although the long evenings, glimpsed occasionally, suggested how it could be. Often they dined early: the old Marchesa would sit afterwards, not in her own apartment but in the salotto where she had first been seen. She played patience, sitting up until at least midnight. Donna Laura crocheted, her head bent, while Eugenio, often unnoticed, would sit rolling his eyes or perhaps staring at the girls – his short legs crossed, showing an expanse of white silk sock. Stefano would have gone to his club, while the Marchese retired to bed almost at once after the meal. He suffered from nervous debility. Attempts to make Eugenio go to bed were usually unsuccessful. The young Marchesa sat with a book, the pages of which were rarely turned. Taddeo played with puzzles, intricate metal links and chains. The third evening of their stay he played chess with Edwina. Fanny said irrelevantly: 'I hate cards.' Later the three of them played backgammon. Edwina thought then:

what must this be like – night after night after night?

Wednesday. Marchesa Vittoria was At Home from five to seven. By a quarter past five all the guests had arrived. She received in the largest of her drawing-rooms, the one with the piano. In her seat by the fireplace, surrounded by flowers and bibelots, she held court, Donna Laura at her side. In the room beyond, a huge round table covered with gleaming white linen, embroidered insets, was spread lavishly with food. Fanny, removing herself as soon as possible from the room where the old Marchesa was, stood there unashamedly stuffing herself. It was in there that Edwina met Ersilia and her husband – a small balding man, evidently forty but looking fifty. Ersilia, very pregnant and nibbling a tiny cake covered in pink sugar, talked to Edwina of hunting. She had the passion, she said, from her mother who was now no longer interested. She had invitations to hunt in England which soon she would take up: 'I wait for a child. But after that . . .' They spoke of Edwina's mother: 'Adelina has told me – she also has the same passion . . . ah, the *tramontana*, that wind – and a fine winter morning, and a good horse, a fine horse . . .'

It was still only half past five. Taddeo had told them: 'It's not necessary to stay too long. You pay your respects to Nonnina of course, then I introduce you perhaps to someone interesting –'

But before this could happen Donna Laura brought the message that Edwina was expected to sit with Marchesa Vittoria. 'She ask you –' She corrected herself: 'She command you –'

The old Marchesa, speaking French, English or Italian, talked with a succession of people: Edwina was bewildered. On each occasion she was introduced. The name of Adelina arose frequently. Uncle Frederick, who'd been there at the beginning, was there again for the last half-hour. The old Marchesa told him: 'Next week Edwina will play the piano.' To another guest, the elderly attaché at the British Embassy, she said: 'Perhaps you can come in next Sunday to meet a few friends *en intimité*? It is possible that she will play for us then.' She spoke as if Edwina were not there. Later, Edwina heard her say in French: 'She is not a beauty. But with care and attention perhaps an *élégante* . . . ?'

'Stefano is not here yet,' Taddeo said, 'but I have the key – Today we visit the gallery. Edwina – you haven't said yet what you thought of yesterday? You are a great success with Nonnina – '

'*I'm* not,' said Fanny.

Taddeo said in a teasing voice, 'You don't know how to butter her – is that the word?' But when Edwina, interrupting indignantly, said: 'I don't do anything special,' he was all penitence. 'I didn't mean – she *likes* you, she is fond. It's only natural. And when she likes, she likes very much.'

'And when she dislikes – ' Fanny began, but Taddeo, hurrying ahead, didn't hear.

'First, more frescoes. I *think* Lanfranco. As we have in some other rooms. Here, two pictures. When we have our earthquake – nineteen hundred fifteen – only little here of course and early before breakfast, in the Abruzzi it was so big – two pictures have fallen. A little damage, you see, to the frames . . .' He held a candelabra to each painting. Chandeliers hung from the ceiling the length of the gallery. There was no electric light. Stefano, who had just joined them, came up behind as Taddeo continued: 'I hope you see well enough. It's Nonnina who has said we don't change the light. Not in her lifetime. Of course after she is dead my father – or at least later certainly Stefano will – '

Stefano interrupted in a cold voice. '*I* decide what I will do.'

'Bully for you – ' Taddeo said lightly. Edwina thought Stefano was going to say something else, but the exchange was arrested. They had come upon the Pope. Paschal III. He was very ordinary, and any resemblance to the family impossible to see; disappointing too, because no cruelty, no arrogance. Nor piety either.

But yes, here and there were faces which glimpsed in the

light of the candles made Edwina gasp almost with recognition: Ersilia's eyes with their fierce curved brows, Taddeo's mouth and sharp chin above an ornate ruff, again and again Stefano's high-bridged nose and almost hooded eyes. An eighteenth-century Eugenio – Simple-mindedness had visited the family before.

'This one on the horse, it is by Velasquez, I think . . .'

'I shall be the guide,' Stefano said, reaching for the candelabra.

'But of course, old boy,' said Taddeo. Then to Edwina: 'He got out of bed upside down. Do you still say "old boy", by the way? I like better "chap". Of course, my dear chap,' he said now to Stefano.

'Oh, be friends,' said Edwina. She thought of herself and Cora. 'For you, yes,' Taddeo said, touching her. They had come to a big ebony cabinet almost covered with ivory panels carved with tiny figures and trees. She had to peer to see the detail. Fanny beside her, leaning forward, bumped against Stefano. 'You knocked into me,' she said to him indignantly: 'You knocked me just then –'

'I beg your pardon.'

'Of course I don't mind – how assy. I rather liked it.' She paused and then she said in a husky voice. 'Do it again, would you?' Stefano coloured. In the candlelight Edwina felt rather than saw his flush. He said: 'This panel here which is painted is the Devil, many devils. I am always afraid, as a child. I had then the key, you understand, to come down –'

Edwina thought that she too would not like to be down here alone. The devils in the dark cracked paint were traditionally gleeful and forked of tail, but standing on the cold marble floor she was reminded suddenly of Clare's story that far-away stormy night: the poor Ampleforth boy and the Black Thing.

She shivered. Taddeo said suddenly, as if part of, ahead of her thoughts: 'And we must show you too where we are all buried – where *we* shall be buried . . .'

Fountains. The Antici-Montani, playing in the courtyard,

two in 'the garden of our friends', and again and again, where Florence had seemed to her a city of bells, Rome was a city of fountains. Not only the expected Trevi and Tritone and Barcaccia, but all the little ones which in gardens, streets, squares would suddenly surprise her. She would have liked to walk about on her own. Occasionally she was able to wander with Uncle Frederick: outings for just the two of them, without any pre-arranged plan. He showed great concern then that she should be enjoying herself in Rome. 'A lifetime here is not long enough . . .' He seemed very interested in her opinion of the family. He said he had questioned the wisdom of bringing Fanny here. 'I have been thinking . . .' But he never said what he'd thought.

Fanny had now met Annette's brother. He'd been seen painting again one time when Edwina had not been of the party. He'd recognized Fanny at once. With his aunt and some cousins he was living in a house and studio in the Via Margutta until October. She said she hadn't spoken for too long because Stefano had become impatient, but she had his card and they were going to be in touch. 'Isn't life exciting?' she cried.

Although she felt guilty afterwards, sometimes Edwina would think simply: I wish you hadn't come, hearing yet again at some meal an account of cleaning out sheep's hooves, the over-animated laugh, the gushing enthusiasm. She and Taddeo seemed to suffer from a twin complaint (although in him it didn't irritate her). Neither knew when to stop. Again and again Taddeo would make jokes at Eugenio's expense, and the old Marchesa, who for Fanny merely looked her disapproval, would drum her forefinger three times. And then always, his charming apology: 'Nonnina, sorry – you're not *cross*?'

A woman in a turban with a long cigarette-holder pushed past, her elbow catching Edwina's rib. She didn't notice. Edwina did.

'Manners!' said the man standing near Edwina's chair. 'I am ashamed. Fortunately she doesn't come into my *ambiente*

– but the people who the dear Principessa . . .'

Edwina agreed. It seemed simpler. She didn't know with whom she was speaking but as she hadn't heard when she should, she felt it was too late to ask. Dressed in white she had been sitting half an hour now on one of the many little gilt chairs round the wall of the long high room. She had had to curtsy to the quite terrifying figure of the Princess: late seventies and heavily made-up, raddled almost, gnarled, bejewelled, enthroned. Uncle Frederick wasn't there; he was already engaged. She had lost Stefano and Taddeo, and others of the family. Established on the little gilt chair it seemed that she must receive whoever came into her orbit.

'Lady Rodd, the wife of your Ambassador – a Beneficenza at the Eliseo, I think. Scenes from Cleopatra – You were not there then? So very well attended, you see . . .' Her companion was pleased with his English so that she supposed he might stay a long time. Too long. He had a manner as if he would like to catch her out – his confident domed forehead at war with his drooping moustache.

'You are only here some *weeks*? Antici-Montani – This family is most interesting. But misfortunate. They have this, I think, which often happens in old families. It is not pretty, naturally. But Stefano he must marry soon, he is one of the best *partis* in Rome. *Many* are interested – I can even now point to you some . . .'

Edwina realized with relief she was not going to have to talk about herself. She sipped at a small yellow drink she had taken from a tray.

'And it is fortunate – not all are so lucky – that he and Taddeo, that they are not killed in the War.'

Edwina said yes, indeed. 'I think that would have meant the end of the family.'

'What end of the family?' He leaned towards her a little, his moustache dampened. 'Eugenio, he of course would marry. It would be arranged. After all it is only necessary he is able to do as the animals – you understand me? Excuse me that I am frank. Naturally, there is the fear always that it may happen again . . .'

A string quartet in the next room could be heard faintly above the hubbub of voices. Her companion had tired now of the Antici-Montani. Cleaning out his earhole with his little finger, he said: 'I am very interested by Shakespeare – you are acquainted with his works? I think you will be interested to learn that he is not the author of his plays. It is the Count of Derby who has written everything. We have a very good book about this just these last days. The *tema* is – '

'Fee fi fo fum, I hear English. And I'm jolly well going to interrupt – ' The voice was booming, the tone joyful and enthusiastic. She was a very large woman: Edwina's companion seemed to shrivel beside her. 'I couldn't resist when I heard. My dear, I know everybody in Rome – and of course you, my dear Alfredo – But who's *this*? I thought I knew all the English . . .'

Edwina was explained, and the woman, who turned out to be a maiden lady called Dora Norrington, hooted with pleasure. 'Such a beautiful home. Some of these palaces are so lovely, Barberini, Pamfili, Colonna . . .' She seemed to be all bust: a platform so that Edwina couldn't really see the remainder. That and her enormously thick lips defied inattention.

'My dear, I must show you English Rome. How long are you here? You don't know the English Tea-Rooms – Babington's? Really? That is a *must*. And poor dear little Keats's house – "Beauty is truth, truth beauty" . . .'

The little gilt chair looked scarcely big enough for her frame. She held her head high and very rigid – necessary perhaps to support the bust? Words and yet more words gushed forth: 'The War – you look too young. I hope, my dear, you were too young to do anything – *my* War work – I had a very busy War. A friend to the Tommies here in Rome. And such *fun*! I'd worried, you see, about these boys stranded sometimes two, three days, and *no* idea of language or food or where to get a shave. The poor darlings. So *every* day, winter and summer, I was down at that station. I took them over completely – "Auntie Dora" they christened me, my dear. Can you imagine? The word was passed round –

Of course I hadn't heard here of the Defence of the Realm Act so I didn't know what a household word "Dora" was – it was all really *very* jolly and touching . . .' On and on. 'Alfredo' had long since disappeared. '. . . Some people of course, have been doing excellent work for *cats*. Your Italian, my dear, is *not* good with animals . . .'

Edwina, looking out into the throng, prayed silently: Oh Taddeo, Oh Stefano, come and rescue me.

They were a foursome. Walking in front, Marchesa Vittoria and Father Gomboli, the chaplain, who at meals was usually silent: he spoke no English and little French. (Often he looked as if he *might* say something, pressing and unpressing his hands as if to pray. But '*Dunque* . . .' or perhaps '*Insomma* . . .' would be all the results.) With his measured step he seemed to have some difficulty now in adjusting himself to the old Marchesa's slow tread. Behind them came Edwina and the young Marchesa. Slowly the procession made its way down the corridor. It was just after midday.

A little scream, high-pitched. The old Marchesa halted. Round the corner, hair coming unpinned, falling in an auburn mass over her face, hurtled Fanny. She stopped short. A tiny 'Oh!' and a giggle.

'Hide and seek, you see,' she said in a little voice, as Taddeo, breathless, stopping only with difficulty, followed her. He put both hands up in a gesture of contrition, smiling. Then with a shrug of his shoulders he blew a kiss to his grandmother and was gone.

They were both gone. The old Marchesa's face had settled into heavy lines of disapproval. Father Gomboli, turning, said something to her quickly – Edwina caught the word '*bambini*', one of the few words she knew. Then in what was obviously meant to be reassuring tones, he added slowly: '*Giocanna ancora a nascondersi* . . .' The Marchesa replied angrily: '*A me sembra invece che giochino a ritrovarsi* –' She began to walk on.

The young Marchesa had not moved. She was looking straight ahead, staring. Edwina turned to her. 'What did they say?' She felt it suddenly to be of importance.

'He has said they are only children, they still play at hiding themselves, but my mother-in-law says no, to her she thinks rather they play at finding each the other – I cannot make it very clear.' She looked ill at ease. The light, shining on her face, emphasized the dark growth, thicker than Edwina had realized, on her upper lip.

'Sometimes she is displeased, you understand. She has plans for them all, for all our children. Stefano – ' she broke off. 'Where is Stefano?' she asked anxiously. 'He said – ' She put her hand to her forehead: 'He tells me nothing.'

'Who is this beautiful woman?'

Edwina glanced quickly at the date beneath the photograph. May 1859. The old Marchesa's finger stabbed at the picture. 'Tell me, who is she?'

'You,' Edwina said. And certainly, in spite of the preposterous dress and the fixed almost astonished face, there was indeed a dark beauty. But looking now at the heavy folds of facial skin, the bloodshot eyes ringed by deep dark circles, the scant elaborately waved hair – she could not take her mind back sixty years. The heavy leather album stayed open at that page. Below was a wedding group. A taller, straighter-haired Stefano stood proudly beside his bride. January 1860. An immense entourage surrounded them. The old Marchesa pointed to a gentle-looking girl whose head hung forward. 'That is Concetta, the mother of Adelina.' She paused: 'You like to see these? This marriage it was a great affair. You see, from two such big families – and we also have been many many years in Rome – there is much wealth. Many estates. But the times were not happy, you understand. Only some years and Rome was quite changed. This business of a king – we are naturally Blacks. Some they are more extreme – The Lancellotti, this family they have shut the front door so it cannot open. To remind of the Pope who is prisoner. When they have a ball – even then, all must go in at the side . . . And the city also, that is quite spoilt – these roads they have made. The new Rome. Everything goes then – Farnesini

Pine, Villa Massimo Negroni, and so many, so many, destroyed.' For a moment she sat quite still, lips pursed, eyes far away. Then turning a page: 'Here you see Gelasio, who now is Marchese – this baby with the hat. He was not of course the best – Niccolo here and Leone, both are better – But he is the first. Here is another, here he looks before he is married – '

Edwina stared at the portrait. In a dapper way, with his wet eyes and look of one who needed protecting, mothering, the present Marchese seemed to have an attraction which he certainly didn't possess now. 'So,' the old Marchesa remarked. 'We have then this nonsense. They are cousins and they meet at a family party – or perhaps hunting? They meet and she is good then, how she was looking. And she, she is blind with love. She *will* have him. There is all this – nonsense. My husband is weak – he allows it. It was only to wait and the passion goes. Something more *convenable* is arranged. But *no*!' She drummed three times on the page. 'No! So we have this fine boy that you see each day at the table, who cannot eat properly, who is thinking nothing – An animal has come into the family.' She was silent for several moments. *'Mah!'* She stared ahead at the firescreen, wrinkled lips pressed together. *'Mah!'*

Then: 'This time, this marriage, we leave Rome.' Her finger drummed on the open page. 'This time – we leave Italy.'

'My word,' Taddeo said, coming up behind her, 'my word if I catch you bending – '

She said laughing, 'Oh Taddeo dear, where do you *learn* these expressions?'

'But I told you – ' He looked hurt. 'Don't you remember when I say things?' She shook her head, laughing at him still. They stood together for a moment in the late afternoon sun. She could feel his restlessness. He reached out and caught hold of her hand. His own was cool and firm. 'Now you tell *me* something.'

'What?'

'Why you are always so sad?'

'Taddeo, I'm not sad – I laugh a lot. You know I do.'

'No, why you are sad even when you laugh?' He whispered in her ear: 'You tell Taddeo. I promise I won't say. Boy scout's honour. You love some Englishman? They don't let you marry someone? What is it – you *tell* me . . .'

She thought for a moment, standing in the gardens of the villa, that she might; that she could tell him everything. In a glance she saw it all. That she could say about even the walk across to Bay.

'But first I tell you something. Here you walk very carefully. These flowers . . .' But already it was too late: water sprayed up from the bed where she had trod, wetting skirt, sleeves. It missed her face. She laughed, shaky with relief that she had told him nothing. 'You might have *said* – '

'I shall just say to you – they're a joke, you see. But when we want to find them we don't. I know only they're somewhere here about. In this villa, you see, there lived an Antici-Montani with a sense of humour . . .'

They had arrived in the middle of the day, motoring over from Rome, the four of them accompanied by Donna Laura. Uncle Frederick was spending three days at Villa D'Este with relations of Adelina's. Stefano had needed to come to this villa, as he did quite often, on behalf of his father. The Marchese had been confined to his room for over a week now. Although he had not after all succumbed to Spanish 'flu he had contracted something unpleasant of his own. Various reports filtered through: some days it was his liver, others his throat, and yet again his legs. The old Marchesa remarked with asperity that the trouble was 'here' – tapping her forehead lightly and with dignity.

The drive, past high walls covered in roses and wisteria, on through olive groves – purple-black berries, silvery foliage gleaming – had enchanted Edwina. They were to stay the night. She felt that this was what she had wanted, to get away from the palace. She had not realized it was so oppressive, feeling now a sudden sense of freedom from the rolling eyes of Eugenio, Father Gomboli and his '*insomma*', the young Marchesa's nervy unhappiness. But most of all perhaps from the interest of the old Marchesa. Morning and evening she was watched, often discussed, she knew, occasionally quizzed. A horrible idea had come to her a few days ago – but she had dismissed it as preposterous.

Fanny of course was not to be escaped. But for the last few days she had been gentler and even a little quieter: easy too, and disposed to find everybody and everything perfect. She told Edwina that she had heard Taddeo's head wound was worse than everyone thought, and that he might not live to be old – or even stay as he was. 'His mother told me. The old dragon knows, naturally, but she doesn't want to admit it. That's why she always forgives him everything.'

Fanny was with Stefano on the terrace when she and Taddeo joined them. The ilex trees threw dark shadows. The garden just below was formal, the flowerbeds – joke sprays and all – elaborately shaped. A little further on it changed to half-wild, tangled bushes of perpetually flowering roses. *'Le rose di ogni mese'*, Stefano called them. They drank a wine from the estate: white, sparkling. Fanny said, stretching luxuriously: 'I've had this wonderful idea of staying on in Rome – '

'But of course,' interrupted Taddeo, 'you stay to marry me. Naturally. That's all arranged.'

Fanny dimpled. Edwina said, 'Marry *me*, so that I don't have to leave Rome either.'

Stefano said, 'He will marry you both – he is quite capable. What do you call this, that you mustn't do?'

'Bigamy,' Edwina said.

'He does bigamy easily. He is like that – '

Taddeo said, only half-laughing, 'What's this, always bad about *me*? And I'm so good. I was always the good one. I gave my toys to Eugenio when he was already twelve and I knew that he would break them. And it was so. Also, I'm nice to Nonnina always. Fanny, Edwina – defend me – '

'You're perfect,' said Edwina.

'You see, Stefano, that I'm thought well of – the cat's whiskers perhaps – somewhere. It is you, Stefano, with the temper. He had a temper then like thunder – he was not always so pleasant. And also – '

Fanny interrupted: 'That's not fair,' and Stefano added, 'It's not just at all. We speak of perhaps ten, fifteen years ago – ' His voice was quite light, but his face was set.

Taddeo said gaily, 'I marry *Cora*, I think. As soon as I'm in England and this nuisance with the head is arranged, I shall go everywhere I am invited, and of course I meet her.' Edwina, glad of the change of subject, told him that her Aunt Josephine had already written. Cora and Mother were in London and apparently enjoying themselves.

'I shall find my way about. Already I have so many introductions. She will certainly wish to marry me when she sees my great beauty and that I'm the youngest son of a great house.'

'What a snob,' said Fanny.

Edwina agreed, teasing him. He was pleased, as if they had ruffled his hair playfully. But Stefano's face – turned now to greet Donna Laura as she joined them on the terrace – was still dark.

They ate some orange-yellow mushrooms, marinated, called *ovoli*, pasta with a green sauce, sour-sweet duck with pine-nuts, and a rich but very light fresh cherry pudding with rum and lemons. The meal was late and leisurely. A neighbour had been invited, a bachelor also – a little older than Stefano. He had lived in the area all his life. With his receding hair, short strong frame and dark lively eyes, he attracted Edwina's attention. He was very assured: of himself, his home, his life, how everything would be. He spoke easily, in excellent English. When Fanny talked he paid her courteous attention. But with Edwina he not only asked questions, he also watched as she answered. His eyes roamed over her unconsciously it seemed. She felt suddenly a blend of gratitude – as if by doing this he had somehow made her different. Excitement too, as if in a darkened room the lights had been summarily lit. Fed by admiration her mood grew, so that, animated, she knew she looked well.

The atmosphere was such that even Donna Laura, separated from her mother, came a little out of her shell. Eating an orange, nervously dipping in the fingerbowl with its small floating flower, she talked to Stefano of the estate. Her questions showed that she knew nothing of it, nor perhaps of any of the others. She told Edwina in halting English: 'I like our little *villino* in Forte dei Marmi . . .'

The talk had drifted on to politics, had settled there uneasily. Fanny, who knew little of the situation, had the most to say, it seemed to Edwina. She had become quite excited. They were speaking of Fiume and D'Annunzio and the outrageous piratical exploits of his *uscocchi*. She said, 'I should just like to *see* him – '

'Ah now,' said Taddeo, 'now I can use such a good word. He is a bounder. No doubt of this.'

Fanny said, 'But he looks a dear little man – '

'Not so.'

Stefano remarked, 'Maddalena, she met him some times. She became of a different opinion. It is the *voice*, I think.'

Donna Laura said, 'All is disgusting.' But his charm was agreed upon. 'Magnetism, I think you call it,' Taddeo said. 'That is all. A gift from God, which of course I have – Oodles of it.'

'What are oodles?' Angelo asked.

'What *are* oodles?' Edwina asked helplessly. 'I don't know. Lots, a lot . . .'

Taddeo was excitable again. Fanny was pulling restlessly at the pearls round her neck. She was wearing the Fortuny frock. She wore it whenever possible. Beside it everything of Edwina's looked either dowdy or excessively *jeune fille*. A few days ago the old Marchesa had surprised and touched her by saying, 'I arrange, I think, that we buy you such a frock as Frances has. It has become necessary . . .'

They must dance. There was no question about it, Taddeo said, arranging everything, looking out records ('everything here is old hat'), finding a tango and dancing it with Fanny in a frenetic showing-off manner. Donna Laura watched with her hands on her lap and an air of disapproval. Stefano insisted that *he* should dance with Fanny next: he was not very good and she stumbled and clung to him at one point. She was laughing almost continually. Edwina was swept round by Taddeo. He smelt clean and scented but had a frailty almost about him. His clasp was gentle as when he had held her hand outside. He was attractive without attracting her – She thought, I would like him for a brother, and was taken up short, sweating, shaking, thinking: Uncle Frederick, Mother. Coming out of hiding, the memory hurtled towards her heart. The word brother, it would no longer do. But then because it was an easy evening, she thought, laughing at something he said, 'cousin', that will do instead.

She would have liked to dance with Stefano. She danced well (Madame Lambert and Cecil had perhaps been more successful than they realized) and thought that she could probably make him appear good too. Also, she felt sorry for him because he had less charm than Taddeo and was perhaps a difficult character.

Angelo, who'd shown little interest in the dancing, asked her for the next, a one-step. Taddeo and Fanny were together again, showing off, Stefano busying himself with the gramophone. Angelo danced with a competent ease, but his attention seemed more on talking to her. They continued the conversation they had had while sitting out. Smiling, lifting his eyebrows at Fanny and Taddeo doing a showy variation of the step, he said: 'I am in Rome next month. I hope I see you then?'

'We'll have left, we have to go back –'

'It's for another time perhaps . . .' There was an easy feeling about it all. If I wished, she thought, I could take this further. And because he so frankly admired her, she thought: it could be quite easy after all, to be alive again.

'That Angelo what's-his-name was boring,' Fanny said. 'Heavens – was he. Usually I like older men but this time

– did I tell you that Prince in Venice, he distinctly felt for my foot under the table – I mean, I couldn't have been mistaken.'

'Perhaps he'll follow you here and marry you,' said Edwina tiredly, suppressing a yawn.

Fanny said quite seriously, 'He's already married as a matter of fact.' She looked round the bedroom: 'You always get a better room than me.' She tapped her foot: '*Don* Stefano, *Don* Taddeo. I never realized, it means "Lord" – Lord Stefano! I got terribly excited when I thought of that the other day . . .'

Edwina wanted to say, 'Oh, go to bed.' Then, suddenly remembering, she said: 'Whatever's this about staying on in Rome?'

'Oh, it's quite serious – I've already told Taddeo, and Stefano. I was going to surprise you and Uncle Frederick. Annette's brother – I've been invited to join the family party. I spent a morning last week with them while you were closeted with the old dragon and it was all arranged. They may go up into the mountains if it gets very hot but the plan is that I stay with them for as long as I want – I thought even of learning some Italian. Mainly I'll be painting and sketching. I've written express to Marmee. I don't think for a moment they'll say "no" – they're worried anyway I'll go off when I'm twenty-one. Now that I know what I know . . . In any case they approve of Annette's family and all that. The aunt's writing too. You don't *mind*?'

Edwina shook her head. 'No, nice for you.' She yawned again. Fanny, stretching, tossed back her unpinned hair: 'I'm thinking seriously of getting it bobbed.' When Edwina, yawning once more, didn't take it up, she moved restlessly, kicking her foot against an oak coffer near the chair.

'Oh,' she said, 'I feel so frantic sometimes, so – I don't know, *pent up* inside me. I feel almost, sometimes, as if I could murder someone . . .'

In her dream she hurried down the long corridors. This figure of eight – no way out. Was she hiding, or seeking?

Certainly she had lost something. Then, running behind her, steps.

She was in a *salotto*, and from behind a gilt screen Stefano appeared suddenly. He said, 'I've been sent to catch you,' and took hold of her wrists. He pulled her towards him, close, so that they were one, pressed from head to toe. It seemed pointless to resist – wrong even. The easy fit surprised her. In her dream she knew she dreamed, but the rightness continued. They didn't speak (indeed how could they?).

And then the scene changed, abruptly, as only in dreams. She heard a bell tolling. She moved away at once, turning to where the breakers, the great white horses could be seen rearing and crashing out in the bay.

Ben was sitting in a coble drawn up in the Dock. He smiled at her. 'I didn't drown.' Arms outstretched, she wanted to rush to him. Her lips, stiff with joy, would not speak. Then she saw that he was surrounded by people. Of course, she thought, they're all here, they've all come to hear the good news. Ben's mother, Damaris, standing beside Edwina, put an arm round her shoulder. Edwina asked: 'Were you angry – about us?' But without looking at her: 'It's *known* . . .' she said only.

Edwina turned back to the boat. It was empty. She was alone, the sea grey and frothy rushing up the Wayfoot. She stood there hearing the low moaning sound she was making. With clenched fists she hit her head. The sense of loss. It was as fresh as yesterday.

When she woke, tears were streaming down her face. The linen sheet was screwed up, damp, where she had been clutching it.

What have I done? she thought, half awake, half asleep still. What have I done?

Taddeo, resplendent in uniform, sword, helmet, of the Noble Guard. It would be his duty to assist at the Pope's deathbed. Edwina wondered sadly whether indeed Benedict would be the first to go? He should have attended at the Vatican more often but hadn't always been thought well enough –

or was it calm enough? It was hard to imagine him for hours on end not talking, not teasing, not cheeking passing Cardinals, Ambassadors, Prime Ministers.

But it was through the family of course that both she and Fanny sat always in privileged positions at every religious ceremony, had effortlessly the best views, the least discomfort. It was all so simply in the very air they breathed, so accustomed a part of life that it was never discussed.

And yet she'd thought she would find the pomp, the beauty of religious Rome, more deeply moving. She found it only exciting. Emotions written on water. It was as if in the old split tug-of-war she had once felt between Bay and the convent, it was Bay after all that had won. She would think suddenly, remember that once she'd feared she might become a nun, might have to become a nun, and that it was Fanny who had rescued her (and for this she could, did feel gratitude). It all seemed so long ago. She took her religion perhaps more from Mother, on whom it seemed to sit very lightly and for a lot of the time was probably irrelevant. When she had imagined (no, known for certain) that she and Ben had only to live happily ever after, their different religions had seemed to her no problem. She had failed to think of them at all.

A letter came for Fanny: everything was in order. They were delighted at this wonderful opportunity for her – A large sum of money would be telegraphed and meanwhile could she try and arrange some formal art lessons to draw full benefit from her time in Italy? She said to Edwina: 'Don't talk to me about Uncle Clive, will you? I never want his name mentioned. Even in passing.'

Time was what passed – Only a few days to Taddeo's departure. On the last Wednesday, Annette's brother, aunt and cousins were invited to the old Marchesa's At Home. By accident or design they managed to avoid meeting their hostess at all. The old Marchesa made no comment: Edwina, who'd been kept by her side the whole afternoon, didn't meet them either.

Although she spent part of every day now with the old Marchesa – such a habit now that no one remarked on it at all (except perhaps Fanny: 'How *could* you?') – she had been lately playing the piano every morning for an hour or two. It had become accepted. Occasionally in the evenings she would play for everyone, usually after Uncle Frederick had sung. The old Marchesa approved of this: she would stop her game of patience to listen. The others seemed uninterested (it was often the occasion for Eugenio to perform some of his worst facial contortions) although Stefano, if there, would come over to the piano. There seemed to be something about her when she played which aroused his admiration. It was the nearest thing to a bond. Once they laughed together over Adelina's singing – Uncle Frederick safely out of earshot. He showed more than a nodding acquaintance with what she played, 'I learned as a boy, some years,' but rather as something he took for granted – as it might be art for another. When, in talking, they moved from pieces to players, he lost interest.

Uncle Frederick, although pleased that she was playing regularly again, was guarded, non-committal about the proposed studying in Paris – his idea in the first place. Franz had understood that he would arrange it all for not later than the autumn. 'Ah yes,' was what he said, when not very pressingly (it was only occasionally she could feel the desire, the energy and the enthusiasm for it) she reminded him of it, 'Ah yes, of course,' and then the subject would go again. Her fault, she thought. It was sometimes as if the horrible habit of the last hopeless two years, the struggle to cure Mother, had sapped something. She didn't want particularly to do it – believed only that she *would* want it when she got it.

But music was still her greatest bond with him. To celebrate nothing in particular he took her one evening to the Costanzi to hear Debussy's *Pelléas and Melisande* ('the critics say it has no leit-motiv and many other deficiencies but I would value your opinion'), and afterwards, supper at the Massimo D'Azeglio in the Via Cavour. He told her then that he had written to Mother – several days ago now – suggesting that she, too, stay on in Rome.

'I have to be back in Florence, but you have nothing to

hurry to Yorkshire for. Josephine misses you, naturally – but she is more than capable.' It was the Marchesa Vittoria, he said, who had suggested it: Fanny's staying on had made it all quite simple.

'She has a special affection for you . . .' He fingered the fern which stood with two pale yellow roses on their table – the narrow-stemmed vase wobbled. 'I think she would like – ' but he took the subject no further. They talked instead of a letter he'd had from Mother, crossing with his, full of Cora's successes – And hers too. She had befriended a White Russian, was taking him everywhere, helping him to accustom himself to English life. 'Andrei thinks this, that . . .' Later in the summer he would be coming to stay in Yorkshire.

Uncle Frederick said, 'It seems the most wonderful thing that, God willing, she is going to be all right.' He said it benevolently, tiredly. She avoided his eyes.

Taddeo, in a great state of excitement, left for England. The next day Fanny, even more excited if possible, moved out – a week earlier than planned. 'We'll meet,' she told Edwina, 'we'll *keep* meeting.' She seemed on top of the world. 'I love to think of notes from me, being brought in to you on silver salvers . . .'

It felt very quiet after they had left. Stefano was away all that day. In only another week Uncle Frederick would be gone. She realized that she had never actually been asked if she wanted to stay on. The old Marchesa had referred to it only as a fact. 'I am glad to hear what Frederick tells me . . .' Edwina thought: Since I don't really want to be anywhere, I might as well be here. Italy, Rome was where she had become the most nearly alive. And for her the rather oppressive feel of the palace had come to be, after only a few weeks, the natural state of affairs. When she thought about it – how could it be worse than home?

The pudding was a brilliant confection. Rich dark chocolate, studded with flaked almonds, laced with rum-flavoured cream, somewhere between a mousse and a cake, it sat on the serving platter wielded so skilfully by Norberto. Edwina, the spoon slipping as she took a helping – a spot falling on to Norberto's glove was taken back to the embarrassments of childhood (and perhaps of her second day at the palace when in an attempt to help herself neatly to spaghetti, she had been left continually with unfinished strands, so that she had taken more and more and more . . .)

But no one had noticed this mishap. The old Marchesa, who had taken a substantial helping, was now concentrating on it. Eugenio, next to Edwina today, had just been served and sat, a beatific smile on his face, spooning in the dark luscious mixture. Father Gomboli took a helping and attacked it with gusto.

Stefano was absent. Donna Laura remarked: 'I wonder how is our dear Taddeo on his voyage?' She said it devoutly, as of a martyr on his way to the stake.

'Comfortable, I imagine,' said her mother.

They spoke English still out of courtesy to Edwina. She felt for that reason that she must be part of the conversation. Although her remarks were often, she thought, stupider even than Donna Laura's, they were treated always with respect by the old Marchesa. 'Ah, you think so, Edwina?' Or, 'That is *most* interesting – '

The Marchese, at last risen from his sick bed, dabbed at his mouth with his napkin. He ate in small, timid mouthfuls, watched anxiously by his wife. Occasionally he put his hand to his forehead.

Norberto was passing the pudding round a second time. Edwina refused, but Eugenio on her left turned and snatched at the serving spoon. Instantly alert the old Marchesa said loudly: 'No!' banging with the palm of her hand on the table. (Plainly fingers were insufficient here.) But Eugenio continued to hold tight, the spoon buried deep in the pudding. Norberto stood there uncomfortably.

'There is no question,' said the old Marchesa. 'Angela, speak to him, please!' The young Marchesa said, a little nervously, 'It is not good, Eugenio – '

'I take,' he announced triumphantly. He did indeed take. His plate was covered completely, piled high. On the serving dish only a small portion remained, sad and limp.

'This I *will not* tolerate,' said the old Marchesa. 'His liver. Chocolate. It is far too rich.' She said something swiftly to Norberto.

'Norberto will remove his plate.' Eugenio clung tightly as Norberto gave a token tug, and then stopped. Father Gomboli closed his eyes.

'I like,' declared Eugenio, his teeth clenched. 'I want.' That the whole affair should be conducted in English (for her benefit) seemed to Edwina the height of absurdity. She noticed then that the old Marchesa was signalling to her, eyebrows raised. 'Edwina – you.'

Edwina put out a hand boldly. 'Let me have some, Eugenio – ' In answer, he upturned the plate in one grand gesture, covering her hand, her cuff, the white linen of the table. Nuts stuck out incongruously from the smeared dark mess.

He stood up. He was very flushed, his cheeks shining, eyes almost popping. He looked at once a child and an old man. He held his napkin in his hand, waving it like a banner, 'I go,' he declared.

'Yes, it is better that you go,' the old Marchesa said.

He strutted out, still waving the napkin. Norberto, accompanied by two maids, arrived with a towel, damp cloths and a basin of warm water.

The old Marchesa did not speak. She behaved as if nothing had happened. Father Gomboli had opened his eyes again. Donna Laura, clearing her throat, remarked that 'dear Taddeo is perhaps, who knows, very seasick today?'

'Ten on the nine, now he is free . . . Sit down, please. You excuse me . . . There is the eight, and the Queen – no! *Yes.* Now the King, and here is almost success. So . . . We stop. Tomorrow I try Réussite . . .'

Edwina was used to interrupting the interminable games of patience with which the old Marchesa whiled away the long hours of her remaining life. Occasionally, as now, some small triumph, aided a little by cheating, would cause her to go on playing after Edwina's arrival.

'And now you tell me how you shall spend today. This afternoon, what are the plans? Tomorrow you and I drive together, we visit a good friend of mine . . .' She rose slowly from the card table. 'You are not unhappy without Frances? Frederick you still have. That is good. And Stefano – do you see sometimes a little more of Stefano?'

'He's out a lot,' Edwina said. 'I think he's often rather busy – '

'Certainly he must see to much. He has now responsibility. His father, Gelasio, again he is ill. That is how it is with him . . . And *she* – she must spend her time always with an invalid. What sort of life is this? But *"Comme on fait son lit on se couche"* – she would have him. It was all this nonsense of *love*. *Convenienza*, that is the only real way for marriage.' She turned to Edwina: 'Is not that so?'

'No, it isn't. Lots and lots of people fall in love, and marry and live happily ever after – '

'You shall give me the name of *one*, Edwina.' Pause. 'Ah, you are silent. You think. But you know of course that I am right. You must only think what is it that happens? This business of love. They are happy one year, two years – perhaps three. And then? It is the same as if there has been no love, except that it is more worse, because there was not choosing to suit. Now they have nothing. What a foolishness . . .'

Abruptly she changed the subject. Resting her chin on hands clasped around her stick, she said: 'Has Frederick spoken to you – on a certain matter?' Edwina said 'No, not really,' and her manner changed again. *'Mah!'* she said twice into the silence.

Edwina was told to ring for some wine. While they were drinking: 'I am very fond of you, Edwina. Frederick naturally has told me many things. He has described to me such a girl as I admire. He is proud also of your great gift.' She paused. 'I would like to ask if you have put all of your heart there?'

Edwina was taken aback. She looked down at her glass.

In a rush she thought of Ben: the twist, the jab. 'No. Not all – '

'Frederick, you see, has spoken of you always as one who – He and Adelina, you understand, it has been very happy. My niece, I was greatly concerned, naturally. A good match – strange, but good, I think it has suited both.' She paused again. 'And you see, Italian and English, two such different bloods – and yet they have come together very well. Each perhaps have what the other have not.'

There was silence for a few moments. A small ormolu clock struck midday.

'And you, Edwina – have you thought ever how it would be if you, also, marry someone who is not English?'

'Antico Caffè Greco,' it said outside. Next door she'd noticed that they sold pianos. She would have liked to go in there. Stefano said: 'We wait only a little. Uncle Frederick has perhaps forgotten. When he is lunching out, you know – ' he smiled affectionately. Then, his attention on Edwina: 'I had described already the table. We sit, you see, underneath a picture of Hans Andersen – where it is written that he stayed here.'

He glanced again towards the fore part of the café. 'I think we will not wait.'

She felt suddenly then, became convinced that he never thought Uncle Frederick would come, that perhaps it had been arranged that Uncle Frederick should *not* come. She saw it as some sort of trap, or test. Perhaps the old Marchesa had commanded, 'Now you sit alone with her, and say something.' Even perhaps, 'Will you marry me?' For it would be not only her idea – but her order also. And (Edwina marvelled) because it was her order, he would of course obey.

But it was not to decide now, this afternoon. That she herself could manage the task of being his wife, she had no doubts – she had merely to learn: the Marchesa Vittoria would at every step guide her, groom her. All these excursions into society, this waiting upon and attendance at the Wednesdays, what else had it been for?

Here at last – she had thought this last night – was something definite, a sacrifice almost, something definite that she could do with her life: to help others, to repair some of the mess she had made so far. Gradually an idea which had seemed at first preposterous, if not impossible, had come to appear tolerable. She could make so many people happy – the names ran through her mind. All that had been wrong, made right. How little, she thought, I've loved God.

'It's certain now he is not coming. You take coffee, of course?'

(Why did God make you? God made me to know Him, love Him and serve Him in this world, and to be happy with Him for ever in the next.) They ate small florentines, wavy lines down their dark chocolate backs, front studded with cherries and almonds. The coffee came in small cups. Stefano drank his black. Their talk edged round topics: he was warily polite – she had never, she realized, been alone with him before. As far as admiration went, Fanny was surely more to his taste – She'd wanted to flirt, *had* flirted.

They spoke about the War. Once, as if they were still waiting, he said: 'Uncle Frederick is absent-minded perhaps – I think he will go home in a dream, or already he has done so – then to his room and sleep. Yes?'

She felt awkward and longed suddenly for Taddeo's presence. Her eyes wandered. At the next table sat two white-haired, bearded men, so alike they must have been twins. She imagined they must have some secret because for several minutes they would say nothing – both had strange coloured drinks they stirred with a spoon – pulling odd shapes with their mouths, jutting out their chins, raising their eyebrows, almost identically. Then suddenly one would lean over and make some momentous remark behind a raised hand . . .

'I would like to visit England. It would give me great pleasure to meet your family . . .'

'Yes, of course,' she agreed, as if they played some hidden game of meanings. And yet any single remark was capable of much simpler interpretations. He had set himself out now to be charming. 'I thought Caffè Greco was a place you are sure to wish to come in. Also we dine one evening at Ranieri's – some steps only from here. I give a small party.' He turned on her a smile of great sweetness. 'I think certainly you like Rome?'

(How are we to deny ourselves? We are to deny ourselves by giving up our own will, and by going against our own humours, inclinations and passions.)

Against expectation she found herself warming to him. Over the weeks, over so many hours spent in his company – albeit never alone – he had grown to be familiar. Family. For years Uncle Frederick had talked of them all as if their doings must interest her and hers them. No matter now that the real link was the hated Aunt Adelina. She thought for the first time, I like to be with him. She watched his face when he was talking but not looking at her. She watched the habitual slight flush, thought: That's a nice mouth, a little spoilt – Nose bent so slightly, it gave his face strength. Eyes, perhaps the best of all because they were dark and soft. She thought it might be possible to say, if I wanted somebody, that is somebody I could want. She would be making not just a sacrifice but receiving also, greatly. Was she not perhaps being rescued, as Father had once rescued Mother? The figure of her childhood memories, riding Mother away to safety. Now Stefano had come (I must see it like that, she thought) riding a white horse, to rescue her from the dragons of apathy, of desolation.

'. . . We are such a family – I am concerned little with politics only so much as I have to . . .' She had not been listening. 'Naturally I must think when it concerns our property. Also I can look about and see what is not right with Italy, with Rome – but I am not eager so much to do something. For a time, yes. Perhaps at twenty, twenty-one . . . I thought also that when I should become Marchese I would then do such and such – but now I'm not certain. It is laziness perhaps, who knows? But to have been in a war, there is a great tiredness after. You understand?'

Her rogue thoughts. She could not control them. Her mind

wandered, her eyes. She wished now that she had accepted a drink. At the next table the two men had left, replaced by a family: unhappy. The son had said something wrong and was sulking. The father, his elbow taking up too much of the small round table, had turned his head away. The mother was trying to make peace; her hand stroked compulsively the thick tablecloth.

'Yes,' and 'No,' she said to Stefano's remarks, wanting now to be alone to think. Why should I mind exile, she thought, since I belong nowhere now? It felt almost as if she had to decide, this moment, here in the Caffè Greco. (And the ghost of Ben?)

'I am not sure just now the way they build Rome – In England, also Berlin, you have – garden city, is it? Perhaps we also should do something of this. Outside Rome we have country which is not touched. Here they can put first tram-lines. Then *casette*. So each have his own house. Then when they are content, they don't open the ear to this Lenin . . .'

Edwina asked some questions about the villages outside Rome, the conditions there. He seemed surprised, and then when she spoke almost passionately, a little uneasy. She said: 'I saw that time we drove – all those little children playing in the mud in the middle of the main street. I thought they were just making mud pies, but Taddeo said it was a sewer . . .'

'I hope you don't have strong ideas? You are not – political?'

'Not at all. But,' she said it with energy, 'if I wanted to be no one would stop me – '

'It is not necessary. It's quite simply man's work, and so – man's worry. It is of course to protect women that I make such a remark.'

(Why are we bound to deny ourselves? We are bound to deny ourselves because our natural inclinations are prone to evil from our very childhood; and if not corrected they will certainly carry us to hell.)

'You allow me to order you more coffee? I think also there are paintings here by Angelica Kauffmann – Frederick has said something, but I don't know where I must find them – '

He broke off suddenly. As he looked up and away from her, she turned and saw that a man had stopped at their table. Very tall, dark, hair smooth and polished, his manner rather stiff as, bowing slightly from the waist: 'Excuse me – and I *do* apologize if I'm mistaken – it's – it is Miss Illingworth?'

'Yes, of course, but – ' And then: Oh, but how could she have failed to recognize him, that wooden soldier of her dancing-class days. So tall, he had grown so tall. 'Laurence! Laurence, oh, but what a wonderful thing – what are you doing, why are you – ' she broke off, and then still excited: 'However did you recognize me?'

It was then she noticed Stefano's face. It had altered, closed up completely, a veil almost over the eyes. His cold anger came over in waves as she tried, hurriedly, to make everything right:

'Laurence, you see, was at these dancing classes . . .' Introductions must be effected at once. She said lamely, 'I haven't seen him since I was *eight*. He's – '

'But you haven't changed at all. I kept looking from the back there, I wanted to make absolutely sure – It's – not a situation where one wants to make a fool of oneself – '

'Perhaps you have in fact done so?' suggested Stefano, eyebrows raised. There was no hint of a joke, even in bad taste. His voice was cold.

'I beg your pardon?' She had not imagined Laurence either so cold.

'Perhaps, I suggest perhaps that you do not realize – there has been no invitation, I think, to join us?'

'Indeed not,' Laurence said. She was stricken dumb, unable to intervene. 'Probably I have said enough.' He added: 'Certainly *you* have – ' He was white with anger. 'You will excuse me, I am sure?' He turned slightly, didn't meet her eyes. 'Edwina also?'

Gone. Her gaze followed him, her mouth slightly open, the saliva dried. Why don't I get up and run after him? Such years of being told how to conduct myself, she thought, that now I can do it no other way. She contented herself with saying, into the silence: 'How *dare* you behave like that?'

He seemed genuinely surprised. 'But I behave as I wish. You are in my company, it is for me to choose with whom we speak.' He paused: 'It is nothing. It is how I felt.'

'You've no business then, feeling like that. He's my friend and I've lost him.'

She was so angry that it was a pleasure almost; she was surprised at the feelings aroused as she belaboured him with words. He shrugged his shoulders only. 'What a nonsense,' he said. Then he refused to speak at all. She knew then that she wanted to hit him, that words were not enough. But fists were a forbidden language, and since she might not speak it, she too for the rest of the outing kept an angry silence.

In her room that night, standing in front of the flowered wash-bowl, squeezing the tube of toothpaste – its moustachioed effigy of Capit. Dott. Cicciarelli gazing back at her – she felt through her still-present anger a sudden sense of belonging. The next afternoon Stefano brought her a present, a de luxe edition of Chopin's Mazurkas. For the remainder of the day he paid her marked attention.

And the old Marchesa watched.

Oh Uncle Frederick, where have you gone, why have you gone? Only to Florence, home, only a few hours away. But I never realized I would be so frightened. Tossed this way and that on the sea – the sea you used to tell me about. I'm not twenty any more but eight nine ten, and when I go to bed at night I cannot sleep unless your arms come round me. '*Ach Bächlein, liebes Bächlein, so singe nur zu . . .*' In the evenings you sang – it didn't matter that *she* played for you – in the evenings you sang and I hid outside to listen. It was so simple. I wanted only you – and music. Now I know nothing about anything. I would like to love God.

> '*Ach Bächlein, liebes Bächlein, du meinst so gut;*
> *Ach Bächlein, aber weisst du, wie Liebe tut?*'

Because it was morning the doors were open right through so that the vista of rooms seemed endless. It had in its own way some of the same beauty as when in the carriage or motor they drove from the Corso to the Piazza del Popolo, the way stretching out before in a great sweeping rise and fall, something always beyond and beyond.

But today the journey was only indoors, and only towards a piano. The old Marchesa had mentioned this one as having been once the best and had sent a message that it had been seen to by master craftsmen, and was once again – the best.

For several days now the old Marchesa had been confined to her room with a chill and Edwina hadn't seen her. She was surprised at how much she missed the visits. They had become part of her life. A life which was in such confusion that she wished only – nothing had been said – that she could be asked outright, by either of them, by both of them, so that she would be forced to say 'yes' or 'no'. Daily, nightly, 'yes' grew nearer. Perhaps it was that she feared.

Sunlight fell in a great shaft across an onyx table. Busts, always with that slightly forward bowing look, stared at her. All of them had been people once. She came out into a corridor: I hope I can remember the way – She thought it wasn't far now, she could relate it to where the old Marchesa's apartment was. Ahead of her a sofa and two chairs, covered in velvet, an onyx table in front. As she came by a door just near opened and Eugenio came out. He was in a dressing-gown – a silk affair with the tie insecurely fastened and trailing. At first he didn't see her, then as her steps came behind he must have heard and turned. His hair looked wet, plastered damply to his head.

'Good morning,' he announced loudly. He was frowning, brows knit angrily, as if perhaps she shouldn't be there. She returned his greeting quickly, smiling at him. She was about to move on when suddenly his hand shot out, barring her way. 'Go,' he said. 'You come.' Both commands were equally definite. But he was staying her with the full force of his arm. He made a deep, throaty sound, seizing one of her hands. His was damp and a little cool.

She said: 'I'm just on my way to play the piano. *Music*, Eugenio.' With her free hand she mimed. But he made another queer noise, more of a moan this time, and then, lowering his head, he butted her in the chest. She moved to get away but his arms had gone round her: his head banged, butting still against her breasts. Grunting, breathing heavily: 'Nice. Nice. I like.'

Her silk blouse felt wet. 'Yes, yes, that's nice, Eugenio. Enough though. *Basta*!' she said sharply. He stopped. But then looking up, he grabbed her head roughly and pushed it to and fro, his hands fat and damp, pulling at her hair. She could scarcely move. She thought that she mustn't call out.

'No,' she said, teeth chattering. 'No. *Not* nice, Eugenio . . .' He let go then, but almost immediately pulled with one hand at her blouse, wrenching it from her skirt. His dressing-gown had fallen open. As he moved back she saw long combinations, half buttoned. When he lunged forward, gripping her in a bear hug, she could feel the warm flab against her stomach, her sore breasts. He smelt of eau de Cologne and sweat. 'Nice,' he said again, into her ear, the sound almost blasting her.

From nowhere there was a sudden banging. His name spoken, harsh, peremptory. *'Eugenio!'* He moved back. The Marchesa Vittoria, approaching, leaning on her stick, said severely, *'Ma cosa fai?'* He made no effort to get away. Edwina, shaking, slipped down on to the sofa. The Marchesa, leaning for support on the back of the chair, said angrily, *'Vestiti – ora!'* Then as he pulled the gown round, looking down for the cord, she lifted her stick and struck him – the head, the shoulders. Surely something would be broken?

'Eh, eh, eh . . .' He had put up his hands. 'Don't,' Edwina pleaded, 'it was only – ' but the Marchesa ignored her.

Then stopping as suddenly as she'd begun, *'Vai!'* she said, shaking the stick in the air, *'vai, vai . . .'* Eugenio, fumbling with the heavy door knob, disappeared to where he had come from. The old Marchesa, without turning to look at Edwina, without showing by any action or gesture that she knew she was there, leaning again on her stick, walked away.

Edwina began to go after her. And then she thought, if she'd wanted to speak to me, she would have done. She realized suddenly what her appearance must be and, turning, made her way back to her room. She met no one on the way.

'My dear, I'm *delighted* to see you again, though a little surprised we haven't met sooner. (I really must lower my voice – the dear Duchessa's At Home isn't the *jolliest* of evenings . . . but then no doubt you are under the wing . . .) My *dear*, I *must* tell you of the most amazing coincidence. I was talking last night – quite the dullest reception, the Favellis' again – to the most charming English boy – at the Embassy here, and quite by chance he told me of a little upset during his very first week. My dear, I *whooped* with delight. "I can help you," I said, "I know *all* the English in Rome." Auntie Dora to the rescue. "And don't worry," I told him, "I know your Roman, I know your aristocrat, they don't *mean* it . . ." He was so solemn, my dear. "If you hope to be a diplomat, you will have to do better," I said. He had a bad time in Mespot, you know, and then too quickly through wartime Oxford. The lamb. He reminded me in a well-bred way of one of my Tommies . . .

'Now, tell me – *have* you found poor, dear little Keats?'

The flowers on the stall were massed – serried ranks of colour, today they seemed all roses and lilies: over all a big white sunshade. She was thirsty and thought of stopping at one of the *bibitari* for fresh lemon juice. But after standing a moment, she changed her mind, walking out of the square. Out alone, she felt uncertainly free.

It was quiet, early in the afternoon. A wine-cart, black-hooded, rattled past. A dog lay asleep by the barrels. The driver brandished his whip above the mule, calling out the same word over and over again. The building she was approaching looked like a school. A piano was playing in one of the upper rooms. It stopped, and then as she came nearer began again. Haltingly, tenderly, through the open window, Brahms's 'Variations on an Original Theme'.

She had only to walk by. How could it be that she wanted : to stop, and yet could not countenance, believe, accept hat it might ever end? The player had gained confidence. ›he felt the notes now in her own fingers. Standing there on he pavement, out of the sun: correcting, hastening, drawing ut, she was at once listener and performer.

And certainly she could not bear it. The familiar dull ache f the poorly mended heart. It was all impossible. Impossible, nprobable to stand alone in a Roman street mourning some- ne who would never return. She could hear 'Ben's Air' still hen half-walking, half-running she found herself out of the arrow street, a short turning now away from the Tiber. The ears coursed down her cheeks.

She leaned for a moment against a tree. '*Signorina* –' A oman touched her shoulder, concerned, but she shook her ead. '*Va bene, grazie . . .*' The tree was heavy with blossom was it lime?) scattered on the ground around. As she stood nere some fell, fluttered down – a little gust of wind – it overed her hair, fell on her hands. Her face, her eyes, in her outh even. Monstrous confetti.

Half of me still crying for Ben. And the other half? I nould have been up in that schoolroom. Where else should ever be but at the piano? Her hands ached. What have I een thinking of? What *can* I have been thinking of?

'he tea-room was on the left of the foyer and had a pink nd red carpet. Inside, the clink of teacups, waiters gliding y. She saw Fanny at once, at a table just near the entrance olumn.

'Isn't this fast, don't you feel *fast*, being here like this?' xcited, animated and, Edwina thought, very pleased with erself.

'Fanny, your hair –'

'I did it. Walked into a hairdresser's – of course you can't e properly with the hat, but the relief, my dear, when the cissors went snip snip . . . whyever I put up with it for so ng –'

'You were going to be a nun,' Edwina said. 'And also, it

was so lovely. Not like my bushy tangle. The old Marches is getting someone to do something about that.'

'You're brave . . . I must eat, we don't usually have any thing till about ten. Tea, toast? The tea won't taste quit like English but what matter when one's sipping it in th *Excelsior*.' She looked about her. 'That man with the monocl – he's eyeing you, and that quite disgusting woman with hir – the sort that if she were English would say "how deevy" – she's seen him looking.'

Everything was wonderful, she told Edwina. The hous the people, the atmosphere. 'I'm so free – it's really quite th bohemian life, you've no idea.'

'I meant to see you earlier,' Edwina said. 'The time's gon so quickly. And of course I play – '

'Music, I wish they'd have some music, I'm sure there wa music in here when I came the other day. I'm doing a lot painting now – you never took my painting seriously, di you – Portraits I'm doing. Not just faces but the whole perso Everyone who'll sit. I'm doing one of the aunt which absolutely tops, everything drapes on her wonderfully – grea heavy jowls in the face. Wonderful. And I'm doing one – Stefano.' She paused.

'Of Stefano?'

'Well, whyever not? You've only to look at him the tinie bit carefully to see his face is just made to be drawn, painted

At the next table a woman had a small white poodle o her lap. She was feeding it with snippets of buttered toas Edwina said, 'Perhaps if it's really good it'll be hung up i the gallery with Pope Paschal – '

'Indeed,' Fanny said. 'Who knows?' She paused, hesitate then stared straight at Edwina. 'In fact, in the circumstance I should think it would be the natural, the obvious thing do.'

'Oh,' said Edwina. 'Oh,' not understanding.

Fanny lowered her voice, first looking around her carefull 'The whole matter of Stefano and me – it's very serious.'

Edwina said, in a stupid voice, 'What do you mean?'

'I mean – that I haven't just been drawing him, paintin

He's – you must have guessed that he was interested.' She glanced around her again. The poodle had jumped down from its owner's lap and was running in fussy circles. 'We arranged this because it makes a good cover really for – He loves me *passionately*. He's in it very deep, he says – I can't tell you the things he says, but when I said to you I wanted – that time I said men were the thing – it's all that and better too. He says he's never known anyone like me.'

Their tea, their toast waited untouched. 'Of course I'm very careful, it's plain what he wants, what could happen if I didn't know exactly how to behave. He's so urgent, so – not like boys, men, I've known – he can't think how he lived before he met me. I've altered his whole life. His passion – sometimes it frightens me. But it can only be a matter of days before he proposes – some of the things he's said already!' She leaned back. 'It's a better life than cleaning sheep's hooves. And you can see why I wanted to stay on . . .'

Lips moist and parted, eyes alive, it was the Fanny of a thousand confidences. And yet it was not. Edwina felt only the most wonderful relief – as if, about to cross a river in torrent, she had seen that it was not that way she must take at all. She found herself praying, blaspheming almost, words of profound letting go, it's all right. It's *all right*.

A waiter paused, hovered. Fanny waved him away. She leaned forward again, closer now to Edwina.

'I keep saying the name over to myself – even out loud sometimes. Frances Antici-Montani. The *Marchesa* Antici-Montani. *Francesca* Antici-Montani . . . Isn't it all too unspeakably, impossibly grand?'

*Valet ancora virtus*. The family motto – engraved, painted, scored, scratched: here, there, everywhere: the gallery, the ballroom, inside the lid of a huge chest . . . 'Virtue serves as an anchor.' The Illingworths had not had to live up to any such precepts.

They seemed to her now, viewed from abroad, to have been someone else's family. She thought, I know more now about the Antici-Montani than of them. But if I had been born sooner, if Grandma Illingworth had lived longer, wouldn't I most certainly have sat with her as I sit now today with the old Marchesa. (Would it not have been me reading *Wuthering Heights*?)

'We go together next week, Edwina. You and I. Stefano also. I forget which is the piece, but they, all of this family, they think they are very good in acting. It is not so.'

The long satin curtains had not been fully drawn back – the room was darker than usual. The rings on the old Marchesa's fingers glowed dully. 'No person in this circle is good in acting just now. The last was the Principessa Paterno. She was most excellent in *Gli Inamorati* of Goldoni – the Duse has admired her . . . This matter some days ago of Eugenio, it is not good. I apologize. It is certain it does not happen again . . . Now we speak of what you wear. I shall present you naturally to the Duchessa's mother . . .'

They drank marsala. She didn't like it, although each time when she smelled it, she thought that she would. Later she was to play for the old Marchesa. Chopin. For half an hour before luncheon.

'Frederick, I hear from him now that he is safely at home. I don't think it is completely a surprise – what I shall speak of. Frederick then, has said something, perhaps?' The words at first flowed. Then they studded, jabbed: '. . . if you can consider to make Italy your home . . . the bride of Stefano . . . for the family it is very good and you certainly, you shall be fortunate, and I think perhaps content . . . if you agree I speak to Stefano – he knows what is in my mind. He will wish to speak to you himself, it is enough to say to me now that you – '

'But I can't – he can't – '

*'Ma che cos'è?* What is this?'

'They're in love – he means to tell you, I'm sure. It's *Fanny* he wants to marry, not me.'

'*Macchè – wants to marry!* This is nonsense. You speak nonsense. Stefano . . this is only a game.' She leaned forward, her face near Edwina's: 'He is naughty boy. You cannot think he *means* something – he plays only. I see from the irst that he is interested. As it might be in – some dancer, ome actress. You understand? I speak frankly of her. It is ıot *serious*. This is *coup de tête* only. Nothing more –'

'I rather thought it was.'

'To her – who knows? But *he* – how can you think this? Ie is *méchant* only. And so weak. That you will have to nderstand. Also to forgive . . .'

She rearranged her skirt. She wore today oyster pleated ilk. Her bracelets ran along the fabric. 'But I speak. We ıake an end to it all. Now – you pass me, please, that box vhich is on the table. This veil is *point d'Alençon*. Open it ut, please. You see – such beauty! It is worn by me, of ourse. Also, naturally, by Angela. It is for you – Yes, you xclaim, you are right to be astonished, that your hands go p. You suit it very well, I am certain . . .'

She took one of Edwina's hands in hers. 'Show me. They re very strong.' She paused. Her bent fingers stroked dwina's knuckles. *'Mah!'* Then, as if to someone else, 'Yes, ou, Edwina, *you* are very strong . . .'

abington's English Tea-Rooms. 'Are you sure this is all ght?' Laurence asked.

'Perfectly. They're very easy these days. The motor at my isposal – I'm in any case on my way to see Fanny, in Via Iargutta. She's asked to see me – but I'd been going any-vay –'

How to say to Fanny that what had happened was not at er bidding? How to face her? ('All is arranged now, I speak vith Stefano and at once there has been end. Now he shall ıy to you . . .') Where to begin to explain? And how to try ow to give Fanny what she wanted?

'Anyone passing who might peer through the windows. t's hardly though, as if we shall be seen by *le tout Rome* –'

'Dora,' she said.

'Ah, Dora,' he said. 'But how can I mock Dora when she as brought us together?'

'Laurence, it was all so wonderful. If you'd known how ngry I was. For *you* –'

'But it's ended well. Two childhood friends, reminiscin
over the teacups.'

'I must be homesick, a bit,' she said, 'or I wouldn't be s
happy, just sitting here.'

'It's not English – quite. The management, of course, ye
I should point out – try not to look now – Miss Babington
partner. She *was* a Miss Cargill, but married her drawin
master and became the Countess da Pozzo.'

'Where do you learn – '

'Information supplied by Dora. The clientele too is n
quite right. And the potted palms. It tries too strenuously –
We deceive ourselves, I think.'

'Tell me about your War – if you want to. (You hear
about Ned?) And Oxford – my brother never finished . .

The tea-shop was quite crowded now at nearly five o'cloc
There was a babble of Italian and English. Two custome
were talking to the Countess da Pozzo. She and Lauren
ate scones in happy companionship. The tea was very stron
She said: 'I don't need all this food – we eat enormously i
the middle of the day, and again at eight.'

'Muffins,' he said, 'I don't feel like muffins. But plu
cake. I shall succumb to plum cake.'

'Laurence – you are just as I remember.'

'I think I have grown a little – '

'I'll allow that, you didn't tower above me so in those day
But decided, you were so decided. That's what I remembe
what hasn't changed. "I shall be a diplomat." '

'Weren't your plans to be a concert pianist just as definite
A snippet of information – Dora tells me you are going t
Paris.'

'Perhaps.' She felt suddenly confused. She had coloured. '
should tell you, I suppose – '

'But – ' She said then about Stefano.

'My God,' he said.

'You seem awfully surprised. Wouldn't I be suitable?'

He considered. 'I don't see why not,' very seriously, though
fully. 'But that is not perhaps the point.'

She sipped her tea. 'It doesn't matter about the poin

3ecause I don't think I can go through with it.'

'No?'

Whatever *had* she been thinking? Now, when her mind ıad become suddenly so clear. And I am not anyway, she hought, I am not what the old Marchesa thinks. Certainly, urely she expects for her grandson, a virgin. What would he say if I told my story? The walk to Bay. The long walk ack – the man who saw me as I went up Albion Street (who erhaps told Ben's mother?), the long walk along the cliff ath, sore, frightened, forced continually to squat amongst he undergrowth. Shakily tired, coming at last into the early ıorning garden. Rounding the corner, meeting Mother 3ede . . .

'I had these thoughts. I had been looking for a sacrifice, think. All – so ridiculous. I mean, I was quite clear-eyed bout how it would be – it would be unlikely for instance hat he would be faithful to me . . .'

Laurence said yes, that would be very unlikely.

'I suppose I would have been able to play, even give small oncerts – when there was time. Talented amateur actors, I nderstand, aren't frustrated in that set. But what small hange . . .' She crumbled the cake on her plate. 'I liked im – *like* him. That alone made it not impossible. I would ave tried – very hard. Making someone happy. Having hildren. And then what I would have received back. He vouldn't be faithful – but he would be loyal. To be proected and cared for . . . Perhaps I don't mean that so much s the warmth. Human warmth. Someone – ' because she ad just thought of it, she said, 'someone to snuggle up to, ı bed at night – '

'You set great store by that?'

'Yes,' she said simply.

'I wish I did. I can understand the – man-woman bit,' he aid. 'But between times, I don't want to touch, be touched.' Ie said it in that same tone of voice which had said all those ears ago, 'My mamma doesn't wear corsets. She thinks ıey're bad . . .' He said now, 'Some people, I think, are just ıade that way.'

'Laurence, I understand.' She felt that she had known hin
all the years in between.

'There's the question of Fanny too . . .'

When she'd done, he said gravely, pouring himself ou
more tea, not waiting for her to do it, 'Exclamation mark,
think. What shall you do?'

'Tell her everything, how I feel. Even if it can't put thing
right. I'd like – Fanny looks so sure, you know, so strong, bu
she needs me to protect her – '

He said, 'Your mind then, you've changed it definitely?

'It's – almost certain. Yes.' She paused. 'False, it was a
false really. I thought yesterday – you know that shop jus
here in the Piazza di Spagna, where they sell artificial pearls
I watched the woman in there. She just sits all day, dippin
the matrix in some liquid to coat it. Very slow and laborious
But her definite work, what she *should* be doing. And th
pearls are false . . .'

'But people buy them?'

'People buy them,' she said. She looked at her plate. Sh
had crumbled the moist cake to nothing. Laurence saw i
and smiled.

'Let me order you some more.'

'No,' she said, 'no, thank you.' She asked him then mor
about Mesopotamia, his wounds, wartime and post-wartim
Oxford. She said, 'I think you're going to be very successfu
Our ambassador in – Pekin? Perhaps Ruritania?'

'Perhaps Ruritania,' he said, smiling.

She saw that it was time to go. She said, 'I think we shoul
meet again. I don't know how long now I'll stay in Rome.'

'You mean if you decide against? As you will . . . A pity
he said solemnly. 'I would have liked to come to your A
Homes – '

'I should always have asked you.'

They stood outside the tea-rooms. The sun beat down o
the awnings. Coming out she was at first dazzled.

'What a duffer I was at dancing,' he said.

'I used to want to be your partner.'

'Actually,' he said, 'I am very good now. I have conside

.ble confidence.'

A mushroom-seller, smoking a long pipe, sat amongst his ›askets and buckets. Laurence said, 'Let me walk you up to he studio – '

'It's nothing. Via Margutta only.'

'I should like to – ' He pressed, she refused. It was only ve minutes away.

'I shall be in touch,' he said then, watching her as she ·alked off across the square.

The door of the house was open. As she drew near, Fanny ame out. There seemed no sign of anyone else about.

'Oh, there you are,' she said dully. She was wearing a long ›ose jacket with deep pockets. She had her hands behind er back. Her face was very white, strained. Her short hair ulled back from her forehead.

'Fanny – '

'If I can't have him – you shan't have him either!'

Fanny's hand coming out suddenly. Sweep of arm, something flung. As the liquid shot out, Edwina's hands flew to er face.

ınd when Sergeant Death . . .'

Night merged into day. Behind the bandages was another orld. The Venetian blinds were raised, were lowered. But hich was which? Her hands lay outside the bedcovers – the ıeet was smooth. Her fingers, stroking, felt something raised, much-washed darn.

Her hands had flown to her face. But they had not flown st enough and now, this sticky world of blurred pain and ırkness. She had heard herself cry and thought it someone se. A croaking sound, which in time would go, would be›me normal – for although her hands had not been quick ıough, she had not opened her mouth. *L'acido giallo* had ›t hurt the vocal cords.

'And you will see,' they told her. 'Only not so well.' The ›rld would not stay dark, as now.

She worried about Fanny. Asked about her daily. 'Is Fanny l right? What will happen to Fanny?' The police it must

have been, that second day – and Uncle Frederick the inter
preter. Where had Fanny obtained the vitriol, what had sh
said, was there anything they ought to know?

Why be more sorry for Fanny than for herself? Worm
of fire crawling over her face, eating the flesh. And what t
do with the burst of anger that came in great waves – a se
of anger. (Are we also bound to love our enemies? We ar
also bound to love our enemies; not only by forgiving ther
from our hearts but also by wishing them well and prayin
for them.)

Uncle Frederick came and sat with her every day. He hel
her hand. She was in the Anglo-American Hospital. Soon sh
would be able to have more visitors. But Mother – she ha
told Mother, Cora, they were not to come to Italy. Uncl
Frederick, by her bedside, explained to her that the re
Edwina was still there, under the scars. That life would g
on, not perhaps 'as if', but *almost* 'as if'. She would not b
beautiful (had she ever been?), but nor on the other han
would she cause people to stare or be embarrassed. For thos
who had not known her before, to strangers, the public pe
haps, she would not be a sight.

Put out a hand and touch Ben. As certainly here as i
those cold summer days of his death. I don't touch him, onl
because he must be left in peace. She thought: if I had take
after all the wrong turning I so nearly chose, he would n
have been a vengeful ghost.

(How are we to love one another? We are to love or
another . . .) Brahms in the taverns, the servant girls on h
knees. I sat on Ben's knee.

Her hands lay very still on the covers. She placed one ov
the other. Life ran through them.

Other senses sharpened. Touch. Hearing. She could he
– so well. Breakers against the sea-wall. Music (and wh
else was she for?) washing over her – waves.

It is in my hands, she thought.